DOUBLE CROSSING

ERIKA HOLZER

TOR

A TOM DOHERTY ASSOCIATES BOOK

DOUBLE CROSSING

Copyright © by Erika Holzer

Reprinted by arrangement with G.P. Putnam's Sons, a member of the Putnam Publishing Group

A TOR Book

Published by Tom Doherty Associates
8-10 West 36 Street
New York, N.Y. 10018

First TOR printing: May 1985

ISBN: 0-812-58375-2
CAN. ED.: 0-812-58376-0

Printed in the United States of America

*To men and women all over the world
who share a common conviction: that
freedom is a right, universal and
inalienable.*

*And to men and women behind the
Iron Curtain who share, with the hero
of this book, a common desire: to be
free.*

Preface

The Glienicker Bridge is an iron bridge reconstructed in 1908–9. Half the bridge belongs to the East Zone and is called "Bruecke der Einheit" [Bridge of Unity] . . . *

In early morning mists we had driven through deserted West Berlin to reach . . . our rendezvous . . . the . . . bridge called "Bridge of Freedom" [Bruecke der Freiheit] in 1945 by our GIs and the Russians . . .†

Glienicker Bridge, which figures prominently in this novel, was marked for destruction by the Nazis during the closing days of World War II—as were all bridges leading to Berlin. Only Glienicker survived their explosives, but it was badly damaged. Later it was repaired, but not in time for the Potsdam Conference in July of 1945. A temporary pontoon (floating) bridge had to be used by President Truman and other representatives of the Western powers to cross the Havel River that separates Berlin from Potsdam.

That GIs were detailed to work on the bridge repairs in 1945 is fact. That Soviet soldiers were detailed to assist them may or may not be fiction. Given the temper of the

---

*The Karl Baedeker Guidebook to Berlin.

†James B. Donovan, American lawyer for convicted Soviet spy Colonel Rudolf Abel, recalling Abel's exchange for U-2 pilot Francis Gary Powers in 1962 on Glienicker Bridge. (*Strangers on a Bridge*, Atheneum House.)

times—the spirit of cooperation that the West was avidly pursuing with the Soviet Union immediately after the War—it is plausible. That such cooperative efforts between GIs and their Soviet counterparts culminated in a "Freedom Bridge" dedication ceremony is invention, sparked by Lawyer James Donovan's terse reference, above, to a "Bridge of Freedom"—a characterization of Glienicker which proved impossible either to verify or disprove.

ERIKA HOLZER

Bedford, New York
September 1980

DOUBLE CROSSING

Prologue

Paul Houston, American diplomat, walked—reluctantly—into a palace he hadn't seen since his foreign correspondent days over thirty years ago. Cecelienhof Palace in Potsdam, East Germany—site of the Potsdam Conference after the war. Site of another conference in—Houston checked his watch—less than an hour. What the hell, he thought as he tracked the overhead noise up some stairs, this was the age of sequels, wasn't it? If they got away with it in the movies, why not in international politics?

The pre-conference cocktail hour was in noisy full swing. Moscow red, transported *ad nauseam* to Potsdam, Houston thought; red walls, red gilt-trimmed chairs like the ones in the conference room downstairs, red tablecloth on a sumptuous buffet table. Clusters of solicitous Russian waiters were serving drinks. Clusters of solicitous delegates—the Americans and British—hovered about the Soviet delegation. The French stood aloof in another corner. The three Soviet delegates, dark and squat like sawed-off tree trunks, were flanked by a tall, blond interpreter in a Soviet air force uniform. The interpreter looked oddly vulnerable among the tree trunks. Houston forced himself to join the animated group.

"—toast to *another* memorable July seventeenth, the anniversary of the original Potsdam Conference!" the head Soviet delegate enthused to a circle of raised glasses.

The interpreter's translation was in a contrasting monotone.

"Gentlemen, the past three months have not been in vain. Negotiations in Democratic Berlin have become snarled, yes? Never mind. We shall untangle the snarls tonight—here—in this splendid setting. Harmony prevailed once at Cecelienhof Palace. It shall prevail again! As a good hunting dog grabs hold of his quarry, we shall grab hold of our doubts, our disagreements! We shall shake loose . . ."

Glasses moved to lips as soon as the toast—and the translation—were done. It's worse than I expected, Houston thought, as the interpreter, Stepan Brodsky, looked pointedly at him; excitement showed in Brodsky's usually solemn eyes, and hope—no, more than hope. It was the look that comes from hopes being realized. He kept his own expression blank.

And he watched blankness seep into Brodsky's expression as he began translating again—the usual Soviet black-is-white refrain: The original Potsdam Conference had eased world tensions in 1945. It had established the principles for a lasting peace! Houston, alone among the dutifully rapt audience, lifted a stale drink and contemplated that conference's true "accomplishments." Postwar Germany, carved into occupation zones: American, British, French, Soviet. Postwar Berlin, the same four-way split—but thanks to the wily negotiating tactics of "Uncle Joe" Stalin, the Western sectors had been locked in, surrounded by the Soviet zone. And within that zone, farms, factories, millions of people—abandoned to Stalin's "denazification" program.

A waiter refilling glasses brought the rhetoric to a halt. He felt free to return Brodsky's pointed look, since no one else was looking at him; interpreters are used, not noticed. In the moment when Brodsky bent to whisper in the head delegate's ear, Houston felt a twinge—part pain, part unaccountable fear. Then Brodsky was off, having gotten permission, no doubt, to excuse himself until conference time. That purposeful stride across the room looked almost buoyant, the smile for the waiter who handed him a package almost carefree. As Brodsky left by a rear exit, Houston sighed and checked his watch: 6:30—in Potsdam, that is. Only 1:30 in New York. A time for leafing through the Sunday papers. For taking a leisurely afternoon walk through empty summer streets. For—

He thought of the man who would not be walking those streets, now . . . and gave himself another few minutes.

"Just the man I have been looking for!" A West German reporter he knew took hold of his arm, pulling him aside. "I am confused by this new cooperative spirit on the part of the Soviet delegation. Perhaps you know the reason behind the rhetoric?"

"Perhaps," Houston said warily.

"Ah, not for publication. Can you tell me, at least, why after months of harassment at every border crossing in West Berlin, the West is suddenly being assured—"

"I can tell you," Houston said, impatient now, "but I won't."

"Will you comment on *this*, then?" The reporter brandished a New York newspaper, tapped a page one headline.

13

Houston took the paper, pretending to read what he'd digested and rankled over a few hours ago. "U.S. Welcomes Suspended Sentence of Dissident," the headline said. His eyes jumped to the last paragraph of the article: "The suspended sentence, coming on the heels of the recent release from prison of several other dissidents, was welcomed by the State Department as a constructive act pointing toward marked improvement in Soviet-American relations. The outlook for human rights—" He wanted to toss the paper out the nearest window. "Sorry," he said, handing it back, "no comment."

"You Embassy types never do, do you? Cecelienhof Palace." The West German reporter's mouth had slipped into contempt. "The historic site of hopes reborn," he said, looking around. "The place where German hopes were dissected on a bargaining table."

"That was the first Potsdam Conference."

"And the second? Whose freedom will be bargained away this time?"

Houston knew the source of the man's rage: August 13, 1961. A day unlike any other, if you were German. The day the free world stood by while eighteen miles of concrete and barbed wire were embedded in the heart of Berlin, mutilating the city, cutting off the flow of refugees to the Western sectors, cutting it off at the two and a half million mark—almost one-tenth of East Germany's population at the time.

The reporter was still glaring at him. "Are we about to witness a new East-West détente, unburdened by the 'nuisance' of a human rights issue?" he said flatly.

"You don't expect me to answer your rhetorical questions, do you? Excuse me. I need some fresh air before things get started." He turned away.

"—a new era of peace and harmony," he heard a British delegate say as he crossed the room, and he thought, Not for some of us. Not for you, Stepan. En route to the rear exit, he passed his image in a mirror. He had always prided himself on the diplomat's stock-in-trade: his inscrutable face. But the eyes that looked back at him—the color and texture of steel, his detractors liked to say—betrayed him now.

He left the room, picking his way down steep steps leading to a dark corridor—moving, one might think, with caution; moving, in fact, with trepidation. The corridor opened onto palace gardens, and twilight. He felt gravel shifting under his feet, saw trees turning into silhouettes, spotted a tall form in the shadow of a hedge—and stifled an impulse to turn on his heel and run. "Stepan?" he called out softly.

A hand gripped his. "Hello, Houston."

It was the old joke between them. Brodsky liked greeting him by his last name—the name of an American city he hoped one day soon to see for himself. One day soon . . .

Brodsky was extending a pack of cigarettes and a lighter.

"No thanks," Houston said.

"Look at the lighter, Paul," Brodsky urged quietly.

It was a flat metal case, the size of a pack of matches—a conventional American make. Houston touched an emblem glued to one side, straining in the thickening darkness to make it out: a crude rendering of a pair of bird's wings. He stared at the black, out-stretched wings, stalling for time, knowing there were questions he should ask.

"It's *true*, what I've been telling you—in spite of your people's skepticism!" Brodsky said in a burst of enthusiasm. "I got what you wanted, what you need to convince them," he said, lowering his voice even though the nearest soldier was a good fifty feet away. "I have proof that my country's sudden peace offensive is a fraud. Tonight's negotiations will blow up, triggered by some prearranged, strongly worded French insults. The Americans and the British will come under fire for insisting that the French attend this conference—"

"And we'll be harshly reminded, no doubt, that it was too soon after the Paris defections for the French and the Soviets to sit down together." Houston sounded more weary than bitter.

"Exactly. The little melodrama we are about to witness has been expertly staged by a member of the French delegation who takes orders from Moscow. As the injured party, my government will demand bold new concessions from the West. And make no mistake, Paul—*this* time, the Soviets are after West Berlin." He held his hand out for the lighter.

Houston handed it back and watched as Brodsky, with a furtive glance around, took the unit out of its metal case and separated two pieces of cotton padding at the bottom of the mechanism. A couple of black fingernail-sized squares lay between the padding. "The proof," he said reverently.

"Anyone else see this film?" Houston asked, masking his uneasiness.

"Only our East German photographer-friend—he's covering the conference. This film," Brodsky said, reassembling the lighter, "has all the incriminating admissions you will need to back up what I've been telling you."

"How did you get it?" he asked, almost afraid to hear the answer.

"With a bit of luck. One of my fellow Soviet delegates is not a delegate at all—he's Colonel Aleksei Andreyev of Soviet Intelligence, in charge of security at these negotiations. His East German counterpart is a Colonel Emil Von Eyssen. Obviously, both men knew in advance about tonight's scheduled blowup. But thanks to our East German photographer-friend and his helpful connections, I also knew something in advance: Andreyev was planning *not* to show up tonight. I was told he'd be communicating some last minute security arrangements to Von Eyssen by way of diplomatic pouch out of Moscow. Paul, I followed a hunch. I arranged to have a Russian friend of mine go to Andreyev's office on some pretext. He managed to photograph a message just before it went off to Von Eyssen—and sure enough, my hunch paid off! Andreyev admits *in writing* he is not about to waste time coming to Potsdam for a conference that won't last half an hour. He is even helpful enough to mention the name of the French agent."

Brodsky's chuckle ran downhill, and he frowned. "You look distressed, my friend."

"When I think of the risk you took to get us this information . . ."

"My Russian friend took the worst risk—he risked his life. That's why I've included him in the deal," he added quietly.

"You *what?*"

"Paul, try to imagine what it's like to be an exile in your own country. We have felt like exiles all our lives, my friend and I. So rather than abandon him, I lied to you about the film in my lighter—a partial lie. My film falls short of conclusive proof about tonight's blowup. It contains those damaging admissions I mentioned but . . . something crucial is left out: the date, and Andreyev's name and signature. My friend has the *complete* piece of film in a cigarette lighter identical to mine—emblem and

17

all. Your people can easily get their hands on it by arranging for my friend's escape. In two weeks' time.''

"In Moscow?" Houston asked incredulously.

"No, no, in West Berlin. My friend will be attending a medical symposium there—his first visit to the West. He will be well guarded," Brodsky said, frowning. "Colonel Andreyev will see to that. As of tomorrow, the symposium is Andreyev's new assignment. It may be difficult, this escape, but . . . surely not impossible? You can arrange it, Paul? And then," he said so faintly that it sounded like a sigh, "then, we will both be free."

You seem so sure of the future—as if your exile were already over, Houston thought with a fresh twist of pain. "Ah, Stepan, Stepan," he said, "I can't even arrange it for *you*. My people have changed their minds about this 'fair exchange' we've been planning. I have no identity papers to give you. I'm afraid the deal is off."

"No papers?" Brodsky stared at him. "But I *must* have them. I must have them by nine-thirty tonight!"

"I fought with them," Houston said lamely. "They know you have your own contact in East Berlin, your own arrangements. I made it clear there'd be no American involvement in your escape. You know what their answer was? Moscow is edgy—too many defections to the West, lately. My government is afraid of rocking the boat, even at the cost of sitting on your information and going along with tonight's farce. What if you're caught? they asked me. What if your papers are traced back to us? God in heaven, how can they talk about 'human rights' and then— you know what they told me? They actually told me it's a bad time for an escape! Stepan, I'm sorry, I'm so sorry. And so damn helpless . . .''

"Take the film anyway," Brodsky said tonelessly. "It

may keep the West from making some terrible concessions which—"

"Like hell I will! That's precisely what those bastards were counting on. The only thing I'm bringing back to the State Department is my resignation. I decided on my way over from West Berlin just now. And you? What will you do next? Won't your knowledge of languages and protocol land you another foreign assignment? From there, we can—"

"No Western assignments—not for me," he said. "Not with long lines of Party faithfuls clamoring for every one of them."

"But you speak colloquial English, French and German, damn it!"

Brodsky shrugged. "I consider myself lucky to have gotten as far as East Berlin. I have no tail, remember?"

"Ah yes, no hostages to guarantee your return to Mother Russia," Houston said acidly.

"We should go in," Brodsky urged, as if he couldn't bear to prolong the conversation.

They walked back in silence.

At the corridor leading inside, Brodsky opened his package: a bottle of vodka and two glasses. "It was to be a celebration toast," he said, filling the glasses. He handed one over and raised his own. "Goodby, my friend."

"Goodby for *now*."

Their glasses touched, and were emptied.

"Aren't you coming?" Houston said.

"Soon."

Houston started down the corridor.

"Paul," Brodsky called after him, "talking with you these past few months was like having a small glimpse of all the things I've missed. Thank you for that."

Houston stopped to answer . . . and walked on. He could not trust his voice.

"Goodby, Houston," Brodsky said softly to an empty corridor. He walked back up the path, feeling hemmed in by the tight configuration of trees, trying to imagine what lay beyond them. Scattered pinpricks of light off to the right—that would be the village of Potsdam. To the left, lights in orderly procession glowing like fireflies: the spans of Glienicker Bridge. And under it, a dividing line: the Havel River. On one side, Potsdam, East Germany; on the other . . . West Berlin. He heard a horn rising from the river—a coal barge on its way to "the other side"? He thought he heard a patrol boat prowling the shoreline. He could almost feel the probing eyes of binoculars, almost see the machine guns peering down from concrete mounds that rose thirty feet in the air. He tried to find them, staked out among the trees—those watchtowers that were never empty—but it was too dark. The coal barge knew nothing of these things, nor did the fireflies. They were free. As he was meant to be.

As he *would* be, papers or no papers!

No one paid him any attention as he slipped into the conference room and took his place at the round table. No eyes strayed from the thin-faced Frenchman with the delicate moustache.

"—over three decades of discussions on the two Germanys, and what do we have to show for it?" the Frenchman was saying with a sneer. "Harassment. Lies. Important concessions by the West in return for unenforceable promises by the Soviet Union. We take *years* to negotiate an agreement, and the Soviet Union takes *months* to break it!"

With each new insult, the head of the Soviet delegation sat up straighter in his chair. He frowned. He grimaced. He pressed plump fists into the red felt tablecloth.

Someone from the British delegation made a halfhearted attempt to intervene.

"But I am not finished!" shrilled the Frenchman as bubbles of whispered protest floated about the conference table. "We French have had to endure snide remarks by our Soviet colleagues because a few of their ballet dancers defected to Paris last month. I have something to say to the esteemed government of the Soviet Union on that subject."

"Enough!" roared the Soviet delegate, leaping up.

Brodsky's deliberately calm voice, as he translated, was a mocking counterpoint.

"The Soviet Union came to Potsdam tonight prompted by a genuine desire for peace!" The head delegate shook an accusing finger at the American and British delegations. "I hold *your* governments responsible for this outrage. The proposals I prepared to make in a spirit of *compassion* for the German peoples are no longer feasible. I have no alternative but to—"

"Walk out on these negotiations?" Paul Houston's voice! It seemed to pierce the entire Soviet delegation like the point of an icicle, even before the words were translated.

Brodsky kept elation out of his own voice. Paul was on his feet, though he seemed unaware of it. His hands gripped the table's edge, as if he were squaring off against the Soviet delegate, and his face—ah, his face told the tale. Here was an American diplomat, Brodsky realized, who had witnessed in silence one Communist charade too many.

"I have no alternative but to . . . to walk out," the head delegate finished lamely, his grand moment shattered.

21

"Then before you go, how about a straight answer to a straight question, for a change?" Houston challenged, the ice in his voice clashing with heat in the dark grey eyes. "Was it *compassion* for the Germans that inspired your Berlin Wall?"

"The Wall was an economic necessity!" one of the other Soviet delegates retorted in English. "We had to stop the mass exodus of traitors who threatened to—"

"Silence!" ordered the head delegate.

"Shut up!" Brodsky translated, on the edge of laughter. Of tears . . .

The head delegate's fleshy cheeks fairly quivered—now comes self-righteousness, Brodsky thought. "The whole world knows," intoned the delegate, "that with the remilitarization and renazification of Western Germany, we *had* to make the borders of the German Democratic Republic secure. We had to protect the people from spies and provocateurs! We had only the people's welfare in mind when we—"

"Now *you* shut up." Houston's quiet ferocity stunned the head delegate into openmouthed silence. "The whole world knows about the Soviet brand of welfare," he went on. "Bullets and barbed wire for anyone who defies your 'special' view of emigration. If neo-Nazi spies are your excuse for the Wall, how do you explain the barbed-wire borders of the Soviet Union? Of Poland? Of Czechoslovakia—Romania—Bulgaria—Hungary—"

Brodsky translated cautiously now, dropping each Russian word like a weighted pearl. He knew his face had gone white. When he saw that the face of the head delegate matched the tablecloth, he knew what would happen next.

The entire Soviet delegation rose as one and marched out of the conference room.

Brodsky remained in his chair, unable to move. But he was able to smile. An open, uncensored smile for an American friend who stood across the vast, unfriendly distance of a bargaining table in Potsdam.

He watched as Houston stuffed papers into a briefcase. And he knew what he had to do. He got up only after Houston started to walk out. He followed at a discreet distance, not wanting to catch up with his own delegation—not quite yet. Outside, he spotted Houston waiting in front of the circular courtyard for his car to be brought round—waiting and staring at a courtyard decoration that hadn't changed since the first Potsdam Conference: a flowerbed shaped into an enormous red star.

"Monstrous, just monstrous. God only knows what the repercussions will be," complained one of the American delegates as he hurried two frowning companions past Brodsky and down the steps toward the head of the American delegation, who stood in the driveway, making obviously hasty plans for departure. And who stood a more than discreet distance from where Paul Houston was standing, Brodsky noted.

. . . Hello, Houston. Brodsky was on the point of approaching him when someone beat him to it: a West German reporter. He was forced to walk on—back to his own delegation.

"—my congratulations," the reporter was saying to Houston as he passed them. "Apparently not everyone in your business is a placating, mealy-mouthed coward with all the scruples of a whore."

The head of the Soviet delegation was in what the Americans would call a blue funk. Brodsky bided his time, finally cornering the man in the narrow space between a curtained limousine and a military jeep. Brodsky explained. He cajoled. He explained again. "It has nothing to do with walkouts or boycotts," he said with a great show of patience. "It is not a matter of retaliatory measures. It is," he said, with what could be discerned as a touch of scorn born of superior knowledge, "a matter of protocol. We *must* have a military escort vehicle lead the diplomatic entourage back to Glienicker Bridge. I myself will ride in it to ensure that no further incidents occur." Except one, comrade, only one . . .

Brodsky was counting, not just on the man's ignorance of protocol, but on the terrifying questions he knew would be spinning out of control in that bureaucratic brain: What kind of reception awaited him in Moscow? Could he have anticipated the outburst of the American diplomat? Would his superiors remember it had been *his* idea to invite the foreign press to Potsdam? What if he were to add a serious breach of protocol to his "crimes"? The head delegate decided. "You!" he barked at a Soviet soldier. "Ride in the jeep with him."

"Thank you, comrade," Brodsky said, deferential now, as a soldier with a submachine gun over his shoulder climbed into the back seat of the jeep.

Brodsky slipped behind the wheel and drove slowly to the front gate—a protocol signal to the six limousines of the Western delegations, which proceeded to line up behind him: two cars for the United States, two for Great Britain, two for France. Four American delegates rode in the front car while Paul Houston, ostracized, sat in the second one with the West German reporter, who had apparently hitched a ride back. The procession followed him through the woods on a road that was bathed in moonlight.

The moon had disappeared behind a cloud by the time the limousines, crawling after one another like disconnected pieces of a caterpillar, reached an obstacle course of protruding cement blocks. After five hundred meters of painful maneuvering, the jeep led them into a cobblestone square and pulled up between the two stone guardhouses—one flying the hammer and sickle, the other East Germany's compass-like figure. But Brodsky had eyes only for the bridge. It waited just beyond the square, its dull yellow-green webbing looking shiny, almost festive, in the wash of floodlights.

He forced himself to look through the open door of the Soviet guardhouse. Guards sat at a table, mugs in hand. Two men stood talking—and one of them was a tall German officer with white-blond hair. Colonel Emil Von Eyssen, head of conference security.

Brodsky jumped to the ground, ignoring the tense alertness on the face of the soldier in the back seat. Fighting back a wave of nausea from the sudden, overpowering smell of coffee, he walked—casually—toward the waiting line of limousines. The first two had moved past his jeep and stopped, single file, behind two red-and-white-striped poles barring their way. Two guards—a Soviet at one pole, an East German at the other—went into body alert; he ignored them. With the air of a man with some last-minute message to convey, he stepped up to the open window of the second limousine.

"Hello . . . Houston," he said. "I wanted to caution you. The guards are looking . . . edgy. Like Moscow, these days." He spoke evenly, no plea in his voice; he knew Paul Houston would see it in his eyes. "Should something out of the ordinary occur," he said softly, "I will be right behind you."

They stared at each other. Then Brodsky walked back to the jeep.

Moscow is edgy—too many defections to the West, lately. Paul Houston felt his throat constrict. He was dimly aware that the reporter was rolling down his window.

"I cannot resist taking advantage of these obscene floodlights to get a shot of the *verboten* side of the bridge," the man said, "but I prefer not to photograph through glass."

"You know the regulations," Houston said absently. "No photographs of bridges. No open windows on your side when the Vopos check you through—" He stopped to stare. That yellow-haired East German guard in charge of one of the striped poles up ahead—the surly, hate-Americans-on-sight gorilla, wasn't it? The Vopo who gave him a hard time whenever he crossed over? Bruno, was his name. "No photographs," he snapped at the reporter. Then, "Switch seats with me. Quickly!" It will work, he told himself. It *must.*

Houston's heart lurched with the forward movement of the first limousine as it pulled up between the two striped poles. He watched the guard Bruno shuffle restlessly while his Soviet counterpart checked the passports of the American delegates in the first limousine. Following the Soviet guard's lead, Bruno raised the striped pole on his side— but with a resentful sweep of an arm—and stared after the limousine as it inched forward.

A hundred or so feet of cobblestone to the mouth of the bridge, Houston thought, watching, and from there, to the midpoint. . . . He stared at the midpoint, at a yellow rectangle which hung from it, spelling out its message—its territorial claim on his friend Brodsky; DEUTSCHE DEMOKRATISCHE REPUBLIK. Below the sign, like living exclamation points, stood two extra East German guards—a formality, in honor of the occasion, Houston knew. That orange-and-white-striped barrier they guarded at stiff attention operated, not by hand, but by remote control. Once again his throat constricted as he watched this final barrier retract silently to one side, permitting the first limousine of American delegates to cross over. They had reached the West Berlin half of the bridge.

His eyes returned to the guard Bruno as his own limousine pulled up between the still-raised poles. He saw Bruno bend to his task at the left-hand window, clearly expecting an ID card and a two-inch-by-four-inch photo of a West German reporter, pressed against glass. And then he saw what he'd hoped for: Bruno, gaping through an open window at the unexpected, at the contemptuous eyes of an American diplomat—at *him*—as he sat on the wrong side of the car, dangling a passport and smoking an American cigarette. In the moment when surprise and annoyance shifted to resentment, Houston blew smoke in the guard's face.

Bruno cursed and snatched Houston's passport.

"Hand it back, you ugly gorilla. Only the Soviets get to touch my passport."

"Big shot American," Bruno hissed, clutching the passport to his massive chest.

"My passport." Houston filled his voice with cold authority. He held out his hand for it. "Or do you intend to search my car?" His eyes did a lightning calculation of the distance from the poles to the mouth of the bridge, from there to the midpoint—

Bruno was staring at him. "You have no authority," Houston taunted. "You would not *dare*."

"I will search," came the answer. Bruno's hand had moved to his holster.

"Out," Houston ordered the reporter—and to his bewildered driver, "Get out. Leave your door open and the motor running." He followed them out.

Stepan Brodsky, an imposing figure in his Soviet air force uniform, strode up to them, a disapproving scowl on his face, a What's-going-on-here! message in his eyes.

Bruno backed away.

It took Brodsky a split second to slip behind the wheel—another to yank the door closed—a third for his foot to find the accelerator, to push it to the floor. Then his back slammed against seat cushions, the limousine shot past a startled Soviet guard, still holding up one striped pole, and Houston pictured the leap of the speedometer needle: 33 kilometers?

The shriek of an alarm shattered the unnatural stillness of stunned men. Houston whirled around in time to recognize Colonel Von Eyssen running out of a guardhouse. "Get down!" he yelled, and behind him heard his driver and the reporter hit the pavement.

"Feuern!" came Von Eyssen's megaphone-amplified shout. Fire!

Houston followed the megaphone's aim—high and to the right—and spotted machine gun emplacements in the watchtowers. Long, hot streaks of red and orange and yellow tore after the fleeing limousine, bursting into sparks as they struck pavement . . . tracer bullets. His eyes pursued the limousine, willing it to go faster. He saw bullets whip past the hood of the car. A guard at the crossing point collapsed into a soft pile.

"Die Reifen!" Von Eyssen's scream carried over the ear-splitting clatter of the guns.

But the men in the watchtowers knew their job. Even as Von Eyssen screamed the order, a rear tire blew apart. Houston had time for a curse, not a prayer, as the limousine veered sharply to the left, rammed into one side of the bridge, bounced off, and swaying crazily, headed for the opposite side, its right flank exposed to the line of fire. "The gas tank!" Houston choked. "Dear God, he's so close!"

A streak of bright orange connected with the tank just as the limousine jumped a strip of sidewalk and smashed into protruding steel—the retractable barrier, folded up, accordion-like, at one side of the midpoint. Flames, the color of the tracer bullet, attacked the car and grappled with steel webbing. Then pieces of rubber and twisted metal burst into the air. Some of the debris fell on the inert form of Stepan Brodsky. He had been thrown clear.

"Feuern aufhören!"

The spit and crackle of flame against steel filled the silence. Then, in the confusion of wailing sirens and shouted orders, three men raced for the burning wreck, their footsteps swallowed by the motor of a patrol boat, hovering underneath the bridge.

Three men—Bruno, Von Eyssen, Houston—got there in time to witness a struggle: Brodsky, crawling through warm liquid that was spilled gasoline and his own blood.

His body was twisted like a piece of the flying steel, yet he dragged himself forward, away from the flames, one outstretched hand reaching toward some objects that had fallen from his pocket—they lay between him and the edge of the bridge. It was a matter of inches. He groaned, slid forward, touched metal—

A black boot nudged the cigarette lighter just out of

reach. Von Eyssen looked down, smiling, as Brodsky tried to raise his head—and dropped it.

"You sadistic—" Houston seized a piece of the twisted steel and swung, barely missing Von Eyssen's skull. He dropped the steel, reached for Brodsky's wrist—and felt the tip of a bayonet between his shoulder blades. Bruno pulled him up and shoved him aside. Von Eyssen, still smiling, clicked his heels in mock deference and moved off to join the soldiers swarming over the bridge—they were examining the wreck, putting out the fire, bending over the dead body of the guard at the midpoint. Bruno stayed put, a look of suspicion on his face; it was directed at a civilian who stood a few discreet feet away.

No one, looking at Houston's inscrutable face, would have noted the glance of recognition that passed between him and this civilian . . . an East German photographer who was his friend and Stepan's. No one, looking at the photographer, would have guessed what Houston knew: that a Minox camera was concealed in one oversized hand. A swift change in the man's expression made Houston drop his eyes.

Brodsky's blond head was inching forward again. One blood-stained hand strained for the cigarette lighter, pushed—and tensed, as the lighter disappeared over the side into a black void. Then the hand, a few inches from freedom, lay still.

1

A dozen pairs of shapely legs spun around a polished rosewood floor. A dozen pairs of high, black boots swung from deep knee bends into gravity-defying leaps. The barelegged women, red-and-black peasant skirts whirling above their waists, held outsized cups and saucers. The blackbooted men, in loose white tunics with red sashes, formed a ring around the women. In the center of the leaping, whirling figures, an upright bear clutched a samovar. The exuberant cries of the dancers threatened to drown out the cheerful strains of an accordion. The women circled faster. The men arched their backs and broke into a heel-stamping, thigh-slapping finale. The bear, with a sidewise crook of its head, surrendered the samovar to outstretched female hands.

The audience was small, select, and enthusiastic, interspersing its applause with bravos and shouts of ''Wonderful! Wonderful!'' The smiling dancers, one with the bear's head tucked under his arm, bowed and waved at the audience in traditional Russian fashion.

When the applause finally died, a butler announced that Mr. and Mrs. Manning were requesting everyone's presence in the garden, where refreshments were about to be served.

The guests passed through French doors that opened onto a brass-railed patio. A marble staircase led from the patio down to a walled-in garden, the size of a basketball court. Shade trees and tall-stemmed flowers ran along the walls and halted at the East River.

The hostess made a fetching picture alongside a sumptuous buffet table, a slight breeze playing with her ruffled skirt and long, prettily disheveled hair—"peasant-style, in keeping with the theme of the party," she'd explained to several of her friends. "Ladies and gentlemen," she called out gaily, "thanks are in order for the 'sneak preview' we've just had of tomorrow night's gala opening. So before we sample some tantalizing Russian delicacies—the recipes were donated by the Soviet Mission—I should like to propose a toast."

Uniformed maids began passing trays of drinks. Butlers hovered about with bottles poised.

The hostess smiled. "This is vodka—the champagne comes later. I propose a *double* toast," she announced. "First, to the wonderfully talented dancers of Omsk, who have brightened what would surely have been a dull Sunday afternoon in July. Second," she continued, as glasses were raised, "to the gentleman who provided us with this exciting glimpse into his country's folk heritage—to Ambassador Zorin—and, of course, to his charming wife."

Ambassador Zorin, a slight, trim-looking man, beamed. His wife smiled shyly, revealing a stainless-steel tooth. Zorin downed his vodka and held out his glass for more. "I, too, should like to propose a toast," he said, raising his glass. "To my distinguished and dedicated host, Russell Manning, whose contribution to the relaxation of world tensions is considerable."

Russell Manning, executive director of Medicine International, the organization that financed symposiums and medical centers and whose slogan—"World Peace Through World Health"—was known in households everywhere, ran a hand through dignified waves of silver hair. "One cannot indulge in toastmaking," he said, "without singling out America's most prominent surgeon and humanitarian, the man who will represent his country at Medicine International's forthcoming symposium in West Berlin—Dr. Kurt Brenner!"

The silver-blue of the river and the brighter blue of the sky served as a perfect backdrop for Kurt Brenner's tall, stately figure in an impeccably tailored, off-white suit. A faint flush of color touched his cheeks, then spread across prominent cheekbones to the corners of dark, velvet-brown eyes. Brenner acknowledged the accolade with a casual nod and a smile. His face looked young and healthy, deeply tanned from the sun. His hair, in stunning contrast, was completely white. He waited for the glasses to be refilled, waited for the small drop of silence that had followed the previous toasts, before he said in his rich baritone, "To my Russian, French and British colleagues, *in absentia*, and to the success of the symposium which all of us look forward to with great anticipation." He held his glass high and smiled again—this time for a photographer from the Soviet News Agency.

Guests began to desert the vodka for champagne and the buffet table. "Isn't this exciting?" breathed one woman, waving her taffeta parasol. "The whole thing is completely authentic. Chicken tabaka—they serve it with a heavy garlic sauce, fish in aspic, pickled cabbage, crab-meat—I understand it's impossible to beg, borrow or steal crabmeat in Moscow, these days, and look—isn't that cute?'' Her parasol hovered over a platter of iced cakes: white with tiny red stars on top.

The dancers were clustered into two groups, like two awkward, oversized bundles, with no trace of the graceful-ness that had characterized their performance. A couple of unsmiling men in baggy serge suits and heavily starched shirts stood among them. A guest beamed at the dancers and a few of them smiled back self-consciously.

''—so I cannot understand why more Americans do not demand a higher standard of medical care, such as that found in my country,'' Ambassador Zorin was saying to Kurt Brenner.

''You're way ahead of us there,'' Brenner said smoothly. ''I've always admired your policy of making the health of your people a public responsibility.''

''Quite so. From the time of birth, every citizen is enrolled in a neighborhood polyclinic. Every medical need is met. We take particularly good care of our children.''

''Medical care for children—now, there's a subject close to Kurt's heart, isn't it, my dear?'' The hostess had come up behind Brenner and slipped her hand possessively into his.

''Who has not heard of your cardiac clinic for underprivi-leged children?'' the Ambassador said politely. ''Very commendable.''

A butler approached the Ambassador about a telephone call in the library.

''Don't look so disappointed,'' the hostess quipped as Brenner watched Zorin hurry away. ''You'll have plenty of time to impress the Ambassador with all the wonderful things your institute is doing, though I can't see why you'd want to bother. You certainly don't expect to get any money out of *him*, do you?"

"Don't be a bitch." Brenner's lips curved into a characteristic smile, half amusement, half contempt.

"Why shouldn't I be?" she retorted, annoyed by the amusement. "You're such a busy man, with your lectures and your charity work. You've been neglecting me. I don't think you'd have come to my party if it hadn't been for Russell. You can't afford to antagonize him, can you, dear heart?"

"I can afford to antagonize anyone I please," he said coldly.

"Not Russell. Not until after his symposium. Think of all that publicity! It should help you raise money for your precious institute—not to mention your own pocket. Russell says you're absolutely desperate for money these days," she said, smiling.

"A combination of the recession and some injudicious personal investments," he said, sounding more indifferent than he felt. "And I've been neglecting you lately because I've been in Washington. Government grants are getting as scarce as hen's teeth."

"Poor darling." She sounded mollified. "How unfortunate for you that most of Russell's handouts go to underdeveloped countries instead of heart institutes on the upper East side of Manhattan." She took out a cigarette and reached for some matches on a table.

Brenner beat her to the matches and lit her cigarette with a graceful movement.

"Darling," she said, "with all this money-chasing you have to do, how ever do you find time for the surgery you're so famous for?"

"I have a competent, highly trained staff at my disposal," he said in a bored voice. "Why don't we talk about something else?"

"Why, certainly. Let's talk about your perfectly enchanting wife. Since she doesn't know about *us*, I think her not being here is downright rude. Was it mere oversight, or am I being snubbed?"

Brenner frowned, wondering who else had noticed Adrienne's absence. What was he supposed to tell people— that his wife refused to socialize with the Soviet ambassador? Or worse yet, that she now refused to socialize with her own husband? It was sheer luck that their latest rift hadn't hit the gossip columns. "You know Adrienne," he said lightly. "She's all wrapped up in that job of hers."

"Medical writer for a news magazine. Charming occupation for a woman with *her* social background, I must say. Doesn't she ever give any teas or anything?"

Brenner threw back his head and laughed. "Adrienne, give a tea?" His arms swung outward, expressing amused incredulity.

The sudden movement caught a passing butler off guard. His tray of drinks swerved, sending the glasses against the garden wall with a crash.

"Clumsy fool!" Brenner's face was pale.

"But Kurt, dear, it was an accident. Is this a demonstration of the famous Brenner temper?" she chided.

Brenner was examining each individual finger with care. "Suppose a piece of flying glass had cut my hands?" he snapped. The hands were long and narrow; people often noticed them.

"Cuts heal, darling. A little cut wouldn't interfere with all that surgery you haven't been doing lately, now would it?" But she realized that she'd gone too far. He looked really angry. "They're perfectly lovely hands," she soothed. "When are you going to let me paint them?"

"Portrait-sitting is a bore," he said, not sounding bored. "The institute commissioned a well-known artist to do my portrait over six months ago, but the hours I've wasted just—"

"Excuse me," she interrupted, her trained hostess' eye catching the expression on the Ambassador's face as he stepped through the French doors. She hurried up the patio stairs.

The Ambassador was leaning over the railing, talking to one of the unsmiling men below. He turned at her approach. "I am sorry to spoil your lovely party, but I must leave at once. We all must." He gestured toward the dancers, being herded into a tight circle in front of a garden door leading to the street.

"How perfectly horrid of you, Mr. Ambassador," she said, "but I forgive you. Shall we see you after the opening, then?"

"I am afraid there will be no opening," he replied—and instantly regretted not having lowered his voice. People had heard.

A small crowd gathered, looking up at them expectantly. "How disappointing," someone whispered. "Did you hear? No opening." "What's happened?" asked someone else.

Kurt Brenner and Russell Manning exchanged apprehensive glances.

A news columnist with a bored expression joined the crowd growing at the foot of the stairs. "Would you care to comment on the cancellation of the opening, Mr. Ambassador?" he asked dutifully.

The Ambassador adjusted his glasses, giving himself a moment to think. He had been waiting for the telephone call.

The expected blowup of negotiations in Potsdam was to have signaled a change in his country's attitude toward the British and the Americans: business as usual, but at a polite, tantalizing distance until further notice. Because of the border incident, however, his instructions were obsolete. Politeness was not called for any longer . . . "I am sorry to report," he said crisply, "that the barbs of Western hostility have pierced my country's good intentions at the bargaining table. Negotiations in Democratic Berlin and in Potsdam have come to a halt—thanks not only to France, who struck the first blow—but to the United States." He glanced at his watch, making a mental adjustment for the five-hour time difference. "Barely an hour ago," he continued, "while we were enjoying Russian folk dancing in New York City and drinking toasts to the relaxation of world tensions, an American diplomat in Potsdam was filling a conference room with harshly worded insults. Even worse, this man aided and abetted a politically and morally depraved person—a common criminal—who tried to leave the German Democratic Republic unlawfully. Fortunately, the criminal was apprehended. Unfortunately, the repercussions touch all of us. There will be no dance performances, no sports events, no—"

"No medical symposium?" Russell Manning interrupted. "Surely, Mr. Ambassador, your government won't find it necessary to withdraw?"

"It is conceivable." Zorin turned away.

"Russell," Brenner said urgently, "suppose the Russians do back out. You're not thinking of cancelling, are you? What about the money you've poured into the new medical center? What about the dedication ceremony we've been planning? It's only a few weeks off!"

"I'm not sure, I'm just not sure," Manning said. "You

know as well as I do that the whole idea of the symposium was to bring the 'Big Four' powers together in a hot-spot like West Berlin, all engrossed in medicine for a change. We're supposed to be in the middle of an East-West thaw, for God's sake! People talk about stepping up cultural and scientific exchanges. Medicine International was first in line, for God's sake! I hate politics," he said. "We could go ahead without the Russians, I suppose, but it wouldn't be the same. I don't know, I just don't know . . ."

Brenner hurried up the stairs just as Zorin was about to come down. "Mr. Ambassador," he said, "I consider myself a patriotic American, but I must confess that I am surprised and offended by my government's behavior. To think that some bureaucrat who takes it upon himself to play God can sabotage *months* of important negotiations—to say nothing about worthwhile scientific exchanges," he added darkly, glaring at Manning. "Did this damn-fool diplomat even consider the consequences of helping some lawbreaker, I wonder?" he said angrily, warming to the subject.

The news columnist no longer looked bored; he was taking notes. So was the man from the Soviet News Agency. The Ambassador was studying Brenner curiously, the suggestion of a smile on his lips.

Brenner lowered his eyes. "It has taken years of dedicated effort for our two countries to establish a bridge of friendship," he said with ringing sincerity. "I only hope that bridge is strong enough to withstand these isolated attacks. I only hope the situation doesn't deteriorate to the point where it threatens the peacemaking endeavors of praiseworthy organizations like Medicine International." He looked at the man from the Soviet News Agency, his glance underscoring his words.

"Mr. Ambassador," the columnist said as Zorin started down the stairs, "the man who created the incident, is he East German or Russian?"

"He was Ukrainian, a minor air force official," the Ambassador said indifferently, and kept walking.

"Was, Mr. Ambassador?"

"He was shot."

"At the border?"

The Ambassador paused reluctantly at the door. "I believe he was stopped on the bridge between Potsdam and West Berlin."

The columnist thought for a moment. "We dedicated a bridge back in '45 for the original Potsdam Conference. Liberty Bridge, I think it was, or Freedom—Bridge of Freedom," he said a shade too innocently. "Are we talking about the same bridge?"

"I know that bridge only as Bruecke der Einheit—Bridge of Unity," the Ambassador said stiffly, "so named in 1949 for 'einheitspartei'—socialist party unity in the German Democratic Republic." He nodded brusquely at the hostess and went out.

Kurt Brenner held onto the brass railing of the patio to keep his hands from shaking. Freedom Bridge. God *damn* that reporter for bringing it up. At least the damn fool hadn't remembered the details, he thought. And what if he had? Brenner let go of the railing defiantly. And had to hold on again. Damn fool, he chastised himself. The bridge business was pure coincidence—just another failed escape that could have happened at any border crossing. Just another poor bastard who— Who was Ukrainian. *Two* coincidences? he thought shakily. You're a fool *and* an idiot! he told himself. Only idiots drag up thirty-year-old ghosts. You're upset about the symposium. You've had too much to drink—goddamn ridiculous Russian toasts! There's nothing to be uneasy about—upset, yes, but not uneasy. He thought of Adrienne and her blind spot about dissidents and political asylum. To hell with her, he decided. And to hell with the damn fool who'd gotten himself shot.

He let go of the railing and examined his hands. Not a tremor. He picked a glass of champagne off a passing tray and headed for a cluster of women, loudly lamenting the loss of their first night. They looked as if they needed cheering up.

2

Dr. Kiril Andreyevich Andreyev sat on a low stool, monitoring the control panel of a boxlike machine on wheels.
He examined three pumpheads on top, then followed the
downward flow of colorless liquid through clear, plastic
tubing. The flow was unimpeded. "What time is it?" he
asked a technician.

"Twenty past eight, Doctor."

He frowned and looked up. Dr. Yanin was late. The
nurses had prepared the patient. The assisting surgeons and
the anesthesiologist moved restlessly about the operating
table. Finally the doors to the operating room swung open,
and Dr. Mikhail V. Yanin burst into the room. He was a
small teddy bear of a man, with thick eyebrows and curly,
graying hair that refused to be confined under his green
surgical cap—round and high, like a baker's hat. "Out!"
he said, simultaneously gesturing at the patient and glaring
at one of the technicians. "Take the patient out. I am not
ready to begin. I have something to say." He tugged

43

impatiently at one sleeve of his green hospital gown until the patient had been wheeled from the room. "I have just learned of a catastrophe—for me—for the hospital that bears my name—for Soviet medicine!" he announced with characteristic melodrama. "I have just been informed that our trip to West Berlin was cancelled last night!" He surveyed a semi-circle of uneasy faces. "So? No one has anything to say?"

Kiril Andreyev heard words, but they were only in his mind. Stepan's words, said only two weeks ago—in casual, unaccented English: "See you in West Berlin." And the two of them, believing it, had grinned at each other.

He heard words said aloud, bitterly: "The State giveth and the State taketh away." It was the anesthesiologist.

He managed to look across the room at Nurse Galina Barkova, her face desolate beneath the white triangle of her kerchief. Only last night, sitting on the bed in his room, laughing in delight, Galya had been saying, "West Berlin! Elegant shops, exotic food, a sumptuous hotel room—do those things really exist? And clothes. Not my shapeless black dress fit for an old woman, anymore. Clothes with style!"

She was looking away now, as one of the surgeons said, "I suppose it's a question of money."

"Not *this* time," Yanin scowled. "This time, it's a question of politics, or so I gather from the doubletalk. It seems we have been insulted by the Americans, so we are going to boycott the symposium."

"There's no chance they'll change their minds?" someone asked.

"Why should they?" Yanin snapped. "What do they care about *my* problems? We have money for space stations and rocket fuel and fancy hotels on Gorky Street, but

I am expected to accomplish miracles with faulty equipment. You all know what I am reduced to—scavenging! The visiting Canadian surgeons leave tomorrow. By tomorrow, I must swallow my pride and ask them to send me some sutures. Sutures! So?'' he repeated.

No one answered. Dr. Yanin was a Party member. Everyone looked properly sympathetic.

Everyone except Kiril. He was hearing Stepan's voice, remembering endless strategy discussions about how to channel their particular skills. "Forget about medical research or surgery, Kiril. The best job is the one that could lead to a trip or an outside post, even in a Soviet bloc country. It's a step in the right direction." "Why?" "Because it's one step closer to a more accessible Western border."

Yanin began to pace. "Cancelling this trip adds insult to injury," he growled. "*Months* of preparation with nothing to show for it! Even worse, I am to be robbed of the opportunity to observe a master surgeon at work."

"Do Dr. Brenner's operating teams really do ten to twelve open-hearts a day?" asked one of the surgeons skeptically.

"Ten or twelve to *our* three or four," moaned Yanin.

Two stone-faced men in dark suits walked through the swinging doors and looked around.

Yanin stared at them, momentarily speechless. Then his bushy eyebrows rose. "How *dare* you enter my operating room unannounced. Get out! Get out at once!"

It was as if Yanin hadn't spoken. "Which one of you is Dr. Andreyev?" asked one of the two men.

"I am." Kiril stepped out from behind the machine. His eyes, deep brown like his hair, were somber. The habitual set of his mouth was firm, suggesting tight control . . . or endurance. Occasionally the control would slip, causing the left corner of his mouth to turn down slightly, suggesting a touch of melancholy. The mouth was in control now.

"Come with us," said one of the men.

"Please," said Yanin in a subdued voice—he knew, now, who the men were. "Please, we have a grueling operating schedule, this morning. I need Dr. Andreyev to operate the heart-lung machine."

"Get someone else."

"You don't understand." Yanin's voice was deferential. "Dr. Andreyev is an expert. He can hook up the machine with his eyes closed. He anticipates every move I make."

No reaction.

"This machine performs a vital function," Yanin pleaded. "It takes the place of a patient's heart and lungs. Even with the best of equipment, dozens of things can go wrong. That plastic tubing," he said, pointing, "is not of the best quality. If it should spring a leak during an operation, it would need immediate repair. If the blood in the oxygenator should drop below a certain level, air could be pumped into the patient's blood stream—only an alert technician could prevent it. If the patient's heart should refuse to start once the operation is over, the technician would have five minutes to get the patient back on the machine—five minutes, or the patient would die."

"Get someone else," repeated one of the stone faces. He motioned for Kiril to follow and walked out. The low-pitched whine of the doors swinging back and forth was the only sound in the room.

A black, high-roofed limousine waited at the curb. Kiril walked down the hospital steps, flanked by the two men. "Am I under arrest?" he asked, as the door of the limousine opened. No answer. "What business does the secret police have with me?'' he persisted, as he climbed into the back seat.

The two men might as well have been deaf mutes. One of them signaled the driver to start the car. The other leaned back and looked out the window.

Kiril's hands dug into the pockets of the hospital gown he'd had no time to remove. His hands were cold . . . as they had been that time when he was only thirteen and had been roughly accosted on the street by a couple of burly police agents and interrogated for seven uninterrupted hours about people he'd never heard of—a group who'd planned to hijack a plane out of the country. Only after it was over had he learned why he'd been seized and questioned: the young daughter of one of the plotters was a casual school acquaintance; and Kiril Andreyev was the son of an Enemy of the People.

I should prepare myself, he thought. I should think up a story or an excuse . . . but for what? Something I said? Something I didn't say? Something to do with Stepan? He closed his eyes, trying to remember. They have no way to connect me with anything, he told himself. Not unless they've found the film in Stepan's lighter.

He forced himself to look out the window. The limousine had paused for a light, near a building with a familiar message blazoned on its facade: GLORY TO THE COMMUNIST PARTY—THE GUIDING FORCE OF THE NEW SOCIETY. They have had me for forty-seven years, he thought. Years of weighing and hoping and scheming, endless years of cautiously discarding one plan after another until the right plan—the workable one. Which was now destroyed by a boycott.

He looked out at the faces on the street. Blank faces. A man who might grumble, but only about the scarcity of oranges in December . . . a woman who might curse the

47

system, but only because it stocked caviar exclusively at hard currency shops for foreigners and government officials . . . faces that resented the tedious shopping queues and the long waiting lists for automobiles and the harsh winters—and nothing else . . . faces of men and women who had grown used to the system. Who took for granted that they were slaves. There was only one defense against sinking into that kind of living death, he knew—never stop dreaming of freedom, never give it up.

The limousine pulled up in front of an imposing building. With its row upon row of windows and its glossy black marble facade, the building had a guileless look—a showplace on tourist itineraries, said to house government offices. This was true. The spacious, windowed offices were occupied by high-ranking members of the secret police; the windowless core of the building, not visible from the street, contained one of Moscow's most infamous prisons.

Which would it be, Kiril wondered as he was hustled out of the limousine, office or prison? . . . Office. He walked with relief into a small anteroom and realized suddenly where he was. Two weeks ago, the room had been empty. Now, the wooden benches hugging the walls were filled with an odd assortment of people—young, old, middle-aged, shabby suits, ostentatiously expensive dresses . . . He looked at tensed shoulders and averted eyes. The one thing they have in common, he thought, is fear. The room was silent.

He sat down next to a young girl. Something about her tugged at his memory. She glanced at him, shyly at first as she took in his hospital gown, then with a kind of intense scrutiny. She tried to smile, but her lower lip began to tremble.

"Don't be afraid," Kiril said gently, knowing she had every reason to be.

"I'm not, really, not for myself," she confided in a whisper. "It's my brother I'm afraid for. He said some things he shouldn't have and now they're looking for him. They'll find him, too, unless I can stop myself from giving him away."

He knew suddenly what she reminded him of; something in her face was faintly like an image from his childhood. A beloved friend who had gotten his first taste of anti-Semitic persecution in kindergarten. Who, at eight years of age, was studying Hebrew and Jewish history in secret. Who, at twelve, was dragged from the room of his devoutly religious parents by three police agents, thrown into a waiting limousine, and installed in a Young Communist camp a thousand miles outside of Moscow. The camp featured loudspeakers blaring propaganda, patriotic marches, and rallies—for the reconditioning and rekindling of the Communist spirit in Soviet children. His friend's bunkmates were threatened with the loss of camp privileges unless they "saved the soul of this victim of Zionism." His friend was kept there, not the usual four weeks, but over eight months. He had never been the same afterward.

The young girl beside him shuddered. "I haven't a chance," she said. "I knew it as soon as I realized where I was."

"What do you mean?"

"Don't you know whose office this is?" Her eyes pitied his ignorance. "They call this place the Confessional. They say no one leaves here without telling everything he knows."

He was wondering how to answer when an unmarked door opened.

A secretary with a pink, bovine face stuck her head out, motioned to a small huddle, and watched impassively while a man and two women filed past. She started to close her door—and spotted Kiril. Her face lost some of its pinkness. She hurried over to him. "Dr. Andreyev, how nice! Won't you join me in my office?"

"Andreyev?" The girl's eyes became enormous.

"It's not what you think," Kiril said quickly. "I'm here for the same reason you are." But he knew that nothing he could say would reassure her. He got up and followed the secretary to her office. When she'd closed them in, he said, "Are you feeling better now, Miss Dimova?"

"Much better, thank you." She licked her lips. "I'm surprised to see you here, Doctor. It isn't because of what happened two weeks ago, is it? You promised not to tell the Colonel. I could lose my job." She sounded on the verge of tears.

Touching, he thought, remembering her impassive features in the fear-filled room outside. "You needn't worry," he said coolly. "I have kept my promise—and your secret." *Our* secret, I hope, he thought.

She sighed. "Thank you. Won't you sit down and— excuse me." She picked up a ringing telephone. "Right away, sir." She hung up and smiled apologetically. "I'm afraid they're ready to see you. First door to your right, Doctor."

The room that he entered had no windows. Two men sat at one end of a long table. An empty chair waited for him at the other end. One of the men was smoothfaced, barely old enough to shave, from the look of him, Kiril thought. The other, a man in his fifties, had a wary expression in his eyes. Just as Kiril sat down, a white flash shattered the dim light, blinding him. When he could see again, he realized that someone had switched on a low-hanging overhead bulb. He felt pinned to his chair by the white glare. He could no longer see the two men clearly.

"We want to ask you some questions about an air force officer named Stepan Brodsky," said the older man.

Kiril felt his hands go cold again.

"Do you deny he is a friend of yours?" The voice of the smoothfaced interrogator was razor sharp, with no trace of his colleague's almost deferential caution.

"He is," Kiril said quietly. "I don't deny it."

"When did you first become acquainted with him?" asked the older interrogator.

"We met about ten years ago. I was a medical officer attached to his air force unit. It was just a chance meeting. I don't remember much about it." But I do remember, he thought. Their response to each other had been immediate and spontaneous. When everyone around you was a potential threat, you learned to sense who was an enemy and who a friend. Like the pathetic girl in the anteroom.

"How do you spend your time with this man? What is your relationship?"

"Purely social. We're friends. How do friends spend their time?" he asked rhetorically, remembering the years they'd spent learning languages: French, German, English with a British accent, English with no accent at all—with contractions and a lot of slang thrown in—"in case we get a chance to pass ourselves off as Americans," Stepan had said, as they'd bent over a radio, hunting for foreign broadcasts. And their excitement at Stepan's discovery of "Operation Travel Bureau," organized by West Berlin students right after the Wall went up. The Bureau had been responsible for hundreds of escapes, its technique simple, but effective. Scour Western Europe for lookalikes—in some cases, exact doubles, like the shopkeeper from Basel and the orthopedist from Leipzig. Then, smuggle European passports into East Germany. For months afterward, Kiril had donated every spare moment to medical exchange programs, while Stepan had haunted diplomatic circles. They had scanned every foreign face in the vain hope of spotting lookalikes of their own.

"Are you aware this Brodsky is a traitor?" said the young interrogator, breaking the long, incriminating silence. "When did he start betraying his country? Before or after he joined the air force?"

"I didn't know him before," Kiril said cautiously. His hands felt colder.

"*Why* did he join the air force?"

"He never said." But he had: "The whole point was to be able to steal a plane with enough range to get me the hell out of here. But they'll never trust me anywhere near one!"

The older interrogator disliked the tone of his brash, young colleague. One could not know exactly the standing of this Dr. Andreyev. The thing to do was to tread carefully. "Do you know any of Brodsky's friends or acquaintances?" he asked in a tone that was neither friendly nor unfriendly.

"I've met a few. I don't know any of them well." But he'd had the chance: they were students, artists, writers, scientists, who were vehemently critical of the system. He had devoured their underground literature, typed and circulated by hand. He had gone with Stepan to a few gatherings and gotten his first heady taste of free-wheeling discussions on forbidden subjects. He had stopped going when he'd begun to suspect he was under some special surveillance. It felt a little like having smallpox—if you walked around with it, you were in danger of contaminating others. Stepan had scoffed at his self-imposed quarantine, even after seeing the wiretap device on his telephone. But Stepan had searched his own room after that, and then Galya's; more wiretaps. "It doesn't matter," Stepan had assured him. "Most of my friends are well known to the secret police, and they just assume their phones are tapped." So he had returned to the gatherings. Until someone discovered his family history. When it became obvious that his presence made people uncomfortable and inhibited conversation, he had stopped going again. It had been like locking himself in mental solitary.

"Did you know Brodsky was planning an escape? Did you know he'd try to crash through the barrier on the bridge between Potsdam and West Berlin?" asked one of the interrogators.

"In an American limousine?" interjected the other.

In the small stretch of silence that followed the questions, both interrogators leaned forward; the subject—up to now imperturbable—looked visibly shocked.

"I didn't know it," Kiril said slowly. His mind was an agony of questions: Where was Stepan? Why had he abandoned the plan? Had his own part in it been discovered? And Stepan's lighter—where was it? He thought suddenly of his own lighter, the twin, foolishly left lying on the table in his room, and the cold that had been in his hands slid down to his stomach.

"We know," said the younger interrogator, "that you met with Brodsky on his brief return to Moscow two weeks ago, before he left again for East Germany. Do you mean to say he revealed nothing about his intended escape?"

"Nothing. Where is he now?"

The two men looked at each other. Cautiously the older one said, "He is dead."

"Shot while trying to escape," snapped the other.

After a while he heard one of them say, "We have no more questions for the present. Thank you for your cooperation. You will remain here, please." They left him in the white glare.

His body was a numb, unfamiliar object. He felt no anger, felt nothing at all. No, it was worse than that—he felt as if the numbness had sunk into his bones, wiping out his capacity to feel. Then something penetrated the numbness: a sense of loneliness so acute that his shoulders slumped from the weight of it.

Why should I fight anymore? he thought, even though he knew he was committing treason to a childhood vow. I am as dead as Stepan, he thought.

He saw Stepan's face, grinning at him across their favorite corner table in the "Western bar" on Gorky Street, where they would go to watch the kids in their blue jeans and miniskirts and shaggy hair. They would lose themselves in the defiant attempts at gaiety and raise their own glasses in the solemn toast that had become a ritual between them, uttered a hundred times while they plotted the future. It was their courage line, his and Stepan's, even though it had been only his long years before they'd met.

Say it now, he thought. Say it! And finally, Stepan's face before him, he did, whispering the toast as both a vow and a farewell. "To Anna and Kolya."

By the time someone came in, a massive figure in a soiled military tunic, and said, "You come with me," he was able to rise calmly and follow.

3

The desk was in friendly disorder: papers, books, assorted pipes, a half-eaten sandwich. The first thing one noticed about the man behind the desk were his eyes, behind pale-rimmed glasses: a moist-looking blue, with a tendency to blink rapidly. Sympathetic eyes. The top of his head was smooth, except for a few strands of faded blond hair. His jacket was loose and ill fitting. Bits of tobacco nestled in the wrinkles of his shirtfront. He had the look of an absent-minded professor, and a smile that seemed benevolent and wise, that seemed to say: "At ease. Let down your guard. Nothing is to be taken seriously in this room." The smile turned to amused condescension while the eyes, alert now, made a rapid but thorough inventory of his visitor. Pale eyebrows contracted into the barest suggestion of a frown—he seemed to be looking for something in Kiril's face.

"What do you want?"

Aleksei Andreyev indicated a chair. He shrugged when

Kiril remained standing in front of his desk. "I might ask *you* the same question. Why did you come to my office two weeks ago?"

"I wanted some information about the symposium—some straight facts, for a change." He said it casually, his mind pushing back the real reason: Aleksei's secretary, a former patient from his first polyclinic, who had a history of fainting spells. It had been easy . . . and terrifying. Coming to the office unannounced, on the pretext of getting information . . . knowing in advance Aleksei wouldn't be here . . . armed only with a miniature camera and fast film, concealed in his medical bag . . . sitting down with the secretary exactly ten minutes before a diplomatic courier was due . . . accepting her offer of tea and complaining that the glass was too hot . . . slipping a powdered drug into her tea as she turned to reach for a metal holder . . . waiting precious, terrifying minutes while she slipped into unconsciousness . . . photographing the message waiting on her desk for the courier . . . injecting her with a fast-acting, antagonist drug. She had pleaded with him, afterward, to keep silent. Fainting on the job was a serious matter. It could mean her dismissal. He had promised to keep her secret.

Apparently, it was still a secret, for Aleksei merely looked thoughtful. "So you were curious about the symposium," he said. "Let's just say I was curious, too. I thought I'd take a firsthand look at my brother after ten long years." He leaned back in his chair. "You've managed to remain young."

"I know all about your curiosity."

"Regrettably, surveillance can't always be done with subtlety. I admit to being well informed where you're concerned. I know, for example, when and where you acquired that healthy-looking suntan—a week ago, at the Black Sea. Why didn't you wait until early September? The weather is delightful then.''

"My vacations are assigned."

"But of course," he said softly. "Your undistinguished career would account for your lack of options in such matters. I must say that after all those childhood pretensions about ambition, I thought you'd amount to much more." He paused. "I know about the bad years, when you couldn't get a job. I know about the menial jobs you did get: putting up intravenous drips for other doctors, holding their instruments for them . . ." The blue eyes probed Kiril's face for a reaction. There was none. "I know about your first semi-decent job at a Moscow polyclinic, the one you gave up in order to become a glorified mechanic for the eminent Dr. Yanin. Now, why did you do that?"

Kiril shrugged. "I'm exactly what I want to be—an indispensable 'mechanic' for the best surgeon in Moscow." Eminent enough to be invited—and reinvited—to the West, he thought.

"How unfortunate that you lost precious years merely acquiring your credentials. I understand you had difficulty getting into a medical school."

Kiril lost track of Aleksei's voice and heard the sound of his own: begging for an education, trying to persuade indifferent faces to let him into college and later into medical school. "Comrade Andreyev, why, after the Young Pioneers, didn't you volunteer for the Young Communist League?" "They wouldn't have accepted me." It had been a plausible lie. "Why should the State educate the son of an Enemy of the People, Comrade Andreyev?" "Because I can serve the people. Let me bind their wounds and cure their illnesses. Let me serve." Let me be a doctor, like my mother . . .

"Your troubles were all very predictable, I'm afraid," Aleksei was saying. "At the risk of sounding boorish, I must admit that being the son of a Traitor to the Country—or was it Enemy of the People, in those days—didn't stand in *my* way."

"So I see."

"I grant you it was hard in the beginning, but I'm a resourceful man. You used to be interested in medical research. Did you know that was how I started—in research? You've heard of the Index?"

Kiril had heard of it—a staggering collection of biographies, international in scope and indiscriminate in content. Anyone of even remote interest to the secret police was part of it.

"I buried myself in the Index. Over the years, I made myself useful to a great many people."

"You mean that over the years, you became an expert blackmailer."

"One tramples, or one is trampled on," Aleksei remarked philosophically. "We had that tarnished family history to contend with, remember? I could have saved you a great deal of unpleasantness, by the way, had you come to me for help. Why didn't you?"

"That's like asking a priest why he never made a pact with the devil."

"You *are* your mother's son, aren't you? Your antisocial attitude is precisely why I've kept an eye on you all these years," Aleksei said calmly. "I could have you arrested, you know. I could have you placed in one of those mental institutions you've had the temerity to decry. But then, I'm a generous person, when it comes to ignoring relatively minor transgressions. That petition business was a meaningless and futile protest, by the way, but I should warn you against venturing into more dangerously overt acts of anti-Soviet slander. Rest assured that if you did, I would be the first to hear about it. And the first to act. You would get one chance to make a public display of yourself—only one."

"I know."

"I wonder if you do. You flirted with Siberia by signing those petitions."

"Did I?" He thought of his years practicing medicine in the Siberian labor camps, his first assigned job. Treating those whose "crime" was to disagree with a government that loudly deplored the Siberian prisons of the Czars, and that planted the symbol of the "new" Siberia—a fist holding a torch—on buildings everywhere. Schoolchildren translated it daily: "Freedom Breaking Through Oppression." He looked at Aleksei. "Unlike you, I don't consider it meaningless to protest against the institutionalization of sane men. As a doctor, I had no choice."

"Really? Judging from the scarcity of protesters, most of our doctors seem to feel otherwise," Aleksei said softly. "Well, no matter, so long as we understand each other. One ruined career because of treason in the family is enough, don't you agree?"

Kiril turned his back on him. He noticed for the first time the booklined walls and comfortable chairs, the indirect lighting and pastel color scheme. "The Confessional," he said. "It doesn't look like one, but that would be part of the technique, wouldn't it? I wish it *were* in my power to ruin your so-called career—I wish I could do for you what Anna did for the old man!"

"You'll never get that chance," Aleksei said. "Even if

your friend Brodsky almost did.'' He was leaning forward slightly, his voice no longer soft. "Brodsky was my responsibility. Had he escaped . . . But then he didn't, did he?''

Kiril stared at his hands, immobile on the chair. If he concentrated, he could make them stay where they were, could keep his fists from smashing out toward the sound of that smile. He succeeded finally and turned to face his brother.

Aleksei sounded irritated. "The timing of that little melodrama Brodsky staged last night was unfortunate. Your Dr. Yanin wasn't alone in wanting an opportunity to observe the famous Dr. Kurt Brenner at close range.''

"What business could the secret police have with a man like Brenner?'' Kiril said.

"So Brenner is a hero of yours, is he?'' Aleksei buzzed his secretary. "Miss Dimova, did those additions to the Brenner file arrive yet? . . . No, don't bother.'' He motioned to the massive figure that stood just inside the door. "Bring me the Brenner file,'' he told him. "My assistant, Lieutenant Luka Rogov,'' he chuckled as the man hurried out. "He's quite valuable to me in his own way. Aren't you, my friend?'' He smiled as Luka lumbered over with a bulky file folder. He opened it and scanned the top sheaf of papers. "Let me read you some recent off-the-cuff remarks by your hero.''

"I never said he was a hero. He's someone I respect professionally.''

"Listen to this,'' Aleksei said. It was when he got to the words "Did this damn-fool diplomat even consider the consequences of helping some lawbreaker?'' that he was rewarded with the first sign of emotion on Kiril's face. It was not the emotion he had been looking for. "Well?

What do you think of that?'' he pressed, even though the twist of his brother's lips told him.

"Let me see that," Kiril said evenly, reaching for the folder.

"Seeing is believing, is it?" Aleksei handed him the top sheaf of papers. He turned his attention to a ringing telephone.

Kiril sat down, his back to Aleksei and Luka. He read Brenner's remarks. He read what had triggered them: the remarks of the Soviet Ambassador. He could understand Zorin's mentality. But a man like Brenner? A heart surgeon who made his living saving lives? The papers twisted in his hands, dislodging a small brown envelope clipped to the back pages. He felt something inside . . . a photograph? He opened the envelope. And met Dr. Kurt Brenner—the name was typed at the bottom of the photograph and initialed by someone from the Soviet News Agency.

Dark brown eyes. High cheekbones. Similar kind of nose. Hard to tell about the mouth, he thought. White hair. Take away the sophistication, the look of wealth and distinction, and with a little cosmetic help, I could be a younger version of this man! he marveled. Three words exploded in his brain: OPERATION TRAVEL BUREAU. He stared at the photograph, unable to believe the resemblance, yet knowing it was possible, recalling the Bureau's case histories of lookalikes, even doubles, recalling the shopkeeper from Basel and the orthopedist from Leipzig. Could this be the way out, after all? *Did those "additions" to the Brenner file arrive?* Aleksei had asked his secretary. Maybe Aleksei hadn't seen the photograph yet. If he had, wouldn't he have commented on the resemblance? Kiril slipped both the photograph and its envelope into the breast pocket of the shirt he was wearing under his hospital gown. He kept the file in plain sight on his lap. He turned his chair around.

"Don't take up my time with your petty squabbles," Aleksei was saying on the phone. "The repairs will have to wait. . . . Because my orders are to keep all unauthorized personnel out of the entire bridge area until I've completed my investigation. *Your* orders are to have the necessary equipment set up before I get there. . . . Next weekend, my friend. . . . Who knows how long? A week, perhaps two. Unless the press of business forces me back to Moscow, I'll work through the weekend, if necessary. I'll expect you to do the same."

He hung up and looked at Kiril expectantly. "Please excuse the interruption. I believe we were talking about your *hero?*" But he saw no trace of violent anger, not even a suggestion of pain. Only a politely attentive expression. "I trust you found Dr. Brenner's lack of sympathy for your friend, Brodsky, disturbing. You must not judge him too harshly, however. A man of Brenner's prominence has many considerations to weigh." He shrugged. "His outburst was premature, as things turned out. They're going ahead with their West Berlin symposium."

"How do you know?"

"How do I know anything—or should I say everything?" *Your Dr. Yanin wasn't alone in wanting an opportunity to observe the famous Dr. Kurt Brenner at close range.* "You never answered my question, Aleksei." Sound *casual,* he ordered himself. "What business does the secret police have with Dr. Brenner?"

"I'll answer you by asking my own question." Aleksei fingered several pipes, chose one, and began filling it, his fingers milky white against the dark wood of the stem.

"As a man familiar with the field of heart surgery, what would you say were the chances of someone like Brenner defecting to the Soviet Union and practicing his craft here?"

"Whatever else you are, I don't think you're a complete fool. Defectors run in the opposite direction, don't they? There's also the small matter of medical facilities. Ours don't begin to compare with what the West has to offer, apparently. Dr. Brenner must have everything he wants. What would be in it for him?"

Aleksei lit his pipe before looking up. "Suppose it wasn't a question of what he had to gain? Suppose it was a question of what he stood to lose?"

"I thought your specialty was extorting confessions?"

"I have any number of specialties. You're forgetting about my background."

"As a blackmailer?"

"Let's just say I've always known how to capitalize on my Index experience. Fascinating work, collecting all those bits and pieces that form the mosaic of a man's past."

"There's something in Dr. Brenner's past you'd like to capitalize on?" Keep it casual, he thought.

"There was." Aleksei followed the lazy, upward drift of the pipesmoke. "Brenner's defection would place me in an enviable position. The man who could reverse a certain trend and persuade prominent people—prominent humanitarians—to run from West to East, for a change, would be held in great esteem in certain circles."

"I see."

"It's a pity we're boycotting that West Berlin symposium. I'd really love to have had a crack at Brenner."

"What if you could have your cake and eat it too?" Kiril said carefully. "What if, despite the boycott, you could have your close-range look at Brenner and a chance to make your . . . proposition?"

"I'm afraid I don't follow you."

"We could hold our own medical conference—with Dr. Kurt Brenner as our guest of honor. We could make it hard for him not to accept by scheduling it a few days before the one in West Berlin—by holding it right next door in East Berlin. We could invite surgeons from the People's Democracies. Dr. Yanin could chair the occasion."

"What an intriguing idea," Aleksei said thoughtfully. "Quite apart from my own private purpose, it has great propaganda possibilities. Not only do we boycott the West Berlin affair, but we steal its thunder, as well."

"You like the idea, then? It can be approved on such short notice?"

"It's possible. If our conference were to be a simple one-day event—some discussion, a demonstration or two, an honorary dinner—I can't be sure, of course. Decisions like this take time. But I'm inclined to think the propaganda aspects will prove irresistible in certain quarters. Let's see . . ." He consulted a calendar on his desk. "The official opening of the West Berlin symposium is at noon on August first, a Tuesday. That's two weeks from today. That doesn't give us much time, does it? If we were to schedule our conference for the day before, on a Monday morning . . . yes, that might work."

"Why not invite Brenner for the weekend before?" Kiril suggested casually.

"Not a bad thought, but I may be tied up in Potsdam that weekend." He started to make some notes.

"Yes, of course. You were making plans on the telephone."

Aleksei looked up. "What gave you the idea for a

conference?'' he asked slowly. ''Why the sudden desire to cooperate with the secret police?''

''I'll cooperate even more, if you let me. In case you're busy just before the conference, I'll entertain Brenner for you until Monday.''

''Don't you think Dr. Yanin would be a more suitable substitute host?''

''He's entertaining some Australian surgeons that weekend.''

''But you don't know Berlin. You don't know East Germany.''

''You're wrong. I know a great deal about both. From my friend, Stepan Brodsky,'' he said evenly. ''Let me borrow Brenner's file, and by the time he arrives, I'll know all I need to know about *him*, as well. Are you thinking I don't have the credentials for the job? I'm your brother, remember? I'm a long-standing member of Dr. Yanin's surgical team. I'm a doctor with almost twenty years of experience—much of it, I admit, behind a heart-lung machine,'' he added with feigned bitterness. ''Don't you think I'm in a position to knowledgeably describe the life of the Soviet heart surgeon? In glowing terms, of course.''

''You amaze me,'' Aleksei said softly. ''I know a great deal about you, Little Brother. Why do you want to do something so out of character?''

''I could say that observing the brilliant Dr. Brenner at work would enliven things at the Yanin Institute. I could say his presence there would mean a great deal to Dr. Yanin . . . a man to whom I may be devoted,'' he said derisively. ''Or,'' he said, his voice hard, ''I could admit that you were right. Running a heart-lung machine is a colossal waste of my talents. If Brenner opted to remain, he'd need his own surgical team, wouldn't he? He and I would have a weekend to get acquainted. What could be more natural than for him to train *me* as his chief assisting surgeon? I'm tired of watching from the sidelines. I've always wanted to get into surgery. I could be as good as Yanin, himself, given half a chance.''

"So childhood ambition dies hard, after all.''

"That, and hero worship,'' Kiril said—a reluctant admission. "Dr. Brenner is a surgeon without peer. Well?''

"I must admit that the thought of you as my co-optee is intriguing.''

"Your what?''

"Co-optee is someone who cooperates with us on a given assignment. It's *you* playing unofficial host for me. What an amusing thought. Why aren't you looking amused? Well, why not? I've always thought of myself as a charitable person. I do think that unofficial hosts should have unofficial bodyguards, however. Tell my brother about *your* credentials, Luka,'' he said softly.

Luka stepped forward. His head was shaved, his face flat, his black eyes deep-set and slanted, his skin neither brown nor yellow but some of each. The coarse black hairs of a mustache framed the sides of his mouth. "In 1945 I help liberate Berlin,'' he said, his eyes gleaming with the memory. "I was six years in Red Army. I was—''

"That will do, Luka. I discovered Luka during the war, but I lost track of him,'' Aleksei explained. "I rediscovered him years later on a Moscow street. He comes from a small town near the Mongolian border. His name has been modernized, but not his soul. He's the kind of man we find invaluable in security matters, a man devoid of imagination. Such men know how to obey orders. They never question them. I don't think I need to add that Luka enjoys his work." Aleksei studied Kiril's impassive face and frowned. "Let me clarify my position," he said. "When you were a child, you used to fear me. I see that this is no longer the case . . . even though you have much more reason to fear me now. Remember this, then. If I permit you to precede me to East Berlin, you will not develop any unpatriotic ideas. Luka will make certain of this. He will have his orders. Should you attempt escape, his orders will be to take extreme action. Understand what I mean by 'extreme.' There is a story that circulates among my colleagues about a general's younger sister, picked up in Moscow for black market speculation during the War. The police contacted the general, expecting him to dismiss the charges. I still have in my possession a copy of the general's order: 'Speculation during wartime is treason. Shoot her.' Any questions, Little Brother?"

"Just one." Kiril tossed the papers from the Brenner file onto Aleksei's desk. "Do you think our guest of honor will come? I understand from Dr. Yanin that he has consistently declined invitations from Communist countries."

"Not *this* time. You read his remarks. Outrage over the Potsdam border incident. Enthusiasm for scientific exchanges. Eagerness to rush to the defense of our country, even at the expense of his own. His remarks have been widely publicized—no small thanks to us. I think the eminent Dr. Brenner would find it extremely awkward to refuse." He chuckled. "He can always say he wants to visit his birthplace—did you know he was born in what is now East Berlin? In the end, however, your hero will accept our invitation for an entirely different reason," Aleksei predicted. "Fear."

4

Adrienne Brenner shut the door of her editor-in-chief's office . . . carefully, because she felt an urge to slam it. She walked away.

"Mrs. Brenner?" It was the man's young secretary.

She stopped, realizing she'd been about to walk past her without saying hello. Goodby was more to the point, she thought glumly.

"Are you all excited about your new assignment?"

"Not exactly. I liked my old one better."

"Oh, West Berlin is old hat," the secretary laughed. "When Mr. Beal told me about the East Berlin conference, I told *him* it couldn't happen to a better person, knowing how you love to travel. Talk about seeing new places and meeting new people!"

"Didn't you hear the raised voices, Maggie? I don't want to go. I'm *not* going," she added, with more determination than she felt.

"But why? I thought you were the adventurous type."

"It's no adventure going into East Germany," she said quietly.

The secretary seemed bewildered for a moment. Then she confided, "Mr. Beal was terribly enthusiastic when he read about your husband's plans in the papers this morning. He kept talking about what a great, old-fashioned scoop it was because the ban on Western reporters couldn't possibly apply to you. He said—"

"That they can't very well exclude the wife of the guest of honor. He told me."

"And you're not going? This couldn't cost you your job, could it?"

Adrienne sighed. "You tell me. You've worked for him longer than I have."

"Oh, Mrs. Brenner," the secretary said, dismayed, "couldn't you reconsider? I mean, wouldn't you—why won't you go?"

There it was again, Adrienne thought, her feeling of disbelief. The answer was *not* self-evident, she reminded herself. It was just a matter of . . . what? "I'll tell you later, Maggie, I'll try to explain. Right now," she said wryly, seeing the time, "I'm late for my lunch appointment at New York's newest 'in' restaurant."

Late again. Only this time it's not my fault, she thought as she hurried up Fifth Avenue. Even so, she found herself pausing in front of a bookstore, wishing she had time to browse . . . Move, she ordered. She walked briskly until she came to a cluster of foreign tourist offices and felt the old excitement taking hold. Greece. Bonaire. Moroccan Tours. Japan Air Lines. And Aeroflot. Nonstop jet service to Moscow. She walked past, quickened her pace . . . and found herself slowing down in front of a department store

window. You coward, she thought. Putting it off, are you?
Afraid to find out if what you read in the papers is true?
She hailed a cab.

Brenner experienced the old stir of excitement, and the
old irritation, as his wife moved through the restaurant
toward him in that easy, rapid stride of hers. Her tall, lithe
figure was attracting the usual admiring glances . . . and
as usual, she seemed oblivious of them, he thought, annoyed.
Sleek copper hair, brushing her cheeks as she walked . . .
lovely. Cool, green eyes with their catlike upward slant
. . . very lovely. And unnerving. She was the only one on
God's green earth who could make him feel guilty—without
reason, he added hastily. He hadn't even made up his
mind yet. The cut and color of her pantsuit, severely
tailored black, stressed her slenderness, making her look
vulnerable. He knew better. "Late as always, but always
worth waiting for," he said, smiling, holding out a chair
for her.

"I was tied up with the editor-in-chief longer than I
expected," she apologized.

"So Carter Beal is acting the slave driver again," Brenner joked. "I'll have to speak to him about making me
wait for you. I mind waiting in one sense," he said,
suddenly serious. "Every minute I get to spend with you is
important now." He reached for her hand. "When are you
coming back to me? The apartment is like a mausoleum
without you."

"That depends, Kurt."

"I'm sorry for pressing. I know we're supposed to settle
things after West Berlin. In Paris!" he said gaily. He
raised his empty martini glass. "Here's to Paris and a long

overdue vacation for both of us. Darling, do you realize how long it's been since we were in Europe together?''

"I might not be going, not to West Berlin, anyway,'' she said unhappily. "I'm on the verge of being fired. Carter was so damn elated by this East Berlin medical conference he read about that he . . . he's insisting I go with you and cover it. Kurt, you're not going, are you? I told Carter you couldn't have accepted that invitation.''

"I haven't accepted it,'' he said firmly. But he felt a flash of uneasiness for the second time; the first was when the invitation had been hand-delivered to his apartment last night and then leaked to the morning papers. By whom? he wondered. And who the hell was Malik, first initial "N''? Colonel N.V. Malik was "looking forward'' to seeing him. Malik was a common Russian name—he'd checked that out. Did the "N'' stand for Nikolai? Another common name. So it couldn't be the man he knew. Not after all these years.

Adrienne was looking openly relieved. "I'm so ashamed of myself,'' she said. "I should have known you wouldn't accept, only those damn newspapers! After what you said at the Manning party, I guess I just assumed you'd go. I suppose the papers did, too.''

"You know you take these things too personally,'' he said.

"What things?''

"Oh, you know . . .'' He waved his hand. "This whole human rights business. Every time you read a headline about someone jumping ship or having his exit visa denied, you . . .'' His voice trailed off.

"I what?''

"You take it too personally,'' he repeated lamely.

"How should I take it, Kurt? Should I ignore the headline and turn to the sports section? Should I label these people 'lawbreakers?' ''

"Look, Adrienne, I didn't mean to get into all this."

"I'm sure you didn't," she said flatly, "but you raised a damn good question just the same. Why *do* I take it so personally? No one else seems to, or if they do, they're bewilderingly selective about it." She shook her head. "Petitions for ballet dancers. Jewish emigration quotas. They're commendable, as far as they go. The trouble is, they don't go far enough. What about all the others who want to get out?" She shrugged. "You know what my problem is? I've been thinking about it lately. It *feels* self-evident to me that free men should care about the men who aren't. What kind of imagination does it take to picture your own wife or husband on one side of a Berlin Wall and you on the other, for God's sake?"

"More imagination than most people have," he observed. "When are you going to realize that and just relax about these things?"

"When are you going to retract what you said at that party? You told me you wanted to make up for it."

"I think you're exaggerating the importance of a few remarks said in the heat of anger. I'm sorry I said what I did about this Brodsky fellow—I really am." He meant it.

A waiter approached with menus. She waved him away. "But you've changed your mind about issuing a retraction, haven't you?"

"Look, I'd be happy to if I thought a good purpose would be served, but it happened over a week ago. Why call it to people's attention all over again? Besides, I'm not eager to get embroiled in politics. I'm a heart surgeon, after all. I have a public image to consider."

"Do you consider anything else, these days? I'm sorry. I shouldn't have said that." She lit a cigarette.

"Why don't you let me do that," he said irritably. "I hate to see a woman light her own cigarettes."

"Charmingly old-fashioned, aren't you? Do you know what *I* hate to see? You—making a production out of it, showing off those hands of yours. Your hands—*and* your face—belong in an operating room, not spread all over the society pages. Damn it, Kurt! What's happened to you? Don't you care about surgery anymore?"

"You'll never understand, will you?" he said resentfully. "We train top people at the institute. We do long-range medical research. Do you have any conception of what it costs just to run operating theaters and a few clinics? *Someone* has to raise the money. My staff alone—"

"But they're *not* your staff. You don't own that institute."

"I'm the institute's star attraction—their biggest fund raiser. My reputation attracts donations."

"I'm not underestimating the importance of money," she said. Her voice sounded suddenly tired. "It's just that your fund-raising activities seem to have become your sole preoccupation in life. You court celebrity, Kurt. You can't seem to get enough of it."

"What an unflattering image," he said tightly. "If you're implying that I've changed, you're quite mistaken. I've *always* known the value of good publicity."

"Maybe you haven't changed," she said dully. "Maybe the things I saw . . . or thought I saw, were only on the surface."

"Is that what you think?"

She shook her head slowly. "I'm not sure. The only thing I'm sure of is what an incredible surgeon you are. I wish you hadn't lost sight of that."

Brenner sensed retreat, not in her words, but in the tone of her voice. "I *have* changed, Adrienne," he said. "These last few years, I've begun to think beyond the narrow boundaries of surgery. Do you realize what a powerful instrument medicine can be in promoting world peace? Russell Manning told me just the other day that a man of my reputation would make an ideal ambassador of good will—an apolitical ambassador, of course. He thinks people like me can accomplish more than all our politicians and diplomats put together. And I've come to agree with him. All these years I've heartily approved of medical exchanges, but I couldn't take part in any. I had to keep peace in the family," he added, gently reproachful.

"You're going to East Berlin."

"Can't you see that I must?"

"I can't see it," she said, getting up.

"Wait. Suppose I told you I had a special reason for going?"

"What reason?"

"I can't tell you that. You'll have to take me on faith."

"No, Kurt."

"Adrienne, dear," he said, as if she were a stubborn child, "your aversion to Communist countries is quite pointless and out of date. What we need is *more* contact with the Communists, not less, more opportunities to learn each other's ways."

"Have you ever asked yourself what my aversion is based on?" she said quietly.

"Political bias, pure and simple."

"Is it?" She picked up a knife and held the point of the blade against his collar. "Put your hands on the table," she said.

He opened his mouth to protest.

"Don't talk. Just do as I say."

He put his hands on the table.

"Don't try to get up. Don't try to leave this room." She counted off thirty seconds, looking at her watch. "Okay, now you can say something—anything at all."

"Have you gone crazy?" he whispered, flushed with embarrassment.

She dropped the knife. "*Now* you can get up, if you want to. Or leave the room. You obey orders very well," she said flatly. "Not that you had much choice, with a knife at your throat."

"What the hell?"

"That's what runs the countries I have an 'aversion' to—a knife or its equivalent," she said. "That's what you sanction with your apolitical good will tours. You wanted an opportunity to learn their ways, didn't you?" She started to leave, but he grabbed her arm.

"Who do you think you are?" he choked. "A self-important socialite-turned-journalist, and you dare to criticize *me*? Why the hell did you marry me? All that fuss and chatter about what a great man I was—how I made the world come *alive* for you. What was all that—some kind of an act?"

She wrenched free and rushed out of the room.

Adrienne stood outside, eyes closed, until her breathing was under control, then she started downtown for her office. Her arm throbbed, a tight band of pressure where he'd grabbed it. He had enormous strength in his hands.

Some kind of an act, she thought bleakly, not wanting to remember but remembering with a vividness that wiped out the past five years. Standing on the balcony of some amphitheater full of excited medical students, excited her-

76

self by her promotion from researcher to medical writer and the challenge of her first assignment . . . the moment when the famous Dr. Kurt Brenner entered the operating room—a moment when excitement turned into something else . . . watching as if from a great distance what seemed like a dance performance, with the most beautiful choreography she had ever seen: every gesture purposeful but unhurried, relaxed but without wasted motion, nurses and assisting surgeons effortlessly maneuvered about the operating table by the sure hand of a master director, the elusive angle of an ·incision being probed by two equally deft hands, a perfectly positioned needle ending the performance—and a jarring exit that forced her back to the real world. But the real world included an interview. Tentative questions awkwardly put—why couldn't she get the awe out of her voice, the schoolgirl adulation? He hadn't seemed to mind. When she asked him about the famous Brenner temper—rumors of elbowing aside flustered assistants in the midst of an operation, flinging an instrument at some nurse whose timing was off by a fraction of a second—he laughed good-naturedly and owned up to the rumors, disarming her, making her lose track of her next question. She apologized, confessing that it was her first interview. He countered with an invitation. Since they both had something to celebrate—her promotion and his new heart surgery clinic for underprivileged children—why not celebrate together with champagne, dinner, dancing?

The courtship had been exhilaratingly brief; the marriage had made headlines. The exhilaration lasted a few months. She felt guilty, at first, when she'd catch herself wondering whether the artistry she'd seen that first day in the operating room had been a delusion, or a dream. Dr. Kurt Brenner, confident, dedicated surgeon, seemed to have metamorphosed into a charming man-about-town with an unpredictable temper, a dazzling smile, and the pseudo-confident style of a playboy. She refused to believe it. She would visit the institute and stand in the balcony, watching him work, recapturing her vision of him. She would lose it again in his office or in the halls, watching scrub nurses fighting to be assigned to his operations—and the spectacle of Dr. Kurt Brenner enjoying the competition, flattered by it. They had talked things out, argued, reconciled, talked some more. There were times when she thought she was getting through, and times when she'd succumb to the famous Brenner charm.

I never got through, she thought, with a sudden burst of clarity. Whatever is driving him was there long before I came into his life. But it's been getting worse. How long before all those distractions and divided interests turn him into a first-rate PR man and a second-rate surgeon? She passed a newsstand and spotted his photograph over a bold caption: EMINENT SURGEON TO ATTEND EASTERN BLOC MEDICAL CONFERENCE. The apolitical ambassador of good will, she thought. Would he praise the latest Soviet anti-smoking campaign? Would his friend Manning prepare a humanitarian award for some doctor who cured sore throats in labor camps—and approved of the camps? Preventive medicine, she thought, for people who needed permission to live. What an article that would make. What parallels one could draw . . . free ambulance service, and forced labor . . . drugs to wipe out pain, and drugs to kill rebellion . . . medical care from cradle to grave, and death waiting at a border crossing . . .

If I accept the assignment, she thought, if I go to East Berlin, I could see it all firsthand: the benign platitudes and the reality underneath—like this Brodsky who'd just been shot. She thought of a lead for the article. It would be tricky—unless she could pull some background material together in a hurry. She checked her watch and stepped into a phone booth.

In the oak-paneled taproom of the Press Club, Adrienne quickly spotted him, sitting in the leather comfort of a dimly lit booth. No signs of strain, she thought, in spite of what was going on.

"Hello, Paul," she said, smiling, sitting down opposite him. "It's been a long time. I wish women aged as gracefully as men. You look wonderful."

Paul Houston grinned. "So you like a touch of gray in a man's hair, do you?"

"I do when it's natural. How are you, anyway?"

"Bearing up. It wouldn't surprise me if half of what you see turned color in the past week," he said dryly.

"That rough?"

He shrugged.

"In that case, I'm doubly grateful you saw me on such short notice."

"Notice?" He laughed. "You're looking at a man with lots of time on his hands."

"Does that mean the Russians have succeeded in getting you fired?"

"Not quite. They've been screaming for it loudly enough, haven't they? No, I've been asked to retire gracefully."

"I'm really sorry."

"Don't be. I was planning to resign when I got back from Potsdam. I'm not sure, now, that I will. I think I'd rather be sacked."

"Why, for God's sake?"

"Because my colleagues are trying to convince the Soviet

Union that what is euphemistically being called the 'border incident' was some unfortunate accident, a bit of carelessness on my part. If they fire me, it will look like an admission that I acted with 'deliberate and premeditated malice,' as the saying goes.''

''*Was* it deliberate?''

''Damn right.''

''That's what I figured. Could we talk about it?''

''Now, wait a minute,'' he said, eyeing her with mock suspicion. ''I thought you were after a briefing on East Berlin in connection with some article you're planning.''

''Not really,'' she said, looking a little guilty. ''It's a reporter's prerogative to lie a little, isn't it, when she's after a story?''

He laughed. ''Not when it means conning an old friend. What's this 'story' business? I thought your field was strictly medicine?''

''It is. You must have seen the morning papers. Paul, as of an hour ago, I'm covering medical conferences in *both* Berlins. I have something special in mind for the first one. I'm going political. I thought of a perfect lead for my East Berlin piece: a Ukrainian named Brodsky on one side of a ledger, and a gathering of so-called humanitarians on the other. The thing I want to dramatize is the hypocrisy behind their goddamn slogans. What do you think?''

''I think you're playing with dynamite.''

''Damn it, Paul!—you just finished tossing the same dynamite in the Russians' faces at that Potsdam conference. I read about what you said. Why do you think I called you?''

''I didn't say I disapproved of dynamite, did I?''

''Then you'll help me?''

''I didn't say that, either. What do you want to know?''

"Everything you can tell me about this Stepan Brodsky—who he was, why he wanted to get out, what lay behind that desperate attempt on Glienicker Bridge—"

"Whoa," he interrupted. "I'm not sure you're ready to tackle that last one. You'd be in some very deep water."

"I can swim."

He frowned. "Level with me, Adrienne. You're doing very well in a nice safe career—no fuss, no complications. The ugliest thing you have to deal with is illness. What do you need this for? What's in it for you?"

"It isn't as if I haven't asked myself the same question—I have. Did you know you'd befriended the unofficial Conscience of the Western World? I have this dubious 'talent' for putting myself in the other person's place."

"Like who, for instance?" He was smiling.

"Oh, the old man hanging onto a subway strap because some kid beat him to the only empty seat. The hot dog vendor who spends more time in court than he does selling his hot dogs because the City won't give him a license. The absentee owner of a parked car that someone is letting their dog urinate on—hell! I don't even own a car. The grocer who was robbed ten times, finally gets himself a .45, shoots some thug—and then finds himself indicted on a gun charge."

"Seems to me there's a common denominator in all that," he said, still smiling.

"What? The hollow ring of injustice? Someone's property rights being stepped on? Both, I guess," she said, answering her own question. "But Paul, the most important property a person has is himself, isn't it? So when I hear about people like this Brodsky, when I see how they're kept locked up, I guess I overreact—at least Kurt says I do. Do you know that ever since I read my first

81

book about Siberian labor camps—gold mines, I think it was—I haven't been able to buy anything made in a Communist country? I made the mistake of telling that to some guy at a cocktail party. He was bragging about his upcoming Grand Tour to the People's Republic of China. He said, 'Who really knows about your little dollar ninety-eight protest? Who cares?' I didn't have an answer.''

"Maybe you'll answer him in that article I'm going to help you out on."

"Thanks, Paul. I really—"

"*If*," he went on, "your magazine is willing to take on the whole damn State Department."

"Why not?" she said gaily. "My editor-in-chief is always talking it up about how controversy sells magazines. Anyway, it's a moot point. He's so eager for me to go with Kurt that he's agreed to print whatever I hand in—over the strenuous objections of my senior editor, I might add." She took out a notebook. "I'm ready."

"I'm not, unfortunately. I promised my lawyer that I'd keep my mouth shut until I'm officially severed from the Department—which shouldn't be long, now," he said dryly. "I'll fill you in when you get back."

"I have this habit of picturing things in newspaper headlines. EX-DIPLOMAT PROSECUTED FOR REVEALING STATE SECRETS."

"Don't worry, they won't prosecute. A legal battle would keep the whole wrangle under a spotlight—the *last* thing they want. And I won't be telling you anything I wasn't planning to say in a press conference. I'll just hold off until you've had your exclusive."

She looked at him with undisguised admiration. "I'll bet you could have any diplomatic post you wanted if you kept quiet. But you won't. Fair's fair, Paul. What's in this for *you*?"

"Satisfaction," he said grimly. "I want the American people to know what a low priority their government placed on a human life."

"Do the American people really care?"

"Some of them. Why else are you writing your article?"

"You're right, I suppose—I hope you're right."

"I also want revenge. I gave my word to Brodsky, and I was forced to break it. Then there's a little matter of robbing the Soviets of the edge they think they'll have the next time they sit down to bargain about Berlin—but more about that later."

"There's no way they can muzzle you, is there?"

"No, but they'll do the next best thing—call me a liar. The problem is, it's my word against theirs, and the only evidence I have is lying at the bottom of the Havel River. Literally buried in mud, no doubt," he added gloomily.

"What do you mean?"

"Brodsky was carrying some film in a cigarette lighter. The lighter . . . went over the side of the bridge. There was other film, but . . ." He shrugged.

"But what?"

"It's as good as buried, in Moscow," he said flatly. "Enough questions for now, okay?"

"Okay." She stood up.

"What, not even *one* drink?"

"I'd love to," she sighed, "but as usual, I'm running behind schedule."

"Give my regards to Kurt. Unless," he added, "he'd just as soon not have the regards of a 'damn fool' diplomat who likes to play God."

"I'm really sorry about that crack. It's no excuse, but I

don't think Kurt realized, at the time, what diplomat he was talking about.''

"How does he feel about your article?"

"I'm not telling him until it hits the presses," she said lightly.

"Be careful you don't cramp his style," he teased.

"How would I do that?"

"By sounding off on all those non-stop slogans you're about to be subjected to—*ad nauseam*. Kurt isn't the only Brenner with a temper."

"I think I'll save it for the article."

"Speaking of articles, that was some write-up Kurt got this morning. He certainly has a better press than I do."

She frowned. "He works harder at it."

"He's also more photogenic than I am. Or is it a question of aging more gracefully?"

"You mean the white hair? He thinks it looks distinguished. Speaking of photographs, do you have one of Brodsky—something you could make a copy of while you still have access to department files?"

"I'll do better than that. There's a good chance you'll be running into a well-connected East German photographer named Roeder. Ernst takes two kinds of pictures: the ones destined for East Germany's Party newspaper, *Neues Deutschland*, and the ones aimed at a very different audience. Ever hear of *Die Mauer—The Wall?*"

She sat down again. "No."

"It's a magazine published out of West Berlin. Leaf through a few copies, if you get a chance. It specializes in picture-stories of East Germany. Very grim stuff, some of it, or very dramatic. Like that famous shot of an East Berlin border guard leaping over barbed wire into the French sector, remember? That was a *Die Mauer* special.

The magazine enlists sympathetic border policemen at the various Allied checkpoints. Whenever they smell something unusual in the air, they alert the nearest *Die Mauer* photographer. But the most dramatic stuff usually comes from within. The only thing that keeps guys like Roeder going is a chance to get in their licks—even if it has to be anonymous.'' Houston lit ? cigarette and stared thoughtfully at his lighter. ''Roeder was on the bridge last Sunday when it happened. He was a friend of Brodsky's. I think he got a photograph of Stepan just before he died.''

''He's allowed to take *those* kinds of photographs?''

Houston smiled faintly. ''You should see this guy, Roeder. He's innocuous looking—more like some timid bank clerk than a celebrated photographer for the Party organ. The kind of man who never takes chances, right?'' He chuckled. ''Wrong. He walks around with this big goddamn camera—that's for the authorized photographs. The unauthorized ones for *Die Mauer* are taken with a miniature camera. He has these big, oversized paws for hands—wonderful for concealing a Minox—but how the hell he managed to—''

''That's very enterprising, carrying two different cameras,'' she said thoughtfully.

''And very dangerous. Don't try it. I've known more than one naive tourist who wound up in a Communist jail for photographing things he shouldn't have, like a beautiful sunset with a piece of some bridge in the background.''

''Bridges are off limits?''

''Bridges and a lot of other things.'' He frowned. ''If Roeder did get a photograph of Stepan on Glienicker Bridge, he may still have it, unless, by now, he's managed to smuggle it out.''

''You say this Roeder is well connected?''

"Very. He has a brother-in-law in East German intelligence."

"Will Roeder give me Brodsky's photograph, if he still has it?"

"He will if he knows he can trust you. I'll take care of it before you leave."

"Thanks for the help, Paul—present *and* future. You won't be sorry." She clasped his hand. "See you."

He watched her walk away. *You won't be sorry.* I hope not, he thought uneasily, already sorry that he'd told her about Roeder's two cameras. "Don't take any chances," he called after her.

But she was too far away to hear.

5

Plush white carpeting swallowed footsteps. Billowy silk drapes and navy chairs of glove-soft leather encircled the room. The soothing strains of a symphony helped muffle the repetitive sound, part whine, part growl, of taxiing jets somewhere beyond the drapery.

"This is a very nice room. Much nicer than the regular waiting area," said Dr. Max Brenner. He sounded vaguely uncomfortable. He was tall and white haired and wore an unfashionably cut suit.

"It's a VIP lounge," Kurt Brenner said, amused.

"For very important persons like my son."

"Just following in my father's footsteps. You were my inspiration."

"Ah, but you flew past *my* footsteps a long time ago!" his father beamed. He looked around. "All these people are friends who've come to see you off?"

"Most of them. Matter of fact, I ought to be circulating."

"Go right ahead. And Kurt, don't be upset about your

mother. I'll talk to her. I hate to see her miss the symposium in West Berlin as much as you do. It's such an
honor, your representing the United States and—"

"If she's willing to go as far as Switzerland with you,
why in hell won't she go with you to the damn symposium?"
Brenner was annoyed. "It's no trip at all from Zurich to
West Berlin."

"I'll talk to her," Max Brenner repeated. He looked
even more uncomfortable.

"I have an idea, Max," Adrienne soothed. "This East
Berlin thing on Monday is going to be a one-day affair—
today and Sunday will be just red-carpet window-dressing,
I gather. Why don't Kurt and I fly to Zurich early Tuesday
instead of going straight to West Berlin? That way, I can
talk to her, too, and help change her mind. Then all four
of us could fly to West Berlin in time for the symposium's
opening at noon on Tuesday."

"You know how I dislike being on time for a party,"
Brenner said irritably. "I wasn't planning to arrive until
the dedication ceremony on Tuesday night."

"Correction, Max," Adrienne said. "We'll pick you up
in Zurich, and all four of us will fly to West Berlin in time
for the ceremony Tuesday night—in time to make a grand
entrance. Is that all right with you, Kurt?"

"Fine, fine," he said, looking around. "Excuse me,
will you?"

He mixed with the crowd, moving easily from person to
person and group to group, spending brief, calculated
minutes. He stopped to talk to a man who stood by himself,
staying longer than usual.

"—which is why we're pleased that you're going,
Doctor," the man concluded. "Officially, things are on
ice right now, but unofficially . . ."

"A little good will at the opportune time can make up for a lot of things, I should think," Brenner said. He was thinking: Officially, I'm going in order to smooth some ruffled Soviet feathers. Unofficially—

"That your wife over there mingling with the natives?" the man asked, crumpling his cocktail napkin into a ball. He dropped it into someone's unfinished drink.

"That's my wife," Brenner said, permitting himself a mental sigh. Adrienne was carrying on an animated conversation with one of his father's friends. He thought of all the people in the room she could have been talking to.

"Wouldn't mind an introduction to the other half of this good will venture," the man said.

Brenner almost choked on his hors d'oeuvre. Christ! he thought, motioning to Adrienne, I hope she knows enough not to sound off.

But she said nothing when he made the introductions, only raised an eyebrow a little when he mentioned the State Department. He wondered, again, why she'd changed her mind and decided to go with him to East Berlin. She had avoided a discussion, too busy with some last-minute shopping. He wondered what the hell was going to be with their marriage. She hadn't avoided *that*—she'd just refused to discuss it.

He continued to wonder after they said their goodbys and boarded the plane. Could she have come round to his way of thinking—too proud to admit it yet? Could he have misjudged her? It wouldn't be the first time, he thought, glancing down at that lovely face, enigmatic in sleep. Hadn't he figured her for an adoring, well-bred young lady who would bend to his will *and* the considerable difference in their ages? Hadn't he attributed her stubborn streak of independence to the willfulness of youth, something she'd eventually outgrow? She hadn't outgrown it—a big factor in their floundering marriage. Not that he wasn't partly to blame, he admitted. Marriage problems took time to work out. He hadn't had much time. And whose fault was that? he thought defensively. Hadn't she come into his life just when he was reaching the acclaim he'd struggled so hard for? He'd been close to the top. Had he reached it yet? Only a couple of other surgeons in the whole country—hell, in the world—could equal his record-breaking schedule of open-heart operations or approximate his skill at the operating table. Approximate it . . . or match it? he wondered uneasily, thinking of his Texas competition. His thoughts moved to Medicine International, to the long list of doctors the organization had considered and rejected, then to his friend Manning's well-publicized accolade of "great humanitarian." The time and effort he'd put into cultivating his humanitarian image, and Manning's wife, were not worth thinking about.

Adrienne stirred restlessly beside him. He remembered, guiltily, the question she'd put to him the other day: "Don't you care about surgery anymore?" It was a good question. A lot of people lost interest in their work, he thought. It happened all the time. It happened to me. Surgery used to challenge and stimulate in the early years. No challenge, now, and not much stimulation, he admitted. What the hell, he thought, money pinch-hits for boredom any day of the week. And the fame—that made up for a lot of things. So what if I courted it? he thought. I earned every admiring glance and sweaty handshake. He smiled, remembering those who admired and envied him at the same time, envied him the glory and the talent and his unbeatable—

He felt a chill of uncertainty, and his mind short-circuited

90

the rest of the thought. The rest of the thought was: No one is unbeatable.

He rang for the stewardess and ordered a cocktail. And because he didn't care to dwell on uncertainty, he thought about his youth. He had excelled at everything he did in his youth, learning to keep one step ahead of everyone else. At nineteen, he had been about to enter the Spring term of his third year of college, planning to double-register in medical school in the Fall. That would have made him the youngest person in the program—but just another first-year med student. Not good enough. One day, in 1945, he spotted a patriotic enlistment poster. Then he knew what to do. The army desperately needed medical corpsmen. After a short training period, he'd be shipped overseas for some first-class experience. After a brief tour of duty—it was sure to be brief, judging from reports on the war's progress—he'd be back home, ready to let the army pay for the rest of his education. Even better, he'd have an edge over his classmates; they'd be green with inexperience. *My* experience, he'd be able to say, was with life and death on the battlefield. So Honor Student Brenner had become Private First Class Brenner.

There'd been times, he thought ruefully, when he'd bitterly regretted making the switch. He stared moodily at the brownish-white liquid swaying torpidly in his cocktail glass with the plane's vibrations. Like the muddy, lethargic waters of the Elbe River, stirred by an anemic breeze, winding its way past the camp where he'd spent the last days of the war, ministering to the sick and the wounded. And the dead . . .

"Medic! Medic!"

Pfc. Brenner raced across the field and dropped to his

knees beside the twisted body of a soldier who'd just stepped on a land mine, trying not to look closely at shattered limbs. He held one eyelid open. The pupil stared back, unseeing. He got up and walked away, wondering how much more of this he could take. God!—two solid months of it. They kept saying it would be over any time now—it was the middle of April, for Chrissake! They kept saying the only casualties from here on in would be German—die-hard Nazis concentrated in small knots of resistance in and around Berlin. They were bracing themselves for one last battle to the death with the Red Army, descending from the north.

"Hey, Brenner, the CO wants you. On the double!"

He headed back to camp, passing a line of bedraggled German refugees on the way. He'd seen hordes of the poor bastards in the last few weeks, plodding along the river-bank with their miserable possessions wrapped in dirty sheets, heading south through the American lines. Fleeing from the advancing Red Army, he thought uneasily. He saw a handful of soldiers clambering into the rear of a canvas-backed truck.

"Medic?" The CO was impatient. "Hop in the back, will you? Let's get this show on the road!"

First Lieutenant Joseph Cherner extended a hand to pull Brenner up.

"Where to, Joe?" Brenner asked.

"Advance reconnaissance to Potsdam, about fifty miles north of here. General Simpson's orders. He's hell-bent on beating the Reds to Berlin, and Potsdam's right on the outskirts. He wants us to look things over," Cherner said eagerly.

"What's the CO want with me, for Chrissake?"

"He figures we could run into some stray Krauts—the

whole area is full of 'em. We might need a medic.''

"What *I* need is sleep, after the day I've put in.''

Cherner looked sympathetic. "Try catching up on some. I'll wake you if there's any action.''

"I'll *bet* you will, you gung ho—'' He bit off the words. You could kid Joe Cherner about a lot of things, but not about fighting for God and country. The only time he'd seen Cherner really mad was in combat. He had one helluva temper—and one helluva combat record to show for it. He looked Cherner over. A big good-natured sonofabitch, he thought—the all-American type, complete with crew cut and football-hero shoulders. He stretched out and closed his eyes. When he opened them again, it was dark, and he was alone in the truck. "Joe?'' he called.

"It's okay.'' Cherner was standing just outside. "There's nothin' going on—not a goddamn thing. The CO just got orders to pull back. Our whole division has to stay put at the Elbe. It seems Eisenhower wants the Reds to have a clear field so they can take Berlin all by themselves.''

"Where's the CO?''

"Down the road a piece. Mad as a tiger.''

"I'll bet. He doesn't think much of the Russkies, does he?''

Cherner glared at him. "Neither do I, buddy. Maybe you forgot that Cherner is short for Chernovsky. Maybe you forgot where my parents are from, huh?''

Brenner drew back. "Okay, okay, so it slipped my mind. The Ukraine, wasn't it?''

"Cherner!'' someone hollered. "You speak Russian, don't you?'' It was the CO's first sergeant.

"I'm a little rusty,'' he yelled back.

"Never mind that. The CO wants you up front. You, too, Brenner. Bring your medical kit.''

They walked up the road in the narrowing path of the truck's headlights, both of them straining to distinguish some silhouettes clustered about a dilapidated jeep with its headlights switched off. When they were almost there, a beam from a flashlight hit them.

"Cherner? Brenner?" It was the CO.

"Yes, sir," they said in unison.

"This is Mr. Johannsen. He's with the Red Cross." The beam shifted, revealing a nondescript man in a shabby overcoat. "Examine these kids, Brenner. See what you can do for them."

"Kids, sir?"

"Yeah, kids." The beam traveled reluctantly along the side of the jeep, paused when it got to a pair of small, bare feet, then moved up to reveal a huddled form, then another . . . and another . . . There were ten of them in all. The oldest, a girl, couldn't have been more than fifteen or sixteen. She was holding tightly to the hand of the youngest, who was about three. The others were somewhere in between. The girls had stringy, matted hair; the boys' heads were shaved. Their tattered clothes and swollen stomachs, their enormous eyes staring out of bruised, emaciated faces, gave them the look, not of children, but of aging dwarfs. As Brenner examined them, one by one, they began to whimper.

The CO angrily stuffed one hand into the pocket of his field jacket. He was a stubby man with sharp, probing eyes that couldn't bear to look at the children. "Talk to them," he said to Cherner. "Say something in Russian to the girl, there. She seems to be in charge of the others. Tell her we're their friends."

Cherner addressed the girl in quiet, reassuring tones. After a few minutes, she began to answer him haltingly.

"I was telling your captain how I came upon these unfortunate children," said the man from the Red Cross. "Sachsenhausen is north of here, and—it's a concentration camp," he explained, noticing Brenner's puzzled expression. "It's directly in the path of a Russian column sweeping down on Berlin. The camp commandant, an SS colonel, had standing orders from Himmler to evacuate before the Russians got there. I was trying to persuade Keindel—that's the commandant—to release the survivors." He shook his head slowly. "Forty thousand survivors out of a hundred thousand. Keindel wouldn't listen, of course. They moved everyone out in two long columns. I followed in my jeep." His voice dropped. "Sick, starving, half-dead creatures, prodded along by bayonets. Those who couldn't keep up were shot and left in a ditch. It was the older girl, here, walking in the rear, who spotted my jeep—I think she took me for an American. I don't know Russian, but it was clear that she and some of the other kids were terrified of being captured by Russian soldiers. I crept along behind them, hoping for a break. Then, when Keindel ran into an advance Russian patrol, I took advantage of the confusion to get the children into my jeep. Then I got the hell out of there, hoping to reach the American lines. Then," he said, looking gratefully at the CO, "I saw your truck."

"The kids are Ukrainians." Cherner's voice sounded peculiar. "Their village surrendered voluntarily to German troops—the villagers apparently welcomed the goddamn Krauts like they were saviors! Their parents had a kind of pact among themselves at the camp. Whoever survived was to keep the kids from being shipped back to Russia—they were terrified of reprisals. The adults are dead. The girl feels it's up to her, now—it's *her* pact to carry on. Little Mother," he said softly, as the girl, wild eyes partly hidden by dark, tangled hair, hugged the smallest child to her chest. "Her older sister was in charge," Cherner went on grimly. "She was shot yesterday, and left in a ditch. Well, Captain, what do I tell her?"

"Tell her we'll hide them someplace where they'll be safe—from the Nazis *and* the Reds," the CO said tightly.

"What about our orders, sir?" Brenner said uneasily. "According to the Yalta agreement, Russian citizens have to be repatriated to the Soviet Union."

"To hell with the Yalta agreement! I'm not letting the goddamn Reds deport these kids. They'd be treated like deserters. You got any idea how the Reds treat deserters?"

"I have to go back," the man from the Red Cross said, climbing into his jeep. "There may be survivors in those ditches."

"Go get the truck," the CO told Cherner. "You and Brenner will take them back alone. The rest of us will walk home. There's a deserted farmhouse a few miles beyond the camp, along the river. Wait for me there. Get moving. And Lieutenant . . ."

"Sir?"

"Keep your lip buttoned. You, too, Brenner. The fewer people who know about this, the better."

"Medic!"

Pfc. Brenner finished his sandwich, tossed an empty beer can into the gray-black water, then watched while the current dragged the reluctant can downstream. He started up the steep incline of the riverbank at a leisurely pace, toward the bridge that was being repaired. Across the river was a line of slow-moving trucks, loaded with plaster of paris and GIs packing picks and shovels. Bound for Potsdam's Cecelienhof Palace to replant hedges and repair ceilings—as if they were getting ready for the British Coronation instead of some dumb conference. I wish they'd repair the smell around here, he thought, wrinkling his nose. It was almost two months since Berlin had fallen, but the odor of dead bodies still clung to the air, like smog. People talked about how you could smell Berlin for miles. Part of the stench was because of last-minute sabotage—the goddamn Krauts had emptied their sewers into the Havel River to contaminate the city's water supply. The Krauts hadn't been so lucky with Glienicker, he thought, looking at the bridge. They'd dynamited the hell out of every bridge leading to Berlin, but sturdy old Glienicker had survived, even if it did have a broken spine.

"Medic! Where the hell are you?"

I have to get out of here, Brenner brooded as he approached the bridge and looked around for his casualty. I *have* to get the hell out of here. He stepped over planks and stray pieces of iron, keeping to the side of the bridge that was propped above the water line by wooden pedestals. Some doctor you'll make, he chastised himself, as he bent down to examine a GI who'd injured his knee. A doctor has no business having a weak stomach. Well, who wouldn't? he thought. Who'd want to examine women weighing in at eighty pounds and men whose necks were too small for their collars and tubercular-looking kids who'd never live out the summer? Not to mention the thought of catching diphtheria or typhoid or scarlet fever. Or even dysentery. Guys were dropping like flies from dysentery. Berliners were dying from it.

When he finished his examination, he caught sight of Joe Cherner in the middle of the bridge. Talking to a major. From the raised voices and the scowl on Joe's face, it looked like one helluva brawl was going on. He went closer. Some GI, nervously shuffling a camera, was standing on the sidelines. So was a tall Russian officer, with a pressed uniform, a carefully starched shirt, and boots with a spit-and-polish shine. *This* Russkie, Brenner thought, hadn't been part of the loot-burn-and-rape brigade that had swarmed over Berlin, that was for damn sure. This one wouldn't smell of fish and leather.

The Russian officer looked up at him, revealing a young, strikingly handsome face and coolly appraising eyes.

The American major's face was flushed. "For the *last* time, Lieutenant Cherner, am I going to get my advance publicity shots or not?"

"For the last time, *sir*, I won't be any part of this!"

The major stalked off, followed by the GI with the camera. The Russian officer tossed Cherner a disdainful salute and walked away.

"What the hell's going on, Joe?" Brenner asked.

"Some sonofabitch brigadier general got the brilliant idea that since GIs and Russians are repairing Glienicker together, why not top it off with some fancy bridge ceremony? It's supposed to be a symbol of Allied friendship and cooperation," he said disgustedly. "They're staging it the day of the big conference, just before the politicians cross over to Potsdam. The major wants me and that Red you just saw—some joker named Malik—to christen the goddamn bridge."

"So what's the problem?"

"The problem is having my picture taken with some sonofabitch Red. I won't do it! Why the hell should I?"

"Because a major and his brigadier general say so, that's why."

"The goddamn Russkies! Ever since they 'liberated' Berlin, they've been boasting about how they practically won the war singlehandedly. We can thank a sonofabitch named Eisenhower for that one.''

"You'd better cool it, buddy. You're still in his army.''

"I almost choked when I heard what they're planning to christen Glienicker—Freedom Bridge, for Chrissake!''

Brenner shrugged. "Maybe if you asked them politely to get somebody else for the ceremony . . .''

"Don't think I haven't. The major is sold on that all-American-looking mug you keep telling me about—that, and my combat record,'' Cherner said with dismay. "Up until now I've been asked to cooperate, but I think they're getting ready to make it an order. Maybe the damn thing won't come off.'' He looked around at the construction debris scattered over the bridge. "We're running behind. If we *do* finish in time for that conference,'' he said, "at least it'll mean a ticket out of this godforsaken place.''

"You kidding me?''

"Nope. They've scheduled a little trip for us bridge-christeners and a few PR types. We visit some European cities, and then it's home, James.''

"Home?"

"That's what the man said. A whirlwind tour of the States so the American people can hear pretty stories about Uncle Joe Stalin and see a good-looking Russkie specimen up close. After that, the major will see that I wind up my tour of duty at the engineering school of my choice.''

"You lucky bastard,'' Brenner said enviously.

It was getting dark when Brenner left the Soviet compound in Berlin. He picked his way gingerly through brick-littered streets, stopped to show his pass to a couple of Russian soldiers, and crossed from the Soviet zone back into the American.

It was all arranged. The Russian, Nikolai Malik, with his excellent command of English and his excellent connections, had worked it all out. Tomorrow morning, the Ukrainian kids would be picked up by the Soviet authorities. They'd be well taken care of—he'd been assured of that. *You got any idea how the Reds treat deserters?* One man's opinion, he thought defensively; they were Russian citizens, weren't they? It was where they belonged. It was the law, damn it! If the President of the United States had seen fit to make it the law, who was *he* to go against it? And who the hell was the CO?

It had been a cinch locating them. The CO's first sergeant had remembered him from the reconnaissance patrol and had talked freely over a few beers one night. The kids had been moved from place to place, ending up in the American zone in Berlin, where arrangements were quietly being made to have them shipped to a DP camp somewhere in France. Once they'd been repatriated, Brenner thought, Joe Cherner could be counted on to balk at taking part in any ceremony with the Russians.

The streets were silent. Brenner walked for a long time, concentrating on a formidable obstacle course of broken pieces of pavement, mounds of rubble, and gaping holes camouflaged by a thin layer of gray-black dust. When something made him look up, he realized where he was; the "criminal," he thought, had been irresistibly drawn to the scene of the "crime." He stared uneasily at the bombed-out ruin . . . a cellar that had been transformed into a refuge—part hideout, part nursery.

He heard angry voices. Then he noticed the Soviet truck parked in front of an American jeep. So much for *tomorrow's* arrangements, he thought. The Russkies always keep one step ahead of you. He'd have to remember that in case he had to deal with them again.

He stepped quickly into the shadows as people began emerging from the cellar: some Russian soldiers led by an officer he'd never seen before, a couple of flustered GIs—a sergeant and a first lieutenant buddy of Joe Cherner's—and ten whimpering children. They were being hustled into the back of the Russian truck. "They're headed for Potsdam," he heard the lieutenant say as the truck pulled away. Potsdam was Soviet territory, now.

The sergeant leapt behind the wheel of the jeep. "I know a shortcut. With any luck, we can beat them to Glienicker Bridge. Maybe somebody can figure out a way to stop them from crossing over."

The lieutenant was about to hop in the jeep when he spotted Brenner.

"I saw the whole disgraceful thing, Jerry," Brenner said, coming forward. The dismay in his voice was genuine. "Isn't there anything we can do?"

"We're sure as hell going to try. Hop in. If nothing else, you can give us a little moral support."

The sergeant gunned the motor. The truck was already out of sight.

When it finally pulled up to Glienicker Bridge, an American soldier was planted firmly in front of the entrance. The lieutenant and the sergeant—and Pfc. Kurt Brenner—were grouped around him. "This bridge is officially closed to vehicular traffic until repairs have been completed," the soldier told the Russian officer.

The officer ordered his men to take the children out of the truck. "We will walk," he announced in perfect English.

"*Do* something!" the lieutenant urged.

The American soldier shrugged helplessly. "What the

hell *can* I do? I wish to God the CO would call back. Nobody knows where he is."

The feeble glow of makeshift lighting—lanterns strung at uneven intervals along the mouth of the bridge—was a blessing, Brenner was thinking; in the semi-darkness, he couldn't see the expressions on those small faces. Tensely, he watched the children being sandwiched between the soldiers, forced, with one exception, to walk single file. The exception was the older girl, who'd insisted, apparently, on carrying the three-year-old in her arms. The Russian officer brought up the rear. The strange-looking procession moved off, the sound of their footsteps mingling with the slapping of the waves against the damaged side of the bridge.

"Keep to the other side," the officer yelled in Russian. The girl had teetered dangerously near the bridge's ruptured stringer.

The girl paused at the spot where the stringer—one of the center spans—was extending its broken limbs in mute agony, one piece sticking straight out, the other hanging limply in the water, leaving a narrow breach. The darkness made it difficult to tell where the sky ended and the river began. Suddenly the girl cried out and leapt into the breach. As if her cry had been a prearranged signal—or a pact—two older boys followed her. Three others hesitated, then jumped. The last three children, the youngest, froze. The soldiers grabbed them.

When Brenner got to the center of the bridge, there was nothing to be seen in the beam of his probing flashlight . . . except a dark patch being dragged reluctantly downstream that could have been the girl's hair, riding on the gray-black surface.

*   *   *

"You're a goddamn blackmailer! How can you think of money in a situation like this?" Brenner's voice was a careful blend of incredulousness and indignation.

Nikolai Malik was unimpressed. His pale gray eyes, like chips of ice, reflected cynical amusement, making him appear much older than his twenty-three years. "The situation was of your own making," he said. "I am merely cashing in on the consequences. And so are you, my friend. Look down there." He gestured toward the scarred landscape at the foot of the hill. "In a few days you will say goodbye to all this."

"Our little ceremony is three weeks overdue," Brenner said.

The repairs on Glienicker hadn't been finished on time; the politicians and diplomats had had to cross the Havel River into Potsdam via a provisional pontoon bridge—and the Potsdam Conference had ended five days ago. But the bridge christening hadn't been scratched, and Glienicker had been ready since yesterday. An announcement about the ceremony had just been posted.

"The delay notwithstanding," Malik said, "you owe it all to me. I must admit I am disappointed by your attitude."

"We had an agreement."

"So we did. I agreed to help you step into the shoes of your friend Cherner. In return for my considerable efforts, you agreed to give me a modest sum of money—*and* help my government regain custody of ten Ukrainian children. I lived up to my part of the bargain, but you did not. My government never got complete delivery, did it? It seems only equitable that you provide me with some extra compensation."

"And if I don't?"

Malik shrugged. "That is up to you, of course. If this

affair were to be made public, it could only help *my* career. I doubt that it would do yours any good at all. Doctors are supposed to be humanitarians, are they not?''

Brenner looked away. "It's not my fault those kids drowned. I couldn't know they'd do something crazy and try to escape.''

"Or try to commit suicide.''

"That's a funny way for a Russian to be talking!'' Brenner snapped.

"I never claimed to be a patriot, my friend. I am a pragmatist. We are both pragmatists. Which is why you should be worrying about your future right now, instead of lamenting your past.''

"Yes,'' said Brenner, his voice low. *Their parents had a kind of pact . . . the adults are dead . . . the girl feels it's up to her, now. . . .*

"Well, do we agree on the slightly altered figures?''

"All right. I think I can raise some more money.''

"I thought as much.''

"Can you wait until we get to New York?''

"Why not? I am a reasonable person. I think you will also find me an amiable traveling companion. I am most eager to see your famous cities and . . .''

Brenner wasn't listening. Someone was climbing up the hill—someone in a hurry. The sun was sinking rapidly, hanging low over the horizon. He had to squint against the interfering rays to see who it was. He caught sight of a figure and lost it again as the path up the hill curved abruptly out of sight. But he could hear, and what he heard was menacing: bushes being savagely trampled, branches being smashed out of the way. He felt suddenly the cornered, immobilized terror of the hunted. The figure that finally emerged from the brush and stood, panting, on the top of the hill, was Joe Cherner—his inflamed eyes and his huge body, outlined in red by the sun's rays at his back, giving him the look of some apparition out of hell.

"I just heard . . . about your being in the . . . ceremony." Cherner was sucking air into his lungs. "You wanted . . . to get out of here . . . didn't you? You wanted it so bad, you were . . . willing to make a deal, you sonofabitch." The apparition advanced menacingly. "Admit it . . . God damn your soul!"

Brenner backed away, his mouth a silent plea for mercy.

"You turned in those kids. That was the deal . . . wasn't it?"

Brenner shook his head wildly. His hand slipped down to the automatic on his hip.

"*Murderer*. You as good as murdered those kids!" Cherner kept advancing. "I'll tear you apart for this! I'll—" He stood suddenly still, stopped by a spot of orange, like a dying ember, from the last of the sun's rays on metal—a gun in Brenner's trembling hand. Cherner's own hand went automatically to his hip. "You bastard," he hissed. The words collided with a sharp noise, like a walnut being cracked open.

Brenner was shaking violently. He let his smoking gun drop to the ground.

Malik bent down to take Cherner's pulse. "You killed him," he said.

"It was self-defense! *You* saw him go for his gun. You're a witness!"

Malik's hands explored the body. "No gun," he announced.

"But . . . I *thought* he had one. He was coming for me. *You* saw him coming for me!"

"What does that prove? He was unarmed. If we had

105

found a weapon on him, or if he had come after me instead of you—"

"That's it!" Brenner made a guttural sound, a cross between a hiccough and a sob of relief. "Cherner hated Russians—everybody knows that. What if you *were* the one he came after? What if I shot him to protect *you?*"

"Most accommodating of you," Malik said. "But if we are talking about self-defense, your story would be more convincing if your friend, Cherner, had a weapon on him." He took a revolver out of his belt.

"But that's a Russian model," Brenner protested.

"No matter. He could have picked it up somewhere. American soldiers are fond of collecting war souvenirs. Incidentally, there is no way your army can trace it back to me. I picked it up myself." Malik fired a bullet into the ground. Then he positioned the revolver in Cherner's hand. "*Now* it is self-defense."

"It really was, you know," Brenner insisted as they started down the hill to get help.

"Of course," Malik soothed, "of course it was."

Self-defense. Kurt Brenner stared, unseeing, at the gently swaying liquid in his glass. He'd been terrified that day—of what Cherner might do to him and of what he might tell the world. Had he really intended to kill him, then? Or had he fired because he'd thought Cherner was going for a gun? There was no way now, he realized, to reproduce the true state of mind of nineteen-year-old Pfc. Kurt Brenner. The truth was no longer accessible; he had repressed it for too many years. And the price of that indulgence? he asked himself. A nagging, guilt-ridden uncertainty that had tortured him for years before he'd managed to put it totally out of his mind. What had brought it back? Reminiscing about his youth, perhaps. Yet he did that all the time without going back to the war. It must have been that remark made at the Manning party about Freedom Bridge. That, and a man's name . . . Malik. Nikolai Malik, perjurer, he thought, remembering how convincingly Malik had lied at Cherner's inquest so that the whole business, with its political overtones, had been hushed up. Nikolai Malik, pragmatist . . . who had blackmailed him for years, then disappeared from his life without a trace. Was it the same Nikolai Malik who had invited him to East Berlin? He looked from Adrienne's face, relaxed in sleep, to the faces of the other passengers on the plane. He could find no comfort in them, no reassurance.

6

SPECIAL COMMISSION ON TRIPS ABROAD, Central Committee, CPSU, said the sign on the table. Next to it was a pile of printed forms, each containing cautiously written answers to carefully drafted questions.

Two men bent over one of the forms, on which the handwriting was bold and carefree, spilling into the margins. One of the men followed the list of questions and answers with a pencil. "I don't like it," he said, tapping the pencil on the question labeled "Family status."

"It's all right, I tell you. His file is in perfect order," reassured the other.

"But look what happened to Simonov last month—a severe reprimand for giving an exit permit to a man with a short tail. *This* man has no tail at all!"

"He has no need of one. You know who his brother is."

"I still don't like it. Whenever something goes wrong, we're always asked the same question: how many hostages were you counting on? What could we answer in a case like this?''

"What a lot of fuss over nothing," grumbled the other. "He's only going to East Berlin."

"Just the same, I want to ask him a few questions."

When his name was called, Kiril noticed that the people standing closest to him inched away. A few glanced at him resentfully, as if he should have known better than to join the group and possibly cast suspicion on them all. He approached the men behind the table innocently . . . as if they really were innocuous bureaucrats, instead of plainclothes officers in the secret police.

"Your residence registration certificate."

Kiril handed over the certificate.

"Your internal passport. Your military card."

"Both those documents were turned over to the proper authorities three months ago."

The man started to leaf through some papers attached to the back of Kiril's questionnaire. "How many forms have you completed in the last three months? How many personal appearances have you made?"

"Hundreds of forms. Dozens of appearances. At the time, I was being cleared for West Berlin," he added, knowing that no other explanation would be necessary.

"How many photographs?"

"About twenty."

"Why, in your more recent photographs, are you wearing these dark sunglasses?"

"I explained that in Question Eleven." Kiril took off the dark glasses he was wearing so they could see for themselves: his left eye was inflamed. "Several days ago I developed a minor infection. My eye is very sensitive to light." He put the glasses back on.

"Tell me, Dr. Andreyev, are you content with your answer to Question Eighteen?"

"Yes, of course," Kiril replied, sensing a trap, certain he'd fallen into it.

"Only *one* person will accompany you to East Berlin?" the man asked softly.

"We have information to the contrary," snapped the other before Kiril could answer. "In addition to Lieutenant Rogov, you will be traveling with Colonel Nikolai Vasilyevich Malik."

Kiril shrugged. "Someone obviously decided it wasn't necessary to give me advance notice of the Colonel's plans," he said, his tone implying that neither he nor his questioners should dare to speculate about the motives of whoever was responsible.

The two men exchanged wary glances; they knew that Malik was a colonel in military intelligence, a hated rival organization. They dismissed Kiril and motioned for the entire group to approach the table. "Has everyone signed the loyalty pledges and the secrecy agreement?" one of them asked.

There was a general murmuring and a nodding of heads.

"Very well. You will not receive *these*"—one hand came down hard on a pile of green leather booklets— "until you have read and memorized these." The other hand patted a pile of red booklets with gold lettering. "*Then* you will be ready to sign the oath of obedience."

Kiril took a red booklet. "Rules of Behavior of Soviet Citizens Abroad," it said on the cover, and under that in smaller letters, "For Internal Use Only," and under that, SECRET. The "rules of behavior," he saw, were written in a style suitable for children: Do not drink. Do not visit places of doubtful entertainment. Do not talk with foreigners outside the presence of a reliable witness. Do not use the normal mail facilities of the host country. Do not fail to report suspicious behavior on the part of your associates and traveling companions. *Above all*, do not forget that every Soviet citizen is a constant target of provocation by mercenary, bourgeois, anti-Communist elements—all of them eager to recruit the unwary into their ranks.

Kiril's lips tightened, cutting off a smile.

Twenty minutes later, he walked out of the building that housed the office of the Special Commission on Trips Abroad. The sound of steel doors slamming behind him gave him a sense of finality. The weight of a green leather booklet in his pocket gave him a sense of lightheadedness. He walked through a courtyard and out into the street before looking back. I'm free to go, he thought wonderingly. Free to leave the building. Free to leave Russia!

He walked slowly, trying to cling to the lightheaded feeling, but after several blocks he felt it slipping away, drained by the sights he had known all his life. He saw ponderous granite structures with six-story-high portraits draped over their ornate facades—comic-strip versions of his country's heroes, past and present. He saw string after string of red flags, waving hypnotically in the breeze. Above the sheer, sprawling flatness of Moscow a few tall buildings rose self-consciously. He felt a moment's kinship with them; they were misfits like himself.

He caught sight of the time—almost two o'clock—and walked faster; the stores were about to reopen for the afternoon. As if by magic, the streets were suddenly full of frenetic shoppers, queuing up to do battle for the family groceries, eager to seize some items from a counter before it disappeared indefinitely from the shelves. A surging, jostling crowd, yards long and three abreast, sprouted in front of a fish shop. When he tried to edge past, he found himself edged right off the sidewalk.

There was no queue at his trolley stop, but people packed themselves into each vehicle with the zealousness of combat soldiers embarking on a mission. When the trolley doors closed behind him, he was struck, as usual, by the contrasting stillness inside. And by the sadness of his fellow passengers' dress. Men in cheap sandals and ill-fitting trousers, their faces as wilted as their collars; women in shapeless cotton dresses that were faded from too much laundering, wearing dull, faded expressions to match. Even the exceptions one sometimes spotted on the streets—a young girl wearing a bright scarf and a touch of lipstick or a chic woman with an expensive, foreign-made outfit—weren't really exceptions, he thought. The spark of liveliness was in their clothes. It never seemed to reach their eyes.

He sat down opposite people who read or stared into space. A few spoke in half-whispers, eyes, and thoughts, averted from their neighbors. He turned away from those guarded expressions and looked out the window. Rows of prefabricated apartment houses rolled past—pale yellow cinderblocks—each a cheerless, functional echo of its neighbor, only bits of green from windowboxes breaking the monotony of their bleached, pathetic shabbiness.

He worked his way to the front of the trolley and got off at one of the cinderblocks—his home for the last ten years. The day he had moved in, he thought as he walked up three flights of stairs, his new Moscow address had sounded impressive: different numbers for the street, the block entrance, the floor, the room. The first time he'd climbed to his room, his eagerness had soured. His floor, like all the floors, housed a dozen different families living off the same drab hallway; he had felt assaulted by a pervasive dinginess. Now, as he walked down his hallway, knowing he would never have to do it again, he felt a sense of detachment. He passed through a communal kitchen and unlocked the door to his room. It was simply furnished for simple needs: a narrow bed, a few shelves and wall hooks for clothes, a small scarred table, a chair. Apart from some medical books, piled at one end of the table and providing the only spot of color, there was nothing to suggest the character or personality of the occupant—as if he expected to be moving at a moment's notice. It was a suitable room, he thought, for a transient-in-spirit.

He closed the door before switching on an overhead light. A plastic suitcase lay open on the bed, next to his raincoat. Some bottles and an eye dropper were on the table. A towel with brown stains hung over the back of the chair. A clock on one of the shelves told him Galya was due any minute. He took off his dark glasses and examined his left eye in a mirror. The redness was almost gone. You may have passed inspection this morning, he told himself, but you may not be so lucky the next time unless you remember to keep after it. Once every hour, at least until people stopped asking questions about the dark glasses. Reminding himself to pack what he needed and get rid of the rest, he opened one of the bottles, stuck the eye dropper in, and with the odor of lemon pulling at his nostrils, put a few drops in his left eye and held his breath against the stinging sensation. He checked the eye once more, noticed a spot of brown on his temple, and wiped it off. Then he checked his scalp gingerly. It still felt raw from the chemicals and repeated rinsing, but the result was a good match—just a little darker than his natural color. Galya was the only one who might notice . . . except in dim light, he thought. He raised the window shade a little before switching the overhead light off. Then he sat down on the bed to wait for her, and remembered that he still had to get rid of the miniature camera. He reached into the inside pocket of his raincoat—and found his cigarette lighter as well. He took it out, thinking that he ought to get rid of it at the same time as the camera, knowing the film inside was useless to him, now. But what about the American State Department? Don't risk it, he told himself . . . and then recalled his own words: "I wish it *were* in my power to ruin your so-called career." It is, Aleksei, he thought, imagining what his brother's colleagues would say and do when they discovered who was responsible for such an embarrassing breach in security.

He tensed at the familiar tap-tap on the door. "It's unlocked," he called out, getting up.

Galya came in, saw his open suitcase, and said nervously, "You must have so much to do yet. I'll just say a quick *bon voyage* and be on my—" She flushed. "After the way I acted two weeks ago, I'm surprised you let me in."

"I'm glad you called," he said, regretting his coolness. He looked at her lovely figure in her plain black dress, made plainer by luxurious honey-blond hair. He looked into wide-set blue eyes and saw regret . . . and a touch of melancholy that reminded him of the women in the trolley. His coolness began to dissipate. He took her hand. "Let's forget what happened. I know you didn't mean to be callous about Stepan's death."

She bit her lip. "It seemed that way, I know. I'm really sorry. I was just so . . . crushed about losing the trip to West Berlin that I guess I lost track of everything else."

"I know what it feels like to want something desperately," he said, his expression gentle, "to dream about it and make plans and then see the plans explode in your face. We all go through it. The worst part is never being able to count on anything.''

"Not for me," she said bitterly. "The worst is never *having* anything."

"That's something we learn to adjust to."

"I never have—God knows I've tried. I know there's more to life than pretty clothes and good food and a flat all to yourself. It's just that—oh God, Kiril!—if only we had a *little* of that, or the hope of getting it some day. Do you know when it hurts the most? After I've been to the cinema—especially the American pictures. I lose track of the story because I get all involved with the background, the clothes and furniture and shop windows filled with wonderful things. And then I start to notice that it *is* background. Kiril, the people in the picture all act so *casual* about their wonderful things! And then I look down at my dress—four years old and as stylish as a muddy overshoe—and I touch the grease on my face they call make-up, and I think about the crabmeat I haven't tasted in four years, and then I start to cry and hope that what I'm seeing on the screen is just American propaganda, like they tell us. Do you . . . do you suppose that's the way it *really* is over there?"

"Never mind," he said, making her sit down on the bed next to him. "One day you'll have some of those things you want so much. Don't ever stop wanting them, not completely."

"Yes," she said, avoiding his eyes. He was puzzled.

In a moment thick with silence, she fingered the dark glasses he'd left on his raincoat. "How much longer must you wear these?" she asked in an awkward effort at conversation.

"A few days, possibly a week."

She took out a cigarette and held out her hand for his lighter. "I've always meant to ask you what the black wings stand for. Did Stepan ever say? He got one for himself, too, didn't he?"

He nodded. "It's for the air force."

"Wouldn't it make more sense to have the wings of an airplane?"

He shrugged and casually tossed the lighter into his suitcase.

"I should let you finish packing," she apologized, getting up.

"Don't go yet. I have plenty of time."

"You look . . . odd," she said.

"I was just thinking about the time we've spent together, the last few years."

"Don't sound so solemn about it," she laughed. "You'll only be away four days. You know what *I* think? I think you've contracted a bad case of first-trip-out-of-the-country-itis. I hear it can have a *very* sobering effect on its victims." She reached over to brush the hair from his forehead, feeling lighthearted again.

"An apt diagnosis, nurse. Shall we drink to it?" He went to get a bottle of vodka from the shelf.

"Can't. I'm late for an appointment." She got up and kissed him quickly. "Be sure and call me the minute you get back," she said, turning around at the door and then stopping, searching his face as if she still found his expression odd. Then she blew him another kiss and went out.

He stared at the closed door, the bottle still in his hand, and thought, Let's drink to *last*-trip-out-of-the-country-itis. I hate to drink alone. Why couldn't you have stayed for one last toast, Galya?

. One last toast. He stared at the mirror, at a spot of gold around his neck. He could feel the weight of it. . . .

"It belonged to Anna," his aunt said. "I think you're ready to have it now."

"What is it, Aunt Maria?" he asked, turning the object over and over in his palm.

"It's a charm made of gold—a miniature scalpel."

"What's that?"

"What, and you a doctor's son? It's the instrument doctors use to make incisions. The scalpel was part of Anna's necklace. She always wore it, even under her white smock. Your grandfather had it made for her the year she entered medical school."

"Were there other charms like mine?"

"Six altogether, and all different—a tiny thermometer, a stethoscope, a little reflex hammer, a doctor's head mirror and, of course Anna's favorite, the microscope."

"I want to wear my scalpel around my neck like Anna did," he announced.

"I'll get you a chain for it."

"Aunt Maria, why did you say I was ready for it? Is it because I'm eleven now?"

"Partly, but it's more than a birthday present. You've never said much about your mother," she added softly, "and you've always called her Anna. I used to think you resented her for taking Kolya away and leaving you behind. After what you said yesterday, I know that you don't. Are you really glad that she's free?"

"Oh yes!" he said. "And I don't resent Anna anymore. I used to," he confessed. "I didn't want her for my mother. The teachers would make me stand up and tell the whole class she was an Enemy of the People, and then everyone would point and call me names. And beat me up after school when I wouldn't say it anymore. I know how to hit back now."

"You should think about our secret talk whenever they talk against Anna like that. She was so unhappy here."

"They were always telling her what to do, weren't they? So she went away and took Kolya . . . but not me," he finished with a sigh.

"You know why it was Kolya and not you, Kiril."

"How lucky Kolya is!" He jumped up from the table and tore a red kerchief from his neck. "I hate it here. I hate them always telling me what to do. I don't *want* to be a Young Pioneer! We had to do it again yesterday for the new members—the eight-year-olds. We had to raise our right arm in a stupid salute, and then when somebody called out—BE READY—we had to answer ALWAYS READY!"

"It's only a ceremony," she said, reaching over to brush the hair off his forehead . . . dark hair, like his mother's. "It doesn't have to mean anything if you don't want it to."

"I hate our Young Pioneer squads most of all. My squad leader says we have to work after school now on social projects—things like making posters and marching in demonstrations and . . . and collecting glass and iron scraps from the junkyards for the Five Year Plan. He says we'll have to go to the country some day and work in the fields. I don't want to," he said stubbornly.

"We have no choice about such things, you know that. You mustn't object." She picked up the kerchief and retied it around his neck.

"I will so!" he said, tugging at the kerchief.

But she stopped him. "Shall I tell you how to object?"

Her tone was softly conspiratorial. "It's the only way we can, but it works."

"Who told you?"

"Your mother."

"How?" he said, fascinated.

"Inside you—that's where to object—quietly, so no one can see and punish you for it. You do realize, don't you, Kiril, that the punishment gets much worse as you get older? Don't you?"

"I guess so. I did that, Aunt Maria. Just yesterday." A note of pride crept into his voice.

"What did you do?"

"What you said. When Sergei Fedorovich—he's my squad leader—called me the son of an Enemy of the People in the lunchroom, I called *him* a dirty name, only I didn't say it out loud. And I didn't feel ashamed of Anna, either. I just stood there wanting to . . . to be with her."

"Sit down and finish your cake," she said gently, seeing his effort not to cry.

"Tell me the story again," he pleaded, "about the day Anna and Kolya left Moscow." When she agreed, he sat down, gravely attentive.

"Your mother had been working late at the polyclinic. Your father was in the bedroom, drunk as usual. Aleksei had gone off with his friends instead of watching you, as he was supposed to. You and Kolya were playing in the parlor. Just as soon as Anna walked in the door, she heard a loud crash—your father had fallen off the bed! She rushed into the bedroom, leaving her medical bag on the parlor floor and—"

"And Kolya and I crawled over to it."

"Walked, more likely," she laughed. "He was a year and a half at the time and you were even older."

"And *then?*"

"Then Kolya got Anna's bag open somehow and pulled out a . . . what?"

"A lancet!"

"Sharp as a knife, the lancet was, and poor little Kolya was holding the sharpest edge next to his chest when he fell, apparently. The lancet pierced the wall of his heart."

"Kolya screamed and then Anna came running back and thought Kolya would die," he prompted. "Our doctors thought so, too, didn't they? But he didn't, did he?"

His aunt busied herself with clearing the table. "They weren't certain they could save him, so Anna made your father send her to Germany, to a famous surgeon in Berlin who was experimenting with the very kind of operation Kolya needed."

"And then they never came back."

"You forgot something. The last thing Anna did before she left—the very last—was to bend down and kiss you . . . like this." She took his small face in her hands and kissed his forehead. "And *that's* when you reached up and tugged at the little scalpel on Anna's necklace until it came off," she laughed. "I tried to take it away, but you screamed so loud that Anna said to let you keep it. When you stopped playing with it, I put it away for you."

"I love my birthday present," he said, turning away to hide tears.

"And Anna loved you, Kiril. Very much. How it must have hurt her to give you up."

"It won't be for always. We'll find her. We'll go to Germany and find them both!" He noticed her expression. "You don't believe me, do you?"

"It's possible," she said unconvincingly.

"You don't believe we'll find Kolya, do you? You think he's dead from the operation."

"Kiril, darling, what *I* think doesn't matter. Believe he's alive, if it helps you. Believe in Germany and Anna and Kolya. It can't hurt to believe."

"I'll find them. I believe it," he said, his tears forgotten. "I'll *never* stop believing it!"

Kiril's fingers held the neck of the bottle in a murderous grip. "A final toast is in order," he said out loud. "To a childhood obsession that became a vow. To an old courage line I won't be needing anymore. To the last time I'll have to say it. To Anna and Kolya!" It was a farewell—not to Stepan, this time, but to Mother Russia. He put the bottle to his lips and drank, then hurled it against the mirror. And watched while glass splintered at his feet and vodka spilled silently to the floor.

Galya hesitated in front of the Metro station. The red letter "M" blinked at her like some fellow conspirator. She hurried into the station, to a row of wooden telephone booths along one wall. She stopped outside a vacant booth to take out a coin and caught the envious glance of the woman next to her, who had spotted her changepurse full of two-kopeck pieces. Galya snapped the purse shut, thinking that this was *one* shortage, at least, that didn't affect her—not for the last two years, anyway.

She shut herself into the narrow booth and dialed. In the silence, as she waited for her call to be put through, she became aware of two competing rhythms: the tapping of her fingertips against the telephone base and the ticking of her wristwatch . . . a frantic ticking, as if the watch were racing to keep ahead of her nervous fingers. She stopped tapping and touched the tiny face of the watch . . . the elegant gold band. Beautiful. Expensive, too; made in West Germany. She shouldn't have worn it today. If Kiril had noticed— But he hadn't. By the time he got back, she'd have a good story to explain it.

"Yes? What is it?" The voice on the other end of the line was uncharacteristically impatient.

"It's Galina Ivanovna."

"Ah. And what have you to report?"

"Nothing," she said nervously.

"Comrade Barkova." The voice was patient, now, and patronizing. "I don't expect you to uncover some dire plot to overthrow the Kremlin. Your assignment is to observe much subtler things—an unguarded remark here, an antisocial view there, an overall state of mind. Incidentally, how *is* his state of mind, these days? Are his spirits unnaturally low since the death of his friend? Has his behavior altered significantly? I find your *non*-report a trifle disconcerting," the voice finished severely.

"I'm sorry. What I meant to say was . . . there's been no change since my last report."

"What about his little sojourn to East Berlin? Is he looking forward to it?"

"Oh, well, yes. That is, he didn't really *say*. He just . . ."

"He just—what?"

She hesitated, feeling trapped by the tight embrace of the phone booth, by the ticking of the watch as it counted off the seconds.

"Well?"

"It wasn't anything he said, really. He was just so solemn when I got up to leave. And he looked at me so strangely.'' As if, she realized suddenly, he never expected to see me again.

''My dear, you are a very attractive young woman—my most charming co-optee, by far. To be parted from you for even half a week could upset any red-blooded man. Shall we see that he is not upset for long?''

''What do you mean?''

''Can you be packed and ready to leave for East Berlin in, say, an hour and a half?''

''*I?* But . . . but I have no papers. No exit permit.''

''I'll take care of the details.''

''Yes. Oh, yes! I can be ready in *half* an hour! But . . . what will I tell Kiril?''

''I'll take care of that, too—with a plausible story. Call me back in twenty minutes.''

''What will I have to do?'' she asked cautiously, remembering.

''No more and no less than what you've been doing for the last two years. Just keep an eye on him for me. You'll have help, of course, but there are things a woman can see—and sense—more easily than a man. And I promise you this, Galina Ivanovna, do a conscientious job for me and you will be amply rewarded on our return. I've been thinking about a private flat. It could prove useful if you had a place of your own.''

She closed her eyes, thinking of her roommates . . . someone's eyes always looking, someone's ears always listening . . . She said shakily, ''You're *sure* nothing bad will happen to Kiril?''

''It's touching, your constant concern for his welfare. But don't lose sight of the fact that his welfare is *precisely* what you've been guarding. Remember what I told you at the start of our little joint venture. Some men have to be protected from other men, but men like my brother have to be protected from themselves. We do understand each other, don't we, comrade?''

''Yes,'' she said quietly, ''we do.''

7

Kiril stood on an unprotected stretch of ground, with Galya shivering beside him. There was nothing within a hundred yards—no buildings, no hangar, no foliage—to serve as a windbreaker. His raincoat slapped against his trousers. His coat collar was raised, partially obscuring the lower half of his face. A cap and dark glasses obscured the rest. Will it obscure enough? he wondered uneasily.

Two official limousines were parked nearby, containing the rest of the welcoming committee: two East German officials, one with a symbolic key to his country's most prestigious hospital for Herr Doktor Kurt Brenner; the Mongolian, Luka Rogov; and Colonel Nikolai Malik, army officer, whose silent scrutiny during the three-hour flight from Moscow to East Berlin had been disquieting.

Kiril had kept the dark glasses on and his face in the pages of a book the whole trip, so Malik wouldn't get a good sense of what he looked like and couldn't make comparisons with Brenner. What was this Malik doing here? Kiril wondered. Part of the blackmail scheme Aleksei had alluded to, probably. What *was* that scheme? Would a man like Brenner succumb to blackmail?

You have until conference-time on Monday to answer both questions, Kiril told himself uneasily. You have until Tuesday to counteract the blackmail and make sure Brenner goes back to America. Damn Aleksei's secretiveness! Before returning to Potsdam, he'd handed over only pieces of Brenner's file, so there was no way to get past "heart surgeon" and get a handle on "private citizen." Then go over what you *have* got one more time, he told himself wearily: Father, first generation American, German descent. Mother, German born, a naturalized American citizen. Both parents employed by the cardiac institute where Brenner was chief surgeon, the father also a surgeon, the mother in some research capacity. A flamboyantly successful career. A long and equally flamboyant bachelorhood interrupted—if Aleksei could be believed—by a well-placed society marriage. A widespread reputation as a humanitarian because of his nonprofit cardiac clinic for indigent children, and because he was known to cancel an entire day's surgical schedule and lock himself in his office on the rare occasion when a patient died under his knife.

A man of contradictions, Kiril thought. A renowned surgeon who'd declined every invitation to medical exchanges in Iron Curtain countries, then had heaped extravagant praise on Medicine International's "peacemaking endeavors." Why had he accepted *this* invitation with such alacrity? Kiril shrugged. He had always admired Brenner—by reputation. The only thing he felt now was contempt. After what Brenner had said about . . . lawbreakers, he could not turn out to be like the other American doctors he'd met through the exchange programs.

A bittersweet experience, those exchanges, he thought: excitement triggered by the mere presence of Americans, then depression after they had gone, leaving only the contrast between what he guessed to be their normal way of life, and his own. They also left behind information, of course, for they were open and generous with their medical expertise. And so friendly. He sighed. Indiscriminately friendly—to Party hacks and government officials and secret policemen, as well as fellow doctors. The Americans saw—there was no way they could help seeing—the rigid controls that their Russian colleagues were forced to work under: no free exchange of ideas, no real opportunity for hosts and guests to be alone, no way to participate without awkwardness in a simple exchange of gifts. Once, some doctor had given him an American detective novel for his own volume of Russian poems, and both books had been examined as if their pages harbored a coded plot to overthrow the Kremlin. Yet the American doctors always kept silent. And kept coming back.

"Look," Galya said, "here they come!"

He saw a tiny speck that was the plane approaching, and he felt a surge of optimism. Whatever else he was, Brenner was an American; he would never succumb to a blackmail threat—not if the price were his American way of life. He felt a touch of the old excitement as the speck became a flying fish, skimming over foamlike clouds. Then the fish acquired a smooth, silver body, circled for a landing and taxied to a halt. In a few days, Kiril thought, the Brenners would be returning home. To America. The left corner of his mouth curved downward . . . the old bittersweet feeling.

The man and woman who got off the plane were Americans—it was in their walk and in the lift of their

129

heads, so different from the East German officials approaching the runway. Kiril zeroed in on the man's walk—jaunty,
with a brisk, authoritative step. Unlike his own slower, more
deliberate way of moving, he thought, frowning with
concentration. The man came toward him, swinging a trim
briefcase the way some American movie hero would cross a
courtyard swinging a tennis racket. He wore movie-hero
clothes and his white hair was smooth-looking. Kiril compared it with his own—dark brown for now, until he washed
the rinse out of it. His hair was thicker, too, more unruly;
he would have to pick up some hair tonic at the hotel . . .

The inventory stopped abruptly. He was staring into
Kurt Brenner's face, only a few feet from his own.

This was no strong resemblance. It was the eerie sensation of staring at his slightly altered perception in a mirror.
In the moment when he reached for Brenner's hand, he
forgot the standing order he had given himself: monitor
people's reactions—especially Galya's.

He needn't have worried. Galya barely noticed Brenner;
she was too fascinated with his wife. Tall, she noted, with
an almost catlike grace. There was something commanding
about her . . . or perhaps it was the long, military-looking
cape she wore, with gold braid on the shoulders and along
the raised collar. And the penetrating green color . . . a
good match for her eyes. Copper glints were all you could
see of her hair. The rest of it was captured under a
wonderful, wide-brimmed hat that slanted provocatively to
one side, shading half her face, giving her an air of mystery.

Galya glanced quickly at Kiril and saw that he seemed
oblivious of everyone but Dr. Brenner. Then she realized
why. Dr. Brenner looked just like him—incredible! No
one else, not even the Brenners, seemed aware of it. But
how could they be? she realized. All they could really see

was Kiril's dark hair and dark glasses. Only by looking closely could they notice the striking similarity in the shape and contour of their faces, the resemblance around the mouth. Only if you knew Kiril's eyes, like I do, she thought, could you know how much Dr. Brenner's were like them. She nearly giggled as Kiril looked at her disbelievingly. Then she lost track of it, her attention drawn once more to the figure in the dark green cape.

A commercial airport, Adrienne was thinking, the largest one in East Germany! All the research she had crammed into the last couple of days hadn't prepared her for her first sight from the air: tethered goats grazing on the grass between runways that were weathered looking and cracked—like rows of abandoned country roads going nowhere. She saw a few scattered buildings and only three planes. Guards holding submachine guns stood like uniformed statues at strategic points around the field.

She turned a polite face to the officials who'd emerged from their rounded limousines and nodded her way through ponderous introductions. Everyone looked so shabby, she thought; even the trim uniform of the very correct Russian officer seemed soft and formless by American army standards. The blond woman was lovely, but oddly disconcerting. The man in the raincoat and dark glasses, doctor whatever-his-name, was disconcerting, too. It wasn't his attitude so much as . . . what? His looks, she concluded; he looked familiar and unfamiliar at the same time. He looked a little like Kurt. He looked, she thought uneasily, studying him, remarkably like Kurt. Tall, with the same kind of build and the same kind of bone structure—what she could see of it, anyway. She realized that the amenities were over. She got into one of the limousines, looked around for Kurt, and sighed. He was following the lovely blond into the other limousine.

Brenner cautiously parted rear window curtains to see which limo the army officer was headed for. Who was he kidding? he thought. The "army officer" was Nikolai Malik. He had known even before the formal introduction. "How do you do," Malik had said—nothing more. Unable to look at Malik's face, his eyes had clung to the red epaulets on Malik's shoulders, blinking hard, so that the epaulets had seemed like danger signals. Cautiously he had looked up . . . at straight, dark hair, streaked with gray now . . . at a mocking quality in the not-quite-hidden recesses of a remembered smile . . . at eyes that were the same glacial pale gray—amused, recognizing, being recognized. He saw that Malik was on his way over.

He let the curtain drop into place. For a moment the dark curtain of his preoccupation parted and he recaptured a peculiar reaction he'd had on the runway, to this Dr. Andreyev. The man's greeting had been proper enough. But intense. Probably because the two of them seemed to be the same physical type, he thought, and then dismissed the matter; Malik had just opened the car door. Brenner turned to the East German official and launched into rapid conversation in his best conversational German. His "best," he thought as the official complimented him, was more than adequate; it was impressive as hell. And it kept him from having to talk to Malik.

Nikolai Malik got into the jumpseat opposite Brenner. Say nothing, Malik was thinking. Smile knowingly. Ominously. It was going to be hard obeying instructions—obeying orders, he corrected himself wryly—and even harder to sit on his hands all weekend. "Make yourself scarce," Colonel Andreyev had told him. "Nothing starts until *I* get there, understand?" The self-important bastard, Malik thought. "Cigarette?" he said, during a brief lull in the conversation. His manner, as he lit Brenner's cigarette,

132

was deferential. "Lovely afternoon, isn't it? Nice weather for sightseeing," he observed, disobeying instructions . . . just a little. Brenner looked so damned uncomfortable. Just like in the old days. "Is this your first trip to East Berlin, Doctor Brenner?" he asked.

So far, so good, Kiril thought as he sat back in the other limousine. Galya's initial reaction was nothing to be alarmed about, and the Brenners . . . He glanced for a moment at Adrienne, sitting next to a window. Nothing to worry about there, either, at least not yet. He felt grateful for the partially drawn curtains; the air was filled with shadow and the smoke of cigarettes. He looked at the back of Rogov's thick neck; he was sitting up front, next to the driver. No reaction from that quarter—predictably. Even if Rogov noticed the likeness, he'd be indifferent to it, thanks to his limited assignment: *Guard this man, this potential traitor.* Rogov was—how had Aleksei put it?—"a man devoid of imagination."

The limousines cut across runways and grassy strips and pulled up in front of a low brick building.

"This is our airport terminal," announced an East German official, extending his hand for Adrienne's passport and her declaration of valuables. "There will be no need for you to leave the car. I shall attend to the formalities."

"I'd like to have a quick look inside, if you don't mind," she said, and got out without waiting to see if he did. She saw him shrug, then head for the other limousine.

"Inside" looked about as commercial as a monastery. No shops or displays of magazines and candy bars. No newspapers, of course. One small dining area; a tired-looking waitress was serving soft drinks and sausages to half a dozen customers.

"The terminal is not impressive, I am afraid," said an apologetic voice behind her.

She turned to see the Russian doctor, Andreyev. "You've seen our airport terminals in the West?" she asked him curiously.

"Only in the cinema. Until yesterday, I was never out of the Soviet Union." The voice had a pronounced Russian accent. "Have you ever been to my country?" he asked, equally curious.

"No. Until today, I was never behind the Iron Curtain."

He started to hold the door of the terminal open for her when it swung outward.

Luka Rogov stood there, frowning. The frown dissolved on visual contact with Kiril.

Kiril ignored him. "Now that you are here, Mrs. Brenner, we must see that your trip is memorable. We Russians have a motto: *Pokazat tovar litsom.* It means 'Show them the best of our goods.' On behalf of my East German comrades, I must apologize for this inauspicious beginning." He smiled. "I shall personally see to it that the view improves." Thanks to a little research and Stepan's vivid descriptions, he thought. "By the time we arrive at our hotel, you will have seen some of the *best* that the Deutsche Demokratische Republik has to offer."

Adrienne stepped out of the limousine and looked around a huge circular plaza ringed with tall buildings.

"The new civic center," Kiril announced, following her out. "Forty blocks of office buildings, housing units and shopping arcades. An expensive new theater. A concert hall." His voice was enthusiastic.

Spacious pedestrian walkways, with no pedestrians, she thought. An enormous traffic artery, with no traffic . . .

She had just read that fewer than one East German in twelve owned a car.

"The famous television tower," he said respectfully, pointing out a thin, tubular structure. "It is the second tallest edifice of its kind in all of Europe—almost twelve hundred feet high. Your hotel," he said, indicating a building that towered over the others. "It has over forty stories and two thousand very modern rooms. It is unique in Eastern Europe—except for one of our Intourist hotels, of course. *Our* hotel overlooks Red Square and the Kremlin and has *three* thousand rooms. There is white marble everywhere—some people find it ostentatious," he added offhandedly.

Adrienne frowned. Another pointed comparison between Russia and East Germany. Her doctor-guide had made one after another throughout their leisurely drive from the airport. He was eager, apparently, to show her that the best of his country's "goods" were better than East Germany's. Could he really be so unsophisticated as to think that his boasts on behalf of either country were not ludicrous to Western ears?

She started to wander through the plaza, feeling the intensity of his glance behind her. It made her uncomfortable. The drive in had been uncomfortable. There had been a kind of grim purposefulness underneath his polite running commentary, like a barely discernible musical theme contradicting some blaring melody. At times, he'd been bewilderingly frank. Like his response to her comment about working women. She had noticed that they seemed to be everywhere—directing traffic, driving trolleys, doing heavy labor on construction sites. He had remarked that Russian women were even more "liberated," that it was a common sight in Moscow to see them digging ditches and hauling heavy equipment side by side with the men. Later, he had pretended not to notice her reaction to "Neue Wache"—a memorial to the "victims of militarism and fascism," he'd explained. It had Greek columns, an eternal flame . . . and heel-clicking, goose-stepping German soldiers who changed guard every hour.

She had sensed his silent scrutiny as he pointed out other landmarks on East Germany's famous Unter den Linden—the Soviet Embassy, a State museum and opera house, the university with its newly renovated clinic where Kurt's medical conference was to take place. The great, broad boulevard, enlivened by four parallel rows of linden trees on each side, was one of the most chillingly barren streets she had ever seen. There were red flags on the official black limousines stacked all along the street's center island, and red flags around the long, thin necks of lampposts that bent obediently over the pavement; they had made her think of tall, gaunt men, tagged and hunched in silent agony. Although it was Saturday, the boulevard had seemed like some abandoned parking lot, except for one place where people milled about aimlessly, the place where Unter den Linden began—or ended—cut off by a mass of shrubbery, designed to hide the Wall, and failing: nothing grew high enough to block the Brandenburg Gate's stone columns, and beyond them, a tantalizing glimpse of West Berlin.

When Unter den Linden had opened onto a large, empty square, her guide had helped her take some photographs with her big, clumsy camera while he translated some of the slogans strung up in clusters over wooden bleachers: "Forward with the Building of Socialism." "To imitate the Soviet Union is to imitate the victor."

"That place seemed familiar," she had confessed on

their way back to the car. "Is it something out of the Nazi era?" "It is Marx-Engels Platz, once part of the famous Lustgarten. Strange, how history repeats itself—Hitler used to hold huge rallies and military displays there, and so do we. But *we* march to the slogans of a noble cause. Only last evening I witnessed a stunning torchlight display of tanks and marching soldiers . . . the Iron Fist of Socialism. Do you like parades?" Andreyev had asked, his tone so innocently inquiring that he could only have been baiting her. "Just the capitalist variety," she had replied. "Kids marching with high school bands and drum majorettes displaying their legs. No tanks," she'd added with heavy sarcasm; "they can be hell on the roads." "But our displays are necessary, even inspirational—people need frequent reminders of their Iron Fist," he'd persisted. "Did you know we have twenty-two combat-ready Soviet divisions—over four hundred thousand soldiers!—stationed in East Germany?" "To keep seventeen million East Germans in line?' "To keep the peace." She had thought her bluntness would offend him. Incredibly, he'd seemed pleased by it.

Later, she'd been struck again by the sense that he approved of her obvious disapproval when he'd showed her a showplace street nicknamed Parrot Colony, because it housed only Party members; its shops had featured TVs, washing machines, small cars—luxuries, he'd explained, that others had to wait years for.

But for him to share her attitude would be preposterous, she thought, glancing at him—*her* turn to stare, now. She noticed even more similarities in his face. A wide brow like Kurt's, a long, straight nose. What were the eyes like behind those dark glasses?

"Very impressive, your civic center," Brenner said,

coming up to Kiril. "Don't you think so?" he said to Galya. "I've seen pictures of your famous television tower, Dr. Andreyev, but they don't do justice to it."

Their mouths are different, Adrienne thought, and the difference isn't in Kurt's favor. She watched Kurt's lips slipping into his characteristic half-smile, as if he were both amused by the world and contemptuous of it. There was no contempt in the set of the doctor's mouth, and no amusement. She saw an odd combination of resoluteness and what looked like endurance. Why resoluteness? Endurance of what? She shrugged, annoyed with herself. What she was really seeing was an iron discipline to go with his Iron Fist of Socialism. And what did a good Party man have to endure, after all? Not even a long waiting list for a new car. One quick look at the Deutsche Demokratische Republik's "goods" with a glib parrot-guide, she thought, and I start making pointless comparisons and reading hidden virtues into the man's face.

She took Brenner's arm. "Let's go in," she said. "I'm eager to see our 'very modern' hotel." Behind her, she felt the intense scrutiny again.

8

"Zum Wohl!" Brenner said as Galya passed around glasses of champagne.

"To the good health of us all," Kiril said, smiling, and tipped his glass to an unsmiling Luka.

Luka, stubbornly empty-handed, gave Kiril a wary, narrowed look.

Adrienne put her glass down. "I'm sure you're eager to see the clinic," she said to Brenner. "Just give me a few minutes to unpack some things." She walked into an adjoining bedroom.

Kiril looked around eagerly. He had never been inside a completely modern hotel suite before. His own room down the corridor—his and Rogov's—was just that: a room with a couple of narrow beds. This was so much more . . . a spacious, cheerful sitting room, trim-looking molded furniture of brightly colored plastic, a bedroom almost as large as the sitting room, with gleaming maplewood bureaus and an enormous bed with an iron bedpost.

The Brenners didn't seem impressed, not even by the elaborate luncheon they'd just been served by two waiters in tuxedos. That, he thought, was a point in his favor; people accustomed to real luxury would be reluctant to give it up.

He watched Mrs. Brenner unpacking in the next room and thought about the ride in from the airport—the first leg of his "guided tour." Had he found himself a potential ally? She wasn't like the other foreign women he'd met through the exchange programs—or the men, either. No excited babble about "exotic" surroundings. No diplomatic responses to his stream of blatant propaganda. No tactful efforts to avoid politically awkward subjects. A police state held some reality for Adrienne Brenner—which meant, he concluded hopefully, that she'd never consent to live in one. Would her husband defect without her? Brenner seemed solicitous toward his wife, yet there was a coolness between them. If Brenner really was a Don Juan, what kind of love could they have for one another? Very little, he thought with satisfaction. He frowned. What was the matter with him? Since Mrs. Brenner seemed to be a political realist, the closer she was to her husband, the more she would help him resist Aleksei's blackmail and return to America. He realized he was staring at her garments on the bed . . . soft and fragile looking against the rough cotton of the bedspread. His glance shifted to the furniture. The maplewood looked tawdry now, put to shame by the russet highlights in her hair. He caught himself frowning at the huge bed. What was the *matter* with him?

He forced himself to look away—at Galya, laughing and talking in halting English to Brenner about an elaborate cellophane-wrapped basket of fruit, compliments of Colonel Aleksei Andreyev. He knew, he thought, what was the matter with him. He looked at Galya enjoying herself, with not-quite-lifeless eyes and not-quite-listless posture—because she had not quite given up. He watched her smile . . . almost like a reflex action; it never reached inside to touch her soul. And Adrienne Brenner? He had not been prepared for an Adrienne Brenner. She was disarmingly direct. Her almost fierce independence intrigued him. He mentally transported her to Moscow and tried to picture her standing, subdued, before some bureaucrat—being told what to do, how to live, what to think; he could not imagine it.

Galya's profile intruded suddenly on his thoughts. She was hungrily staring past him into the bedroom, at the rich array of garments strewn across the bed. *Kiril, the people act so* casual *about their wonderful things!* It was so cruel, so unfair, to make comparisons, he realized. Adrienne Brenner was one of the fortunate ones. There was no way Galya could hide her bleak heritage; it was like a second skin one could never shed. Not even on the other side? he wondered. Not even if there were someone like Adrienne Brenner to help one forget—Fool! Forget Brenner's wife. Concentrate on Brenner. Get *through* to him.

He had to remind himself as they were all going down in the elevator. He happened to be standing close to Adrienne Brenner . . . so close that he caught the faint scent of perfume in her hair. He reminded himself again as they stood waiting for a limousine. The wind was tugging at the long folds of her cape. He felt in league with the wind, urging it on, wondering about her body under the cape.

He needed no more reminders as they drove to the university clinic. Something was wrong with Brenner. He was being complimentary about Unter den Linden, but the glib phrases seemed to slip out automatically; he seemed in the grip of some fierce preoccupation. I must cut through it, Kiril thought, even at the risk of being obvious. Even in front of two witnesses? he wondered uneasily . . . and shrugged. The Mongolian spoke almost no English and understood even less. And Galya, what was there to fear from her?

He held off until the five of them were walking through the long corridors of the clinic. When Brenner made some offhand remark about medicine, Kiril launched into the standard Party lecture, speaking eloquently of the fifty-odd years of Soviet medical progress, contrasting it harshly with the shortcomings of the Czarist regime. Then he slipped in a few liabilities. It was true that Soviet medical schools graduated thirty thousand physicians a year. He "had to admit," however, that many of them qualified to be little more than technicians. Soviet hospitals were *far* better staffed than their Western counterparts. Not that (regretful tone) surplus medical personnel were a good substitute for modern electronic devices. The Soviet medical community was *appalled* by the shocking waste of equipment so typical of Western hospitals—disposable surgical gloves, towels discarded after a single use. Of course (rueful smile), his country's chronic paper shortage left its doctors little option regarding disposable products. He noticed, between verbal thrusts, that Adrienne Brenner was taking notes. Brenner was looking politely attentive.

When they came to an area marked off-limits to visitors, Kiril dismissed the warning sign with a wave and led them to an empty room, eager "to show you some modern X-ray equipment I saw yesterday." But in the adjoining room lay a patient, his chest covered with short, black tubelike objects. To Brenner's raised eyebrow and Adrienne's pained expression, he explained, "Leech therapy—

an almost barbaric contrast with the X-ray equipment next door, but the patient is a Russian soldier wedded to the old ways. This kind of anti-coagulation therapy is still common in some parts of the Soviet Union.'' Adrienne Brenner was looking at the patient as if her eyes could substitute for the camera she'd been forced to leave at the reception desk. Brenner was frowning vaguely.

As they walked to their waiting limousine, Kiril talked about the practice of medicine in East Germany, where doctors were regarded as members of the elite. In Russia, he explained, medical personnel were among the poorest paid of the professions. Not that East Germany's Ministry of Health was without its own problems. Did Dr. Brenner have any idea how many doctors had left East Germany since 1958—right after the Party had launched a campaign to improve the quality of political and ideological dogma in the medical profession? Had Dr. Brenner heard that by the time the Wall went up a few years later, there was such an acute medical crisis that hospitals and clinics had been forced to limit their services to emergencies? Did Dr. Brenner realize there was one doctor to every eight thousand inhabitants, compared to the West German ratio of one to eight hundred? Did Dr. Brenner know that until recently, doctors in East Germany had been restricted to the inferior medicines produced in Communist bloc countries?

Dr. Brenner did not know. He did not seem to care, either.

When they got to the limousine, Kiril parted the heavy curtains while Galya and the Brenners settled themselves in the back.

Luka waited until everyone had taken a seat and the

back doors were closed, checking that his two charges were in the middle before he got in next to the driver.

"I thought we would take a quick drive before dinner, just to give you a sense of the city," Kiril told the Brenners as the car pulled away, thinking that the route he had chosen, described by Stepan, happily was not on the special list entitled "Areas of Democratic Berlin closed to foreigners."

As the car left the Unter den Linden area, the change was swift—from starkly modern apartment houses to seedy housing projects. Between buildings so caked with grime that it was impossible to guess at their original color, vacant lots with crumbling plaster grimaced—the bombed-out ruins of another era. Some half-collapsed structures, with sections of walls sagging from their moorings, gave evidence of being occupied.

Everyone but Luka was silent, made uncomfortable by the furtive, resentful stares their limousine was attracting on uncrowded streets. When Brenner muttered something about the somberness of the architecture, Kiril said automatically, without conviction, "A nation's progress is not always self-evident. East Germany has the highest standard of living of any Soviet bloc country." When Adrienne commented on the patience of the shoppers lined up at a street vendor's vegetable cart, his remark was again automatic: "Queues are a way of life with us. Patience is not a virtue, it is a necessity." He shrugged. "The average Soviet citizen spends over four hundred hours a year waiting on line for basic necessities," he said.

He had said it, he realized, not to draw pointed comparisons for the Brenners but simply because the comparison was so apt. It occurred to him that he felt too much at home here, almost as if he had never left Moscow. Different streets, he thought, totally different cities; Moscow was pale yellow—washed out, while East Berlin was tarnished and gray with a kind of grittiness in the air, as if the whole place could use a good scrubbing down. And yet . . . this ominous familiarity with a place he'd never seen before.

It was the silence, he realized; it was the absence of bright lights. It was the way people hurried, as if their biggest desire were to get off the streets and out of sight. It was the people themselves, men and women with German hairstyles and dress but with the same ill-fitting clothes he'd looked on all his life, and the same expressions: part lethargy, part despair. Was this the face of the whole world? No, he reassured himself quickly.

No, he repeated—and stopped himself from staring at Adrienne Brenner, from looking at her as hungrily as Galya had stared at her clothes. But he had no need to stare. She was already etched in his memory . . . an outward look in the cool, green eyes, unconscious pride in the set of her mouth and the lift of her head, unstated confidence in the way she moved. All proof, he thought, that somewhere beyond his existence was another world— another universe—that was just across a wall. He felt the empty ache of longing. Then longing switched to a sudden, searing impatience that blurred his vision.

This was a new experience. His whole life had been a litany to patience that had kept him alive and brought him to the edge of freedom. He had taught himself to sit on his anger, to scoff at his bitterness, to go slowly. Don't stop now! he pleaded with himself. Don't abandon your oldest ally—your best weapon! Don't fall victim to the sights and sounds meant only for the Brenners. Keep a vision of those people lined up for their vegetables—of the patience stamped on their faces . . .

But he knew, even as he listened to his mind, that his emotions were in revolt. He knew that after forty-seven years of waiting on line for his freedom, his patience had burned itself out.

9

The limousine swerved to avoid a pothole, and Galya slid a little with the movement. She wrinkled her nose, irritated by the musty odor of the worn velvet upholstery. Her eyes flitted about the car's interior . . . thick driver-passenger partition, thick-curtains, thick Oriental rug under her feet. The rug had been expensive once, she thought, a real luxury. She glanced at her only luxury, her wristwatch, and caught her breath at the thought of the flat Colonel Andreyev had promised her. Then she remembered the things she would have to tell him first—innocuous things, she told herself quickly. There was nothing wrong, nothing dangerous, in what Kiril had been saying, just . . . odd. I won't go into details, that's all, she thought, and felt her uneasiness drop away. "What now?" she asked Kiril in Russian.

"We could visit the Soviet War Memorial in Treptower Park," he answered in English. "There is still time before dinner," he told the Brenners. "Treptower is a famous tourist attraction not far from our hotel."

"I am so tired," Galya said in grudging English. "I would like so much the return to our hotel."

"Not a bad idea," Brenner chimed in. He needed a drink. "Had enough for one day, dear?" he asked Adrienne. "I have a feeling jet lag is just around the corner."

"I'll catch up with myself tomorrow. We're having a restful day at the beach, right?" she asked Kiril.

"The Baltic shore will be restful but we must travel several hours by plane to get there," he said.

"I'm really not tired. I'd like to see the memorial."

"All right. The limousine will drop us off, and we can walk back."

When the limousine headed for the hotel, it was three persons lighter. Brenner pretended to stare out the window, hoping to avoid conversation. But Galya, sitting next to him, made no attempt to talk.

He relaxed against the cushions—tried to. How the hell could he relax when he was about to be blackmailed? The stakes would be higher than in the old days, he thought, and the cash would be harder to raise. Could he convince Malik that he was in a real financial bind? What if he stood his ground and refused to pay the bastard a sou? —after all, the World War II episode was ancient history. When you came right down to it, it was his word against Malik's. And these days, his word counted for something.

When they got to the hotel, he and Galya parted company—he to a cocktail lounge on the thirty-eighth floor, she to her room. But before the elevator stopped on her floor, she said to him shyly, "In your rooms, this champagne that we taste, I like very much. There was left a little. Do you mind I finish before resting?"

"Not at all," he said, handing her his key. "Just leave the door unlocked when you leave."

She hurried to the Brenner suite, oblivious for once of the odor of disinfectant in the corridor. She had trouble unlocking the door because her hand was shaking with anticipation.

Adrienne was uncomfortably aware of her leather shoulder bag and slim-heeled sandals as she crossed the hotel lobby. She had carried her cape for blocks, rather than attract attention, but it hadn't worked; they had stared at her suit, her shoes, her shoulderbag. Even here, even in the so-called better part of town, she thought, they never stopped staring. In the elevator, she thought about her depressing walk through Treptower Park, the stares that had followed her down every path. She hadn't been able to name what she was seeing, knowing that it wasn't envy or malice. Dr. Andreyev had named it for her: fear, and a touch of resentment. "Western clothes stand out because of their rich fabrics and stylish lines," he'd explained, "and there is no mistaking the fit—so perfect it could not possibly be some hand-me-down from an aunt or older sister." "Why fear?" she'd asked him. "Such clothes are the trademark of the privileged—Party bosses, their friends and mistresses." "Is it the same in your country?" "Why would it be any different?" Then he had drawn her a thoroughly depressing picture of Soviet women, always yearning for something better.

Why does it hurt me to think about it? she wondered as she walked down the corridor to the suite. I'm not my brother's keeper—I've never believed in that wretched slogan. Why do I take these things *personally?* She shrugged, impatient with the same old question she had never found a satisfying answer to. The door of the suite was unlocked. She opened it, went in, and stopped.

From the entranceway she saw a black dress lying like an abandoned dustrag on the bedroom floor, most of her own wardrobe spread out on the bed . . . and Galya.

Wearing a cream-colored gown, the one that seemed to flow in an unbroken line from its high virginal neckline to the floor, Galya was sweeping about the room. She was graceful elegance in motion—head high, shoulders straight, arms slightly apart—as if she didn't quite know whether to hold in the wonder of what she was feeling or let it take wing. The beginnings of a smile pulled irresistibly at the corners of her mouth. Her eyes had the luminous look of unshed tears. She glided to a slightly breathless halt in front of a long mirror. "Tell me, sir," she said softly to an imaginary figure in the mirror, "is still green gown which is best you like? *This* one is most wonderful, I think. The color is—how do you say in America?—sympathetic to me."

"It really is," Adrienne said, coming into the sitting room and stopping just outside the bedroom door.

Galya whirled around. She started to fumble with the clasp at the back of her neck.

"Please don't be embarrassed," Adrienne said, her voice as soft as Galya's had been. "The gown is so lovely with your coloring and your blond hair. Would you allow me to give it to you?"

"You are too much generous." Galya's voice was dipped in starch. "Are all American ladies so generous as you? But I have no need for such a generosity. Quite soon I am having money to buy beautiful gown, same like this one." She slammed the bedroom door.

As she began to change, so did her expression—from resentment to something darker.

* * *

Adrienne stepped off the bleached planks of a board-walk and sank ankle deep into hot white sand. She arched her back, stretched luxuriously, looked around at her fellow sunbathers, and for the first time lost the tension that had ridden with her, like an uninvited guest, through the streets of East Berlin. I could be anywhere in the world right now, she mused, reminded of travel brochure clichés: sun and surf, castles in the sand, picnic baskets and carefree chatter. But there were no picnic baskets, she noticed, and no carefree chatter; people were quiet. It was probably because of the blare from the damn loudspeakers—they were all over the beach, perched on top of long poles, sticking up from the sand like disembodied periscopes. The strident notes of a military march oom-pahed their way to a clash of cymbals, followed by the razored cadence of carefully enunciated German. She saw that people didn't seem the least bit interested. "What's going on?" she asked Galya, standing next to her. "Can you understand German?"

Seeing the politely aloof face that turned to her, she wished for the tenth time that she'd bitten her tongue before making her tactless offer. Last night's apology, and this morning's, hadn't cleared the air, apparently.

"I understand only few words," Galya said. "For me, the foreign language is hard."

"Your English is a lot better than my nonexistent Russian and German."

"How kind to give me compliment on my not good English," Galya said stiffly.

Adrienne restrained a sigh. They started toward the shoreline, their silence mocked by the relentless staccato of the loudspeaker voice. A strong sea breeze caught fringes of the beach umbrellas they passed, snapping them with the same staccato beat. Lieutenant Rogov was sitting under their own umbrella next to an empty chair. Adrienne almost laughed; Captain Ahab, she thought, in a perspiration-stained Russian uniform, staring out to sea for his Moby Dick. That's curious, she thought, since the object of his constant attention is standing right next to him. Then she felt a stab of disappointment . . . Dr. Andreyev was wearing his inevitable dark glasses, but instead of giving him an air of mystery, they seemed ordinary on a beach. He had on an incongruous yachting cap, tipped jauntily to one side—

The sudden blast of another march jumbled her thoughts just as he turned in her direction. "Dr. Andreyev," she called, gesturing at the nearest loudspeaker, "can you explain what they're saying on these damn . . ." The question fell away, as Kurt Brenner took off his sunglasses.

"Dr. Andreyev is getting his feet wet," he said, pointing.

"I . . . it was the dark glasses."

"Darling! I didn't think you knew how to blush. Well, don't be embarrassed. I admit we have a lot in common—physically, anyway. You wanted to know about the loudspeakers?"

"Yes," she said, glad to be off the subject of Andreyev. "Apart from the militant music, what is it they're broadcasting so insistently?"

"Lectures, announcements, that sort of thing."

"They're broadcasting lectures to people on a beach?"

"Amazing, isn't it?" he said with a faintly incredulous smile. "They're also checking identity cards—see that uniformed guard over there?" He started to put his dark glasses back on. "Is it safe?" he teased, "or are you apt to confuse me again with our mysterious host?"

"There is no mystery in dark glasses," Galya observed.

"Dr. Andreyev must keep away light from eye infection. But is big mystery," she said sweetly, "why Mrs. Brenner is mistaking him for husband. I tell difference if *my* husband," she purred, reaching up to adjust Brenner's yachting cap at a more rakish angle, then looking him over with a mock frown. "Maybe Mrs. Brenner tell from white hair showing under cap," she said, "or from this"—she touched a mole on Brenner's shoulder—"or this"—her finger followed a thin line on his skin, white against the deep tan of his chest. She dropped her hand, laughing. Then, like a defiant child expecting anger, she faced Adrienne.

Damn you— Adrienne almost said it aloud, to Kurt, not the Barkova woman. To his arched eyebrow and to that half-smile which meant he was flattered, as he was flattered by his nurses and by hostesses at cocktail parties and— "Oh, the hell with it," she said, startling both of them. She dropped onto the sand with her beach towel.

The sun was a lightweight blanket on her body; she closed her eyes, surrendering to its warmth, trying not to think about anything. But yesterday was hard not to think about. Her article was practically writing itself, now; whole paragraphs kept darting in and out of her mind. The only thing she'd dared to write down were a few memory-jogging words that would be meaningless to anyone else. Photographs were more accurate than memory, and more incriminating, if only she could manage to take the ones she really wanted. Lugging her conspicuously large camera around was great camouflage for the tiny Minox in her shoulderbag, but so far, she thought ruefully, she had almost nothing to show for her trouble.

"—couldn't have asked for better weather," she heard Kurt saying.

They're so different, she thought, comparing his voice with Andreyev's; their styles were different. How could she have made such an embarrassing mistake? Yet she felt uneasy about the undeniable likeness. She felt uneasy about *him*. For a walking propaganda machine, he was too damn purposeful. Even when he was pretending a callous indifference to some of the things he— She caught herself. Pretending? Now, what makes you think that?

She felt the delicious warmth of her sun-blanket slip away, as if some presumptuous cloud had crossed the almost cloudless sky. She smiled and turned lazily on her side, reaching with half-closed eyes for the robe she'd dropped on the sand next to her towel. Her arm stalled in mid-air, as if someone had grabbed it.

Kiril was looking down at her. His shadow across her body had blotted out the sun.

She felt the weight of his glance and her own tight breathing—the shock of seeing his body outside the prison of an ill-fitting suit. She was conscious of smooth, wet skin . . . the shape of his shoulders . . . his hands reaching for a towel . . . the insolent line of his legs, braced against the hard-driving wind. She was conscious, suddenly, of her own body, pinned beneath his shadow . . . bare legs, the curve of her hip, a bathing suit that covered her up to the neck but left her shoulders exposed . . .

The shadow broke. He had turned to respond to something Brenner was saying. She dropped back and closed her eyes, feeling cold, even though the sun was back.

10

The Soviet army jet helicopter that had flown them to the beach in the morning was parked on the lawn of the resort hotel where they had just had lunch. It was almost all plexiglass, a playful-looking bubble on skis, and a crowd had surrounded it as if it were something from outer space. Adrienne watched the crowd because it was an excuse not to watch what was going on behind her: as he had done this morning, Lieutenant Rogov was methodically searching Dr. Andreyev and Miss Barkova.

She had been spared that indignity; Rogov had been interested only in her shoulderbag. He still was, she thought, feeling a tap on the shoulder and turning around to find him looking at her expectantly. She noticed that he'd left his calling card—a smear of dust on her white dress. She handed over her bag and watched his thick fingers explore all the side pockets; apparently he still didn't give a damn about the Minox inside one of them. Dr. Andreyev had joked about him once: "My shadow. He is 'nyekulturny'

—uncouth, but he makes a good bodyguard. We Russians are not too popular with our East German comrades." But Rogov's assignment, she suspected, had nothing to do with hostile Germans.

In the helicopter, sitting across from Kiril and Galya, Adrienne watched Luka heave himself inside. He was surprisingly agile for a man of his bulk, she thought, and wondered why he hadn't searched the pilot. Maybe that was the co-pilot's job—if the tightlipped, tensely alert man in the front compartment really was a co-pilot. She felt comforted by the two radio receivers that allowed communication between the pilot and the sealed-off passenger compartment. But she still felt uneasy, as if they were in the detachable part of a command module and at any moment might be set adrift in space. She looked at her Russian fellow passengers who, judging from their impassive faces, were used to the lack of seat belts, and then braced herself in time with the blast of the motor, watching the violence of the whirling rotor blades in the flattened hair and wildly flapping clothes of the bystanders outside. The copter went straight up, as if pulled by a giant magnet.

Kiril stood up after the helicopter leveled off, spoke to the pilot on the radio, then sat down again and translated. "We will soon be flying at what is called chimney or tree-top level. This will afford us an excellent view of the countryside as we approach Berlin—and a good view of the Berlin Wall."

He turned to Adrienne, acknowledging her surprise. "Did you think I would avoid showing it to you? Perhaps you think the authorities regard the Wall as a thing of shame, to be hidden from sensitive Western eyes? On the contrary. The Deutsche Demokratische Republik is one of the great industrial powers now—one of the twelve most productive nations in the world. The Wall contributed significantly to its economic development.''

"How?" Adrienne asked.

"Every able-bodied citizen is an economic asset of the State. The government has an investment in him. Until 1961, over four thousand productive citizens a week were leaving. In 1961 alone, the rate exceeded 250,000 a year. The month before the Wall was constructed, 30,000 people—more than half of them under twenty-five years of age—left the country.''

"*Fled* the country—you like precision, don't you, Dr. Andreyev?" she said, feeling the tight knot of her latest resolve to keep silent come undone. "Since you like Soviet comparisons, perhaps you can enlighten me about similar methods in your own country. You do have the same economic policy, don't you? I've always had trouble pinning down exact figures on the forced labor that mined your gold and dug your canals and chopped your timber. Was it only nine million productive citizens? Some people put the total as high as thirty million—or would you say that's an exaggeration? And now the Siberian pipeline . . ."

She watched as the combination of mock politeness and contempt in her voice seemed momentarily to stun him. "We were talking about the DDR," he said finally.

"All right, let's talk about the DDR." No polite contempt, now; just grimness. "Exactly how many people have been killed trying to scale that Wall?"

His face was impassive, but he lowered his eyes. "My figures may not be up-to-date, but I believe the number of official registered deaths has been put at one hundred and eighty—seventy-five people killed at the Wall itself, the rest at other border sites. The unofficial total is obviously higher. A West German agency I know of claims ninety-six persons were killed in one year alone.''

He looked up, and went on matter-of-factly. ''The statistics become more meaningful the more one knows about the Wall. It is a unique piece of construction because it is in a constant state of flux, always being repaired or rebuilt or added to: stone and brick into concrete slabs, concrete into blocks of cement, cement into solid chunks of wall. The Wall itself is almost thirty kilometers long—roughly eighteen miles. In some places it is only six feet high, in others, twenty.

''Most people know about the border patrols between the DDR and the Federal Republic of Germany in the West. Few, perhaps, are aware that the patrols are continuous. Fifteen thousand hand-picked guards work the entire border area in two-man sentry units. They carry lightweight submachine guns, tracer ammunition and tear gas bombs, and they have standing orders: Shoot to kill.

''An elaborate obstacle course was designed. It is constantly being improved to make their job easier—at a cost of half a million dollars per mile of improvement. There is a strip of land that no one may enter without a special pass, followed by a strip of beets and potatoes—low-lying crops that cannot obstruct a view of the border, followed by another unobstructed view—the 'security or protection strip'; all buildings and trees have been razed. In some places six-foot boundary posts stake out the border; each stake has an inverted nail on top imbedded in cement. Then there is a strip of barren sand 100 yards wide that has been raked smooth to capture footprints, and beyond that, a concrete-lined trench—nine feet deep, fifteen feet across; a trap for vehicles. Next is a 60-yard-wide mine field—no warning signs, of course, followed by what I call the 'hunting strip'—I like the irony of the name. Hungry police dogs range back and forth on wire leads that are a hundred meters long—over three hundred feet; it gives the animals great freedom of movement.

"Finally, there is a barbed-wire mesh fence that is ten feet high and three feet underground—to prevent tunneling. The fence is armed with sophisticated weaponry. Every fifteen feet there is either an 'antipersonnel' explosive device—the most recent, when tripped, hurls shrapnel into the body—or automatically firing machine guns. The guns are triggered by an electronic eye and set up to hit at knee, chest or head level. The fence is studded with watchtowers— over six hundred of them. They used to be made of wood; now they consist of concrete cylinders set one on top of another, crowned by a platform with searchlights and ports for machine guns. There are miles and miles of barbed wire in the fence. People speculate that should the wire strands be laid end to end, they could encircle the globe."

He paused. Adrienne had stopped taking notes after his first few sentences. Her face felt oddly still, like a wax figure's.

Kiril went on in the dry, methodical tone of a military report. "The area popularly referred to as the 'death strip' must be seen to be fully grasped because it . . ."

Hands pressed against the plexiglass, she lost track of Andreyev's voice as his description began to come alive. The copter had dropped to "tree-top" level, but there were no trees—there was nothing; the "security strip," she thought, where everything had been bulldozed or dynamited away. They were cruising over winding, parallel ribbons of dark soil. One of them, she knew, was planted with trip wires and explosives. Irregular rows of what looked like jagged, upright crosses floated by—"dragon's teeth''; they were pointed, spiked-steel protrusions ''guaranteed to stop a tank.'' Beyond the spiked-steel crosses, past a tangle of coils that looked like a row of tumbleweed but was an electrified, barbed-wire fence, was the Wall itself. It was an angular snake that could change its shape and texture at will . . . now, the smooth gray of concrete . . . now, the grainy unevenness of cement . . . now, the still-intact wall of some forgotten house . . . now, an unbroken series of bricked-up windows. A bright gold speck signaled malevolently to her and went on signaling . . . the sun's reflection, caught and held by razor-sharp glass shards all along the top of the Wall.

Why tack such an old-fashioned Cold War theme onto a nice cut-and-dry medical piece? Her editor-in-chief had said it, at their last conference.

The Cold War is a bit of a dead issue, you know, her senior editor had chimed in. *Not to mention your ''hypocrisy behind the slogans'' idea. Your theme isn't relevant anymore—a few years ago, maybe, but not now. Not with détente.*

She stared out at the top of the Wall, her glance bearing down on the narrow concrete strip like a sewing-machine needle on a band of infinitely retreating fabric. She saw the roller device Andreyev had described: lengths of pipe forging a path through the broken glass, so someone groping for a handhold would slip. The pipe ran out, its place taken by metal shafts with outspread arms, like miniature telephone poles. But the taut wire stretching from pole to pole was barbed.

A death strip, Andreyev had said.

''A bit of a dead issue.''

* * *

Kurt Brenner was feeling desperate for a drink. This was some goddamn red carpet tour—especially for people who were supposed to be past masters at displaying their treasures and hiding their sores, he thought with mounting irritation . . . and an uneasiness he didn't care to examine. Surely his hosts could have arranged a more appropriate itinerary. "I'm sorry you had to see this," he said as Adrienne turned away from the window.

She sighed. "I'm sorry it's here to be seen."

"Tell me about your visit to Treptower Park," he said, trying to divert her.

"It had manicured lawns and elaborate flower beds. Very pretty." She turned back to the window. A square dirt plot with neat rows of white tablets drifted past. "It was horrible," she said. "Treptower is one enormous mass grave. Five thousand soldiers are buried in it. The flowers made things worse somehow. What is it about mass burials and unmarked graves that seems so ugly?"

"Their callousness." It was Kiril. "When a man dies, he should be permitted the dignity and solitude of a private resting place, not . . ." His mouth twisted. "Not lowered into some anonymous collection of humanity."

Luka understood little of the conversation, but a few English words connected with the cemetery below . . . Treptower . . . mass grave . . . soldiers. He aimed his binoculars at the passing headstones, erected long before the Wall became their neighbor, and he smiled—certain, now, of his bearings. "Look down there," he said to Kiril in Russian, handing him the binoculars.

"I see an empty field and a few border guards. What of it?" Kiril asked. "Or do you mean the cemetery we just flew over?"

"No, no, not cemetery. Look at field beyond it. Field is secret," he said conspiratorially.

"Then why tell me about it?" Kiril asked warily.

"I tell you from kindness," Luka said with his sly, setting-a-trap smile. "Field is new. But not empty. You like to know what is in it."

"I don't think so." Kiril handed back the binoculars.

"Your friend, Brodsky, is in it!" Luka announced triumphantly. "Your friend and other traitors who try to leave—all together in mass grave, like garbage in garbage dump. Look—look quickly." He brandished the binoculars. "You still have time to say goodbye."

Kiril's head snapped back as if he had just caught the sting of a whip. Not Stepan. Not in such a place! Dimly, he felt Galya's hand on his arm, heard Luka again . . . "Shot down like wild pig, your friend." He heard his own words, that sensible inner voice of his, pleading: *Don't act—don't move—don't throw away your plans, your hopes, your future—don't bring down on your head—*"Too quick a death for that one," Luka said. "Not so quick if *we* had been there." Smashing the binoculars out of his way, he lunged for Luka's throat.

With a swift upward motion, Luka's bear-arms broke the hold. One hand whipped high—a gun in it. He brought the gun down expertly against the side of Kiril's head.

Kiril staggered backward and fell, violently striking Adrienne's knees.

She stared at a thin trickle of blood seeping into her white skirt—and at Rogov's gun, aimed at Andreyev's chest.

The gun shifted imperceptibly; Kiril was reaching slowly for a handkerchief. With one hand, he wiped the blood away. With the other, he pushed himself up. He swayed, steadied himself, turned his back on the gun, and barked a Russian command into the radio. Abruptly, the helicopter swerved and spun around, tilting at a crazy, zig-zag angle.

We're losing altitude, Adrienne realized with alarm. She heard the Barkova woman scream—saw Rogov stumble in the narrow passageway—felt Kurt gripping her shoulder—was mesmerized by a rush of black, filling the plastic bubble with shadow— The death strip! Her arm shot up to shield her face. "My God," she cried, "Andreyev is trying to kill us!"

11

Adrienne dropped her arm. And saw blue sky and the black furrows of a plowed field.

Kiril opened the helicopter door and dropped to the ground. Luka went after him. Two uniformed guards came rushing over, submachine guns swinging wildly from shoulder straps.

Kurt Brenner caught snatches of German—angry demands for an explanation—Andreyev's authoritative voice saying something about an inspection. "What the hell's going on?" he asked Galya.

"It is better not know—better not be mixed in," she said, staring at the bloodstain on Adrienne's skirt.

"What was that fight all about?" Adrienne asked. No answer. She shrugged and reached for her shoulderbag.

"Please not to leave!" Galya gasped. "We have no permit to be in this place. We could have trouble."

"Why?"

"Because of this place."

Adrienne looked out. "It seems harmless enough."

"It is graveyard . . . mass grave," Galya said in a hushed voice. "But not for like Treptower and heroes of Great Patriotic War. I think this is secret place for people who try escape."

"I see." Adrienne went over to the open door.

"What do you think you're doing?" Brenner said in alarm.

"Adding another mass grave to my itinerary."

She landed on soft ground, feeling deceptively calm, knowing the only way to make it last was to keep herself from feeling anything else. She looked at freshly plowed dirt, a field big enough for maybe a hundred conventional graves. How many bodies could you bury in a human dumping ground—a thousand? Five thousand? She looked around quickly: Andreyev was walking slowly along a barbed-wire fence that surrounded the field, his "shadow," Rogov, following a few feet behind; one guard had his binoculars trained on them, the other was in deep, angry-sounding conversation with some people near a gate. The helicopter, its blades still rotating, was perched on the field like some wary animal poised for flight. She felt around in her bag for a slim, silver object, the length of a pocket comb. With her back to the copter and the two guards, she slowly pivoted, focusing on the field . . . the barbed wire . . . the signs that said VERBOTEN . . .

Above her, Galya watched through the plexiglass.

Adrienne slipped the Minox back into her bag and headed for the copter, impeded by the wind, her struggle through the deep furrows made awkward by her high-heeled sandals.

She caught sight of Andreyev, standing near the gate. On his rigid features was a mixture of pain and quiet horror that even his dark glasses couldn't hide. She went

over to him and touched his arm, a gesture of support.
"Dr. Andreyev . . ." she began uncertainly.

"I have seen their barbed wire and submachine guns,"
he said slowly as if to a stranger. "I have been to their
concentration camps and mental wards. I have seen how
they punish the living. But this . . . this is a form of
vindictiveness I had not imagined. To punish the dead by
robbing them of a decent burial . . ."

"The dead are beyond punishment," she said gently.

"That's true. But not the people who mourn them. A
grave is for remembering, even honoring. That's why we
keep going back, isn't it? To think quietly, to remember? I
must spend the rest of my life trying to forget this place . . ."

He wandered away. How strange he sounds, she thought,
how totally different. Then she realized he'd spoken without his heavy Russian accent. She forgot the accent in the
next moment. She was thinking—with absolute certainty
and with confusion—that her parrot-guide was no apolo-
gist of the regime. He was one of its victims.

"Are you denying what we both know? This *is* a burial
ground. This is—"

The angry words nudged Kiril out of his somber reverie.
He looked beyond the gate at the man who had uttered
them. A short, muscular man dressed in laborer's clothes.
Three other men, looking uncomfortable in neatly pressed
suits, stood next to him, one man with a protective arm
around the shoulder of an old woman in black shawl and
babushka. Not so old, he realized, going closer, just bent
and weary, with deep crevices running down parched cheeks.
"What's going on here?" he said in German.

"The name is Zind, Albert Zind," said the man in the
laborer's clothes. He indicated the others. "Erich and

Gunther, my brothers. Our friend, Otto Dorf. And my mother. We've come all the way from Potsdam to visit the grave of my sister. Our papers . . ." He reached over the gate and handed some papers to Kiril. "You can see they're in order, and *still* they refuse to let us in." His hair was the color of sand. His blue eyes were expressionless.

"These people are a pack of fools," grumbled one of the guards. "They have special permission to visit some grave. Where do you see any graves around here, huh? Where are the headstones?" He flashed Kiril a conspirator's wink. "Let them visit every cemetery in Democratic Berlin for all I care," he said with feigned indifference.

"I am losing patience with all of you!" the other guard barked. "No more arguments, do you hear? Leave!"

"My sister is buried in this field," Zind persisted. "My mother is not well. The trip has tired her. I promised her she could say a few words over her daughter's grave. Only a few words. *Then* we'll leave."

For once, Kiril was grateful to have the Mongolian behind him, with the grim authority of his Soviet uniform and the red star on his cap. "Let them in," he told the guards, putting the same kind of authority into his voice. And before either guard could stop him, he unlatched the gate and held it open.

"Are you crazy?" one of them muttered. The other looked more resentful than startled.

Kiril shrugged. "Since they know the truth, what harm can it do? Come," he said to the Zinds. As they entered the field, he saw bitter hopelessness drain from their faces— all except one face, their spokesman's. He remained expressionless. "How did you learn of this place?" Kiril asked, walking with him.

"Through my job. I'm in bridge construction. Foreman

on the repair work being done on Unity—that's what they're calling Glienicker Bridge, these days.''

''The bridge between Potsdam and West Berlin,'' Kiril said. His voice seemed strangled.

Zind looked at him curiously, then at Luka—at his uniform. ''One of your fellow Russians crashed into the bridge recently. Poor bastard tried to make it across in some diplomat's limousine—and almost did, from what I hear.'' His voice was as expressionless as his eyes. ''I heard something about burial arrangements and asked a few discreet questions. That's how I knew where to find my sister. She and the Russian had the same idea, only she tried it from East Berlin instead of Potsdam.''

His mother was tugging at his sleeve. ''But where is Eva? You promised me, Albert, you promised . . .''

''She's here, Mama, just as I told you. We don't know exactly where—I told you how it would be, remember? —but she *is* here. I said I'd take you to her, and I've kept my promise. Now you must keep yours. Just say a brief prayer and we'll go home.''

She shook her head, uncomprehending. Tears ran down the ravaged cheeks.

Kiril took the miniature gold scalpel from the chain around his neck. He knelt on the ground and began to smooth a patch of soil with his hand. Then he carved out a large, rectangular shape—the outline of a headstone. He carved four German words inside the rectangle: HERE LIES EVA ZIND.

''Eighteen years old,'' Albert Zind said tonelessly.

Kiril went on carving.

''Late of Number 13 Holländische Siedlung, Potsdam,'' said one of the brothers.

"Beloved daughter of Frieda. Adored sister of Albert, Gunther and . . . Erich," said Erich Zind.

"Beloved by Otto," said another voice.

Kiril bent to his task, tiny letters so all the words would fit inside the rectangle-headstone.

The woman had already dropped to her knees beside him. When he was through, she crossed herself. Her lips moved in silent prayer. She had stopped crying.

When Kiril rose, Albert Zind gripped his hand. The blue eyes were no longer expressionless.

12

A drop of water landed unceremoniously on Aleksei Andreyev's head. He wiped it away, oblivious of the dampness and the beads of water that clung precariously to the underbelly of Glienicker Bridge; he was too intent on the action in front of him. Even after ten fitful and unproductive days, interrupted by a side trip to Moscow, he was still fascinated by the dredging operation. The scooping device at the end of the boom came up from the river looking like a giant, dripping clamshell with a mouthful of mud.

A lanky man in a windbreaker stuck his head out of the East German guardhouse, spotted Aleksei, hesitated, then walked down the steps to him. He cleared his throat.

"Yes, Mueller, what is it now?" Aleksei didn't turn around. He was watching a sleek, gray-green patrol boat pass silently under the bridge. A sunray picked up the glint of binoculars.

Mueller hesitated again. "Colonel, maybe you shouldn't

be standing down here in all this wind. There's still some loose debris on the bridge. You never know where the wind might take it.''

"I'm touched by your solicitude. What is it you *really* want to talk to me about?" He turned around, aware that his expression was all patience and kindness . . . with just a hint of the patronizing about it, aware that even his dress was unsettling: a casual, almost sloppy look, meant to relax, to inspire trust. "Well?" he asked, looking into Mueller's face and smiling because he had inspired something quite different.

"I was just wondering . . . uh, they've been at it over a week now, and I was wondering why you don't use a skindiver, since the object you're looking for is so small. Be a lot less expensive than dredging and, uh, not quite so time consuming.''

"Have I presumed to tell you how you should go about repairing the bridge after I'm gone, Mueller?"

"No, sir, Colonel, but—"

"Then don't presume to tell me *my* job. The river is too muddy for your inexpensive skindiver." He held out the checked sportsjacket he was carrying so Mueller could help him into it. "As for being held up, learn from it, Mueller. Develop patience. Patience is one of man's most underrated virtues, did you know that?" He started up the steps.

"Patience is a luxury I can't afford," Mueller mumbled, hurrying after him. "The structural efficiency of the bridge has been damaged, and they expect me to get it fixed and reopened to traffic in a week. I'll need a *month,* with what I have to do. They keep calling and I keep telling them I haven't even gotten started. And then they—"

"Well, why don't you start?" Aleksei surveyed the

bridge from the top of the steps. "What's to prevent you from putting some men to work repairing that center barrier or removing some of the twisted steel?"

Mueller sighed. "Not in this wind, not with the dredging still going on. Riveting means a lot of sparks. We could have a fire on our hands. Apart from checking the stresses and putting in a request for new steel struts—I did that a week ago—I'll just have to let everything else wait," he said, trying to sound philosophical. "But Colonel," he persisted, visibly frustrated but still deferential, "how much longer will you be?"

"How much longer, indeed," Aleksei said thoughtfully as the clamshell hit the water and sank to the bottom. "I'm beginning to wonder if we've been concentrating on the wrong spot. Is that guard around—the one who filed the report? I think I should talk to him again."

"He's been reassigned to the nine A.M. shift. I'll see if he's here yet."

Aleksei watched Mueller hurry across the cobblestone square and enter the East German guardhouse. He always enjoyed these conversations with Mueller.

The door of the guardhouse flew open and banged against a stone wall.

The guard walking toward Aleksei in long, impatient strides had a kind of raw, seething vitality . . . like Luka, Aleksei thought. But unlike Luka, this man resented him—resented all Russians, probably. A pity. Men like Luka were becoming extinct.

"You wanted to see me?" the guard said gruffly, coming up to him.

"I want you to answer a few more questions," Aleksei said, studying alert blue eyes, yellow hair escaping from an authoritative gray-green cap, the man's almost loving grip on an automatic rifle. "Tell me again—Bruno, isn't it?—where you saw Comrade Brodsky's cigarette lighter go over the side, the exact spot."

Bruno's eyes went to the lefthand side of the bridge. He pointed to a space between two lower parallel iron bars, just opposite a mass of twisted steel. "Right through there he dropped it. Like I told you before," he added sullenly.

"So you did. It seems I will be holding up bridge traffic a while longer."

"So what? The traffic's mostly military brass attached to the Allied Mission in Potsdam. Mostly big shot Americans," Bruno growled.

"So you dislike Americans, do you?" And Russians even more, he thought, catching a flicker in the man's eyes. "You have a point, my friend, this *is* a do-nothing post. Still, we must get on with the job. I want you to repeat everything you told me before—everything you saw, heard, smelled, from the moment the bridge formalities began."

"The American limousines were parked single file behind the poles. This Russian air force officer got out of his jeep and—"

Aleksei had a gift for visualizing. As Bruno talked, he pictured the first limousine moving leisurely across . . . the second stalled by an angry exchange of words. He saw Brodsky's sudden move, heard screeching tires, the clatter of machine guns, saw an automobile smashing into the retractable barrier, then Brodsky's body arching through the air—thrown clear just as the automobile burst into flame. He touched the blackened members of the bridge, picturing the patrol boats, with dogs on deck and searchlights turned on, cruising restlessly back and forth under the bridge, ready to swing into action the moment— Under the bridge? he thought. *Under* it? He seized Bruno's arm. "Were the patrol boats near this point? *Anywhere* near it?"

Bruno frowned. "They might've been, but I don't see—"

Aleksei walked rapidly toward the Soviet guardhouse.

Bruno shrugged and went after him. He was curious. He was paid extra to be curious.

A few telephone calls brought forth a list of every patrol boat in the vicinity of the bridge that night, a rundown on the size of the crews, the names of every man on the night shift. Within half an hour, a sheepish-looking officer was standing in front of Aleksei's desk, an American cigarette lighter in the outstretched palm of his hand. His explanation was part apology, part defensiveness. How could he have known the purpose of the dredging operation? Two weeks ago today he had found the lighter on the deck of his boat, and since there'd been no way to identify the owner . . . He looked regretful as Aleksei took the lighter, and relieved when Aleksei waved him away.

Bruno's fellow border guards were talking and drinking coffee. Only Bruno watched Aleksei finger the lighter curiously, frown over the black-winged emblem on one side, test the flame, examine the lighting mechanism. Only Bruno saw him remove the mechanism from its metal case, stare for a moment, then dig into one end of its cottom padding with his index finger. Bruno edged closer.

Aleksei tapped the base of the mechanism, and shook a few tiny, black squares onto his spread-out handkerchief. He called a Soviet officer from the other side of the room. "How long will it take to get some blowups?"

"A few hours, perhaps?"

Aleksei handed him the film, wrapped in his handkerchief. "I'll see you in East Berlin within the hour—an hour and a half, tops. I've wasted enough time on this business," he said testily, frowning at his watch.

"It's roughly forty kilometers to the Embassy. You can be there in thirty minutes—less, if you hurry," the officer said helpfully.

"I won't be at the Embassy. I have a breakfast function to attend. Bring the blowups to the Humboldt University Clinic on Unter den Linden. Bring them to *me*."

Bruno crossed the square to his own guardhouse, reached for a telephone, and dialed a familiar number. "Colonel Von Eyssen, please," he said.

Aleksei opened the curtains of his limousine, chasing the semi-darkness from the back seat, letting in a different kind of gloom: a colorless, flat landscape, a gray sky that had swallowed up an earlier promise of sunshine. His eyes kept returning to the front seat, reinforcing the fact that the place next to his driver's—Luka's seat—was uncharacteristically empty. He puffed on his pipe, thinking of Luka's soothing presence, his usefulness, his reliability. One could relax with Luka. It's because of his total loyalty, he thought, and that incredible strength of his. Just thinking of Luka's strength gave him comfort.

He did not try to clarify the nature of that comfort. He merely thought of it, relaxed, and let images and memories drift into his mind . . .

Aleksei Andreyevich Andreyev was no more than three years old when he encountered fear. He feared the fat boy on his block who would grab his toys and run off with them. And the ugly, skinny girl who kicked him in the ankle once and left a throbbing bruise. And the red-bearded man who came regularly to his family's flat, dragging huge, clanking milk cans behind him. And his father—his own father!—who had a booming voice and large, rough hands that hoisted him high in the air whenever his breath had that funny, sour smell. Aleksei never wondered why such things made him feel helpless and bewildered. He took his fear for granted, as much a fact of life as the sidewalk in front of his building.

He was eight years old when he made a double discovery: that *grown-ups* had fears, and that—wonder of wonders—*he*, Aleksei Andreyevich, could make them afraid. The day had started out like any other: school, homework afterward, a visit with his best friend, Ilya, the same old invitation to stay for supper. But at supper he had reached past Ilya for a platter of meat, instead of asking for it as he'd been taught, and his elbow had knocked against a bowl of brown gravy. Ilya's older sister, Dasha, had jumped up in a rage. "Look how you've splattered gravy all over my new blouse, you clumsy fool!" she'd screamed at him, and he'd jerked away from her, eyes squeezed shut with terror, sure that she would strike him. Nothing happened. He opened his eyes a crack, then all the way. He saw it first in her parents' eyes, and then in hers: fear. They kept pushing apologies at him. Dasha's mother kept saying he shouldn't tell his father. What had his father to do with his bad manners and spilled gravy? he wondered. It was only when he was walking home later that he realized what they were all afraid of—his father. But why? He made up his mind to find out.

His father, he learned, was a charter member of "Cheka." Spelled out, that meant "The Extraordinary Commission for the Struggle against Counterrevolution and Sabotage"— whatever *that* meant. But Cheka had been born six weeks after the Great Socialist Revolution in 1917 and it was dead, now, so the reason couldn't be Cheka. He learned that his father held an important job—"high-ranking," someone called it—in the "OGPU." Spelled out, it was the "United Political Administration." Whatever it meant, people spoke of it in whispers. He tried to understand what his father did but gave it up when he realized after a while that it didn't really matter. Whatever his father did, it made people like Dasha and her parents afraid. He heard two things repeated about his father: that he was a "powerful" man, and that he was in "intelligence." He was told that "intelligence" meant looking into the "secret" activities of counterrevolutionaries. He shook his head over that one. But no one had to tell him about "powerful." His father, he discovered, could have whole families arrested or sent to Siberia. Or even shot.

Once he knew this, things began to happen—or rather, he *made* them happen. Like mentioning his father's name in a roomful of people and watching the air become suddenly thick with fear. One day he discovered that in the face of other people's fears, he forgot his own. He began to study people. With a word or a hint, he found that he could always get his way, and no arguments. He got lots of presents and invitations to parties. He began to experience a secret pride—and a heady new feeling of power—whenever he was able to trigger the fears of others and lose his own in the process. He became a sort of crown prince, reigning in the dark shadow of his father.

When he was not quite ten, the presents and invitations ceased abruptly. His mother had gone away to Germany with his little brother Kolya and then had disappeared. They blamed his father for letting her leave the country. At first he had feared for his father's personal safety. But what happened turned out to be worse. They held a "troika"—a secret trial by three judges from his father's own OGPU—and branded his mother an "Enemy of the People." What did it matter that his father was cleared of the charges of "co-conspirator" and "wrecker," since they took away his "rank and privileges"?

Aleksei had never particularly noticed his family's style of living; he noticed its absence. No more five-room flat in Moscow filled with furniture and paintings and Oriental rugs. No more country home or horses or motorboats. No more delicious food that hardly anyone else could get. No money for Western clothes, no limousines. Gone—all of it—just like blinking an eye. One day the Andreyevs were at home; the next, they were dumped on the highroad, seventy-five kilometers out of Moscow. But physical hardship was not the worst of it. Overnight, Aleksei's sense of being crown prince in a secure world collapsed into raw terror, one that transcended his old feelings of helplessness and bewilderment. This was a *knowledgeable* terror that sprang from all the fear-inducing tools he had learned to use against others and could now be used against *him*. Who knew better about the informers planted in every apartment building, factory, and office in the city? How often had his father joked about the way his country meted out punishment to criminals?—a thief or a murderer faring better than a Betrayer of the Revolution. His own mother had betrayed the Revolution. It was *her* shame, not his! But from now on, it would be his and his father's.

He was twelve before he realized that his father would never rehabilitate himself and take up his old career; his father was drinking himself to death. That year, Aleksei swore that he would win back the family honor—that someday he would hold his father's post. In the midst of making bold plans, he noticed something peculiar: just thinking about such a future brought him a sense of relief.

The terror he always carried with him, like a knapsack on his shoulders, wasn't bearing down quite so heavily.

It took him over twenty years. By the time he was in his early thirties, the terror had disappeared—for good, this time, he would reassure himself over and over. This time it wasn't just a matter of feeling secure; he was actually enjoying himself! The years he'd invested in the Archives Section of the Information Directorate—his "mole years," he was to call them later—had finally paid off: he'd been given access to the Classified Library. He learned to use the Library as no one ever had . . . lovingly, like a violinist with his Stradivarius. He became an expert researcher. He stole files. He developed the ability to ferret out, and to file away in a steel-trap memory, the secrets and misdeeds of people who were in a position to help him, or might be in the future. He became adept at applying just the right combination of hints and pressure, promises and threats. At first he merely survived. Then he prospered.

The terror struck again on the day he realized his whole career could be toppled as swiftly as his father's had been—and by the same kind of sledgehammer. His brother Kiril was leaving a trail of unhealthy rumors in his wake. Allusions were being made to diversionist tendencies and an unpatriotic attitude. Aleksei had cursed himself for his lack of foresight and put into immediate operation a tight surveillance program. But the damage had been done; he felt vulnerable again. The old feeling of terror had been resurrected.

The feeling dogged him, undermining his work, interfering with his sanity and his sleep—until the day Luka Rogov, that enduring apparition who had served under him during the war, reentered his life on a Moscow street.

Luka, the awesome primitive, who enjoyed simple things, like the satisfaction—the pleasure, even—of extracting pain from his enemies. Luka, the human torture machine, introduced into a world where his services were always in demand, doing what he was told and doing it well, incapable of entertaining a scruple inside his sluggish brain. Luka, who *feared no one*. Luka, his loyal servant. His friend. His comfort.

Over the years, the two of them had developed into a memorable interrogation team with a conventional but effective approach: the carrot and the stick. Aleksei contributed a subtle mind, a patient, literate reasonableness, and a carefully researched dossier on the "subject." Luka's contribution was often more symbolic than real—a presence in the interrogation room like a bulky piece of furniture that was noticeable but unused—unless it became necessary. The word got around, making it even easier to deal with recalcitrant subjects. Plum security assignments came Aleksei's way, the latest being the prestigious East Berlin-Potsdam negotiations. And in recognition of his achievements, he was close—very close—to being rewarded with the biggest plum of all: the intelligence position equivalent to the one held by his father in the now defunct OGPU.

That reward, he thought, tapping his pipe idly against the limousine's glass partition and following the drift of cold ashes onto the rug, had been jeopardized by the Brodsky escape attempt. True, it was no more than a blemish on his otherwise clean record, but no one in intelligence could afford blemishes. The Brenner business would resolve everything. The thought that he was about to reclaim the family honor, a lifetime goal, gave him pleasure—muted by the picture in his mind of one cowed subject after another. The average Soviet citizen was no match for his talents, he admitted; they were used to threats, and to the power of his office to make good on them. But Dr. Kurt Brenner? A prominent heart surgeon who was used to giving orders, not taking them? An American reared in a decadent culture which nurtured independence? *There* was a challenge . . .

13

"Zum Wohl!" The Direktor of the Humboldt University Clinic smiled at the honored guest.

Glasses were raised. The bottle of cognac was passed. One by one, the doctors rose to toast the good health of Dr. Kurt Brenner—in Russian, Hungarian, Polish, Bulgarian, Romanian, Czech. Someone proposed a toast in honor of the ladies. Galya, seated unobtrusively near a desk in a corner of the spacious room, smiled shyly. Adrienne, sitting on the arm of an easy chair, inclined her head. Herr Direktor was toasted for having arranged such an excellent breakfast in the clinic cafeteria. Formalities over, the doctors began positioning their chairs in a loose semi-circle around Brenner.

Kiril, standing behind Adrienne's chair, whispered, "Now it begins."

She turned to him. "What do you mean?"

"They are about to pick your husband's brain for the latest techniques in Western medicine, the ones that relate to their particular specialties. All through the meal and the toasts afterward, they have thought of nothing else. But first, they will go through the ritual of suggesting that doctors in the People's Democracies have the best of everything.''

''Our electronic monitoring system is an impressive achievement, is it not?'' Dr. Yanin pressed, leaning toward Brenner's chair. ''A patient's heartbeat speeds up—a second attack seems imminent—but we are ready! A new drug—a thousand-volt electrical charge to the chest . . .''

Adrienne whispered to Kiril, ''I know a doctor who went on an exchange program last year, eager for a glimpse of your pioneering coronary care units. He didn't see a single one in operation.'' Kiril nodded.

''—and our vascular stapling machine, a superb invention, makes suturing obsolete,'' a Polish surgeon was saying.

Kiril looked at Adrienne, wondering if she remembered about the suture shortage.

''—surgical breakthroughs in congenital heart lesions.''

''—original research on organ and tissue transplants.''

''—medical helicopters swiftly dispatched to remote areas.''

Kiril thought of his three years of forced internship in the remotest area of them all, when the sight of such a helicopter would have been a godsend, and restrained a bitter smile.

A movement caught his attention. A door behind Brenner opened and Aleksei came in. Only Rogov and Colonel Malik seemed to notice him standing there, taking in the room and the semi-circle of eager faces.

Kiril kept his face impassive to hide his sudden panic. He thought, The moment of truth—when Brenner turns around and Aleksei sees the likeness . . . as Yanin had seen it at breakfast, and some of the other doctors, too, even though they couldn't see his eyes. Would Aleksei remember the reference, carefully placed in his travel documents, to an eye infection—his excuse for wearing dark glasses? His panic increased as he realized he'd forgotten to apply the drops of lemon juice after breakfast.

Don't do it, Aleksei, he pleaded silently; don't ask me to take off the glasses so you can compare faces . . . and see the redness that isn't there.

Aleksei looked at the rapt faces of the doctors and listened to the voice of the man to whom the faces were turned.

"Medicine is international," the voice said. "Great contributions come from every corner of the globe. The United States, in my judgment, has much to learn from your great countries. That's why I've always applauded medical exchanges, and the more the better."

Aleksei watched Dr. Yanin's head bob in enthusiastic agreement. "The continuing progress of mankind rests on shared technology and culture—on a free flow of people between nations."

Aleksei saw a woman he did not recognize—clearly a foreigner—make a movement of protest, then stifle it. So, he thought, calculating quickly, could this be the lovely reason behind all those Iron Curtain medical exchanges Dr. Brenner had declined to attend?

His eyes moved to his brother, standing behind her. He noticed Kiril's dark glasses and frowned.

"Colonel Andreyev!" cried the Direktor, spotting him. "We are pleased and honored that you could spare the time to join us."

The semi-circle came apart as doctors turned to look or

185

moved their chairs. They are not pleased by the interruption, Aleksei thought. No doubt, every moment with their knowledgeable guest is precious to them . . . too bad.

The guest of honor turned to greet him. "Colonel Andreyev," he said politely, "Colonel Malik tells me I have you to thank for this occasion. I am Kurt Brenner."

Aleksei's voice seemed to stall, like the motor of a car left too long in the cold. *How was it possible?* he thought. After an awkward pause, his voice turned over, but even as he responded to the amenities, questions buzzed in his brain like annoying insects: How could there be such an uncanny likeness without his being aware of it? Why hadn't the Brenner file tipped him off? No file photographs? He frowned, trying to remember, then realized the file *had* contained a few newspaper reproductions—poor ones—so he had ordered a photograph from New York. What happened to it? he wondered, feeling uneasy. Some bungler from the Soviet News Agency must have forgotten to wire it, along with Brenner's remarks at that Russian folk dancing party—either that, or his secretary had misplaced it. Unlikely. Something is misplaced somewhere, he thought with a fresh rush of uneasiness. He turned to look at his brother again.

Malik's voice pulled his attention away; he had just asked Dr. Brenner the first of the questions.

Brenner answered Malik with a deprecating smile. "Yes, as a matter of fact, I was—Seventh Army. I was very low on the totem pole. A private first class."

How bored you sound, Dr. Brenner, Aleksei thought, pulling out his pipe. But how nervous you look. And Mrs. Brenner? he wondered as she joined the group. Genuinely bored, he concluded. Perhaps she did not like war stories. But then, she did not know this one.

"Seventh Army. Berlin, 1945. I thought as much," Malik said, as if warmed by reminiscence. "We look to be the same age, Dr. Brenner. Odd, the things one remembers and the things one forgets. For me, the battles are a blank—ah, but not the weapons we won them with. I have fond memories of the semi-automatic pistols we used in those days—the Tokarev Model 1933 comes to mind. And then . . ."

Spare me the irrelevant patter of the weapons fancier, Aleksei thought, and transferred his impatience to his pipe, tapping out tobacco that had refused to start.

"I'll wager you were one of those American GIs who wanted the old 7.62mm Nagant Model 1895 revolver for a war souvenir. Do you remember the Nagants, Dr. Brenner?" Malik asked.

The look on Brenner's face told Aleksei that he remembered one particular Nagant only too well.

The look on Malik's face told Aleksei that the Colonel was starting to enjoy himself—some compensation, perhaps, for being forced to interrupt his own work in West Berlin. Not that he had any choice.

He got his pipe going on fresh tobacco and said cheerfully, "Come now, gentlemen, enough of this wartime reminiscing." The relief in Brenner's eyes was so transparent that he almost laughed. Do you believe, my big fish, he thought, that you have wriggled off the hook? "Not that most of us here could not reflect on the war without colliding with some memories of our own—painful ones in my case," he observed solemnly. "I spent time in Berlin after the hostilities were over. I have vivid memories of the repatriation problem we encountered with over ten million of my fellow citizens who had been kidnapped by the Nazis. Some of them had been prisoners of war, but many had been forced into slave labor, poor creatures. They were eager to return to their homeland, of course, but some stubborn holdouts, obviously deranged by their ordeal, made things unpleasant for those of us working on the problem. We had a particularly hard time with Ukrainians."

He watched Brenner's hand reach into his vest pocket for a cigarette; it was steady. "I remember one story that ended in tragedy," he went on. "It seems that a group of orphaned Ukrainian children—refugees from one of the Nazi death camps—became unwitting pawns in an exchange of favors between one of our soldiers and an American GI. By the time the children were turned over to us, they were in a frightful state, having been shunted from one place to another. And then . . ." He paused to shake his head regretfully and to enjoy Brenner's fixed stare at some flowers on a coffee table. "Then, those being chaotic times, none of us thought to ease their transition and reassure them that a Soviet uniform was different from a Nazi's. Poor children," he said, soberly reflective. "As they were led away for repatriation, seven of them committed suicide—leaped into the Havel River before anyone could stop them. Tragic. Don't you think so, Mrs. Brenner?"

"Very tragic," she agreed tonelessly, looking as if she were swallowing other words.

"Of course, as an American, you could hardly criticize our repatriation policy of the time, could you? Quite a few of our people were repatriated with official American help," he said softly, offering to light her cigarette.

She let him light it. "You're wrong, Colonel . . ."

"Yes?" he prompted, breaking the uncomfortable silence as she paused.

"I was reading only recently about America's part in

your postwar manhunt. You really are too modest about our contribution—quite a few, you said? We repatriated over a million refugees for our Soviet allies,'' she observed flatly. "But then, as you pointed out, the refugees were eager to go home. People had such odd ways of showing eagerness in those days, didn't they? Slashing their wrists. Jumping off roofs. Leaping out of windows. All very anxious to return to your Soviet paradise.''

Good girl, Aleksei thought, aware that he was the only one in the room enjoying the heavy silence and averted eyes. He looked pointedly at Brenner, as if willing the man to read his thoughts: Now that you know—fully— what to expect should your wife discover your past, your options narrow, don't they? Defect—and you keep your secret. Defy me—and be exposed. In either case, he realized suddenly, Brenner might not get to keep his lovely, outspoken wife.

Beside him, he heard the Direktor, relief in his voice as he welcomed a new arrival. "Herr Roeder! Herr Ernst Roeder, ladies and gentlemen, here to take photographs for *Neues Deutschland*. Let me introduce you . . .''

Aleksei had time to note Adrienne's recognition of the name, but no time to speculate; an officer had come in behind Roeder. He took an envelope from the man and dismissed him. "I fear my presence here has been somewhat disruptive,'' he apologized to the room at large. "Please go on with your medical discussion while I attend to a private matter.'' He gestured toward Kiril. "I am sure my brother would enjoy reciting for Dr. Brenner the new oath our young physicians take before entering their profession. It should make an inspiring photograph for *Neues Deutschland*, Herr Roeder, especially if you write some inspiring copy to go with it.'' Smiling, he motioned for Luka to follow him across the room to the desk near where Galya was sitting. Behind him, he heard snatches of Kiril's strained monotone: ". . . work in good conscience wherever the interests of society require . . . guided in all actions by the principles of Communist morality . . . always to remember my responsibility before the people and the Soviet State . . ."

Still smiling, Aleksei tore open the envelope—and saw the blowups from the cigarette lighter. When his mind could function again, his first thought was: The Brodsky affair has a new twist. His second was: I am in deep trouble. *A security leak.* Linked to *me*. He stared at his own last-minute instructions to Von Eyssen about a political charade—a peace offensive that the Soviet government was publicizing highly but planned to sabotage. Then he noticed that his letterhead was missing; so was his signature at the end of the message. His words . . . but unidentified. Why?

He felt a hand on his shoulder, and read confusion and concern in Luka's dark scowl. Then he realized that the tight bumps all over his skin and the numbness in his limbs had nothing to do with the room's air conditioning. He was in the first stage of the old terror. Even with Luka standing right beside him? He heard an inner voice speaking urgently, explaining, asking things Luka would have no capacity to understand, but it was all right so long as Luka was there, so long as he could see the fearlessness of Luka and the strength. Questions began to spill out, mingling until they formed a solid core: Where was the missing part of the film? Why was it missing? Why not include it with the body of his message? Which member of his staff had leaked the information? Who had had access to it? For that matter, who had access to a miniature camera?

"A flat, silver thing, cold to touch." It was Luka's voice. "The American lady," he said, smiling, "she hide one inside pocketbook. But not use once. She takes pictures only with big camera."

Aleksei caught a signal from Galya; she had overheard and was shaking her head in slow disagreement. He held out a pencil and slip of paper. She wrote: "I saw Mrs. Brenner using a very small camera to photograph . . ." She hesitated, then pressed down hard on the pencil. ". . . the secret place for burying deserters—the place near the Wall."

Aleksei stared at the note. He stared at Adrienne Brenner. Her chair turned away from a vigorous medical discussion, she was in earnest conversation with Ernst Roeder. Roeder, he thought, Colonel Emil Von Eyssen's *photographer* brother-in-law! Fool, he berated himself. Fool! he exulted. A security leak, from *my* staff? How—when I tested each one for political impurities more diligently than a chemist tests a new drug? The message went directly from my office to Von Eyssen's. This is *his* leak.

And the missing letterhead and signature? he wondered again. Perhaps there was more film—a second installment of some kind, and this Roeder was saving the best for last. But why? He shrugged. Whatever the reason, one thing was clear: Roeder needed a courier to get the film out of East Germany.

What an amateur you are, my dear Mrs. Brenner, he thought. You recognize a name you are supposed to be hearing for the first time, and carry on a "casual" *tête-à-tête* with the most purposeful of expressions. You toss your anti-Communist sentiments in my face and then expect me to think you are here to see the sights or take part in a medical exchange that clearly bores you. What *are* you

191

doing in East Berlin? Traveling with your husband like a loving, dutiful wife? Even though your husband is flagrantly unfaithful and you haven't lived with him for months? From Roeder to Mrs. Brenner to the CIA, he thought, in a nice, neat recapture of the ball Comrade Brodsky had fumbled. Over my dead body! Too true, he thought, holding his stomach, the scissor-sharp pain making him long for numbness. The terror was accelerating.

When he could think again, he thought of his human appendage, of Luka. Dare he turn Kiril's bodyguard into Ernst Roeder's shadow? Too obvious, he decided; if Roeder were alerted, he'd never make his move. Better to save Luka for a showdown, in case Roeder proved to be obstinate. He looked over at his "most charming co-optee," then wrote on the bottom of the note she'd passed him: "From now on, whenever Mrs. Brenner is not in her room, you are not to let her out of your sight." When she took it, he leaned back in his chair, eyes closed. Nothing to do now but wait, he thought. And watch. Just as someone else is waiting and watching me.

Because not for a moment did he delude himself. Not for a moment did he think that he and the officer who'd delivered the envelope were the only ones who knew of its contents.

Colonel Emil Von Eyssen stood in his office doorway long after his most trusted field officer had disappeared down the corridor. He had to force himself to move, to go back inside to the photographs that were now resting placidly on his desk. He made himself sit down and leaf through them again. Colonel Aleksei Andreyev has a grave problem on his hands—Colonel Andreyev, he thought, not I. But he ran a list of names through his mind again. A face loomed with each name, like a roll call: This one is in no position to betray me . . . that one is but would not dare . . . this one has no access to classified information . . . that one used to—not any more . . . When he came to the name of his brother-in-law, Ernst Roeder, he paused.

Damn my sister! he thought. His chair tilted forward with his sudden, lurching movement, and his hand hit the small stack of photographs and sent them skittering across the desk top. As he restacked them with abrupt gestures, he could hear his sister's voice: "My Ernst must have an *important* position in life, the kind that allows him to mingle with *important* people." And I gave in to her, in spite of my better judgment, he groaned. In spite of the fact that I never liked that mousy husband of hers, with his self-effacing manner and his pale eyes . . . with something in them that made you distrust him. If Ernst *is* responsible for the security leak, he thought, that bastard, Andreyev, will find a way to prove it. Can I buy his silence? he wondered. Impossible. The man is impervious to every human feeling, even greed. He recalled the German guard who had been killed at Glienicker Bridge, and how Andreyev had reacted to the news: with amused indifference. That a soldier—a German!—died because of some Soviet swine who never should have been allowed near a border area— outrageous. And the incident itself? Very costly, he thought sullenly, remembering the criticism heaped on him by his superiors.

The word had filtered down from high places right before the Potsdam meeting: *Keep the borders quiet.* No incidents during the negotiations or after their collapse. No incidents during the expected new round of talks, when bold proposals would be put on the bargaining table for the first time. There were rumors about them; perhaps the authorities would try to make a reality of Khruschev's dream: Turn West Berlin into a "Free City"; demilitarize it, change it into a separate political entity, strip it of Allied protection. Make it ripe for takeover.

Had the border incident upset the delicate balance of things? he wondered nervously, damning the Soviets for admitting the Western press to the conference, and the press for turning the spotlight on him. Potsdam isn't even in my jurisdiction, he thought, irritated. I just happened on that scene. What should I have done—let this Brodsky escape to peddle his espionage wares to the West? What would have happened to the delicate balance of things then? It was *my* decisive action that saved the day.

He knew that he had aborted a crucially important intelligence leak. But when the authorities discovered it, they would think only of the leak itself, and the security breach— *his* breach. The very action that should have made him a hero loomed instead as a threat. He thought of how carefully, how cautiously, he had nurtured his career. No sacrifice had been too great—not even the humiliation of being patronized by inferiors. Who are the Soviets to patronize *me?* he raged. Barbarians—all of them!—who raped my country and carried off twenty billion dollars' worth of German industry, calling it "reparations." Once-proud Germans had been turned into tools of the Soviet occupation forces, he brooded, but there would be a day of reckoning, a day when Germany's leaders, East *and* West, would be replaced by men of vision and courage. I must be ready for that day. I must—I will—keep my record spotless, my career intact.

He reached for a telephone on his desk and told his secretary to cancel his appointments and hold all calls— except for the one he was expecting from his field officer, who had returned to his surveillance of Roeder. He lit a cigarette, thinking of Roeder, took a few drags—and ground the cigarette in an ashtray. The gesture summoned images from his memory, images of flesh: bellies . . . buttocks . . . breasts . . . all the soft parts of the body where one could feel the cigarette go in . . . grind deep . . . deeper . . . To get quick results, he interjected. An uncooperative mouth usually had the soft belly of a traitor to go with it. They never stayed uncooperative for long, he thought, lighting another cigarette to calm himself. But the roll call of images started again, earlier ones: The flesh of women he had known . . . love bites inscribed in soft thighs and tender necks and later in the most excruciating places he could think of . . . nipples of pregnant young girls, squeezed for their milk and the blood he could coax from them . . . All in the game of sex, he reassured himself, erotic, sophisticated sex—not perversity, not whips and chains. But the images kept slipping backward in time. Bulging yellow eyes and the contorted dancing of cats with tin cans tied to their tails . . . the placid expression of a sleeping dog moments before a firecracker exploded under its belly . . . Childish pranks, he reminded himself; all the boys had done them—the daring ones. And the snakes didn't count because everyone hated snakes. How the girls would cheer his marksmanship with a rock . . . and squeal at the sudden gush of pink, the color and texture of bubble gum . . . And before that, there had been the vivid yellows and pale greens and the squishing sound when you stepped on all the tiny things that moved . . . "Such a curious little fellow, so fascinated with Nature!" his mother had exclaimed uneasily to anyone who caught him. The image of his mother's face merged unexpectedly with his sister's.

Damn my sister! He stood up and walked over to a

floor-length mirror. The sight that greeted him was as reassuring as ever: a tall, broad-shouldered, robust specimen of a man, with thick white-blond hair and clear blue eyes . . . the man of the future, in neat green tunic and high black boots.

It will be all right, nothing can destroy you, nothing can destroy your career, he told himself, believing it. He experienced a wave of relief then, which he knew dimly had nothing to do with the Old Order or the New, but with his Aryan purity. He clicked his heels to the image of physical perfection in the mirror, and, feeling cleansed, returned to his desk.

14

Everything was in readiness for the high point of the conference—the operation. The patient, unconscious on the operating table, was lying between a sheet and the hypothermia mattress that had lowered his body temperature to the required coolness; doctors, nurses and technicians were stationed around the table; behind them, in customary white smocks and masks, were the honored guests—Adrienne, Galya, Kiril, Yanin, and the other visiting doctors from the various People's Republics. A semicircle of German doctors and their medical students peered down on the operating theater from a balcony. A technician sat placidly behind the control panel of a heart-lung machine.

At a signal from the clinic Direktor, the chief surgeon leaned over the patient, made an incision from collarbone to diaphragm, sawed through breastbone, spread open the rib cage, and exposed a gleaming fibrous membrane ribboned with blood vessels: the pericardial sac. At that precise moment, Dr. Kurt Brenner entered the operating room. He walked to the table, held out a gloved hand for an instrument, and with a quick, deft movement, cut open the sac to reveal the heart. Then, quietly authoritative, he began issuing the orders that would stop the heart and delegate its functions to the heart-lung machine. He frowned once or twice because the balloonlike device hanging above the machine was a bubble oxygenator rather than the more efficient disc version he was accustomed to, and because the technician's responses to his orders were a touch too lethargic.

For a long time the only sounds in the room were the rhythmical breathing of the operating team and the onlookers, as the operation progressed . . . the gentle whir of an electric motor, as blood and oxygen were rerouted . . . the repetitive blips of an electrocardiac machine . . . Brenner's terse commands, swiftly translated into action around the table.

Adrienne, struck by the grace and economy of movement of the performance before her, glancing once at the balcony of mesmerized students, felt herself transported against her will back to the balcony of another operating theater, to her own admiration and excitement, as she watched Kurt assume responsibility for someone's life, in full command of his own.

A noise from the hypothermia mattress signaled the gradual warming of the patient's body. The patient was injected with a drug to neutralize the effects of the anti-coagulant in his bloodstream. An electric shock jolted the patient's heart. The lifeline between heart and heart-lung machine was severed, now; the heart was expected to start beating on its own.

The operating team waited for the contractions to begin.

Nothing happened. The eyes of every doctor in the room leaped to the technician behind the control panel. The man looked stunned, out of reach of Brenner's urgent commands.

Someone shouldered the technician aside. One hand whipped off dark glasses; the other shot out for the spare oxygenator that stood by as a precaution, then reached for a bottle of fresh fluid to wash the lines of tubing free of blood and avoid fatal clots to the brain. Kiril went to work, pausing only once: to exchange a glance, like a firm handshake, with Kurt Brenner, who could do nothing but massage the heart and wait.

In less than five minutes, the waiting was over, the heart-lung machine ready to function again as the patient's heart. But valuable minutes had been lost. The operating team bent over the form on the table, going through motions that everyone knew were as futile as they were routine; the patient was dead.

One after another, the visiting doctors silently left the room. Brenner stood immobile at an operating table ringed with solemn faces.

Galya made her way toward Kiril to console him on his valiant race with the clock—and stopped, frowning. Kiril had retrieved his dark glasses, quickly putting them on again, but not before she saw that there was no redness, no trace of an infection, in his left eye. There never *was* an infection, she realized. Then why . . .

Her glance moved back and forth between two faces in the room. She suddenly remembered Dr. Yanin's little joke this morning at breakfast, when he'd first noticed the likeness: "Like a modern version of the Prisoner of Zenda! Don't try to bring literature to life by playing the king of American surgery, Dr. Andreyev. I should hate to part with you."

I should, too, she thought, knowing, now, why Kiril had looked at her in Moscow as if he never expected to see her again.

Brenner lay on the bed and stared at the ceiling. He had locked himself in the bedroom of his hotel suite, excusing himself from lunch. His East European colleagues had understood and sympathized, having heard how he always shut himself away to mourn a patient's death.

He was genuinely distressed that someone should die under his knife, but the fact that it was *his* knife accounted for the acute anxiety he was experiencing. It was a familiar feeling, he acknowledged, one that descended on him whenever something major went wrong during an operation. It didn't matter that nine-and-a-half times out of ten, it was someone else's mistake—things were not supposed to go wrong in Dr. Kurt Brenner's operating room. Patients were not supposed to die.

When did the anxiety attacks start? he asked himself. About the time I began to go public, he admitted reluctantly; round after round of guest appearances, coast to coast, then abroad . . . Unbidden, the thought of a renowned publicity-loving pianist of his acquaintance came into his mind. The pianist had once admitted to approaching the stage with great trepidation whenever he'd neglected his practicing—fearful, he'd said, of blowing the performance.

Brenner put the pianist out of his mind before his mind could draw a full comparison. It was not his habit to analyze such things. Anxiety was a time, not for thinking, but for feeling: first, ugly crippling emotions, and then soothing ones to crank up his operating-room manner of easy confidence.

I'm no damn good in there. I never was any good! . . .

A patient is dead, and I'm responsible. . . . I've had it—I'm through, finished! . . . I've got to retire while I still have any honor left to retire with! Then the soothing, familiar process of restoration began: *You're a fool. You're respected and admired all over the world, for Christ's sake! . . . Think of the surgeons who emulate you. Think of how they use you as a model for their medical students. . . . Remember earlier this morning?—all those prominent surgeons doting on every word, every gesture? . . . Think of the people attending the West Berlin symposium tomorrow. Think of the toasts and speeches in your honor . . .*

When Adrienne spoke through the bedroom door, closed even to her, telling him she was going for a walk, he didn't even hear her. He was hearing the awe in Dr. Yanin's voice when he'd said to his colleagues: "Dr. Kurt Brenner can accomplish in forty-five minutes what it takes most surgeons two hours to attempt!"

Kiril chose a grouping of chairs near the hotel lobby's only row of telephone booths. He took the end chair, and Luka sank down heavily in the next one.

He had deliberately skipped lunch. There was a cafeteria just off the lobby; if the Mongolian got hungry enough . . . He eyed the telephones almost wistfully. One call, he thought, and he would know where he stood. Then a brief meeting, if he could manage it. What if Stepan's contact man were out, or had moved? Or been caught? But the address Stepan had made him memorize was less than a year old; nothing could have changed in so short a time.

He looked around the lobby, desperate for distraction. There was nothing to provide one in the huge room, with its ostentatious display of marble and random scattering of functional furniture—no inviting nooks or corners anywhere. But then, everyone in the lobby seemed to be on some urgent errand. He leaned forward in sudden anticipation. Adrienne Brenner had just gotten off an elevator and was heading in his direction. He sat back again, disappointed. She had walked past without seeing him, intent, like all the others, on some urgent errand of her own.

He concentrated once more on the telephones, silently rehearsing his end of a conversation that had to be vague and pointed at the same time. And brief. Travel plans for one person. I'm sorry, Galya, he thought, his head bent in painful acceptance of the guilt he felt, even though she had never been his responsibility or his love . . . just a vulnerable child-woman who would be lost without him. You were part of the bargain I was going to strike with the Americans in West Berlin, he told her silently—our escape in exchange for the film. But now I am in no position to bargain with anyone. There is nothing I can do for you . . . except, perhaps, not to leave without saying goodby. You will hate me if I do, won't you? You will hate me for not having trusted you enough. Can I spare you that, at least? No, he decided reluctantly, because for some inexplicable reason, it was true. He did not trust her enough.

"Yes, Colonel." Galya hung up. Her hand stayed on the telephone receiver, stubbornly refusing to move. Then she shrugged and reached for her purse. Don't resent this, she scolded herself as she hurried down the corridor, propelled by a gust of nervousness. Just remember what it can mean for your future. Not that I have any choice—not now, she thought with a shudder, as she stepped quickly into an express elevator.

When she stepped off, she saw Kiril. She wanted desperately to run across the lobby to him, to tell him what she suspected. To hear him say it wasn't true. But all she had time for was a smile and a wave. Damn the Colonel, she thought, hurrying through the lobby and into the street. And not a moment too soon, she told herself, relieved. Mrs. Brenner had just crossed the plaza and was about to enter one of the ground floor shopping arcades.

Adrienne checked her watch. Three o'clock, he had said. She spotted him at a refreshment booth. She sauntered past him, pausing to watch a saleslady arrange meat patties on a large tray.

"Would you care to sample one of our boulettes, Mrs. Brenner?"

She turned. "Mr. Roeder. How nice to see you again." She gestured at the tray. "I'm really not hungry, just curious. Your 'boulettes' look just like our hamburgers."

"Perhaps I can tempt you with one of these?" He tilted the mug he was holding so she could see the pink liquid inside. "Weisse mit Schuss—beer and raspberry juice. It is popular with Berliners in the summer."

"Thank you, no." His hands *are* enormous, she marveled. Maneuvering a miniature camera must be child's play compared to what I've been going through.

"I know what might interest you, Mrs. Brenner. Some souvenir to take back to America. Something for your kitchen from Czechoslovakia, perhaps? Or a Polish raincoat? A bottle of rose petal oil made in Bulgaria?"

"I don't think so."

"I shall not suggest a Russian fur cap or a samovar—they have become such bromides. Well, let me see . . . there is material for curtains from my country—very lovely. There are wooden toys from the People's Republic of

China—handcarved—a delightful gift for a child. You have children, Mrs. Brenner?''

"I have a young nephew who's pretty handy at carving his own wooden figures. Davey would probably love something like that."

"Wonderful." He led her to the toy counter and picked out a wooden figure. "Look at the labor that has gone into this. See how easily you can move the tiny limbs about— very flexible."

"How is it done, with elastic?"

But he was no longer examining the toy. His eyes scanned the arcade's long, uncrowded aisles. "So Paul Houston is about to defy his government a second time." He kept his voice low. "A remarkable man, Paul. He is determined, is he, to avenge our friend Brodsky's death by exposing the dark side of the American State Department? Tell him I shall anticipate the sound and fury of his deed with great relish. And gratitude."

How deceiving appearances can be, she thought, taking in his glasses, medium height and build—medium everything—measuring his words and tone of voice against his milquetoast expression. She said, "I gather there's more involved than avenging Brodsky's death."

"Yes, of course. New negotiations are in the making, new concessions to the Soviet Union in the air. Paul's revelations about the sham conference in Potsdam will shatter them."

"Is that what the film in Brodsky's cigarette lighter was all about—the recent conference? What's the matter?"

Roeder's expression had turned grim. "I was thinking about Stepan. It was because your State Department double-crossed him that he made that desperate, last-ditch attempt to escape on his own. An impossible gamble, and yet, how close he came to winning. Do you know how he spent his last excruciating moments on earth? Getting rid of his cigarette lighter. I saw him drag himself forward . . . inch by inch . . . until he had pushed it over the side of the bridge.''

"Why? What was so important about that lighter?''

Roeder shrugged. ''It was just an ordinary American lighter with an emblem on it—black wings of some kind. What was important was the film inside. He had to destroy it, I suppose, because if it fell into the wrong hands, it could implicate the man who took the pictures in Moscow.''

"What happened to *him*, I wonder?''

"I have also wondered. I never knew his name, only that he was a good friend of Stepan's and that, until the Soviet boycott, he was scheduled to attend tomorrow's medical symposium in West Berlin. Bearing gifts to your State Department in an identical cigarette lighter.''

"You mean, more film?''

"So Stepan said.''

Could it be the *other* film Paul had alluded to, she wondered, the evidence he needed to back up his story? As good as buried in Moscow, he'd said. *Was* it?

"And now, Mrs. Brenner . . .'' Roeder's eyes were making another sweep of the arcade, ''allow me to conclude our business.'' He signaled a saleswoman at the far end of the toy counter.

Dr. Andreyev, she thought, had been scheduled to attend the West Berlin symposium. Andreyev, with his crudely disparaging statistics and his baiting remarks. All those studied looks . . . the undertone. As if he'd been taking her measure. To see if he could trust her? Their unexpected side trip in the copter . . . the way Andreyev had acted when they got there . . . *I must spend the rest of my*

life trying to forget this place. Why would he say that
unless a good friend of his was buried in that—how had he
put it?—anonymous collection of humanity. A secret place
for people who try to escape, the Barkova woman had
admitted. Dr. Andreyev *must* be Brodsky's friend, she
concluded. She closed her eyes for a moment. And he
must have *me* in mind as a courier for his film!

"We should leave now." Roeder took her arm. "You
will find what you asked me for wedged behind the left leg
of one of the figures. I cannot vouch for the quality,
however, even with fast film and a pre-set camera. I
had floodlights in place of a flash, and I had to work
quickly." He handed her the package the saleswoman had
wrapped.

Galya, standing at the far end of the arcade, watched
with interest as a package changed hands. It was the signal
she had been waiting for. "If Mrs. Brenner meets with the
photographer, Roeder, and if anything passes between them,
anything at all, let me know immediately," the Colonel
had told her—emphatically. She stepped into a phone
booth, closed the door, then opened it again and peered
out. They were walking down an aisle, stopping to look at
things and talking, obviously not in a hurry. It was so
inoffensive, the photographer's purchase of a few objects
from a toy counter, Galya reasoned. Of what importance
could it be? Why should she make trouble for a total
stranger? Not that she would mind making trouble for Mrs.
Brenner, she thought. If the fine American lady with the
elegant clothes were in trouble, maybe she would have no
time to whisper with Kiril or exchange long, lingering
glances.

Her hand on the door of the booth trembled for a moment. Then she pulled the door shut, inserted a coin, and dialed.

Adrienne and Roeder paused just inside one of the exits. "Thanks for your help with the Oriental figures," she said to him in a tourist's voice. "My nephew will be happy I ran into you. Will I . . . be seeing you before I leave tomorrow?" she asked in a more normal tone.

He consulted his watch. "Not for the cocktail hour coming up, but I shall certainly be on hand for the dinner reception in your husband's honor—as a member of the press, I have no choice in the matter. I am looking forward to tonight's occasion, however." He held the door open for her. "We will share a very special toast, you and I," he said softly.

She half-turned in the doorway to respond—and in the next instant was knocked off balance and sent spinning by someone's bulky shoulder. She caught her breath and her balance, her face flushed with anger. Then anger congealed into ice.

Luka Rogov stood in the doorway, blocking Roeder's exit.

Roeder looked frozen, too, and terrified, she thought. There was no color in his face, no expression. She made herself tap Rogov on the shoulder. "Mr. Roeder was about to see me to my hotel. You will step out of the way, please," she said with authority.

Luka looked at her. "Give me toys," he said in Russian, reaching for the package she was holding.

She took a step backward, clutching the package.

"Give him what he wants," Roeder said. His voice

sounded queer. "Give it to him and go. Please. It is all right—I will be all right."

Adrienne thrust the package in Luka's face. "I'll see you tonight," she told Roeder. "I'll be looking for you," she promised, more for Luka's benefit than Roeder's. She walked away quickly.

From the other side of the plaza, Galya watched Mrs. Brenner head for the hotel—free to leave, apparently, she thought. Mr. Ernst Roeder was not. She watched him being hustled toward a waiting limousine. So it was the photographer they had wanted, after all, she concluded. I don't care! I *had* to make that call. If this Roeder has nothing to hide, then he had nothing to worry about. But who doesn't have something to hide . . . especially from Colonel Andreyev? I don't care, she repeated with uneasy defiance. I must think of myself. And Kiril. He's alone now, she realized, pried loose from his revolting bodyguard. We can be alone to talk.

She hurried into the hotel lobby, and spotted him just outside a telephone booth. But as he approached, he seemed to be heading right past her.

"Kiril!" She stopped him, incredulous. "What are you— I *must* speak with you."

"Not now," he said.

"But it's important. It can't wait."

"It will have to." He walked out.

She stared after him, thinking that she was nothing to him anymore, not even someone to be courteous to. It was uncharacteristic of him to be rude and insensitive, a voice reminded her; had he ever behaved like this before? He has *other* things on his mind, she shot back, ignoring the question. Now that he has *her* to think about, he has no time for me. How foolish of him, how shortsighted. I have no way, now, to ask him certain questions. I have no choice but to make a full report. For your own good, Kiril, she added righteously, remembering what the Colonel had said: *Men like my brother have to be protected from themselves.*

15

The limousine was spacious enough to accommodate four passengers, six if the jumpseats were used. Luka, enjoying the novelty of sitting in back, sprawled comfortably across two seats.

Ernst Roeder sat as close as he could to the window on the opposite side of the car.

Luka's military cap, upturned, rested on one large knee. Chuckling, he began rolling the Oriental figures around inside his cap; the flat, clacking sound of wood against wood kept pace with the chuckles.

Roeder stared straight ahead, looking like the timid bank clerk who has just breached some time-honored banking tradition and is steeling himself to face his superiors. But there was a trapped-animal look in his eyes that went beyond fear. He dug into his pocket for a small bottle and slipped a pill under his tongue. His breathing was labored; he took out another pill.

Luka's burly arm whiplashed across the distance between them, catching his wrist in mid-air.

Roeder recoiled as if he'd been struck by a snake. "Medicine," he said hoarsely in Russian, "it is only medicine."

Luka sniffed the contents of the bottle, shrugged, and dropped it into his cap with the wooden figures.

Roeder closed his eyes and tried to relax. He felt so ashamed. He had worked so hard to prepare himself for this moment, to meet it without fear when it came. He had known it would come, some day; he had calculated the risks in advance—even preparing himself for the prospect of a firing squad, or worse, if his cold-eyed brother-in-law took charge of things. The risks had been worth the consequences, he thought, because I hate them, I hate my own countrymen and their obscene claims on me. To hold a man against his will—to hold him, and then dictate how he should live, he thought, *that* was what had made him fight back. A poor weapon, his stark photographs that graced the grim pages of *Die Mauer* whenever he could smuggle them out, but without them—without the risks he incurred—he could not have survived for long. My kind of survival has a price tag, he reminded himself. It is time to pay. But with dignity, Ernst, with dignity!

But he could not stop the palpitations. *Why* couldn't he? Foolish question, he thought. The answer was sitting right next to him, in a soiled military tunic. He made himself look. Shaved head, large, flat face, slanted eyes that would gleam if they happened on terror and helplessness. A creature who provoked memories.

He had caught a glimpse of Rogov three months ago, at the opening session of the negotiations in East Berlin. A small fissure had developed in the mental block that sealed off his memories, and a few had come trickling through. He had managed, after that, to keep his distance, not seeing Rogov again, not up close, until this morning at the clinic. He had felt the fissure widen. Like the Dutch boy who stuffed his finger in a leaking dike, he had stuffed the fissure in his memory block with fragments of conversation—with hard concentration while he set up the group photographs—with the interesting diversion of his talk with Mrs. Brenner.

But there was no stopping the flood, he knew, not in the narrow confines of a curtained limousine. He sat back and let it engulf him . . .

In May 1945, the creatures turned loose on Berlin, on the last remnants of the Third Reich, found mostly old people, women, and children.

The first thing Ernst did after his mother disappeared was blacken his sister's face with coal dust—all the women did it to make themselves ugly to the Russian soldiers. But his sister hated it and kept rubbing it off. So he made her wear a pair of his trousers—the baggiest he could find— and he hid her long, blond hair under a cap. But his sister was twelve, two years older than he, and her girl's body was hard to disguise. So he kept her with him as much as he could, afraid to let her out of his sight, especially at night. She slept next to him on a piece of old mattress in a vacant cellar. He slept on hard cement. He had trained himself to hear faint noises, to wake up when he heard them. What he heard that morning was boisterous laughter and a string of Russian curses. What he smelled was the queer, overpowering odor of fish and leather. What he saw were dirty soldiers' uniforms. When they were so close he could smell their breath, he looked at swarthy skin and slanted eyes—and malice, gleaming at the sight of his shrinking helplessness, his terror. When his sister stirred in her sleep and her cap slipped, loosening a long, golden

213

strand, he watched malice turn into something else. When they went at her like a wolf pack—tearing at her clothes and laughing and cursing and covering her screams with their laughter—he knew he should fling himself at them, and fight. But all he did was sob and call his sister's name. He was still calling it long after the soldiers had left, but she wouldn't answer. He would not let her out of his sight. Not for five days. After that, he buried her in a corner of the cellar that had a dirt floor.

Roeder took his glasses off and wiped his forehead and upper lip; beads of moisture melted into his handkerchief. "Please," he said to Luka without looking at him, "let me have another pill."

Twenty minutes later, Roeder's agitation began to subside even without the aid of medication. He had been brought to an unpretentious little house, into a room that was half kitchen, half parlor. Through an open bathroom door he saw a pair of stockings drying on a shower bar, and he could smell cheap perfume—signs that the place had been vacated hastily. He felt grateful for the overstuffed chair he'd been offered and for the little tables cluttered with dusty bric-a-brac; nothing threatening could happen to him in such surroundings.

There was nothing threatening about Colonel Aleksei Andreyev, either. He told himself Andreyev had always seemed a civilized sort. He felt a fresh rush of gratitude for the man's friendly, deferential tone. Obviously, Andreyev was aware that he was dealing with someone who had connections in high places. He wondered why Andreyev had summoned him to a private house instead of the Soviet Embassy.

"—so in order to save us both time, which for me, at least, is essential," Aleksei was saying in colloquial German,

214

"I will tell you what I already know. You will then tell me what I do not know—it's called 'fill in the blanks.' " He stopped to light his pipe. "I know, for example, that you are in the business of selling secrets to the West. I know that one of your partners-in-crime was the Ukrainian traitor, Stepan Brodsky. I know that the two of you conspired to pass certain information to our enemies concerning the Potsdam negotiations, and that your partner was planning, for reasons not yet clear to me, to deliver what I shall call a teaser"—he held up Brodsky's cigarette lighter—"in this object I rescued from a river, or more accurately, that a patrol boat rescued." He paused. "I know you were about to finalize the sale—your 'second installment' of film—with the help of an American courier, the lovely Mrs. Kurt Brenner," he continued. "Did you guess the reason for that stop my limousine made on the way over here? The film which you concealed on one of those wooden toys and then passed to Mrs. Brenner is being developed right now." He leaned forward. "Tell me, please, who else is involved in your little enterprise. Who are your contacts? I want the name of every person who has any knowledge of this Potsdam affair."

Roeder returned Aleksei's stare with dazed eyes.

"You must trust me . . . confide in me," Aleksei intoned, sounding as gently forgiving as a father confessor. "I can help you. My friend, we can help one another," he said, sounding like a sympathetic co-conspirator. "Come now," he coaxed, "the truth sits on the tip of your tongue. Release it."

Roeder opened his mouth, but no sound came out. A sudden fog had settled in his brain and he lost his bearings in it. Where to begin? How to explain that yes, he *was* involved, but no, he was not—not in the way that was

215

meant? What if something he said accidentally implicated someone else? *I have nothing to do with espionage—with the film concealed in Stepan's lighter!* he wanted to cry our. *My* pictures are of his death.

But when he looked into intelligent blue eyes . . . blinking . . . blinking, he shuddered at what he had missed on his first appraisal. "You are wrong," were the only words he was able to form out of the fog.

Aleksei motioned for Luka to follow him to the kitchen area, to a door that he opened with ominous slowness, and on darkness. "I wish I had time to play the usual cat and mouse games, Herr Roeder, but unfortunately you are not a man I can afford to detain too long—not until I have something incriminating in hand. A confession would do nicely. For that, I must rely on my associate, here. Lieutenant Rogov does his best work in a cellar," he said. "You will go with him, please."

A cellar! Roeder's fingers curled, digging into the arms of his chair.

"The place is in deplorable shape," Aleksei apologized. "Dirty and cluttered, quite damp for this time of year. But it's well equipped for my associate's needs—rubber truncheons, iron bars—that sort of thing. I can't promise you he'll use them, since he's developed a preference for more subtle methods—my influence, I'm afraid. Not long ago, he drove a man insane by making him lean against a wall on two forefingers. Luka?"

Like a tank edging into battle, Luka advanced slowly on Roeder's chair; his eyes gleamed.

Those eyes! Roeder screamed without sound. He gasped, choking on his helplessness. His ears burst: curses—sobbing—laughter—screams. He struggled to separate the sounds, he struggled to move; he had turned to stone.

Calling . . . calling . . . rocking in his arms . . . all bloody and broken . . . calling and sobbing and rocking . . . I'm sorry, I'm sorry . . . so lovely and golden . . . so still. *No!*

One oversized hand began to claw at his chest.

Von Eyssen strode up to a parked car where his field officer was waiting for him. "Which house?" he rasped—and realized the man had noticed his agitation. "My brother-in-law has a history of heart disease—scarlet fever—you remember how it was in Berlin after the war," he explained off-handedly. "Prolonged stress could be dangerous," he added. "How long have they had him?"

"About a quarter of an hour, not counting the time he was in the limousine."

"Which house?" Von Eyssen repeated in a tone that substituted for clenched teeth.

The man pointed it out.

"Wait here unless I call you," Von Eyssen told him. He moved quickly toward the house and took the steps two at a time. He kicked at the front door with his boot. They have had no time, he was thinking. They cannot have a confession yet.

A scowling Luka Rogov opened the door.

Aleksei was kneeling beside Roeder's body, taking his pulse. He dropped the wrist and stood up. "I've been expecting you, Colonel," he said. "I'm afraid there's been a regrettable accident. Your brother-in-law has had a heart attack. A fatal one."

"As a result of *your* interrogation. By what right did you subject him to—"

"I assure you, he was subjected to nothing."

"I do not believe you." Von Eyssen glanced pointedly

at Luka. "My poor sister," he said, his voice lowered respectfully. He bent over the body, then stood up. "You have made my poor sister a widow. I will see to it that you pay dearly for this."

"You're bluffing," Aleksei scoffed. "Your quick pursuit of your brother-in-law can mean only one thing. You've obviously bribed someone to get you copies of certain photographs in my possession, so you know about the security leak."

"I do," Von Eyssen acknowledged, thinking of the cost of that information: two people to take care of—the border guard Bruno, and the man who'd developed the film in the lighter Bruno had called him about.

"What you do *not* know, my dear Colonel," Aleksei said, "is that I happened on some more film—a sort of second installment, I believe. The pictures are on their way right now. They will prove that your 'poor' sister was married to a traitor and a spy—who was caught in the act, I might add."

"You are mistaken," Von Eyssen retorted hotly. "The message that was photographed—*and* the security leak—originated in *your* office, not mine."

"The crucial issue is not where something begins, but where it ends, isn't it?" Aleksei said, gesturing to a chair. "Shall we both reserve judgment until the jury arrives?"

Von Eyssen snorted, as if to say: Why should I lend myself to this charade? But he sat down, burying his tension under an expression of disdain.

When the doorbell rang, Aleksei stopped Luka with a glance and went to answer it himself. He took an envelope from one of his officers and, with the smugness of a poker player who raises his bet without looking at the last card dealt to him, tossed the unopened envelope to Von Eyssen.

"Herr Roeder was caught passing these to an American courier," he said, smiling as Von Eyssen hastily tore the envelope open.

"But . . ." Von Eyssen went through the photographs once—twice. "But this is nothing!" he exclaimed, waving the photographs in front of Aleksei's startled face. "Of what significance are a few harmless pictures of a dead man—a *Soviet* traitor? As a matter of fact," he said, calm now, "Ernst took these pictures on *my* orders—a memento for my files. A consolation prize for the widow of the German border guard killed at the bridge," he added thinly. He stuck his head out the door and yelled for his officer.

Aleksei grabbed the photographs out of his hand.

"You have killed a prominent citizen of the German Democratic Republic, my dear Colonel," Von Eyssen said in a voice suitable for reading proclamations. "You have killed him in a crude attempt to cover up your ineptitude and someone else's treason. I will not allow you to point the finger of suspicion at a dead man by—"

His officer burst into the room, revolver drawn.

Aleksei looked up from the photographs—and went back to them, his expression that of a man who carefully follows a road map and winds up on a dead-end street.

"How many times have we Germans been encouraged to get on the 'hot line' and call critical matters to the attention of our Soviet friends?" Von Eyssen went on caustically. "Rest assured that the wires between Berlin and Moscow are about to heat up. By tomorrow morning, Colonel, you will be up to your neck in 'critical' investigation—your own." He glared at Luka. "And yours." He turned to his officer. "See that no one touches the body until I return." He stalked out of the house, forgetting to click his heels, not bothering to close the door, barely noticing the woman he passed on his way down the steps.

Galya stared after the imposing German officer, thinking that something important must be going on, wondering if she should leave and come back later. Stop procrastinating, she scolded herself. What you have to tell Colonel Andreyev is important, too. Besides, he expects you—a matter of great urgency, you told him.

It *was* urgent, she thought. Someone had to stop Kiril before he did something terribly dangerous and . . . well, dangerous. She walked up to the partly open door, pushed it tentatively, and went in.

Colonel Andreyev—cool, imperturbable Colonel Andreyev! she marveled—was pacing the room. She gasped when she saw a man with a gun in his hand standing over another man who'd fallen or— She pressed her hand to her mouth to choke off the scream in her throat. "Is he . . . is Mr. Roeder dead?" she whispered to no one in particular.

"What does it look like—a beauty nap?" Aleksei snapped. "Get out of here!"

Galya backed out the door as cautiously as if she had a vial of nitroglycerine in her purse and eased her way down the steps, into the street. She walked slowly, unaware of distance or direction. Only the approaching darkness made her pause and look around. She was on a quiet residential street, deserted except for an old woman, bent over the flattened tire of a bicycle. She felt her lower lip trembling and bit down hard to stop it. She could not stop the rest of her body from trembling. She could not stop the thoughts that came at her in a sudden, terrible rush— *Murderer. Mr. Ernst Roeder's murderer.* The thoughts slowed, giving her time to see . . . to examine with luminous, unforgiving clarity what she had done, and why. A telephone call leading to the death of an innocent man because of . . . ? Envy, she thought bleakly; envy of another woman's good fortune—a woman who had tried to be kind. And jealousy, she admitted, even though I had no right to be jealous. She let Kiril's face take form, let it hurt. He had given her everything a man who wasn't in love could give: affection, the tenderest of lovemaking, a steady, gentle optimism. How can I measure what I owe you . . . my love?

Then the most unwelcome thought of all fell on her, shattering his image. The least of what I owed you was loyalty, she realized, thinking of how easily she had bartered it, and for what. She stood, head bowed, arms rigid at her sides, and silently cursed her obsession for glamour, for all the wonderful things that had lured her into the ugliest of human activities: spying on someone who trusts you.

Another image began to form—she squeezed her eyes shut to stop it—but the body of Ernst Roeder, sprawled on the carpet, loomed. Only it wasn't Roeder, it was Kiril. She shuddered, knowing she'd been a breath away from delivering Kiril to Ernst Roeder's fate.

She went up to the old woman who was still muttering over her disabled bicycle, and pressed something into the woman's hand. "I hope it brings you better luck," she said in faltering German.

The old woman would relate it endlessly to friends and relatives—to whoever would listen: the story of the crazy Russian lady who, with tears streaming down her face, made her a gift of a wristwatch—solid gold!—and look, look at the markings—the watch comes from "the other side!"

16

The express elevator opened onto the 38th floor. Adrienne, late as usual, hurried through a deserted cocktail lounge, following the unmistakable sounds of a party—and stopped, caught by the view. When have I ever been able to resist the city at night—any city? she thought, smiling. But her glance was drawn involuntarily to a streamer of red lights pulsating from the upper stem of the television tower— East Berlin's proud landmark; her smile developed uneasy edges. She could almost feel the pulse of those lights . . . like exposed heartbeats, she thought, captured and strung together. Then she heard it again—the amplified sound of a beating heart, regular, rhythmic—followed by the awful sound of silence in the operating room and the pounding of her own heart, filling a void. Poor Kurt. What a thing to have to live through. She glanced at her watch. He was going to be really late, this time, she thought, hurrying through the lounge and into the hotel banquet room.

Every table was full, every booth. A long table centered

on a raised platform had some empty places, the most conspicuous being the place of honor; she couldn't help wondering whether it was because of the outcome of the operation or because of Kurt's penchant for making an entrance. Even the television cameras looked impatient, and the press— She moved closer, frowning at a small cluster of newsmen. Where was Ernst Roeder?

A man wearing white tie and tails stuck a drink unceremoniously in her hand and walked off. She stared after him, wondering how she was supposed to distinguish the waiters from the guests—and smiled. Not all of the guests presented a problem.

Dr. Andreyev, wearing a blue suit that looked tired, saw her and broke away from a conversation.

She watched him crossing the room to her, watched that slow, measured way he had of moving, and thought that underneath the surface slowness was a coiled spring. She remembered the ominous stillness in the helicopter, shattered by his lunge for Rogov's throat. She saw dark glasses sailing across an operating room and his hands reaching— discarding—smashing out of the way—moving swiftly and expertly over the control panel of a heart-lung machine . . .

"Good evening," he said softly.

She was suddenly conscious of her gown, pale green with a faint suggestion of silver, of how weightlessly cool she felt even though the fabric enveloped her like a wave, freeing only her hands and her throat.

He spoke again, his voice self-consciously louder. "Where is the guest of honor?"

"Fashionably late, I'm afraid," she answered without thinking, and flushed. "I shouldn't have said that. Kurt is always shaken after a patient dies. Is there anything else you'd like to show me before I leave tomorrow?" she asked pointedly, thinking that now was the time for him to mention the film he was carrying.

"The only thing left on my itinerary is a private goodby. May I come to your suite later this evening?"

"Yes, of course," she said, relieved. "If my husband is with me, I'll just—"

"Please tell him to expect me. I would not want to miss him."

"Oh?" she said, bewildered, wondering how he could possibly pass her the film in front of Kurt—who would never let her take the risk of smuggling it out. She wondered, suddenly, if Dr. Andreyev really *were* the Russian friend Brodsky had told Ernst Roeder about. "Do you regret missing tomorrow's symposium in West Berlin?" she asked him. "You *were* invited, weren't you?"

"Yes, I was. And yes, I do regret it. Why do you ask?"

"I was just curious. Why do you regret it?" She saw a quick, bitter smile before he sidestepped her question.

"I wasn't the only one to have regrets," he said. "Miss Barkova regrets it, and Dr. Yanin, and my brother the Colonel. We all had our reasons."

His smile seemed suddenly, inexplicably personal—as if the joke were on her.

"The Colonel found the Soviet boycott inconvenient," he said wryly, "but only temporarily, as it turned out." He offered her a cigarette and took one himself.

She leaned forward for a light but dropped her hand, watching Colonel Andreyev, with Rogov at his heels, come bursting into the banquet room. The two of them scanned the center table and went out again. Looking for Ernst Roeder? she wondered. "It looks as if your satellite has found himself a new moon," she said reflectively.

"For now, at least. I expect my brother will aim him back in my direction soon."

"What does this Rogov have to do with your brother?" she asked, puzzled.

"That's who Rogov takes his orders from. He—"

"Would you excuse me?" she said abruptly. She walked quickly out of the room and caught up with the Colonel in the deserted cocktail lounge. He was talking to Rogov in Russian; she thought she heard the name Malik. She saw Rogov nod and head for the elevator.

Colonel Andreyev sat down on a barstool—heavily, as if his weight would no longer hold him. He had not seen her yet. As she came up to him, she saw that he was turning an object over and over in his hand reflectively. She stopped cold, thinking that it had to be her imagination, just as he swung around, startled.

"Yes?" he said, openly suspicious.

"I'm looking for Ernst Roeder. I believe you can tell me where he is."

"You are mistaken."

"I was with him when your Lieutenant Rogov took him away this afternoon," she persisted. "Against his will."

"How interesting."

"Rogov takes his orders from you, Colonel."

"How astute! We could have a mutually enlightening conversation, you and I, were it not for another pressing engagement. I am on my way to see your husband."

She extended the unlit cigarette she was still holding. "Perhaps you'll offer me a light first."

He hesitated, then shrugged. "Permit me," he said with mock deference.

She tensed as he extended his lighter; then, in the moment when her cigarette caught, she confirmed what

226

she thought she had seen: an emblem. In the quivering flame, the black outstretched wings seemed to be moving.

"Is something wrong, Mrs. Brenner?"

"No," she said faintly.

"Then you will excuse me. I shall try not to delay the festivities too much longer."

She heard the elevator doors open and close. It took her long minutes to identify a murky feeling, and more minutes to shake it off; it was disappointment, and the enormity of it unnerved her. I can't believe it! she thought. I *have* to believe it, she admitted. The cigarette lighter Brodsky had pushed off a bridge was an American make—bird's wings of some kind, Roeder had told her. And Brodsky's Russian "friend" had an "identical" lighter . . . like the one the Colonel had just used. Hadn't Dr. Andreyev said his brother the Colonel had planned to be at the West Berlin symposium? *The Colonel found the Soviet boycott inconvenient.* I'll say! she thought. No way to get his film out. She frowned, remembering the rest of that sentence: the Colonel found the boycott inconvenient—but only temporarily. What was *that* supposed to mean? Unless—

She had to lean against the bar for support because she knew that what she was thinking had a certain logic to it. The Colonel had just mentioned a "pressing engagement" with Kurt. She shook her head slowly. Kurt Brenner . . . courier? Kurt, willing to risk his neck to smuggle some film out of East Germany? And Colonel Andreyev, not the cold, calculating bastard she'd thought he was? The Colonel, enlisting Kurt's help on the spur of the moment like this? It *wasn't* logical. It was impossible! No, she thought, reconsidering, no, it wasn't. The Colonel obviously was not what he seemed. And who says this whole business is spur of the moment? What if he's giving Kurt the film right now, but everything else was arranged between the two of them before we even got here? Like right after the Russians backed out of the West Berlin symposium and issued Kurt their own invitation, she thought, and groaned. That was it, of course. It was one way, she realized, for Kurt to make up for the rotten things he'd said at that Manning party, wasn't it?

You tried to warn me, didn't you, Kurt? she thought ruefully. You hinted at some special reason for making this trip. But when I pressed you for the reason, damn it, why didn't you—She wanted to block her ears, not to hear Kurt's answer: "I can't tell you. You'll have to take me on faith." Or trust. I'm sorry, Kurt, she thought, really sorry. . . .

The elevator's swift descent to the 21st floor was a good omen, Aleksei thought. Act swiftly, he told himself, and you can checkmate Von Eyssen. Pull this off, and you can go back to Moscow in triumph instead of disgrace. The elevator slowed.

The prospect of disgrace, of his recall to Moscow in the morning to give an account of himself in the Roeder affair, was more terrifyingly real than his grandiose scheme involving Brenner. But I'm *right*, he thought, nervously fingering Brodsky's lighter in his pocket. Roeder was a friend of Brodsky's, and Roeder's photographs link him to the intelligence leak. But turning a link into an incriminating chain that led to treason—that took proof. And proof took time.

He stepped off the elevator. You can buy the time, he consoled himself. Just hand Moscow a monumental distraction in the person of Dr. Kurt Brenner. Just move up your timetable a little, he thought, and sighed. Moving up the timetable meant dispensing with preliminaries. There could be no more toying with the fish.

Malik was waiting for him outside Kurt Brenner's suite.

Brenner, looking refreshed and elegant in an impeccably tailored tuxedo, opened the door and turned an untroubled face to his visitors. Perhaps, Aleksei thought, he views us as petty blackmailers. He dropped into a chair. "Get rid of the bugs," he told Malik.

Malik moved with smooth precision—prying open telephone bases, checking each hanging picture, tampering with the overhead light fixture. "All clear," he announced. "Where do you want this?" He held up a plump black briefcase.

Aleksei waved at a coffee table. "Dump the stuff on that."

Malik took a decrepit wire recorder, a spool of wire, and a thin sheaf of papers out of the briefcase. Then he took something out of his own trim briefcase: a revolver and a single cartridge. He placed them on the coffee table along with the other items.

"You may have guessed the reason for this meeting, at least in a general way, Dr. Brenner," Aleksei said.

Brenner's eyes did not leave the gun on the table.

"How does it feel, seeing it after all these years—the old 7.62mm Nagant Model?" Malik asked. "I managed to reacquire it just before we left Berlin—before our American tour. It has been hibernating ever since, but I have kept it in perfect operating condition." He smiled. "I could not resist bringing it. She is a little beauty of a weapon, is she not?"

"Must we get sidetracked by your special interests, Colonel Malik?" Aleksei said impatiently. "Those papers are all we need. They prove, Dr. Brenner, that Colonel

Malik took that 'little beauty of a weapon' from the body of a dead Russian comrade after the siege of Berlin. And since the gun was *Malik's* war souvenir and not your friend, Cherner's, why then, we must conclude that Cherner was unarmed at the time of the incident in question.''

"I brought this with me," Malik said, holding up the cartridge, "because I could not resist reminding you of the bullet Cherner is supposed to have fired at me. It was *I* who fired into the ground, remember? And while we had no tape recorders in those days, the contraption you see here will speak for itself—literally.'' He threaded the wire recorder with the spool of wire, activated it, and released the past.

The voice of Pfc. Kurt Brenner—youthful, petulant—haggled over the details of a sale. A voice with a Russian accent—youthful, more authoritative—kept insisting on American dollars . . . on an installament plan. A bargain was struck . . .

"How naive you were in those days, how inexperienced," Malik said softly. "You should have known I would make a record of our mutually profitable business transaction.''

"And *you* should have known that records have a way of turning up—like bad pennies," Aleksei couldn't resist saying.

"Without records, how would you have blackmailed *me?*" Malik shot back angrily.

"Let us not stray from our purpose. The evidence on the table adds up to premeditated murder. Are you with me so far, Dr. Brenner?''

Brenner opened his mouth to protest.

"No," Malik said, cutting him off, "you cannot plead self-defense, in spite of what they ruled at the investigation—not with what I am in a position to divulge. Are you thinking that the passage of time will save you? Then think again. You were never tried for the murder of Joe Cherner. With new evidence, you could be.''

"And will be, unless you do as I say." Aleksei wiped his forehead. Unless, he thought, you are smart enough to realize that your honorable discharge protects you from prosecution. "Leave us alone," he ordered Malik.

"And the briefcase, Colonel?"

"It stays."

Malik picked up his own briefcase and started to reach for the Nagant revolver.

"You may as well leave the gun, Colonel, now that you have brought it and had your little melodramatic triumph," Aleksei said acidly. "I will see that you get it back when this thing is over."

Malik shrugged. "As you wish."

Brenner's eyes followed Malik to the door, a look of panic seeming to cross his face as the door closed—amusing, Aleksei thought. He said, "Have you considered the publicity a murder trial would generate even if you were acquitted, Dr. Brenner? Have you considered what would become of your reputation as a humanitarian?" He paused, letting the rhetorical question sink in.

"Name your price," Brenner said in the patronizing tone of a rich man who buys without a thought for cost.

"Money," Aleksei spat contemptuously. "A typical American reaction. Whatever the problem, money will make it go away. I have no interest in money. I have something else in mind."

"What?" Brenner said, clearly bewildered.

Aleksei leaned forward. "Your defection to the Soviet Union."

Too much at once, he realized, recording the shock in

231

Brenner's face. All stick and no carrot. "You must know that your talents would be a boon to my country. Think of our greater need. Think of the challenge. I am talking, Dr. Brenner," he said to a blank face, "about the humanitarian goals and slogans of your Medicine International. And then," he said, managing to sound simultaneously pragmatic and solicitous, "there *is* the little matter of your financial difficulties—I am fully aware of them. If you come over to us, your difficulties will be at an end. You look skeptical. No doubt you have heard rumors about our Soviet physician who spends half his life filling out forms for grants. You are forgetting that my country is a land of exception making, and who better to make exceptions for than our most eminent people? Dr. Yanin is a perfect example."

Brenner jumped to his feet, sputtering, "You're crazy! You expect me to leave my country for good just like—like switching off a light bulb?"

"Not for good," Aleksei soothed, "not necessarily."

"Not at all. Never!"

"You are not thinking straight," Aleksei said, all business again. "You will come over to us for, let us say, an indefinite period. You will make a public announcement and mouth some of the platitudes about medicine belonging to the world—all very familiar territory, eh?—and then you will conclude on the note that you have decided to spread your considerable talents around, beginning with the place of the future—the Soviet Union. End of public announcement. In a few years you will be allowed to stay or leave, whatever your preference—an exception we are not in the habit of making," he said dryly.

"You expect me to abandon my family? Desert my institute?" Brenner said incredulously.

"Your institute will desert *you* once you have become embroiled in a sensational murder trial. As for your family, let us be frank. I am not impressed with your record as a faithful and loving husband. Are you? Should you harbor any genuine concern for your wife, however, it should please you to know you are now in a position to extricate her from a very serious situation."

"What the hell are you talking about?"

"Early this afternoon your wife committed a crime against the German Democratic Republic, possibly against my country as well. Whatever the case, I can detain her merely on the grounds that she was caught with film negatives of a strategic bridge. I *will* detain her if you refuse my terms."

"Terms? What terms?" Brenner's voice had turned shrill. "You lose nothing. I give up everything!"

Aleksei got up and swept the items on the coffee table into his briefcase. "You capitalists believe in trade, do you not? You lend my country a few years of your life, and I guarantee to keep your reputation intact so that ultimately you can reclaim everything you have lost. Refuse me, on the other hand, and I promise you the consequences will be permanent."

Brenner groaned, lowering himself into a chair.

At the door, Aleksei paused, one hand on the doorknob. "They say you are an imaginative man in the operating room," he said, smiling benignly. "Imagine this, then: your family and friends, your colleagues, your public—everyone who admires those magnificent hands of yours for their capacity to save life—imagine them looking at your hands and seeing on them the blood of innocent children and of your old army buddy. I shall expect your answer—upstairs—in the next fifteen minutes, Dr. Brenner.

Do not keep me—or the press and the television cameras—waiting. Either way, we shall have a newsworthy announcement to make, you and I.''

Aleksei wiped his forehead as he strode down the hall. The perspiration flowed freely now, but the pressure in his chest was gone. Gone! His instincts told him Brenner was hooked. He stood waiting for the elevator . . . and for the elation to come. Instead he felt the rumblings of an anger that bordered on rage. He knew its object, and wanted to spit out the name: Von Eyssen. The bastard had forced him to act swiftly—to concentrate on the end, with no time to dwell on the means. No time, he thought, to dangle and twist and play with the most challenging specimen he had ever had on his hook.

He stood in the corridor, jabbing the elevator button. What was the point of owning a bagful of sophisticated fishing lures, he thought, if in the end you caught your exotic fish with a net?

17

"Dr. Kurt Brenner." He stared at his image in the bathroom mirror as if expecting an answer. "I am *Dr. Kurt Brenner*," he asserted, as if someone were challenging that fact. "I am not—I *will not be*—intimidated." The image, haggard looking, was unconvinced. "They cannot destroy my career—they cannot." The image said they could, and would. "They'll never get away with it! In a showdown, people will believe *me*, not them." The image looked doubtful. "I will not be intimidated," he repeated uncertainly—a parting shot—and went quickly into the sitting room before the image could disagree.

The coffee table was waiting for him—empty, now, except for an ashtray. But the wire recorder that Colonel Andreyev had taken with him seemed to be there still, spinning out its secrets. And the thin sheaf of papers was there, rustling, whispering, "Proof . . . proof . . . we're the proof . . . ." He pictured the Nagant revolver, loaded with a single cartridge . . . waiting for an order: *Shoot to kill*.

Kill Dr. Kurt Brenner's reputation. Kill Dr. Kurt Brenner's career. Make Dr. Kurt Brenner a man as good as dead!

He sent the ashtray to the floor in a cloud of ashes. A vintage World War II memento and a wire recording of a thirty-year-old conversation—who would take them seriously? The word of the Soviet secret police over the word—the vehement denial—of an eminent heart surgeon, what in hell was he worried about? No one would pay any attention to this Colonel Andreyev—why should they? Because he has proof—facts, a voice insisted before he could cut it off.

"Facts," he sniffed, as if he could make them go away, keeping at mental arm's length his reverence for facts the minute he stepped into an operating room. Fact: a clogged line on a heart-lung machine will send blood clots to the brain. Fact: a patient five or six minutes off the machine will turn into a vegetable. By a process of association—his substitute for thinking in a personal crisis—he saw a vivid picture of an operating theater, with a balcony full of admiring faces. The picture faded, its signal too weak to compete with the certain knowledge that he had a choice to make, that he had to make it now. When a patient's life hung in the balance, he knew that he chose unhesitatingly between alternatives. Now, in the worst personal crisis of his life, he was immobilized.

The unpalatable and the unthinkable, he groaned. To defect to the Soviet Union? Never. To see his past exposed and his career in a shambles? Never. He cursed, visualizing his tormentors. Malik's face lingered in his mind, and for a moment, he was able to shove emotions aside. Malik was a pragmatist—hadn't he always been the first to admit it? The gun and the wire recording were a ploy to frighten me into upping the ante, he thought hopefully. But Malik wasn't running the show. Hadn't he accused Andreyev of blackmailing *him* as well?

What's left to me, then? he asked himself. Cunning, said a voice. My instinct for survival, he corrected hastily. But the only advice his instinct had for him was: Buy Andreyev off. Andreyev's contemptuous face loomed in his memory, and his voice: "I have no interest in money."

In the end, what was left was the famous Brenner temper—a process of exploding first and picking up the pieces afterward. What ignited the explosion this time was the sight of his hands—*his* hands—shaking as if he were some alcoholic with a case of the DT's. He seized the telephone and snapped at the person on the other end of the line. The last thing he said was, "See that my message is delivered promptly to Colonel Aleksei Andreyev in the banquet room on the thirty-eighth floor." He slammed down the receiver and grabbed a suitcase.

Kiril kept his expression calm as he walked out of the dining room and into the empty lounge, to wait for the elevator. But once inside, he had to concentrate hard to keep the drink he was holding from spilling.

The message had been delivered while he and Adrienne Brenner were talking with Aleksei, waiting, like everyone else, for the guest of honor to appear. In between round after round of toasts reverberating from one end of the room to the other, their amenities had sounded strained. Mrs. Brenner had seemed tensely watchful of Aleksei, who in turn had studied her with open curiosity. She had been talking about the Brenners' plan to pick up her father-in-law the next day in Zurich, when she had been stopped in mid-sentence by the look on Aleksei's face as he opened a message from her husband. "What is it?" she had asked, and dazedly he had read the message out loud: Brenner was leaving. Now. The "tragic outcome" of today's operation had left him "too despondent to cope with the demands of the occasion." Would Colonel Andreyev be good enough to arrange for an immediate flight to Zurich for his wife and himself?

Kiril's first thought had been to keep either of them from going into action. "Let me see what I can do," he had said to Aleksei pointedly. "Perhaps a drink and a sympathetic talk with another doctor will change his mind. You can stall things a little longer here, can't you?"

Aleksei had nodded, looking stunned.

The elevator slowed. The drink he was bringing for Brenner still had not spilled. Then, at the door of Brenner's suite, faced with the reality of what he planned to do, he felt some liquid lurch from the glass.

Brenner was in the bedroom with one packed suitcase and another half full. "If you came here to try and change my mind," he said angrily, looking up, "you're wasting your time." He resumed his packing.

Kiril left the drink and his dark glasses on the bureau and went into the bathroom.

Brenner looked up again at the sound of running water. "You don't need to drown out our voices," he snapped. "Your brother already de-bugged this place."

The water in the sink where Kiril had submerged his head a few times had turned brown. He toweled it dry and stepped out of the bathroom.

Brenner's hands, in the process of folding a sports jacket, stopped moving. He stared.

"Don't be alarmed," Kiril said quietly. "A few weeks ago I saw your photograph for the first time and I . . . how can I explain what it felt like, seeing the incredible resemblance?'' But he saw that Brenner knew what it felt like. "Call it coincidence,'' he went on, "call it Fate, but all I know is, it's given me a crack at the biggest stakes in the world.''

"What stakes?'' Brenner said nervously. "Money? You want money when your brother sneers at it? Why is your English so good all of a sudden—what happened to your thick accent?''

"It's a long story. I haven't had an accent for years—I just pretend to have one. It's easy enough to fake. You see, for years I've been preparing myself for certain contingencies.''

"Having to do with *me?*''

"Only recently with you.''

"Your white hair . . .'' Brenner said uneasily; he was staring again.

"My natural color is dark brown. Just before I left Moscow, I bleached it white, then I covered up the white with a brown rinse.''

"Your eyes,'' Brenner said slowly, "why haven't I noticed them before—ah,'' he said, following Kiril's glance, "the dark glasses.''

"I've been observing you closely, Dr. Brenner—ever since you stepped off the plane. I've watched the way you walk, the way you light a cigarette. I know the way your voice sounds when you—''

"Why?'' Brenner started to back away. "Are you planning to force me into defecting against my will? You'll take my place in front of the television cameras and pretend to be me—is *that* it?''

Kiril laughed softly. "I have spent the entire weekend trying to *prevent* your defection. Everything I said and did, every place I took you to, was carefully calculated to make you resist my brother's blackmail. I want you to go back to America.''

Brenner sat down on the edge of the bed. "I don't understand," he said tensely.

"Listen to me. I don't know what my brother has on you, but whatever it is, buying his silence *can't* be worth the price he's demanding."

"Then you can help me?" Brenner said eagerly. "You can stop him from revealing what he knows?"

"I'm sorry, I have no way to do that. No, it is you who can help me. I had planned to approach you later this evening, but since you intend to leave now, let me explain quickly. I met with a man this afternoon who has agreed to help me get across the border—he knows how to arrange these things. He has everything he needs except for one crucial item. I need your passport, Dr. Brenner. With it, I can pass myself off as—" He saw that Brenner was about to refuse, and he dropped his voice to a whisper to disguise desperation. "Please give me that passport. Not here. Not now. I'll be going with you to the airport. They check passports only at the terminal. Once you've boarded your plane, the only thing they'll ask for is a special identity card they check against your ticket. Our limousine will drive you right to the plane. You could slip me your passport on the way and no one would notice."

Brenner burst out laughing, but there was something wrong with its sound; it lasted too long, and when it was over, it left him gasping for breath. "The Brothers Andreyev," he said bitterly. "One of you wants to transplant me to Moscow, and the other wants to get me thrown into some Communist jail. Five years—isn't that the penalty for helping people escape?"

Kiril spoke cautiously; Brenner was balanced on the thin

edge of hysteria. "There's no real risk, can't you see that? Why should the airport authorities deviate from established procedures? Once you're in Zurich, no one can do anything to you."

"What about my wife? Did you know your brother has some trumped-up charge against my wife in his bag of tricks?"

Kiril frowned. "I didn't know. Maybe he's bluffing. Has it occurred to you that he could be bluffing about everything? Maybe the blackmail—"

"It's no bluff," Brenner said wearily. "His fat little briefcase is full of proof—right down to an incriminating revolver and the cartridge that goes with it."

"What does he have proof of?" Kiril pressed.

"You heard the conversation this morning—that subtle prelude to blackmail. He can prove I turned in those Ukrainian children who committed— Who died on their way to being repatriated." Brenner closed his eyes. "He can prove I killed a man to cover it up, although that might have been self-defense. It was a long time ago—right after the War. I was very young . . ."

Kiril was glad the man's eyes were closed. "Dr. Brenner," he said, his mouth taut with the effort to keep the disgust from his voice, "I'm not any kind of Soviet patriot who makes excuses for the people who run my country—men like my brother. But I'm forced to be part of their whole rotten system—I'm locked in, do you understand? All my life I've wanted only one thing. Did I say before that I was after the biggest stakes in the world? What's bigger than a man's freedom? You take yours for granted. I expected that, and it's right that you should. It's . . . healthy. I've met Americans before, you see. They're good people, kind. But they're naive. They visit a place like this, and they accept surface things or they don't look too closely. Perhaps they're squeamish, I don't know. So I thought that if I lifted up the rug and forced you to look closely, I could cut through all that. You're an American. You have a Constitution that really means what it says. You have rights. Can't you grasp . . . even a little, what it's like to be without them? If *I* were an American . . ." He closed his eyes for a moment. "If I had been born in a free country, I would feel a great sympathy for every man less free than myself. I would feel outrage against freedom's destroyers. I would want to help a man break free if I could."

Brenner was staring at his shoes.

"But you don't want to help, I can see that," Kiril said bleakly. "Let me appeal to your conscience, then. This is a chance for you to make some small retribution for those children who died because of you, or the ones who ended up in the Gulag. Isn't it time for a new beginning, when your conscience still has the power to disturb you after all these years?"

"You're no different from your blackmailing brother," Brenner hissed. "You both pretend to offer me a trade when *I* have nothing to trade with." His shoulders sagged. "I told him he was crazy, but you're even worse. Risk five years as a salve to my goddamn conscience?"

"How can you compare me with my brother? The only thing we have in common is my mother's womb," Kiril lashed out. His anger died at the sight of Brenner's sudden expression.

"Maybe I *will* give you my passport. It depends," Brenner said.

An obstruction in his throat stopped Kiril from asking the most crucial question of his life. It was an eternity—it was a full thirty seconds—before he could say, "Depends on what?"

"Whether you can convince me I wouldn't be in any real danger of getting caught. My wife tells me this Rogov never lets you out of his sight. You even share the same room. How were you planning to handle him?"

"With diazepam," Kiril said eagerly. "You know how fast it works—ten milligrams injected intravenously when Rogov's asleep and he'll stay that way for at least four hours. I have some in my room."

"What if you run into trouble between here and the border? Did you manage to smuggle in a gun?"

"They search us too well for that. I picked up a bottle of morphine sulphate and a hypodermic needle in the clinic this morning."

"That can be lethal, all right, but not very practical in an emergency unless the victim cooperates."

Kiril shrugged. "Victims cooperate if you knock them out first."

"Your familiarity with American slang is remarkable. How did you manage it?"

"Long years of practice. They can't jam *all* the foreign radio broadcasts. Sometimes they don't even try."

"You practiced American slang so you could impersonate an American?"

"That was one hope. Among many others."

"Your escape plan won't work."

Kiril closed his eyes. "Why not?"

"Our hair—how can both of us walk out of here with white hair?"

"Oh that," he said, opening his eyes. "I have more brown rinse. We walk out of here exactly as we walked in."

"Then the rinse washes right out?"

"What do you think I was doing in your bathroom a few minutes ago?"

Brenner got up from the bed, one hand gripping the iron bedpost for support. He took a deep breath and let it out slowly. "I have to go," he said.

"But you haven't finished packing."

"I have to see a man about a trade," Brenner said as if he hadn't been interrupted. "Colonel Andreyev's silence for mine. A briefcase full of blackmail in exchange for the morphine and diazepam in his brother's room—and the leftover brown rinse. The authorities would never believe he wasn't in on his own brother's escape plan, even if his name wasn't on the goddamn invitation that got me here! He put Malik up to it, didn't he? Who's to say he wasn't in on the passport business as well? Brothers help each other, don't they?" Brenner laughed harshly. "You people don't operate on proof over here. All you need are suspicious circumstances." He looked at Kiril, then, as if he'd just remembered who he was. "He's smart, your brother. He'll agree to *my* terms, now," he said.

"You know your man—he'll agree, all right," Kiril said bitterly. "He'll also frame me for something that can't reflect on him in any way. Then he'll have me shot. For God's sake, Brenner! You can't—"

"You're exaggerating. He's your own brother."

"Look at me. Look under that rug I've been pulling up for you all weekend. *Then* tell me I'm exaggerating."

Brenner did not look up. "You'd say anything to stop me," he mumbled.

And *do* anything, Kiril thought. He caught Brenner off balance with a single blow.

18

The man half-sprawled on the couch in the Brenner suite wore a shabby blue suit and dark glasses. His hair was dark brown. The man bending over him wore a black tuxedo. His hair was white.

The white-haired man straightened up, went into the bedroom, and examined himself in the floor-length mirror. His lips curved into a smile, amused and contemptuous. With an impatient gesture, he brushed away a few rebellious strands of hair that had fallen onto his forehead, then stepped back for a final survey. He closed Adrienne's suitcase, still on the bed, and put the other suitcase in the closet. A gown and a bathrobe hung there, along with a raincoat and a cape. He put on the raincoat, took the cape, and picked up Adrienne's suitcase.

He was about to shut the bedroom door when he spotted the drink on the bureau—gin and tonic with a twist of lime. He went back for it. He squeezed a few drops of lime juice into the man's left eye, adjusted the dark glasses on his face, and did a last check for brown spots on the neck.

He picked up the telephone. When he heard the tense voice on the other end, he said in Russian, "Sorry it's taken so long since my first call. You must have been worried. . . . I know I said I'd call right back, but things got a little unpleasant." He said "unpleasant" sarcastically—in English. "No, nothing like that. The initial panic is over," he continued in Russian. "Yes, he's agreed to everything. He has one precondition, however—wait, he wants to tell you himself." He held the receiver away, certain that the wires were picking up the rapid beating of his heart. After a few seconds, he lifted the receiver again, a string of American slang expressions flashing through his mind. "You win, Colonel," he said in English, in a voice that was deeper and more sonorous—and more than a little belligerent. "But get this straight. Any blackmail plans you might have on the side for my wife are out. I'm taking her to Zurich myself—*now*. That way, I'm not in the untenable position of having to trust your word on that score. It will also give me a chance to see my parents and try to explain—or say goodby, if nothing else. Well, is it a deal? . . . Right. One more thing. That unpleasantness your brother alluded to just now involved an argument over my wife. It seems he wants her included in our deal—he wants her in Moscow. I'm about to give him my full answer."

He hung up before there could be a reply, grabbed the suitcase and cape, and rushed down an empty corridor to another room. He took a half-empty bottle that was labeled hair tonic, but was diazepam, out of his pocket and flushed what was left of it down the toilet. He buried the hypodermic needle under some papers in the bathroom wastebasket.

He looked around the bedroom. Forgotten anything? Someone's future, he thought, and dug a cigarette lighter out of a suitcase. He spotted the bottle of morphine sulphate there, and realizing he wouldn't be needing it, tossed it into the wastebasket.

He hurried down the corridor to the elevator walking, not with the usual jauntiness, but with brisk authority. He knew, as he began to swing the suitcase as if it were a tennis racket, that he had things under control. That he had a chance.

As Kiril stepped out of the elevator, he saw Aleksei pacing from one end of the long, empty cocktail lounge to the other. Then he saw him eye the suitcase in his hand suspiciously. "My wife's things," he explained.

"Where is my brother?"

"Flat on his back on the couch in my suite. I trust you won't take it personally," he said—and allowed himself to swallow the air piled up in his throat.

Aleksei smiled. "I *always* take family matters personally. Not in the way you mean, however. I noticed my brother's attraction to your wife. Were *you* aware that the attraction seemed to be mutual? But all that is irrelevant now, isn't it? What will you tell her about your forced separation?"

"I'll think of something on the plane."

"Is my brother badly hurt?"

"Only his pride. Oh, he'll wake up with an aching jaw and a good-sized lump on his cranium where his head hit an iron bedpost. Does that disturb you?"

"Actually, it pleases me. His pride has always needed a few hard knocks."

"And now, on to business. I presume you have a car waiting, Colonel?"

"A car to take you to the airport and a special plane to whisk you to Zurich and back—the same plane that will fly us to Moscow in the morning." He paused, then said, "I have my *own* precondition, Dr. Brenner. A group of extremely curious newsmen are waiting impatiently in the next room to hear something out of the ordinary. I cannot disappoint them, can I? I want you to announce your intention to defect. *Then* you may escort your wife to Zurich."

"Once I leave here, you want to make it hard for me to change my mind, is that it?" he asked, stalling for time.

"Can you blame me? But you also benefit. Think of how this will soften the blow for your parents. By the time you reach Zurich, they will know the worst. Everything has been arranged. Certain people in key Western cities, including the press, have been alerted. They are waiting by their television sets and radios to hear this mysterious announcement you are expected to make. You are then expected in Zurich for a brief family reunion. I imagine you will find quite a reception committee waiting."

"In that case, I'll make my big announcement to the reception committee in Zurich," he said, aware that his tense impatience was becoming obvious.

"Not unless you want to make it without your wife," Aleksei said softly.

The ultimate argument, he thought. "The hostage game, and I'm not even on Russian soil yet. My congratulations, Colonel," he said, arching an eyebrow contemptuously. "You win, again. All right, let's get it over with. Where is my wife?"

"Waiting for you in the dining room. Everyone is waiting. Correction: everyone except your old friend, Nikolai Malik."

"Meaning?" he said tensely.

"Colonel Malik has returned to pressing duties in West Berlin, but he will take time out to attend tomorrow's medical symposium in that city—strictly as an observer, you understand. He has high hopes that circumstances will not force him to, shall we say, take a more active role in the proceedings by making public a rather unsavory transaction from his youth. You see, the transaction involved one of the symposium's honored guests."

Sound bitter. "Don't worry, Colonel Malik won't have to go public."

"I did not think so. One last piece of advice. Your announcement can be as short and sweet as you like. Just make sure it lacks the flavor of blackmail. A decision to defect is not made on the spur of the moment, between cocktails and dinner. You might follow the lead I gave you earlier."

What lead? "Don't expect too much. I think well on my feet only in an operating room. Give me a moment alone with my wife, will you?" he said, and strode briskly into the banquet room. *A moment alone with my wife.*

What a mob scene! Adrienne thought, eyeing a distant hors d'oeuvres table almost desperately. The damn table was beginning to look blurry around the edges. So were the faces of people whose names she couldn't remember five minutes after she'd been introduced. All that vodka on an empty stomach, she groaned. If anybody starts one more toast, she decided, I'll drop my cocktail glass. No I won't. Some overdressed waiter would just stick another one in my hand. I'll raise my glass and shout: "Let the vodka turn into water!" *That* shouldn't take a miracle. It's either that, she thought, or the honorable wife of the honorable guest of honor gets quietly inebriated, not to mention smashed. It will be time for breakfast before we have—

"Adrienne?" She heard a voice behind her. A hand edged her into a private corner. "Anything wrong?"

"Nothing that a pot of black coffee won't fix—not to mention my dinner. Honestly, Kurt," she said, turning around, "don't you think you've carried this entrance business—" She stared at him. "—too far," she finished. "You look . . . funny," she said slowly, as he draped her cape protectively around her shoulders. It gave her a funny sensation.

"We're leaving right away. I want you to—"

"Why?" she said suspiciously. What was *wrong* with him? His eyes—

"I'll fill you in as soon as I can. Trust me."

"Thanks for the second chance," she said, dropping her glance. "I'm not sure I deserve it." She noticed the suitcase in his hand. "Where's yours?" she said, looking up again.

"No time. Adrienne, I have to make an announcement you won't understand until after we've talked. I don't want people to see you reacting to it. Do you mind waiting for me in the lounge outside?"

"No," she said reluctantly.

"Do you mind not asking questions until we get to Zurich?"

"All right." I *must* be smashed, she thought. I keep thinking he isn't Kurt. He even sounds different.

"Are you all right?"

"I . . . I've just had a little too much to drink. Give me a cigarette, will you?" *Give me a light, too. Let me see whether—*

Her eyes, watchful as he held out a cigarette, widened as he lit it with a flourish and slipped a cigarette lighter back into his pocket.

"The lounge, Adrienne," he said urgently. "I want to get this over with." He turned away.

"Kurt?" she said suddenly—and half expected him not to turn around.

"Yes?"

His impatience was so damn typical, she thought. "Nothing. I just thought I'd take my suitcase so you won't have to bother with it."

"Thanks." He left it with her.

She watched him maneuver his way through an obstacle course of eager, pressing bodies. He looked tense and very determined. It was true, then, she thought. Colonel Andreyev had passed him the lighter with the black wings. Kurt's "special" reason for coming to East Berlin was to make up for what he'd said about a damn-fool diplomat helping a "lawbreaker." Getting the film Paul needed to back up his story—and risking his neck to get it out of the country— that *would* make up for it, she thought. And it explained so many things . . . Why he'd refused to issue a retraction. Why he'd insisted on accepting the Russians' invitation. Why he'd carried on such a long, serious conversation in the airport lounge with a man from the State Department— some friend of Paul's, probably. Paul must have sworn Kurt to secrecy. Wasn't that how the intelligence community operated—telling people things only on a need-to-know basis? Hadn't Paul even hinted she might be in Kurt's way if she made the trip with him?

I'm in his way right now, she realized; I'm supposed to be in the lounge. She saw that he'd reached the speaker's table on the raised platform. She wished him a silent good luck and hurried out of the room.

* * *

Aleksei watched him on the platform, watched him reach for a microphone. As soon as it was in his hand, Aleksei gave the cue, and the television cameras swung into action.

"Ladies and gentlemen, I think I have spoiled your dinner, or at least delayed it unconscionably, for which I apologize." A good beginning, Aleksei thought. "I feel that I owe you more than an apology, however. I owe you an explanation." The voice had become more authoritative. "I have kept you waiting because I was in the throes of a difficult decision—the culmination of a great deal of soul searching. The soul searching has been going on for a long time," the voice confessed. Aleksei restrained a smile. "I have decided to make my home in the Soviet Union, to live and work there. I'm sorry to be so brief, but I can't say anything more at this time." Curious, Aleksei mused as he watched an excited throng of well-wishers mob the platform. Brenner hadn't stuck to the script, after all. Nothing about medicine's belonging to the world. Nothing about the indefinite duration of his stay in the Soviet Union.

Kiril managed to fight his way off the platform and onto the main floor of the banquet room, swept along by a frenetic tide of people. At least the tide was moving inexorably toward the exit, he thought gratefully. The cocktail lounge was engulfed just before he got to it, and he saw Adrienne being hit with a rush of eager faces and unintelligible questions.

"Mrs. Brenner," he heard a reporter from *Neues Deutschland* say, "I ask you again. Do you plan to join your husband in Moscow?"

She looked around, her expression dazed, and saw him struggling to reach her. "No comment," she said. "Please, I have nothing to say."

He was at her side, finally, saying, "No comment" over and over to the people pressing in on them. His hand on her arm was propelling her toward the bank of elevators.

He scanned the progress of an elevator on its way up, urging it to rise faster, telling himself there was nothing to be afraid of now, he had pulled it off, nothing could possibly go wrong— But when the elevator doors opened, Galya stood there.

Go to them. You must say goodby . . . especially to her. Hurry, before it's too late. The inner command had broken through Galya's lethargy after a telephone call to her room informed her of "the Brenners' imminent departure for Zurich." She had managed the corridor, the elevator button, the ride up to the banquet room.

She had run out of fuel. She couldn't move.

She felt a steadying hand and realized Dr. Brenner had dropped his wife's arm in order to grasp hers. It gave her the support she needed. She accomplished the small feat of stepping out of the elevator and into the lounge. The elevator doors closed, and she leaned against them.

"I'm glad you're here, Miss Barkova. My wife and I would have regretted not saying goodby."

Galya was looking at Adrienne. Impulsively she reached for her hand. "You will please to forgive," she whispered. "I have answered your kindness . . . so wonderful kindness . . . with insults. I am ashamed." The hollow pressure in back of her eyes was unshed tears.

"Please don't," Adrienne said gently.

But this is crazy, Galya thought, unable to understand

her own deep response to what she was reading in the American woman's face. *I feel as if I am saying goodby to a very old friend.* She said out loud, choking over the word: ''Goodby,'' and dropped the woman's hand. She turned to Dr. Brenner.

Oh God, she thought, her polite smile congealed on her face, *oh God! Don't let it show. Don't let me give him away! You're making it hard—don't look at me the way you did in Moscow—* ''Good luck to you, Dr. Brenner,'' she got out finally, forcing the hollow words past a barrier of fear and pain—fear that she would not make it through the next moment, and pain because she knew what would happen the moment after next. ''Whatever you do,'' she said, ''wherever you go, always good luck.'' The words were no longer hollow.

''You're very kind,'' he said, reaching for her hand, then dropping it as he pressed his lips against her forehead. ''Goodby, Galya dear,'' he whispered against her hair.

She pushed the elevator button herself. The doors opened obediently; the car had waited. She listened as the elevator carried them away.

She leaned against the closed doors again. How ironic, she thought. To fight such a violent emotion, to keep it under control, and then to almost give everything away. It had taken every shred of tattered resolve to stop herself from brushing away a few strands of hair that had fallen onto his forehead.

A voice cut into her thoughts. ''I think your services may be needed elsewhere, Nurse Barkova.''

''What do you mean, Colonel?'' she asked, turning slowly to face him.

''My brother is unconscious in the Brenner suite. I'll let *him* give you the embarrassing details when he wakes up.''

"I'll go to him at once." She became aware, suddenly, of the chaos all around her. "*Your* services seem to be needed right here," she remarked, puzzled.

"I've just pulled off an incredible coup—Dr. Brenner has defected," Aleksei said smugly. "He's coming over to us as soon as he deposits his intractable wife in Zurich."

"Congratulations," she said, and pressed the elevator button. And may Moscow take it out of your hide, she thought as she got into an elevator, for the "incredible coup" that is about to blow up in your face.

In the suite, she bent over the inert figure on the couch. Bravo, Kiril! she marveled. You seem to have thought of everything—even down to the redness in the left eye.

She opened the man's shirt, looking for the thin scar she had lightly followed with her finger on the beach yesterday—was it only yesterday? She rebuttoned the shirt . . . Kiril's shirt, she thought, and straightened the tie. She raised the head, pressed the eyelids open, and saw pupils shrunken to the size of pinpricks. She wondered what drug Kiril had used and how long it would last. She lifted one wrist, then lifted her own to check the pulse—and smiled bitterly at the memory of what had happened to her watch.

She wondered how much time Kiril would need. Not much, she thought, for the short drive to the airport and for takeoff. Not much for the flight itself. By the time the Colonel got through upstairs, the plane would be in Zurich.

She took a last look at the figure on the couch. "Good luck to you, Dr. Brenner," she said with a faint smile.

She smiled in sad reminiscence as she passed by the bedroom and saw, through the open closet door, a few garments hanging inside. She saw a patch of beige . . . a gown the color of rich cream? She went into the room. So you have given me your gift, after all, she thought bleakly. Thank you, my new . . . and very old . . . friend.

She left it there. She left the suite and walked slowly back toward her own room, accompanied by the odor of disinfectant. She stopped outside another door—Kiril's— and tried it; it was unlocked. The sight of his suitcase, lying empty on his bed, was hard to bear. The harder sight was the closet that wasn't empty. She went over to touch the things he had left behind . . . a robe, a few shirts and a pair of shoes, the new gray trousers they had picked out together the day they left Moscow.

I've been spared the hardest thing of all, she consoled herself. He never knew what I did. What I became.

She took a last, lingering look around, then a more purposeful one, in case something incriminating had been left behind—in case Dr. Brenner woke up ahead of schedule. Nothing. She checked out the bathroom. Nothing.

She scanned the metal shelf above the wash basin, moving closer for a better look. Her foot knocked over a wastebasket near the door. No razor on the shelf. None in the medicine cabinet. She shrugged, automatically stooping to pick up what had spilled out of the wastebasket. She saw a hypodermic needle. She saw a bottle labeled "morphine sulphate." Two-thirds full—about twenty cc's, she noted, staring at the objects in her hand.

She walked purposefully toward one of the beds, and passing a mirror, caught sight of her reflection. Drab black dress that matched the circles under her eyes. Hair pulled back, giving her the pinched, dry look of a spinster.

She rushed out of the room and down the corridor to the Brenner suite, to the bedroom.

Then she was standing, once more, in front of a long mirror in a cream-colored, floor-length gown, her hair flowing about her shoulders, a stale drink—a gin and tonic—in her hand. She tried to drink away her terror, her regrets, her desolation. She stopped herself before the glass was empty and raised it to her image, smiling defiantly. Again, she ordered. *Again.* She put the glass down and walked about the room until she was quite breathless, her head held high and her arms slightly apart, catching glimpses of herself whenever she passed the mirror, ending with a graceful pirouette. She smiled again, and the tears didn't matter—they really didn't—because *this* time her smile was right and true. She finished the drink and lay down on the bed.

How still he is, Aleksei thought. He should have revived by now.

He checked the time. Midnight. Could someone remain unconscious for over *two* hours from a simple blow on the head? And where the hell was the ministering angel? He leaned over to press his fingertips along the back of the scalp until he found the lump. Of course there was a lump! Why would Brenner lie about that? There was no reason to be uneasy, he thought, knowing he had been uneasy since he'd first laid eyes on Dr. Kurt Brenner. Understandable, in view of the uncanny likeness to Kiril. He reminded himself that there was nothing unique about men who bore a strong or even identical resemblance to other men—the Index was full of them. A trick of Nature, he thought, shrugging.

But the something-is-missing feeling, liberated now from the mental turmoil of a long, tension-filled day, leaped out at him. A clever man, he thought, would know how to turn a trick of Nature to his advantage. Was Kiril *that* clever—that devious? Or that desperate? Why didn't the man wake up? Could he be drugged? Dr. Brenner would have no conceivable reason to drug Kiril, but— He finished the thought reluctantly. Kiril would have good reason to drug Brenner, wouldn't he? Why didn't the possibility occur to me sooner? he groaned, and heard Luka stir restlessly behind him.

He knew why. There had been too many distractions, too much pressure, and no time for his usual attention to detail. No time to track down uneasiness and follow it through to its source . . .

He stared at the form on the couch, thinking that the hair looked peculiar. He pulled at a few strands, wishing he could pull the brain into consciousness. He went at it systematically, choosing hairs at random. The hair was real. It was also slightly damp. Odd. He took off the dark glasses, remembering suddenly that Kiril was supposed to have some kind of an eye infection. Left eye, he thought tensely, lifting the lid. Then he released it. He turned to Luka, the relief obvious in his face. "See if Miss Barkova is back in her room."

"She is asleep," Luka said.

"Really? You checked her room again?"

Luka smiled, as if he had been saving a small joke. "She is asleep *here*," he said, pointing to the partly open bedroom door.

What's the matter with her? Aleksei wondered, frowning. She was stretched out on the bed, fully clothed. "Galina," he said sharply. Then he noticed the belt of a black dress tied around her arm. And a hypodermic needle.

"Why?" he said aloud, fear in his voice and numbness in his chest, as Luka, suddenly alert, began to examine the body.

There are things a woman can see—and sense—more easily than a man. Had he been prophetic when he'd told her that in Moscow? Had she indeed sensed what he had not? What was the matter of "great urgency" she had wanted to speak to him about this afternoon? he thought in sudden panic. "I *must* know. I can't stand not to know!" he cried to a bewildered Luka. "There are *three* different possibilities, do you realize that? If it's Kiril Andreyevich on that couch, unconscious from a blow, then Brenner will be back. But if Kiril has been drugged, then he must have tried to stop Brenner from leaving—and then Brenner *won't* be back!"

Aleksei started to pace; the numbness in chest and arms had slipped down to his feet. "Do I turn Malik loose tomorrow? Do I consult first with Moscow? If I expose Brenner, does that help *my* situation, or make it worse?" Worse, he concluded silently. In East Berlin, Dr. Kurt Brenner plans to defect, but in Zurich, he does not. How can Malik confess his ugly secret on the heels of *that* without it looking like failed blackmail?

He felt Luka's eyes loyally pursuing him back and forth across the room. He stopped abruptly. "The third possibility is *much* worse," he said slowly to those eyes, even though he knew their function was, not to comprehend, but to reassure. And to distract him from the scissor cuts in his stomach. "If the man on the couch is Dr. Brenner, then Kiril is on his way to Zurich." Why *else* would this woman kill herself? If he's escaped, that means the resurrection of my family history and no way, this time, to bury it. *Two* traitors—two Enemies of the People! I was a boy when my mother left with Kolya, so no one could hold me responsible. But look what they did to my father. *What will they do to me?*

He knew what they would do. An outraged Dr. Kurt Brenner would go home and display his bruises to the world, confirming what the world had seen on its television screens: a clever impersonation by the brother of a colonel in the Soviet secret police—a trick played on a banquet hall full of Party dignitaries. The joke of the century! A joke my country will not live down for a long time, he thought. As for me, I will not live at all.

He jammed his eyes shut, as if the terrifying rush of disaster could be stemmed by turning off his eyesight. "They looked and sounded so much alike," he groaned. "How could I have told them apart? How could anyone?" He opened his eyes to check the time, and closed them again. Too late to call the airport and radio the pilot to return—even if he dared, not knowing which possibility he was confronting. Too late, too late. When I release Brenner tomorrow—

His eyes flashed open. "When," he said slowly, "or *if*? Suppose we claim that Brenner changed his mind about the family reunion in Zurich, deciding to go straight to Moscow from here? Who could prove otherwise? Who could prove it really wasn't Brenner speaking into that microphone at the banquet? What if, in all the confusion that broke out *after* Brenner's announcement, my brother waited for his chance, pretended to be Brenner, and faked his way out of East Berlin?"

Aleksei grabbed the telephone on the night table and gave the operator a Zurich number. He replaced the receiver cautiously. "We may survive," he told Luka shakily. "We may salvage something from the disaster . . . if the worst is true. We won't know until he meets with the press in Zurich." He gritted his teeth in an agony of frustration. "Whoever *'he'* is," he said.

19

The plane shuddered. The cabin seemed to roll over on its side.

"We'll be running into some turbulence over the Alps," the pilot had predicted euphemistically. The ultimate irony, Kiril thought. I am going to crash on my unobstructed way from East Berlin to Zurich.

Adrienne moaned beside him, apparently still on the edge of airsickness.

He looked at her. Her eyes were still closed. She'd been asleep a good part of the trip, or as good as asleep, from the effects of the alcohol. It had made things easier.

The sky cleared abruptly and turned calm. The plane shifted direction.

"We're going down."

Adrienne nodded. Her eyes opened, then closed again.

Kiril stared out the window, transfixed by the most luxurious lighting display he had ever seen. Blues and greens, reds and yellows and whites . . . the blinking, cheerful exuberance of neon. Zurich, flashing a welcome to a being from another planet. I'm forty-seven, he thought wonderingly. I have no work, no money, no friends. I don't even own the clothes on my back. I have never felt so young or so confident of the future. Future? The word had no meaning in the Soviet Union. One lived from day to day. All the days are mine, now, he thought. I will need time to get used to that. I have all the time in the world. What shall I do with it? Dream without restraint, he promised himself. Make plans. Change them, if I feel like it. Make frivolous decisions, or serious ones, or none at all. What was the American expression that summed it all up? No holds barred. *No holds barred.*

He glanced at Adrienne. I'll be free to fall in love, he thought, remembering how emotional commitments in his country had been pitfalls to be avoided; lurking at the bottom of the pit was the hostage system.

He tensed with the sudden thud of the plane's wheels on the runway, the vibrations streaking through his body like hot wires. He almost bolted from his seat, and had to grip both its arms while he counted the seconds. Taxiing . . . slowing and turning . . . halt. Someone opened a door. He forgot about Adrienne's suitcase. He forgot to help her out of the window seat and stand aside so she could go first. He saw an open door and he moved toward it. A noisy cluster of people waiting at the bottom of the steps didn't register. He saw pavement. I want to kneel on it, he thought. I want to kiss the ground. But the instant his foot made contact, he was overwhelmed by a sweet, solemn wonder. He had to stop himself from shouting: I made it, Stepan! Anna . . . Kolya . . . look at me! *I'm here!*

"Look this way, please, Dr. Brenner."

A flashbulb went off in his face, then an unbroken series

of them, popping like firecrackers, reducing the runway to white glare. He raised his arm like a shield, blinking to clear his vision.

"Is it true that you're defecting to the Soviet Union?"

"Are you here to say goodby to your parents?"

"What about your wife? Does she stay or go?"

"When do you leave for Moscow?"

"What's behind the defection? Was your family aware of your plans all along?"

"What *are* your plans, Dr. Brenner?"

Most of the questions pitched at him were in rapid-fire English. A few were in German. He waited.

Adrienne stood groggily at his side.

As soon as the voices began to subside, he said quietly, "I want to make a statement." He took a cautious few steps away from the plane. "But not here. Is there someplace we could go at this hour?"

"One of the VIP lounges," someone suggested.

"Right this way, Dr. Brenner . . . Mrs. Brenner. It's a short walk to the terminal," an American newsman said. A hint of disapproval crossed his face. "Your mother and father are in a bad way," he said. "They've refused to make a statement until they've talked to you."

"Where are they?" Kiril said tensely.

"Somewhere on the terminal grounds. No one knew exactly what time your plane was due. Or whether you'd even show up. A few of us diehards hung around just in case. I'm pretty sure your parents are still here. Would you like me to find them and bring them to the VIP lounge?"

"I would, yes. I must talk with them before I talk to the press. Can you arrange it?"

"Sure. I'll see that no one disturbs your privacy. How long will it take?"

"Not long," Kiril said unhappily, as they walked briskly toward the main terminal. There was no way, he knew, to spare Brenner's parents, no way to explain why he was here in their son's place without also revealing what Brenner had threatened to do to him. And why. *Even if I skip over the details,* he realized, *it will all come out when Brenner arrives tomorrow. The only thing I can do is deliver the blow in private. And the blow to Adrienne Brenner, how can I bring myself to deliver that?* he thought, conscious of her hand on his arm, of the way she'd been looking at him all evening—*as Brenner, or as myself?* he wondered. She was smiling up at him now, as he held the door of the lounge open. *The polite distance between her and her husband—did I dream it?* he asked himself. *Perhaps it had all been wishful thinking.*

The American newsman was saying something to a sleepy-eyed bartender at an empty bar; the two men left.

"Tell me everything!" Adrienne said as soon as the door closed. She shrugged off her cape.

How incongruous we both look, he thought. *Evening clothes in some darkened airport lounge in the middle of the night.* He thought that her manner of dressing was as intriguing as she was: a cape with thick, protective folds . . . a black bathing suit with a modest neckline . . . the severe lines of a pantsuit, softened by ruffles of foam at her throat and her thin wrists. And this ice-green gown that revealed nothing and suggested everything.

"Kurt," she said softly, and came into his arms.

The shock of sudden contact fused with a succession of blazing images: her body elusive under a wind-blown cape— her body half exposed to the sun, lying submissive at his feet—her body pressed against his, thin layers of silk stressing the curves and hollows he'd drawn so many times in his imagination—

"—so when I saw the lighter with the emblem, I guessed your real intention," she was saying against his ear. "I'm so proud of you, darling. I feel so full of love and pride that I—"

He held her to him with a hungry, punishing violence. He sought her lips with the same kind of violence and went on seeking even after he'd found them, indifferent to her sudden resistance.

She broke free and backed away from him, breathing in gasps, the back of one hand pressed against her mouth.

"I'm sorry," he said when his own breathing was normal. "I had no right to do that."

She dropped her hand. "What have you done to Kurt?"

"He's still in East Berlin."

"Of his own free will? What kind of masquerade is this?"

"I never intended it to happen this way. Your husband left me no choice. At the moment he's unconscious from a harmless drug."

"*You* did that to him?"

"Yes," he said, his voice hard.

"Why, for God's sake? What did you hope to gain?"

"My freedom."

She stared at him. "What about Kurt's?"

"Don't worry, he's safe enough. After I reveal my identity to those newsmen outside and expose the Dr. Kurt Brenner defection hoax, your husband will be free to leave. They wouldn't dare to detain a man of his prominence—especially after the publicity."

"Who wouldn't dare? Why would they want to detain him?"

"My brother Aleksei is embroiled in some kind of a propaganda game. I can only guess at the other players—his particular branch of the secret police, military intelligence, the higher echelons of the Kremlin."

"Then your brother really is in the secret police," she said, looking confused, "and not—" She broke off, shaking her head. "I don't understand any of this. Why did you make that announcement and pretend to be Kurt? Or was it really Kurt at the podium? It was you in the cocktail lounge afterward and you on the plane—I know, because we were together the whole time. But how do I know *who* it was in the banquet room? You could have switched places or . . ." She closed her eyes for a moment, then said quietly, "You wouldn't be trying to hide the truth from me, would you? Kurt really isn't going to defect, is he?"

Kiril sat down, not looking at her.

"*Is* he?"

"Your husband is not defecting. I am the one who made that announcement."

"Then what's the *matter* with you?"

"Something you said. Something that never occurred to me. I hope to God it doesn't occur to my brother."

"Are you implying they might *not* let him go?"

"It's possible. If Dr. Brenner's *wife* could suspect the defection was genuine, why not the rest of the world? My brother is entirely capable of claiming what you were afraid of just now—that, for reasons of my own, I switched places with Dr. Brenner *after* the announcement. If your husband were kept in a semi-drugged state and paraded in front of the cameras—not too close, just close enough to make it look good—they could get away with it. After a while, they might even trust him with a microphone and a rehearsed speech," he added grimly. "Drugs and black-mail make a powerful persuader."

"What are you going to do about this?"

He spread his hands in a gesture of futility. "The only thing I can—tell the truth and hope people believe me. Aleksei would make it look like a personal vendetta of some kind and claim I'd say or do anything to embarrass the regime." He shrugged. "I can't believe people would take him seriously, not unless your husband cooperated."

"But they might take him seriously? Kurt might cooperate?"

"Look, none of this may have even occurred to my brother."

"But it's possible?"

He sighed. "It's possible."

"*Damn you*. You had no right to do this."

"You're wrong. I acted in self-defense. Your husband trades in human lives. I never wished this on him, God knows," he said angrily, "but if they won't let him go, it will be the most eloquent justice ever visited on a man."

"They're here." Adrienne rose reluctantly to answer the knock on the door. "What are you going to tell them?"

"What I lost the courage to tell you."

"Will you tell them their son trades in human lives?" she said flatly. "They're under the impression that he saves them." She crossed the room and pulled the door open.

The press was buzzing with impatience, held in check by the American newsman, who'd assumed unofficial command. Dr. Max Brenner, grim and ashen, entered the lounge with his wife. He paused to clasp Adrienne's shoulder for a moment. Then he closed the four of them inside.

Adrienne remained, like a sentinel, by the door.

Max Brenner held his wife's arm—a useless restraint that she shrugged off. She crossed the room to Kiril.

He stood up to meet her . . . and felt a rush of gratitude for the strength he recognized in the set of her mouth and in the dark, vital eyes that searched his without flinching. It would make what he had to tell her easier, he thought. She was a step away when he recognized more than strength in her eyes; he saw such a smoldering anger that for a moment he thought she was going to strike him.

"Tell me," she said evenly. "Tell me to my face."

He dropped his eyes, needing a moment to gather his own strength. In that moment, his glance touched her throat.

It was the tiny gold microscope that registered first. His aunt had drawn a picture of it once. He picked out the others, suspended from a flat gold band by threadlike pieces of wire: the thermometer . . . the stethoscope . . . the reflex hammer . . . the doctor's head mirror. A sixth piece of wire, from which nothing hung, was faintly visible against her skin.

"Tell me how you can do this, Kurt. And then tell me why."

Kurt. He felt like a tightrope walker on a windy day, fighting for balance.

Kolya. He felt himself slip and fall into the abyss.

He looked into a face he had loved all his life and said goodby to when he was not yet three. A face forever with him, forever lost. He reached out to touch it—and felt nothing. His arms had not moved from his sides.

"Are you going to tell me or not?"

He saw her mouth moving, that was all. He seemed to

have lost every sense but sight. He stood there, drinking in the sight of her.

"My *son*," she said. There was something menacing in the sound of that word on her tongue. "You are going to do this thing?"

He saw a look that seemed to border on hate, and even though he knew it was meant for Kurt Brenner, he accepted it as penance for the wrong he had done her. He sensed the pain and horror that lay beneath the iron control which was keeping her body erect and her voice calm. How can you endure this? he asked her silently. To spend a lifetime of guilt and pain over a hostage child you had to abandon in order to save his brother—and to hear the object of that bitter sacrifice say calmly on television: I have decided to make my home in the Soviet Union!

His eyes grew full but hers were dry, he thought, with no forgiveness in them.

He forgave her instantly. Did you think I wouldn't understand? That I would hate you for leaving me behind? Oh Anna, Anna, I have had only one obsession in my life—to find you again. To tell you that what you did was right, and to set you free of a guilt you should never have had to bear. To free you as you freed Kolya.

And now they'll know Kurt Brenner is Kolya Andreyev and they'll never let him go.

Can you endure a little longer? he thought. Give me twenty-four hours and I will send your son back to you . . . if I can.

Then he thought of the first welcoming lights of Zurich—of the moment when his foot touched freedom.

I can't do it. Not even for you!

He felt his chest burning . . . or was it only the tiny

gold scalpel around his neck, demanding to take its place on a flat, gold band?

He walked across the lounge with brisk authority. He flung open the door. "Gentlemen," he said, as newsmen poured into the room and jockeyed for position around him, "my statement will be brief. I plan to practice heart surgery in the Soviet Union. My decision has been a long time in coming. It is final. I came here tonight because I wanted no doubt in anyone's mind about the genuineness of the announcement I made in East Berlin a few hours ago. You asked me about my immediate plans. They are to get back on the plane that brought me here. Tomorrow, I will begin my new life in Moscow."

The newsmen broke away when they saw Anna Brenner advancing like some avenging angel.

She slapped Kiril across the face.

His head reeled—from the impact and from the terrible irony.

Flashbulbs popped, recording the slap for posterity and a readership of millions. Cameras panned for reaction shots of a family in chaos. And retreat; Max and Anna Brenner left the lounge.

Adrienne hadn't moved from her post by the door. "Gentlemen, listen to me! Will someone please listen to me?" She was shouting over the din. "I have a statement of my own to make, and it will *not* be brief. I—"

"Wait."

The commotion in the room collapsed into silence as Kiril walked over to her.

"Wait," he repeated.

"You can't stop me," she said coldly.

He grabbed her arm and pulled her through the door, slamming it before anyone could react. "Say one more word and you throw away the only chance I have of rescuing your husband," he said in a low voice.

"You're going back for him?"

"I must. But it has to be as Kurt Brenner, not Kiril Andreyev."

"Why did you change your mind?"

He wouldn't answer.

"I don't trust you."

"You'll have to. If we're not out in twenty-four hours, make your statement. Tell them your husband was being blackmailed for something he did a long time ago. Tell them that he resisted and is being held against his will." He took off the gold charm and pressed it into her hand. "Tell them I was an imposter and then give this to your mother-in-law. She'll be able to back up your story."

"I *still* don't trust you." She dropped the charm into his jacket pocket without looking at it. She went back inside and spoke to a circle of tense, startled faces. "That statement I wanted to make will be brief, after all," she said. "I have decided to accompany my husband to East Berlin. If necessary, I'll accompany him to Moscow. I hope to persuade him to change his mind about this."

Kiril watched from the doorway while they mobbed her with questions.

"I can't answer you," she told them, "but I have a request to make." They waited. "Wish me luck," she said quietly.

20

Max Brenner sat up in bed, awakened by a dull thud. "Anna?" he said cautiously.

"I'm sorry. I dropped my shoe."

"Can't you sleep?"

"No. I'm going for a walk."

He got up, turned on the light, and sat beside her on the other bed while she finished dressing. "It's two o'clock in the morning," he said gently. "We have an early plane to catch."

"There are other planes to New York. We'll catch a later flight."

"I'll come with you," he offered. "The streets will be empty."

She shook her head. "Zurich is an old friend. I want to be alone with her." She touched his face for a moment, then dropped her hand and got up.

"Anna?"

She turned around at the door.

"Take a doctor's advice. Cry, if you can."

"I don't know how."

No, he thought, as the door closed, no tears. Never any tears for Anna.

Zurich is an old friend, Anna repeated to herself as she stepped out of the hotel lobby. It was a long walk down a steep hill to the center of the city, but she knew she wouldn't notice the distance; she never had. She had walked up and down this hill and along these streets over and over, to pass the time. To make the waiting easier. Because Zurich had been the stopping-off point, the bridge that led from Berlin to New York, and a new life in a new country.

The waiting had been hard because there had been so much to wait for. For fear to be replaced, with each passing day, by the conviction that she was safe from the long arm of Soviet retribution. For the visits of a young American doctor—a surgeon she had met in Berlin, and admired, as he assisted in an operation that had saved her baby's life. For her young doctor to complete the last days of his two-year training program under the greatest heart surgeon in Germany; perhaps in all of Europe. For papers to come through which would "prove" she was a native-born German, and more papers which would "document" that the young doctor was the father of her year-and-a-half-old son.

When the waiting was over, the captain of a ship bound for America had no reason not to "legitimize" the baby and grant her the happiness—the honor—of becoming Mrs. Max Brenner. The world-renowned heart surgeon from Berlin, she realized that morning on the ship, had given

Kolya back his life. Max Brenner had given him a name and the chance to live that life to the fullest.

Kurt never really had, she thought. His spectacular achievements—and they were spectacular—had always been marred by his ugly, self-defeating need for approval and his taste for flattery. He had been flattered by his first invitation to a widely publicized medical exchange in Russia and had accepted without telling her—in stubborn defiance of the one thing she had asked him never to do. She had made him back down by the sheer force of her will and persistence, so it had not been necessary to tell him things he was better off not knowing. "You're unreasonable," he had told her resentfully. "What have the Communists ever done to you that you should hate them so?"

Nothing special, she had wanted to say, nothing they hadn't done to countless others. She was only one student among many whose careers were disrupted by the Revolution and whose husbands were inspired to quit school and join the Red Army. She had been left the awkward task of explaining to her family a secret marriage and a baby on the way. She was only one wife among many who saw their love turn to contempt, felt contempt turn to fear, as their husbands took an active role in implementing the New Order. "Become a doctor for both of us," her husband had told her. "I've lost my taste for medicine." What he hadn't said was that he'd acquired a taste for blood.

There was nothing she could do about it. She had lost the ability to reach him. She was left with three goals in life. Keep her husband isolated from their young son, Aleksei. Avoid her husband whenever possible. Keep herself isolated from the nightmare universe produced by the "Great October Socialist Revolution." She had accomplished two of her goals—at first, through long hours of study that kept her away from their flat and semi-detached from politics, and later, through an exhausting work schedule at the polyclinic that left her no time to think or feel. It also left her with little time to offset what was happening to her son. She had known almost from the beginning that she would lose the battle for Aleksei, no matter how much time she put into it—that she was out-maneuvered for reasons she had never been able to comprehend. Horrified, she witnessed her son's gradual conversion, under his father's sometimes patient, sometimes boisterous tutelage, from a timid, introverted boy into a sadistic little bully.

She had vowed never to have another child. She had lost that battle, too. Twice. Kiril was conceived on a night when her usual deftness at putting her husband off with an excuse was met with unusual resistance, fortified by vodka. Kolya was conceived under the same circumstances, and born less than a year later. She had not wanted to bring them into the chamber of horrors that was her world. But strangely, their coming had filled her life with an impossible optimism. It was hard not to feel it in the presence of two such wholesome little beings, with their boundless energy and their playful inquisitiveness—qualities, her own father used to remind her, they had inherited from their mother. They had also inherited her features, miniature mirrors of her face and each other's.

It was a combination of vodka and inquisitiveness that brought about the accident: Her husband, seemingly injured from a drunken fall, calling for her; the boys alone for a moment with her medical bag; a scream that pierced her heart an instant after the lancet pierced Kolya's, missing the actual chamber but slicing into the muscle of the left ventricle. The lack of bleeding, the dusky complexion, the

276

feeble pulse, all suggested that a layer of muscle had temporarily closed over the small opening made by the instrument. Her colleagues had voiced guarded opinions; no one was sure how best to proceed. But she had been sure. Kolya needed an immediate operation that was not available in the Soviet Union; no doctor was capable of performing it. She knew of one in Germany who was. She argued and pleaded with her husband. Then, in desperation, she resorted to one of his own interrogation tactics: she capitalized on his guilt. With a mercilessness she hadn't known she possessed, she turned his remorse over the accident against him, pressing and bullying until he capitulated. He ranked high enough in the Party and the secret police to get her the necessary permission to go to Berlin and engage the surgeon who had recently done the first successful suture of a human heart—and whose patients were given only a forty per cent chance of recovery. She even got permission to go by plane—a train was out of the question in 1925; Kolya had fifteen or twenty hours and they had over a thousand miles to cover. She had had no thoughts of defecting while she sat in a flimsy, wind-tossed aircraft, hugging her baby to her, checking the hour and clocking the mileage each interminable time the plane set down to refuel. They had made Berlin in thirteen and a half hours.

Only when Kolya was recuperating from the operation did she consider not going back, a natural consequence of falling in love. A tentative hope became a possibility, thanks to the right documents provided by Max's relatives in Berlin, and to friends who had previous experience outwitting the Soviet watchdog mentality. His parents in America came through with money—more than enough to arrange for hospital records showing that patient Nikolai

Andreyevich Andreyev had expired on the operating table. "Kolya" had to die so that "Kurt" could live. The chance to live again was hers, too, if she wanted it.

She wanted it. She just didn't want to make the decision to go—or, more precisely, to leave behind. She was only one parent, among God knows how many, forced to choose between freedom and family. There were moments when she was ready to die rather than make that choice. Her family included a son already lost to her, and a son who would be lost without her—who would have only his Aunt Maria, the sister of an Enemy of the People, to act as a buffer for the terrible blows in store for him.

In the end she did not have to choose between freedom and family after all, but between one family member over another. Whatever she could do for Kiril if she went back, she knew, was infinitely less than what she could do for Kolya if she didn't. Kólya had narrowly escaped a death sentence. How could she sentence him to life imprisonment? In the end she chose, not her own freedom, but his.

Did I sacrifice one child to the other? No, she told herself, weary with the question she had been asking and answering all these years. What I made possible for Kurt was never open to Kiril. Had I gone back, it would truly have been a sacrifice of brother to brother. Then why, after so many years, can't I hear the word "abandonment" without a shudder of guilt? Must I now add remorse to it?

In the years since, she thought, haven't I compounded my original crime against Kiril by not making inquiries, by not even trying to let him know that a day never passes without his name on my lips? She sighed deeply. Another question with no easy answer. Max had been persuasive: any attempt to make contact would have been more than painful to Kiril, and worse than futile; it would have been dangerous. Would it have? she wondered. Would it still? Kurt had benefited by that decision, too. He had never known any father but Max, not even in his imagination.

She stopped walking. It was time, she thought, that Kurt be introduced to the father he deserved, that he know his true heritage. Son of a dedicated surgeon? Of a loving, gentle man to emulate and be proud of? No, by God! Son of a drunkard. Son of a man who could have been a doctor and chose instead to be jailer and murderer.

She hailed a taxi. It was time, she decided, to communicate with her other sons as well, if only indirectly. It was time for justice. Justice was truth, wasn't it?

The taxi was climbing the hill when it occurred to her that everything she wanted to say to Kiril could be summed up by a simple fact of her existence, by the necklace she put on each morning. Not because of the gold charms on it, she thought; because of a tiny, almost weightless piece of wire. The touch of it on her skin kept him with her even when she closed her eyes.

Her eyes were open when the tears began, like raindrops spilling down the carved features of a statue in a park.

21

Outside the window was a black void. Somewhere below, two rows of harsh yellow circles cut parallel paths through the darkness. They blinked hypnotically, and the plane, unresisting, went down.

Adrienne studied the man sitting next to her. "For the last time," she said, when his glance shifted from the window to her face, "will you *please* tell me your plan?"

"I'll tell you this much. If anything goes wrong with it, you'll wish you'd stayed in Zurich," Kiril said, preoccupied.

"Won't you at least give me some idea of what to expect?"

"Sorry. I don't trust you any more than you trust me. Let's leave it at that."

Impulsively, she reached into his jacket pocket and pulled out his cigarette lighter. "Why didn't you leave the film safely behind in Zurich, Dr. Andreyev?"

He snatched the lighter back. "What in God's name do you know about that?"

"I'll tell you. *After* you tell me your plan."

The plane's wheels had just jolted onto the runway. "No time now," he said tensely. "Not a word about this in front of my brother, Aleksei, do you understand me?"

As the plane taxied to a stop, Adrienne stared at the pocket into which Kiril had slipped the lighter. She looked puzzled.

He caught her glance, and looked worried.

They got up as soon as the door was opened, and Kiril helped her to the ground. Just before Aleksei walked up to them from a parked limousine, Kiril said to her, "Trust me."

Aleksei, rumpled and red-eyed from lack of sleep, surveyed them silently.

"Where is my husband?" Adrienne finally demanded.

"So you know." Aleksei sounded weary. "I just found out myself—barely an hour ago. Dr. Brenner is still at the hotel, quite recovered from the effects of a drug called diazepam." He turned to Kiril, ignoring the hand extended to him in greeting. "You played your part to perfection," he said in Russian. "I know what you did in Zurich—what you told the Western press. What I don't know is why. Or why you came back. Brenner told me all about the elaborate preparations you made." His eyes traveled to Kiril's hair, then shifted abruptly back to his face. "When Brenner told me what you've been up to," he said slowly, "I calculated things quite differently."

"I'm sure you did," Kiril said dryly in unaccented English. He glanced at Adrienne, as if willing her to listen carefully. "All those years of surveillance, when you tracked every move I made," he went on, "what did they add up to? That, given half a chance, I would have defected to the West? True enough. But you never asked yourself one thing: What is he *really* after? A future, Aleksei. I had no future in my own country, no way to rise above the level of a glorified mechanic—*your* words, remember? How right you were!" His face looked bitter. "*You* had the magic formula, didn't you? You knew how to cope with the family stigma. You asked me last week why I never went to you for help, and I answered with an insult. You could have guessed the real reason—pride. You never sought me out or offered your help. You waited for me to come begging for it. I don't like to beg." He smiled thinly. "Permit me to gloat a little, Brother," he said. "After my performance tonight, I won't have to beg for my future, will I?"

Aleksei was frowning with concentration. "I begin to understand. Your English," he said cautiously, reverting to English himself, "it is very impressive, very colloquial. There is no trace of an accent. How did you manage to hide such an achievement?"

"Ask me what you *really* want to know—why I went to Zurich and came back again. From this point on, I want no more secrets between us."

"Until tonight," Aleksei said thoughtfully, "I never thought there were any."

"Until your little talk with Brenner, you mean? Everything he told you was true. Why deny it? I *did* make elaborate preparations in Moscow—as soon as I chanced on a certain photograph in Brenner's file."

"So it was you . . ."

"My preparations climaxed in Brenner's room tonight. I didn't go there to stop him from leaving. I went to persuade him to leave his passport behind just before he boarded for Zurich. He refused me. Playing the good samaritan isn't exactly his style," Kiril said caustically.

He glanced again at Adrienne. She had been listening intently. Now, her eyes seemed wider.

"Brenner agreed to help me only if I helped him first." Kiril shrugged. "Naturally, I was in no position to do that. I didn't even know what the blackmail business was all about. I did know that your plans for him were big. Then it hit me! I was in a unique position to make a substantial contribution to those important plans of yours. I thought that if I could just take Brenner's place on *this* side of the Curtain and get away with it, if I could pull a switch and fool my own brother—not to mention Brenner's wife— then my chances of fooling people on the other side would be excellent. I gave it a try. What the hell did I have to lose, compared with what I had to gain? And I succeeded admirably, didn't I? My future here is secure, now." A touch of anxiety crept into his voice. "Isn't it, Aleksei? It's far more secure than if I'd fled like some beggar to the West, with nothing waiting for me on the other side. No work. No money. No . . . friends." As if to underscore this last, he slipped his arm familiarly around Adrienne's shoulder. She pulled away, glaring. "See what I mean?" he said resentfully.

"Let's go," Aleksei said, steering Adrienne toward his waiting limousine.

"You know the rest," Kiril continued as they walked. "The details aren't important. Just consider that I've made you a gift of *two* press conferences. The one here might have convinced the world that Brenner defected voluntarily— might. It was restricted to newsmen from the Soviet bloc, after all. The one in Zurich left no room for doubt, did it?" He laughed. "I even fooled Brenner's own mother."

Adrienne was walking stiffly ahead of them.

"And his wife?" Aleksei asked, watching her.

Kiril lowered his voice. "She suspected nothing until we were back on the plane." He chuckled.

"Mrs. Brenner seems understandably distraught. You seem incredibly pleased with yourself."

"Shouldn't I be? *Your* plan failed. Brenner was leaving, wasn't he? It gives me great satisfaction to turn your defeat into my victory—I admit it."

"Does it also amuse you to have made a fool of me?"

"By masquerading as Brenner? No," Kiril said slowly, "no, I was just being practical. If I'd confessed my plan ahead of time, would you have trusted me out of the country?"

Aleksei smiled in tentative surrender, then shook his head slowly as if to shake off remaining doubts. "It will take getting used to, this new conception of a brother who is an asset instead of a thorny liability. It still seems preposterous."

They had reached the limousine. Kiril blocked his way. "I came back, didn't I?" he said quietly.

The intensity of Aleksei's glance matched Kiril's. "You came back. An unanswerable argument." He extended his hand to complete the greeting Kiril had offered outside the plane, as if sealing their new understanding. "I seldom make mistakes of judgment. It seems I made a bad one in your case." He helped Adrienne into the car. "It is much too late to celebrate," he said to Kiril, who followed him inside. "Suppose we do it tomorrow morning before leaving for Moscow. We shall have a leisurely breakfast in my suite—and toast our triumphant homecoming."

Kiril clapped Aleksei on the back. "I can see it now: a couple of returning heroes who managed to snatch victory from the jaws of defeat." He was smiling.

Adrienne sank back against the cushions, remembering

what Kiril had told her: trust me. Do I really have any choice? she thought, wondering how much of what she'd overheard was really true. Then she thought about the help he had sought—and been refused—unwilling to believe it. But when she remembered about the blackmail hanging over Kurt's head, she wasn't sure.

About anything.

Kiril smiled at the morning sunshine streaming through the windows of the hotel lobby as he and Aleksei stepped off an elevator. They started across the room, their steps leisurely, in perfect unison. Aleksei talked with animated gestures. Kiril's hands were occupied: he carried his plastic suitcase in one hand and Aleksei's plump briefcase in the other. As they approached a couch on which the Brenners were sitting, Kiril noticed that the two of them were staring: Mrs. Brenner at him and Aleksei, and Brenner at Aleksei's briefcase.

"I trust you had a substantial breakfast to fortify you for the trip to Moscow," Aleksei said, smiling down on them benignly. "Since we make up the entire passenger list, I expect the crew will not be serving refreshments. No, don't get up," he said as Adrienne started out of her seat. "We are not quite ready to leave." He paused, looking from Brenner to Kiril, as if he were struck, once again, by the likeness.

Kiril's eyes moved to Brenner—and stayed there. He felt on the edge of some violent emotion: he caught it and pushed it back. He noticed, again, Brenner's too-obvious interest in the briefcase. He said, to distract him, "I see that you've opted to go back to white hair, Dr. Brenner. How amusing that you chose to get rid of the rinse, while I chose to put it back. But then, the masquerade is over, isn't it?'' As Brenner arched a contemptuous eyebrow, Kiril found himself wondering about the hair. Prematurely white? Or did he bleach it—an affectation to make him look distinguished?

"You two are surprisingly docile," Aleksei observed. "Getting resigned to a lengthy sojourn in Moscow, are you? I do hope you understand my position, Mrs. Brenner. I cannot possibly let you go now."

Adrienne shrugged. "My place is with my husband," she said flatly.

"Charming. Ah, here is Luka. We can leave, after all."

"Not without Galya, I hope." Kiril looked around the lobby. "She's always so prompt. It's not like her to keep people waiting."

"I'm sorry," Aleksei said in Russian, touching Kiril's shoulder sympathetically.

"Sorry about what?" Kiril said tensely in Russian. "Has something happened to Galya?"

"Something irrevocable. She's dead, Kiril. She killed herself right after you left for Zurich."

He sat down, forgetting to let go of the luggage.

"I've made the necessary arrangements. Her body will be shipped back to Moscow. Kiril, there's nothing you can do."

"Why didn't you tell me?"

"And mar an otherwise perfect homecoming? Frankly, I put off telling you as long as possible." He glanced meaningfully at Adrienne. "Don't blame yourself too much. Galina's unrequited love had tarnished edges. She's been spying on you for the last two years in exchange for a few trinkets." Aleksei looked thoughtful for a moment. "She didn't give you away in the end, though, did she?"

Kiril stood up. But he dropped the luggage.

Pick up the briefcase, he ordered himself. You can leave your suitcase, but *not* the briefcase, because you are automatically being helpful—Aleksei won't be suspicious if you take it with you. Now, walk away slowly. You are a stunned man—Aleksei will expect that. You need a few minutes to grieve in private . . . to grope for some kind of meaning in this . . .

He walked out of the lobby. Slowly. A stunned man, needing privacy and groping for some kind of meaning. It was true enough.

Spying on him, he thought. For two years. For things like her new gold watch? He had been right not to trust her. And yet, he had trusted her in the end—impulsively— and she hadn't betrayed him. Had she killed herself out of a sense of loss and abandonment? No, he thought, that may have been part of it, but guilt had to have been the greater part. He had seen it happen so often in the camps, in Siberia. A desperate man or woman, driven to abandon honor or scruples in order to stay alive for one more day, and when the next day came, unable to live with whatever they had done. Galya had been driven, too, in her own way, struggling to keep a dying spirit alive with a few pathetic symbols of that better life she craved. Trinkets, Aleksei had called them!

Don't blame yourself too much—he repeated Aleksei's words as he watched his brother emerge from the hotel with the Brenners in tow. It's *you* I blame, Aleksei, he thought, you and your insidious system of co-optees.

He waited for them in the limousine, sitting next to the window on the left side after putting the briefcase on the jumpseat in front of him. He watched the Mongolian carrying the suitcase he'd abandoned in the lobby.

Aleksei opened the car door. "Feeling better?" he asked, sitting next to him.

"I'm all right."

Adrienne got in, leaving Brenner with the window seat on the right. Luka took his usual place next to the driver.

"I know what will cheer you up," Aleksei said in Russian as the limousine pulled away from the curb. "It's close to noon. The symposium in West Berlin should be getting under way. Would you care to eavesdrop on a little pandemonium, courtesy of one Kiril Andreyev—alias Dr. Kurt Brenner?" He slid open the glass partition.

"I don't feel much like gloating," Kiril answered.

"It's an acquired taste. Why not give it a try? Luka, turn on the radio so we can all hear."

"Our friend might not find it so amusing," Kiril said, looking over at Brenner. Our . . . friend.

"We're a little early," Aleksei commented over the rippling chords of a Chopin étude.

The music was loud, masking the silence, making conversation unnecessary. Kiril felt it again—an emotion he had no need to push back now. Kolya—he almost said it aloud. How I loved you, he thought, the memory of you. The two of us together. Why did you have to destroy the memories? There was no answer from the mirror-image profile on the other side of the car. Why did you have to take that precious chance I never had and never regretted your having in my place, and make a mockery of it? *How could you let yourself become what you've become?* You and your "bridge of friendship" and your "worthwhile scientific exchanges"—those are *my* keepers you flatter and share toasts with. They could have been yours—would have been, if not for Anna.

Do you realize we have had *one* moment of kinship

since we met—that moment in the operating room when we tried to save a life? Brotherhood has nothing to do with blood, does it? You've proved that—if I needed proof after Aleksei. There wasn't a single moment of recognition between us, was there? How could I have recognized *you* as my Kolya? Even with the clue of that scar on your chest that I spotted at the beach—from your operation, wasn't it? Your white hair confused me, adding years in my mind; Kolya was younger than I was. Your records were misleading—*Mother, German born*. Anna went to Berlin for your operation. *Employed by a cardiac clinic in some research capacity*. Anna's love was medical research, her favorite charm, the microscope. You could have looked like Aleksei, you know, instead of like me. A three-year-old child's recollections are unreliable. I remember only the things we *did* together, how we played and fought and laughed. How you screamed just before they took you away from me . . . And when I was old enough to think—to fight back—to pray a young atheist's prayer—I said: "To Anna and Kolya," over and over, like a precious litany. Do you know what I am feeling at this moment? Like a monk who had dedicated his life to God only to discover that half the time, he'd been invoking the devil.

The radio coughed, the static muffling some English-speaking voices. The symposium had begun. Aleksei and Adrienne leaned forward, straining to hear. Brenner's attention was divided—his ears tuned to the broadcast, his eyes fixed on the briefcase.

Kiril took out his cigarettes and leaned past Aleksei to extend the pack to the Brenners. He started to reach into his jacket pocket and then stopped himself. "Let me have a light, will you?" he said to Aleksei.

Aleksei, deeply preoccupied, dropped Brodsky's cigarette lighter into Kiril's outstretched hand.

Adrienne never saw the stunned expression on Kiril's face. She was staring at the emblem on the lighter. She grabbed it out of his hand. "You have no intention of getting us out of here—you never did!" she lashed out. "I don't know *why* you and your brother keep passing this thing back and forth—obviously, you don't give a damn about the film. But if your so-called plan is to dupe us into going to Moscow voluntarily, you miscalculated. You'll have to shoot me first."

"Passing *this* back and forth?" Aleksei took the lighter from her. "What is she talking about?" he asked Kiril slowly. "This lighter has not been out of my sight since I took it from the officer of a patrol boat in Potsdam yesterday morning. *He* took it off the deck of his boat the morning after your late friend, Brodsky, dropped it over the side of Glienicker Bridge." He turned abruptly to Adrienne—in time with her startled gasp.

A look of comprehension flashed in her eyes, then changed to horror as she stared at Kiril.

"You said something about film. I found some film in Brodsky's lighter, but it was a puzzle with some key pieces missing," Aleksei said carefully. "Are you suggesting that my brother has a lighter like this one with film in it—the missing pieces to my puzzle, perhaps? *Is* that what you are suggesting?"

"Oh, God, I don't . . ."

"You don't know what to say. How about you, Little Brother? Do you have anything to say to me? What is this so-called plan for helping the Brenners, eh? What about this film Mrs. Brenner speaks of?"

Kiril took his own lighter out of his pocket. "A leftover

from yet another of my obsolete escape plans,'' he said sheepishly, handing it to Aleksei. ''The lady is right. I don't give a damn about the film in it. I had intended to destroy it when we got back to Moscow. As for a plan to help them, why, the lady is right again. I filled her gullible ears full of false hopes in order to keep the two of them docile during our trip.''

''Ah, Kiril, Kiril.'' Aleksei shook his head as he looked at the two identical lighters in the palm of his hand. ''I suppose the film in *your* lighter is the same as in Brodsky's, except that yours contains my letterhead—my signature?''

''I'm afraid so. Look,'' Kiril said earnestly. ''I know that I just finished saying there would be no more secrets between us, but surely, you wouldn't have expected me to volunteer something like this. There's no harm done, is there?''

''A great deal, unfortunately. I mistakenly thought the missing pieces of my puzzle—your film—were photographed by another man. *His* photographs were not what I expected, and someone has a vested interest in making *me* pay for what happened. The dead man, Roeder, was—''

''Oh, no!'' Adrienne cried.

''Oh, yes, my little homing pigeon, Ernst Roeder is dead,'' Aleksei said to her with a harsh laugh. ''You led me straight to the wrong man. You may as well keep the fruits of our meddling flight.'' He pulled an envelope from his pocket. ''A bequest from your photographer friend,'' he said viciously.

Adrienne looked through the photographs without taking them out of the envelope. She closed her eyes.

Brenner's eyes strayed from the briefcase to the envelope to the photograph on top. He looked away quickly.

''—so in order to save my own neck,'' Aleksei was

saying in Russian to Kiril, "I must sacrifice yours." He leaned forward. "Stop the car, Sergei, so Luka can get in back. I warned you once about not forcing my hand," he told Kiril as the car stopped at the side of the road. "I regret having to restore you to your bodyguard, but . . ." He shrugged as Luka started to climb in. "I'd be a fool not to take certain precautions, under the circumstances."

"So I came back for nothing, then?" Kiril said incredulously. He moved the briefcase to the rug on his left, as if to make room for Luka on the jumpseat. "Can't you find a way to place the blame on this dead man?" he urged, gesturing emphatically with his right hand. His left hand was fumbling with the catch on the briefcase at his feet. "Can't you swear that you found the damn lighter on this Ernst Roeder's body?"

"Impossible. The body was searched and then guarded until it was removed."

The preliminary remarks that signaled the start of the guest-speaker portion of the West Berlin symposium were a cloying counterpoint to the tension in the air. No one paid any attention to the radio voices.

Kiril groaned and sat back, like a man painfully resigned to his fate.

"Now," Aleksei went on, "suppose we work our way backward, if you don't mind. You knew about my reputation, I'm sure. You *had* to know I'd find you out sooner or later over this cigarette-lighter business. What on earth made you come back?"

Kiril opened his mouth to answer, but was silenced by the first words of the symposium's first speaker—an unscheduled speaker. The words, in English, stunned the limousine's other occupants into instant attention.

"I came here with a sense of mission," said the voice

of Anna Brenner. "My mission is justice. I came to speak the truth about my three sons. I lost my first son, and because of the *way* I lost him, I abandoned my second son in order to save my third. He is listed on your program as a participant in this symposium. Since, as you all know from the newspapers, my third son will not be here today, I wish to speak in his absence. But first, there is an error in your program that should be corrected. Please delete the name Dr. Kurt Brenner and insert in its place Nikolai Andreyevich Andreyev—known, in his native Russia, as 'Kolya.' And now, I have something to say to my sons. To each of them."

22

The close of Anna Brenner's speech brought silence in West Berlin, as a distinguished gathering of doctors, scientists and politicians pondered her words. In East Berlin, three men and a woman looked at each other, pondering their new relationship.

Kiril's mouth was bent with the violence of his emotion.

Brenner's harsh laughter rose above a sudden, raucous mix of voices and static coming from the radio. "The Brothers Andreyev!" he exclaimed, looking from Kiril to Aleksei as one would look at a couple of bastards who had abruptly sprouted on an impeccable family tree.

"You," Aleksei choked, staring at the radio as if the speaker waited there for his reaction. His mouth revealed his reaction—twisted with what looked like the bitter taste of memories. His features hardened, then melted into amiability, as he turned to Brenner. "Well, well, little Kolya, is it?" he said softly. "And all these years, I thought you were dead. My father—excuse me, I think I

should have said *our* father—never realized, apparently, that hospital records could be forged. A forty per cent chance of recovery . . ." He laughed. "You certainly have recovered, haven't you? And prospered. Time to share the wealth, Kolya. You look stricken, Little Brother. I do not mean that literally, in spite of the fact that I am a good Communist. Smile! When life plays its little jokes on us, we must retain our sense of humor."

"Oh my God," Brenner muttered, groping for Adrienne's hand. But she was watching Kiril.

"Just as I thought, no sense of humor," Aleksei said. "Has your soft American life bred it out of you? Surely you must see the humor in this situation—the joke on our dear mother. Three sons, and the only one who merits her undying devotion—her precious Kiril—is the very one who tricked her. *He* delivered *you* into *my* hands. And now, Madame," he said slowly, his glance shifting to the radio, "Mother Russia has all three of your sons. How you must be suffering . . ."

The static yielded to the animated voice of the announcer. "—but the biggest surprise in this afternoon of surprises, ladies and gentlemen, is how the woman whose revelations set off the tumult you're hearing right now is bearing up. The mother of Dr. Kurt Brenner is waiting, microphone in hand, for people to quiet down, ready to answer all those painful, probing questions that are sure to come up. She is—believe this or not—the very picture of that old cliché: calm, cool and collected! Actually, she looks relieved, as if—"

"Tell Sergei to turn that thing off!" Aleksei snapped at Luka.

Luka leaned forward to speak through the narrow opening in the partition. And missed the gun that suddenly appeared in Kiril's hand.

Aleksei missed it, too. In the next instant, its muzzle was against his temple.

Luka turned around and froze.

"Tell your trained bear to let his gun be taken away, or I pull the trigger," Kiril said quietly, so the driver wouldn't hear.

"And do what?" Aleksei said in Russian, "Fire a thirty-year-old revolver that isn't even loaded?"

Kiril applied a slight pressure with the muzzle. "I loaded it in your room this morning after our celebration breakfast."

"With what, your traitorous intentions?" Aleksei scoffed.

"With the cartridge I found in your briefcase—only one round, but it's all I need to put a hole in your head. Tell Rogov—unless you're sure the gun won't fire."

"Let him take your gun, Luka," Aleksei said reluctantly. Reluctantly, Luka spread his elbows wide. "Now move to the jumpseat in front of Dr. Brenner," Kiril told Luka. He obeyed. "Dr. Brenner, take Rogov's—"

But Brenner didn't wait for Kiril to finish. He took the gun from Luka's holster, frisked him, then trained the gun on his stomach, keeping it low, out of the driver's range of vision.

"Tell your driver to stop again." Kiril spoke to Aleksei in English now. "He's to get out and come back here. You have something to show him." Aleksei obeyed.

"I'll answer your question now," Kiril said as the car pulled over to the side of the road. "I came back because I saw Anna in Zurich. I came back for my brother Kolya."

The back door started to open. Kiril shifted position so the first thing the driver would see would be the gun against Aleksei's neck. It was the first thing the driver

297

saw. His hands went up. "Tell Sergei to give the lady his gun," Kiril ordered.

Adrienne stretched out her hand for it as Aleksei gave the order in Russian.

"Now, tell Sergei to raise his hands again while the lady keeps his gun aimed at *your* head, so I can get out of the car."

The driver understood English, apparently. His hands rose even before Adrienne pressed the barrel under Aleksei's left ear.

Kiril edged out the door, walked behind the driver, looked around. There were no cars in sight. He brought the butt of his gun down hard against the back of the driver's head, and the man's legs collapsed under him. "Out," he ordered Luka, motioning with the gun. Then, to Brenner, "Follow him out. Keep that gun on him every second."

"Don't worry," Brenner said grimly.

"Turn around, Rogov," Kiril ordered.

"No. Don't!" The voice was Aleksei's.

Kiril prodded Luka with the revolver. "Move, I said." As soon as Luka's back was to him, Kiril came down hard with the gun butt. Luka staggered and regained balance. Kiril hit him again, and then again, his arm straining with the force of each blow. Luka crashed to the ground.

"Don't kill him! Please! He can't harm you now—don't kill him!" Aleksei had scrambled out of the car, defying the gun at his head. Or forgetting it. "You've killed him," he groaned, bending over Luka's body.

The others stared at him, shocked by the transformation.

"Your trained bear is as strong as one of those wild pigs he likes to hunt," Kiril said. "He'll survive a few blows on the head. Get my brother Aleksei back in the car,'' he said to Adrienne. "You take the driver,'' he told Brenner.

Brenner had already pulled off his tie. He secured the man's hands with an intricate knot. Kiril did the same with Luka. Then the two of them pulled up the heavy Oriental rug on the limousine floor, carried it down a slight embankment, dragged the two bodies over, and threw the rug over them.

"Is the airport far from here?'' Brenner asked as they hurried back to the car.

"No. I'll drive. Sit behind that opening in the partition, but keep your gun out of sight. Just be ready to use it.''

"Right.''

"Get my brother up front with me,'' Kiril told Adrienne as he got behind the wheel.

"You heard him, Colonel.'' She nudged Aleksei with the gun, looking as if she couldn't quite believe what she was doing.

"That plan you wouldn't tell my wife about,'' Brenner said to Kiril as the car moved off, "I take it you wanted to win your brother's trust long enough to get hold of a gun—like the one in the briefcase I told you about.''

"That was a starting point. We have three guns, now.''

"What happens next?''

"Why don't you tell him, Aleksei?'' Kiril taunted.

"I suppose we drive to the airport as scheduled,'' he said, calm again. "We board the plane waiting to take us to Moscow—and you attempt to divert it to West Berlin. You won't get away with it.''

"Who's to stop us—the guards on the plane? That special handpicked airline crew of loyalists you told me about at breakfast? Do you really think they'll argue with three guns, especially after we take them by surprise? With

your help, of course. I want us on that plane fast, Aleksei,"
he said with sudden, quiet menace. "I want you to bypass
the usual boarding procedure."

"I'll have trouble at the terminal."

"A high-ranking member of the Soviet secret police
having trouble with some East German airport lackeys? All
you have to do is speak out of the corner of your mouth
about some secret, urgent mission involving your high-
powered guest of honor." Kiril laughed harshly.

"Very amusing."

"We must retain our sense of humor. Give me back
those cigarette lighters, by the way—both of them. Drop
them into my jacket pocket."

Aleksei shot him a murderous look. "Is there anything I
can say or do to change your mind?" he said slowly as he
dropped the lighters into Kiril's pocket. "A promise of
immunity in connection with this lighter business? A special citation for what you did in Zurich?" He had switched
to Russian.

"Why would I give a damn about your promises or your
citations?"

"Listen to me, Kiril. I can turn you into a *real* hero
with all those important people you alluded to last night.
Go through with this suicidal mission of yours, and if you
don't end up dead, you'll end up back here, as good as
dead. You'll be a common criminal—a hijacker. You'll be
extradited. And I'll be waiting for you."

"That's your trouble, Aleksei—too much experience
with uncivilized countries. I'm flying *West,* Brother! Where
I'm going, they know the difference between a man fleeing
a dictatorship and a hijacker who extorts his way out of a
free country."

"I'm wasting my breath," Aleksei muttered.

"Just concentrate on not making it your last." Kiril's hands had tightened on the steering wheel. The airport was dead ahead. "Roll down your window," he told Aleksei, "and remember, it's three against one, now, and all three of us are armed." He pulled up outside the terminal and stopped a few feet short of some guards talking to a German officer.

Aleksei spoke in brusque, rapid German to the officer, then shoved some papers through the open window. The officer bit his lip as he examined the papers, then handed them back.

"Well done." Kiril pulled away before Aleksei had time to react. "You managed to impress and frighten him at the same time." He cut a purposefully random path across runways and grassy areas, keeping up the speed that befitted an official car on a mission. He slowed down, frowning, at the sight of a limousine parked next to their plane. He pulled alongside and kept the motor running; a German officer was sitting in back, smoking a cigarette.

Von Eyssen got out of the limousine, flipped his cigarette to the pavement, and walked over to Aleksei's side of the car. He peered into the back seat and clicked his heels to the Brenners with an expression of deference that bordered on insolence. "I hope your prominent guests will pardon me if I briefly delay their much heralded flight to Moscow," he said to Aleksei in polite English. "You know, of course, why I could not resist coming here," he added in not-so-polite German, leaning on the window base with folded arms. "Before you depart with your prize pigeon, I wanted to remind you that your glorious homecoming will be short-lived. If you think I will let you cover up what has happened and divert the blame to my—"

Aleksei shoved the car door open, slamming it against Von Eyssen's chest. "Hijackers!" he yelled. "Stop them!"

Kiril's foot slammed down on the gas pedal and the door swung wide, flinging Aleksei out, knocking Von Eyssen to the pavement. Kiril pulled the door shut on the rebound and steered a wild, zig-zag course across runways and grass, past the terminal building, back onto the airport road. He hit the brakes just before the road split abruptly in two directions: left, East Berlin; right, Potsdam. He took the right-hand turn.

"Do we have a chance?" Brenner said hoarsely.

"A chance."

Adrienne parted the back curtains. The signs at the intersection were almost out of sight. "You have friends in Potsdam?"

"I hope so." He was thinking of a handshake and a look of profound gratitude in a man's eyes. He was seeing letters carved in dirt. He was remembering an address.

The sky was a gigantic battlefield, with the casualties—torn pieces of cloud—strewn all over the horizon. Below, on the narrow, winding strip of gray that was a country road pock-marked with potholes and strewn with rocks, another battle was in progress. The road skirted a pale blue lake, a serene witness who refused to take sides between adversaries, knowing the road must eventually win over the black limousine. The limousine moved ponderously, like a shiny, black snail. Suddenly its pace slackened; it seemed on the point of capitulating.

"They can't be far behind," Brenner said, swinging around to the back window, "not if they took the turn to Potsdam instead of East Berlin."

"They'll take *both* turns," Kiril said, stopping the car on a sharp curve.

Beyond the shoulder, which had no guard rails, an embankment sloped gradually for a few deceptive feet before dropping without warning. The lake waited.

"Bail-out time, is it?" Brenner muttered, as Kiril nosed the car around to face the embankment.

"We've run out of road time. Even if the limousine lasts, it will be too conspicuous from here on."

"We walk, then?"

"We walk."

"Won't we be just as conspicuous on the road?" Adrienne asked.

"We won't be seeing much besides bicycles and buses between here and Potsdam. Let's get the car into the lake," he pressed.

"But we've detoured off the main highway," Brenner said, obviously reluctant to get out. "Will they really bother to search the back roads?"

"They will, eventually—sooner than I'd like. If this thing sinks, they'll keep looking for three people in a black limousine—or close to an abandoned limousine," he said, getting out of the car. "If it doesn't sink, at least we'll buy some time while they look for our bodies." He stared at the embankment. "Let's go."

Brenner went around to the trunk and started pulling out suitcases.

"Hold it—everything stays except money and jewelry," Kiril said. "We'll leave our jackets, too."

Brenner took a leather pouch from his suitcase. "What about you?" he asked Adrienne.

"Everything I need is in my shoulderbag."

"Leave it here," Kiril said. "Just wrap what you're

taking in a scarf or handkerchief.'' He took a small bottle out of his own suitcase. ''The brown rinse,'' he told Brenner, ''in case you need it later.''

''I suppose my white hair is as conspicuous as the damn limousine,'' Brenner said, frowning, as he tossed his jacket in the back seat.

''Stand clear when we start to push,'' Kiril warned Adrienne as he went through his pockets. He started to hook his jacket onto the inside door handle by the driver's seat, but was distracted by a movement behind him. Brenner's hand had just closed over the handle of Aleksei's briefcase.

''Just money and jewelry, Kurt,'' Adrienne said, and looked puzzled when Brenner, ignoring her, took the brief-case out of the car.

''Let's get this show *off* the road,'' he told Kiril.

The sight of a black hulk of a car slowly filling with water, and Kiril's jacket floating on the surface, filled Adrienne with uneasiness. During the next four hours, she had no time to think of anything but the need to keep jungle-alert: Four hours of being forced off the road and into scrubby underbrush whenever a family on bicycles, a half-empty bus, or an occasional car came along. Of cutting through fields or woods whenever an isolated farm-house lay too close to the road. Of heat and dirt and painful scratches from quick forays into the bushes.

Kiril's hand shot out in sudden warning, and she caught a glimpse of another farmhouse below them just before she dropped to the ground. She looked at him, lying a few feet away, and felt a surge of gratitude. Our scout, straight out of some Western, guiding a couple of tenderfoots through alien territory, she thought, smiling. He faces danger with such equanimity—almost with exhilaration, she marveled.

In the next instant, she realized why. He was being hunted down just like those postwar refugees she'd read about, he was literally running for his life. But he was free to run—for the first time, probably.

She looked at Kurt, only inches away, and felt a new respect for him. A doctor—a heart surgeon—totally out of his element in a terrifying situation, she thought, who was as calm as their guide. True, he wasn't running for his life, but his freedom was just as precious, wasn't it? Then she remembered Brodsky the "lawbreaker," and she shook her head slowly at the irony.

"It's after five," Kiril said, checking his watch. "We've covered roughly sixteen kilometers—about ten miles. It's too late to mingle with people returning from work. Either we try to slip into Potsdam after it gets dark, or we wait on this hill until morning and chance talking the people in that farmhouse into giving us clothes and bicycles in exchange for money and jewelry. Then we ride into town with people *going* to work."

"It's a risky proposition, either way," Brenner observed. "Let's look at the odds. The way I figure it, we can—"

Look at the two of you, Adrienne mused. Brothers, in a deeper than literal sense, ever since that moment in the car—your joined response to danger, and a chance to escape. You work so well together.

"Well, what do *you* say?" Brenner asked her.

"If we try it tonight, the odds are?"

"Worse than if we wait."

"Why?"

"Weren't you listening? We'd be too damn conspicuous in these clothes."

"If we're stopped as we enter the town," Kiril explained,

"we'd have no identity cards or travel authority to show them."

"But they'll automatically check us at the Potsdam border, won't they?" she asked.

"Not necessarily. I've been told they check only when they have reason to be suspicious."

"Well, if the idea is to look inconspicuous," she said, examining long rips in her black pantsuit and smudges on her ruffled blouse, "I guess we trust the people in the farmhouse, don't we?"

Kiril looked at Brenner. "Are we agreed, then?"

"Agreed."

The lake, still serene, still refusing to take sides, was darker now, almost indistinguishable from the sky. The vehicles lined up along the embankment, two limousines and a military jeep, were turning into silhouettes, along with the standing figures of two men. They talked, looking not at each other but at the water below.

"*You* are the dredging expert, from what I hear. You tell me how long it will take to find three bodies in this light."

"I have a feeling we won't be finding any bodies, no matter how long it takes," Aleksei said. "Still, we must be sure, one way or the other. I want you to mobilize the necessary people and equipment immediately."

"I think you should find someone else to take your orders." A scowl marred Von Eyssen's perfect profile.

"Have you forgotten how much you stand to lose if my brother Kiril makes it across the border? The film he's carrying is your only proof that he was responsible for the intelligence leak. If he gets away, I'll swear it was your brother-in-law Roeder who was responsible. Brother versus brother-in-law—your word against mine. Trouble for us both, my friend. Help me to capture my brother, however, and I guarantee you he'll stand trial. And be executed.''

"Your brother has caused me deep concern," Von Eyssen said slowly. "I think you should turn him over to me, first. I will personally see that he makes a full confession.''

"From what *I* hear, your approach in that department differs from mine," Aleksei quipped. He looked Von Eyssen over and smiled. "Have you ever read Oscar Wilde?''

"Do you think you are the only intellectual in intelligence work?" Von Eyssen snapped. "Of course, I have. Why?''

"I was thinking of Dorian Gray.''

"A trite piece of melodrama," Von Eyssen said, looking uneasy.

"Really? I rather like the symbolism. A man retains his youth and beauty while his portrait ages and grows ugly, revealing the sores of the soul. I didn't think you'd like that story.''

"Are we having a literary discussion, damn you, or are we talking about your brother? Which brother are you *really* after? If you don't deliver the eminent Dr. Brenner to Moscow, it seems to me your brother Kiril won't be the only Andreyev on trial.''

"Quite true," Aleksei brooded. "I intend to capture them both—with or without your help. Do I have it?''

Von Eyssen sighed. "You have it." He got into his limousine. "I'll make the necessary arrangements at once. Where can I contact you?''

"You won't be able to. Once I've picked up my aide, I'll be on the road, making sure every border unit and checkpoint between East Berlin and Potsdam is on full alert. Our three birds only *think* they've flown the coop.

With the detailed descriptions I've circulated, I'll have them back in my net in a matter of days.''

"Look at that sharp bend in the road. Your birds are at the bottom of the lake.''

"Perhaps. But my intuition tells me that my brother Kiril, being a clever fellow, abandoned the car, and being a sentimental fellow, headed straight for Potsdam.''

"Why?''

"His dear, departed friend, Brodsky, made a final stand at Potsdam, before succumbing to the authority of your good German bullets—or were they ours?''

"Both. But they were German, as far as the world is concerned,'' Von Eyssen said bitterly.

"Better be on your way,'' Aleksei advised. "I'll keep in touch with you. Incidentally, Colonel, I want him alive.''

"Who?''

"Brenner, of course.''

Adrienne shivered. The combination of night air and cold ground made her long for Kurt's jacket, left behind in the car. Or Kiril's.

"Cold?'' Brenner whispered over her face. And covered her with his body.

"Kurt, don't.''

"He's asleep.''

"How do you know?''

"Listen to his breathing. Then listen to mine . . .''

"I—he might wake up. Kurt, please.''

"We could all be dead tomorrow, or the day after tomorrow. It's like being in the trenches in the middle of a goddamn war. I want you. I've never wanted you so damn much.''

She tried to struggle without making noise. Impossible. "Kurt, we haven't even—"

"Adrienne . . . Adrienne, I've missed you. I never knew how much until this moment." He took her face in both hands.

It was dark; what little there was of the moon she could see in his eyes. "I love you," he told her, and she tried to see if he meant it. When he kissed her, she responded to his urgency, feeling what she'd started to feel again in the operating room, and today, on the run from danger— She pulled back abruptly, remembering his real reason for coming here. And his refusal to help Kiril. As she turned her head away, her eyes picked out a dark form, outlined against a less dark sky. The warmth on her lips fled into the darkness.

"Adrienne . . ."

"*No*, Kurt."

But her struggle had become a challenge. And a losing battle, all the more desperate because it was fought in silence. She closed her eyes, fighting each wordless demand on her flesh with an image of Kiril . . . her first sight of him at an airport terminal . . . the way he'd looked crossing a banquet room to meet her . . . his expression just before she went into his arms in an airport lounge. She had wanted him. She had wanted him from the moment he had claimed her—possessed her—on a crowded beach.

Her eyes flashed open, and she saw that the dark form had shifted—or the moon; she saw moonlight reflected in his eyes. *He was awake*. She felt the ground, cold against her bare skin, and the night air—cold—and neither of them cold enough to bank the liquid heat that rushed into her limbs. "Oh no," she whispered helplessly, knowing the images had betrayed her senses . . . wanting *him,* not the man who was entering her body . . . Her fingers dug into earth as her body arched, reaching beyond her protesting mind, greedily reaching for the unreachable—and with a shudder, finding it.

She lay there, eyes open to the sky, unable to look in his direction. Kiril, she whispered, but only in her mind. She wept as silently as she had fought.

23

Kiril went first, taking the hill in long, quick strides. The farmhouse was two stories of gray fieldstone, with the top one boarded up. The place looked abandoned—no farm animals or outbuildings, apart from a dilapidated shed. But a plot of rich, black soil in the back was plowed. He moved to a window and looked in. "A man and a woman," he whispered. "Retired farmers, too old to be put into the collectivization program, probably." He took out his handkerchief. "We can wrap the money and jewelry in this."

"All of it?" Brenner asked. "Aren't we saving any for the people in Potsdam?"

"If they help us, it won't be for money."

Brenner, looking skeptical, emptied his pockets and his leather pouch. Adrienne unwrapped her scarf and handed Kiril money and jewelry.

Kiril looked uncomfortable. "I'm sorry I have nothing to contribute."

"We'd never have gotten this far without you," she said quickly, and hoped he didn't notice Kurt's frown of annoyance.

"Do we all go in?" Brenner asked.

"No. Wait here. I'll come back for you." When he reappeared he was no longer wearing his watch. "Come," he said. "We can change inside while the old man is getting the bicycles."

The room they entered was almost all wood—floor, ceiling, walls, furniture—but no firewood to spare, Adrienne realized, looking at a spotless stone fireplace. The place smelled of raw potatoes which an old woman, indifferent to their presence, was cutting up at a metal sink. Adrienne turned her back and slipped into the clothes Kiril had handed her. The hem of the long dress hit just below the knee, and the fabric strained under her arms and across her breasts. "I have my own scarf," she said, turning around—and smiled mirthlessly even before Kiril shook his head, because hers was a designer scarf from Bloomingdale's. She folded a square of rough cotton and tied it, babushka style, on her head.

"Good fit, even if they are a bit threadbare," Brenner remarked, examining the trousers he'd just put on.

Kiril had on a similar pair—coarse serge, wide and gathered at the waist. He pulled on a formless gray cap. "Ready?" he said, holding the back door open.

A tall, dignified old man who seemed more like a businessman than a farmer was waiting outside. Against the back of the house, three bicycles leaned, their scrawny tires and tinny-looking bodies giving them the look of pre-war relics. The old man said something in German and went back in the house.

"He wished us good luck," Brenner told her. "He said

this is a good hour to enter the town because people will be going to work.''

''We'll be able to ask directions,'' Kiril said.

''Is he a retired farmer?'' she asked.

''His brother was the farmer. He and his wife lived here too, but worked on the other side. He owned a couple of shops.''

''And got trapped behind the Wall?''

Kiril nodded. ''Like so many others.''

''I hope he meant it, about the good luck.''

''Don't worry. They need that money. And the jewelry is worth a lot on the black market. They won't turn us in.''

But will you? she wondered, when a smartly dressed youth riding a conspicuously new motorcycle fixed them with a curious stare. Or you? she asked a shabbily clothed family of three that examined them before pedaling off in the opposite direction. Will *you* turn us in? she asked the guards at the Potsdam border as she tried not to stare at a prominent sign that read: ''Undying friendship and alliance with the Soviet Union,'' and waited fatalistically to hear a German command and the dreaded word ''Ausweis''—documents. Don't turn us in, she pleaded, when Kurt or Kiril asked directions. Don't talk, she reminded herself over and over, envying them their fluent, flawless German. No one followed them down narrow cobblestone streets, but every passing face seemed a threat, every frown a betrayal. The unbroken gray stucco on both sides of them seemed less like rows of connecting houses than solid, impregnable walls.

Only when gray stucco gave way to red brick did fear give way to hope; she recognized the cheerful Dutch influence not just in the red brick, but in the high, rounded tops of the attached houses, with their white trim and black shutters. Then she spotted a sign on an iron post that read, HOLLÄNDISCHE SIEDLUNG. Kurt found Number Thirteen. Kiril rang the bell. She felt a hand in hers—Kiril's. The tightness of her answering grip became a substitute for breathing. The door opened and a pair of expressionless blue eyes looked them over curiously, then intently. A muscular arm reached out and pulled her inside. A voice as expressionless as the eyes said, "Come in. Quickly."

The door was closed and bolted behind them.

Albert Zind sat on the passenger side of a panel truck, absorbed in thought.

Bruno, the East German border guard who always drove him to and from the bridge site, glanced at him once in a while as he maneuvered the truck around the U-turns leading away from Glienicker Bridge, his visibility sharply reduced by the sudden downpour. "Cat got your tongue?" he finally growled.

"Just wondering what my supervisor will say when he finds out I pulled the crew off an hour before quitting time," Albert said impassively.

"Who the hell could work in all this rain?" Bruno retorted. "You're the foreman. A foreman's got to make decisions, right?"

"Right. Only problem is my supervisor is nervous about this job. He's in a big goddamn hurry to get it done." There *has* to be some way to take advantage of that, Albert was thinking. But he hadn't been able to come up with anything; he hadn't come up with a goddamn thing all day.

Bruno drove past two roadsigns. One was new: a white triangle with a red border and a black silhouette of a man bending over a shovel; the weatherbeaten sign next to it said: BRIDGE, 500 METERS, with an arrow pointing back the way they had just come. A third sign was tacked over the front door of a nearby guard-duty shack: NO CIVILIANS BEYOND THIS POINT. Bruno pulled up in front of the shack.

He started to get out, then glanced at the gas gauge. "Hey, Zind, I thought you was Mr. Efficient. You know you're almost on empty?"

Albert shrugged. "My mind was on other things this morning."

"Well, hell, since you don't carry spare petrol—"

"Why bother, when it's such a short haul from here to the marshalling yard?"

"Well, we don't have no spare petrol around here, so don't go making the same mistake tomorrow," Bruno said officiously. "What if you ran out on the bridge or the square and we had to leave the truck overnight?"

"Can't have that," Albert said placidly, "not with all that traffic going on between a couple of guardhouses."

"Wiseguy," Bruno said with gruff good nature, as he got out. "See you tomorrow morning." He headed for the shack.

Albert slid behind the wheel and looked out the window while the workcrew scrambled from the back of the truck and lined up for the count—looked without seeing them; he was deep in thought again. A foolproof escape plan was impossible when all the old approaches were unworkable. In the beginning things had been different—there were buildings all along the border, and people could leap from windows and rooftops into the safety of fire nets on the other side of the Wall. But the windows had been bricked up long ago, and the buildings emptied or demolished. Sewers and the underground system of canals had been good in the beginning—if you didn't drown because of a sudden rainfall like today's, or suffocate from accumulated gases. They had grates now, and bolted manhole covers, and an electrical warning system of some kind. People used to actually scramble over the Wall in the old days, he thought, or crawl under barbed wire, or cross rivers in broad daylight. But swimming, even at night, wasn't a matter of dodging bullets and searchlight beams anymore; there were underwater barbed wire obstructions to worry about. The Wall had grown higher and thicker, and all along the border where there was no Wall, barriers had sprung up like mushrooms; it was virtually impossible to get through all of them. People had always tried to ram through the border barricades—tried it in everything from trucks and tanks to improvised armored cars. They still tried, but they never seemed to make it . . . people like his sister Eva. Everyone said the border was almost escape-proof now. Some West German magazine had just estimated the escape rate at a hundred or so a year—a mere trickle compared with the 34,000 escapes during the first thirteen years of the Wall's existence.

A trickle is better than a dry faucet, he thought hopefully.

His brothers Erich and Gunther climbed into the front seat. "The crew's all set back there," Gunther said.

"Come up with anything?" Erich asked.

"All the things that won't work anymore," Albert said as he started the truck.

He headed for the marshalling yard, where they would leave the truck and catch a bus home. They rode in uneasy silence.

Something unique and unrepeatable is what we need, Albert reasoned, some idea you could get away with once, because the border patrols haven't anticipated it yet. Like the kid, armed only with guts and a railroad ticket, who'd smuggled out his fiancée in a hand truck. Or the two families with eleven children between them who'd buried themselves under a refrigerator truckload of frozen meat. Or the worker who'd scurried hand over hand, across a momentarily disconnected high-tension cable. Or the former border-guard medical students, wearing homemade uniforms and driving a car with false military markings, who were familiar with army code signals that got them permission to inspect the Wall—collapsible ladders and all . . .

Mueller, his supervisor, was waiting for him at the yard, pacing outside the engineering office. "I know, I know," Albert told him, as he got out of the truck, "we lost a precious hour out of your schedule."

"That's not the worst of it! Those steel struts I ordered are being delivered the day after tomorrow and I'll be in Berlin that day," Mueller groaned. "Trying to explain the delays in getting this goddamn bridge repaired, instead of being on the site when the new steel goes up."

"What are you worried about? I'm an engineer too, you know. We'll talk about it tomorrow." He turned away before Mueller could give him an argument and headed for the bus stop where his brothers are waiting.

"Can you manage not to be late again tomorrow, since nothing starts until you get here?" Mueller called out sullenly.

"You're in charge. *You* tell me how to make the bus come on time," Albert shot back.

They waited in the rain for the bus. A rivulet floated some dirt and debris down the gutter and Albert thought of tunnels. A lot of them had been successful—dramatically so. Like the one a hundred and forty meters long and twelve meters deep, with a record-breaking sixty escapes to its credit. But it had taken months to build, and he had to think in terms of days; it was only a matter of days before the whole town would be put through a house-to-house search—the Russian and the American couple were important enough for that, apparently. And tunnels were unreliable—too likely to cave in under sandy German soil and too easy to discover when you ran out of places to hide the sand. Besides, the guards were alert to all the signs. They knew what to look for with everything, now—fake military uniforms, people "innocently" swimming in border lakes or sailing on excursion steamers, secret compartments in automobiles . . .

When the bus pulled up, Albert studied its side doors—one for passengers and one for the driver. The buses that regularly crossed to the West had the identical door arrangement—and the same impregnable barrier between the driver and those passengers who had more than a bus ride in mind: a locked door and a partition made of bullet-proof glass.

He followed his brothers into the bus. When they were seated in the back, he said, "I'm stumped."

"Looks like what we need right now is time," Albert said slowly. They were all sitting around the dining-room table. The dinner dishes had been cleared away hours ago.

"Time for what?" Brenner said tensely. "You just finished saying that a house-to-house search is imminent."

"So I'm suggesting we relocate the three of you to a safer place away from the border area until we come up with something."

"No." Kiril's quiet emphasis startled all of them. "This is the time to do it, this is the place. Glienicker Bridge."

Albert's eyes narrowed. "Are you thinking you'll have better luck than your Russian air force friend?"

"Whatever else you've guessed about me, I'm not irresponsible. I'm no symbolist, even if I do have a strong sense of irony."

"Then, why?"

"We're so damn close. We've pressed our luck just getting this far. Unless I'm convinced there's no way to get across, I can't see pressing it any further. How many trustworthy people do you think we'll find out there?" he asked, gesturing at a window. "We *must* find a way to get on that bridge. Couldn't we pose as members of your construction crew?" he asked hopefully.

"Impossible," Erich said. "They have a spread-the-work arrangement—a labor pool. Albert has to pick a different crew from it every morning."

"Pick?" Gunther guffawed. "Pot luck is more like it!"

"It's for security reasons," Erich said with a wry grin. "If some welder, say, were to know ahead of time that he'd be working a strategic spot like Glienicker, he might make some long-range travel plans."

"But you two work on a regular basis, don't you?" Kiril asked, puzzled.

"Because Gunther and I are the best damn ironworkers Mueller could hope to lay his paws on, that's why. With his breakneck schedule, he knows it's in his interests to bend the rules a little."

Albert leaned forward. "That's it," he said matter-of-factly. "An empty petrol tank, steel struts arriving, a bus that's never on time, and Mueller. That will do it."

The room turned quiet.

"The day after tomorrow," Albert said to Kiril, "you and the Brenners will take the place of Erich and Gunther and our friend Otto Dorf—you saw him the day we met."

Kiril nodded.

"Our supervisor expects new steel struts the day after tomorrow. I'll tell him I can get to them bright and early *if* I can avoid having to take the bus. And if," he said slowly, "I can take the flatbed truck home with me the night before."

"Where in hell could we store it?" Gunther asked.

"In that half-empty warehouse of Otto's uncle. In return for this favor, I will tell Mueller that Otto demands—"

"To be slipped into the labor pool for one day so he can earn some extra money!" Erich finished enthusiastically. "Which gives us *three* workmen to change places with our visitors."

"Exactly. The night before," Albert went on, "we'll build a secret compartment—a false back wall—on the workers' hut in the flatbed. That," he explained, "is a small wooden house at one end of the truck, for spare tools and work clothes and shelter from the rain." He looked from Brenner to Kiril. "In the morning, the day after tomorrow, the three of you will hide in this compartment while I drive the truck to the yard to pick up the steel struts." He turned to Gunther. "You and Otto, as crew members, will ride in the back to make sure no one else goes near there." His glance moved to Erich's face. "On our way from the yard to the bridge site, you will be right behind, driving the rest of the crew in the panel truck." He frowned. "Here it becomes difficult. At the site, as soon as the crew leaves the panel truck to be searched and counted, Otto, Erich and Gunther must slip *into* it—and stay there all day. At the same time, Dr. Andreyev and the Brenners must slip *out* of *their* hiding place and into the ranks of the crew."

Erich was smiling broadly.

"So far, so good," Gunther said, "but what about the tear gas?"

"What do you mean?" Brenner said sharply.

"I'm driven to and from the site by a border guard, and just before we take off for the bridge, they routinely spray the back of the panel truck with tear gas," Albert explained. "This time, the guard will be driving the flatbed full of steel, and the panel truck will be left behind so"—he turned to Gunther—"there won't be any need to spray it. But there *is* a risk. You know that mentality—creatures of habit who go by the literal book."

"Let's assume they don't get literal," Erich said calmly. "What's next?"

"All three of us are now on the bridge, aren't we?" Kiril cut in. He was looking at Adrienne.

"You'll walk there with the rest of the crew. The guard will park the flatbed truck behind what I call a rivet pen—it's on the right side of the bridge near the crossing point. That's where you'll be heating up rivets until I come up with a reason to end the workday ahead of schedule and get the crew onto the flatbed, ready to be driven back. The truck won't start, of course."

"Why not?" Brenner asked.

"Because at the same time we build your hiding place, we also drill a small hole in the petrol tank, which we then fill with just enough petrol to get to the bridge in the morning. If there's any petrol left, it will leak out during the day. Which is why, when the crew is ready to leave, our driver-guard will discover an empty tank—and no spare petrol anywhere in the vicinity. The crew must now get out and walk. But you three—you and your wife and Dr. Andreyev—will manage to slip back into your hiding place as soon as the rest of us leave. Within a few hours,

321

the two guards posted at the middle of the bridge—uncomfortably near where you are parked—will change shifts. Then one of you will crawl through the front end of the hut—I'll show you where—and out onto a coupler to pour the can of petrol I will have left for you in your secret compartment. It will be enough to get you going, so you can ram through the rivet pen and across the bridge.''

Brenner and Kiril looked at each other.

''And,'' Erich said, breaking the silence, ''when the crew gets back to the panel truck, we're ready to slip out for the end-of-the-day nose count. It's fantastic, Albert!''

There was silence again as Brenner looked at Erich and Gunther. ''You're so much younger than we are,'' he said.

''They've only been on the job a few days—the construction work just got started,'' Albert reassured him. ''There's a good chance no one's noticed what they look like, except the supervisor, of course. He'll be in Berlin that day.''

''What about this rivet pen—you're sure it will give way when we ram it?'' Kiril asked. ''There won't be time to pull around.''

''It's made of wood. The carpenters just put it up yesterday.'' Albert grinned. ''They did a lousy job.''

''Why don't we hedge our bets? You said we'd be heating rivets in there. What if the fire accidentally got out of control at some point? It would weaken the wood *and* give you a good excuse to close down early for the day.''

Albert grinned. ''Kiril, my friend—I may call you Kiril?—''

''Or friend.''

''It's a perfect touch,'' Albert finished appreciatively.

''To a perfect plan.''

''But far from foolproof. Too many things can go wrong.''

"The thing I don't want to go wrong is to have you and your brothers get caught in the middle. Aren't you making it easy for the authorities to trace the escape right back to you?" Kiril frowned. "An empty truck with no petrol suddenly springs to life and streaks across the border."

"Nothing to worry about," Albert said impassively. "I have my fall guy picked out—the guard at the wheel when the flatbed won't start. He'll swear we were out of petrol. He'll swear the truck was empty when he escorted the crew out of the area before returning to his post." He finished the cold coffee in his cup. "His superiors will swear he's an incompetent and a fool."

"What about your supervisor? He'll know you had the flatbed overnight."

"Mueller will cover for us. He'll know it's his neck, too, if he doesn't."

"If you two are going to pass muster the day after tomorrow," Erich said, looking from Kiril to Brenner, "you'll need a quick education."

"We have a lot to go over," Albert agreed. "We're going to need a fresh pot of coffee." He looked around for his mother and realized she'd gone upstairs to bed.

When he stood up with his empty coffee cup, Adrienne waved him back down. "Since I can't make any contribution to this discussion," she said to Kiril, "the least I can do is make the coffee. Besides, I'm getting bored trying to read facial expressions. Also, nervous."

He smiled. "I'll fill you in when it's over. All you'll be required to do is spend a day posing as a construction worker on Glienicker Bridge."

24

Adrienne started to help Frieda Zind scrape remnants of sausage and black bread from the dinner plates and was rewarded with a tentative smile that looked pathetic on that ravaged face.

Albert pushed his chair back. "We have work to do," he announced, getting up from the table. "Otto will be waiting."

"We'll go with you," Kiril offered.

Brenner stared at his hands. They were starting to form callouses from the trip through the countryside. He frowned over a small scratch. "You don't really need me, do you?" he asked.

"Stay here, both of you. No point in your taking unnecessary risks," Albert said. "Otto has tools and lumber for us at the warehouse. It shouldn't take us too long."

"Is there anything we can do here?" Kiril asked.

"Just get to bed early," Albert advised. "Tomorrow won't be any picnic."

"Not for any of us," Kiril frowned. "I wish there were another way that didn't involve you."

"There isn't. Don't worry about it. We knew the risks when we made the offer. If worst comes to worst, we have an ace in the hole."

"We do? Ah, the layaway plan," Gunther said with a wry smile.

"The what?"

"My government has been doing a brisk barter business with West Germany for some twenty years now," Albert said. He wasn't smiling. "In exchange for large quantities of luxury consumer goods—coffee, butter, spare parts— West Germany gets people. Not just any people, of course; they have to have skills or a profession. It helps to be a political prisoner. Doctors bring the highest rate among political prisoners—*there's* an irony for you, Kiril. You and Dr. Brenner are worth too damn much to be bartered. A structural engineer and a couple of talented ironworkers, on the other hand, could bring anywhere from twelve to twenty thousand marks apiece."

"Some ace in the hole," Kiril said grimly.

"I have a pipeline to the lawyer who arranges these things. It's an option not open to everyone," Albert said philosophically.

"Why do you call it a layaway plan?" Brenner asked.

"Because we don't plan to take advantage of it until our mother reaches retirement age and they let her out. Retired people are considered a drain on the assets of the State." He glanced at his mother through a doorway leading to the parlor. "We'll be home in a few hours," he called out. "Mama? What's the matter, Mama?"

Frieda Zind had just flicked on the television set in the parlor and stood frozen as a program from West Berlin flashed on the screen. "I . . . I forgot," she whispered in German, looking guardedly from Kiril to the Brenners.

Erich laughed softly. "It's all *right,* Mama," he said, going over to put a reassuring arm around her shoulders. "You can do it in front of these people."

Albert shrugged at the question on Kiril's face. "They don't suppress what we watch—not literally. But the unwritten code is never to turn on the set in front of strangers. That's why we missed your speech Monday night. We had dinner guests. Let's go," he said to his brothers.

"Before you leave, would you mind showing me the way to the cellar?" Brenner said.

"That door off the kitchen." Albert pointed it out. "Gunther started a fire in the furnace for you."

"Thank you."

Kiril watched the three men leave, then told the room at large that he was going upstairs for some cigarettes.

Brenner waited until Adrienne started to help Frieda Zind with the dishes before going into the parlor to retrieve the briefcase from behind a couch. He walked back into the kitchen and headed for the cellar door.

Adrienne stopped him with a question. "Can Mrs. Zind understand English?"

"No. Why?"

"I wanted to talk freely without embarrassing her. You've been acting like a snob ever since we got here, Kurt. Maybe you didn't realize it, but—"

"Don't lecture me."

"Please, Kurt. I can't follow most of what you and the Zinds say to each other, but your attitude is so obvious it leaps over the language barrier like an Olympic pole vaulter." He laughed. "I'm serious. Can't you show a little gratitude?"

"I thanked the older brother for what they're all doing."

"I know the German word for 'thank you.' You said it once—in that manner you reserve for hired help."

"You're coming unstrung," he said coldly. "You're imagining things."

She flushed. "Am I? I'm beginning to think the accommodations here are too modest for your tastes. You could always go back to that hotel suite in East Berlin."

"You have an irritating sense of humor."

"And you have a callous side to you that's worse than I suspected. You can be affable to people who'd slam their collective doors in your face right now, yet you're barely civil to a family that took you in without a question."

"You know," he said slowly, "I think you're enjoying this little melodrama. It's just your style, isn't it? All these people you can feel sorry for and identify with."

"Stop it! It's maddening how your mood shifts. I can't keep up with you. You seemed so different when things fell apart in East Berlin, after your mother said . . . what she said on the radio. I thought she got through to you, finally. I thought this whole experience got through. When the three of us were on the road the other day, fighting to—"

"Don't remind me," he said with an expression of distaste.

Kiril came downstairs, smiling at Frieda Zind, who smiled back and put on some fresh coffee. "Let's go into the parlor," he said to Brenner.

"I have something to do first."

Kiril glanced at the briefcase. "Need any help?"

"No, thanks."

"Kolya." He said it softly.

"Don't call me that."

Adrienne came over. "Kurt! Will you—"

"Keep out of this."

"Little Brother," Kiril amended solemnly.

"Don't call me that, either, damn it!" Brenner's face was flushed.

"Why do you act as if I'm your enemy? Is it because I came back for you? Because you feel yourself in my debt? You're not. I came back for Anna. I'm glad, now, that I did."

"Even after what *I* almost did?" Brenner said harshly, seeming to direct the harshness outward.

They looked at each other. Brenner's hand touched the lump on the back of his skull gingerly, as if it were still throbbing.

Adrienne touched his other hand. "Kurt, please try to—"

"I said, keep out of this."

"How can I?" she said unhappily. "I'm right in the middle of it. We were talking about the Zinds while you were upstairs," she said, unable to look at either of them. "Is it true that the East Germans are mostly concerned with 'getting on'—that they're determinedly apolitical? I read that somewheree."

"It's generally true, yes," Kiril answered.

"That makes the Zind family pretty special, doesn't it? Sticking a political neck out in a place like this, getting ready to risk their lives in order to save ours."

"There you go, being melodramatic again," Brenner said sharply. "Lives aren't at stake, particularly not mine or yours. If they catch us, they can't hold us—not after I finish what you keep interrupting." He opened the cellar door.

"You're wrong . . . Dr. Brenner."

The tone of Kiril's voice stopped Brenner halfway down the cellar steps.

"You've forgotten Anna's broadcast, haven't you? As far as the Soviet authorities are concerned, you're a Russian citizen, now. You left Berlin for America without permission. That makes you a fugitive. A . . . lawbreaker."

"But that's ridiculous! I was a baby at the time."

"A mere detail that our—that Colonel Andreyev will overlook, if he gets his hands on you again. He doesn't even need an excuse to hold you now, don't you see that? As far as the world is concerned, you've defected voluntarily. All he has to do is keep both of us out of the public view for as long as it suits his purpose."

"Christ!"

"Aleksei has some kind of a personal stake in all this," Kiril said reflectively. "He probably regrets losing you even more than me."

"First things first." Brenner's voice was shaky. "I'm getting rid of this stuff right now. At least I'll make sure they can't blackmail me anymore."

Adrienne followed him into the cellar. Kiril stayed at the top of the steps.

"What's in that briefcase? What are you getting rid of?" she asked.

"I thought we settled the issue of my past on our last night in East Berlin."

"We settled nothing. You put me off, that's all. I didn't want to press at the time."

"And you do now. Sorry. This is something you're better off not knowing."

"You can't be serious."

"It happened a long time ago. I've made up for it

since—that children's clinic of mine, all the charity work." He turned his attention to the furnace.

"What did you do to make Kiril tell me you traded in human lives?"

"It's 'Kiril,' is it? I accused him of offering me a lousy trade. Maybe that's what he was talking about."

She looked unconvinced.

"I accused your husband of trading when he wouldn't give me his passport, that's all," Kiril volunteered from the top of the steps.

"Is it true about the passport, Kurt? Did you actually hold out for some kind of a deal for yourself?"

"I had to!" Brenner was half turned away from her, trapped between the furnace and a pile of debris. "His goddamn brother was blackmailing me and he wouldn't take money—he sneered at it! I needed leverage. I figured that once he heard about the passport business, he'd have to let me—"

"You tried to turn Kiril in?" she whispered.

"To his *brother,* for Christ's sake."

"To a brother who's a colonel in the secret police?"

"Yes, goddamn it, yes! I had no choice—they didn't leave me any. *Everything* was at stake—my career, my reputation, my whole future. How could I face people once they knew what I'd done to those kids? You think people would care that it happened over thirty years ago? You think they'd believe it was self-defense, even if they never put me on trial for killing Joe Cherner?"

She stared at him. "The Ukrainian refugee children who'd been in a concentration camp? The ones who killed themselves because an American GI—" She swung around, looking wildly at Kiril.

"I didn't want you to know," he said gently.

Brenner was tossing papers into the furnace, one by one, and staring into the fire, his lips slightly parted. He reached into the briefcase and brought out a spool of wire.

She went over and yanked him around to face her. "This is from Anna." She slapped him hard across the face. "Didn't you feel it all the way from Zurich—that slap that was meant for you?"

He moved as if to hit her back, but Kiril had come quickly down the steps. Brenner backed away from the look in his eyes.

Adrienne shook her head slowly as she turned to Kiril. "And I told you in Zurich you had no right to do what you did. Only a fool repays treachery with loyalty. You shouldn't have come back for him."

"He's my brother."

"He's not your brother. He doesn't know the meaning of the word." She watched Brenner turn his back on them, toss the wire spool into the flames, then empty the rest of the briefcase into the furnace. "You sacrificed your freedom for his," she said dully, "and he resents you for it."

"I don't believe in sacrifice. My country is one big sewer of sacrifice," Kiril said. "I'd never have risked slipping back into that sewer if I hadn't been convinced of my chances. I had a better than even chance of diverting that plane to the West."

"Which *I* destroyed. When I think that when you were in Zurich, you were safe. If they catch you now, what will it mean? A labor camp? A firing squad?" He didn't answer. "A firing squad," she said.

"They won't catch me. Thanks to the Zinds, there's still a better than even chance."

"I don't believe you," she said. She walked up to him and went into his arms.

"You're still my wife, damn you!"

They heard a click as the furnace door swung shut. They turned to see Brenner staring at them, fury in his voice and eyes—and contempt in the set of his mouth. " 'My place is with my husband,' " he mimicked. "That's the noble little sentiment you expressed the day before yesterday, you—"

"That was the day before yesterday."

"And the *night* before yesterday?" He looked at Kiril when he said it.

"That was rape."

"That's not the way it ended, is it? Or am I being too crude?"

"I'm not crude enough to tell you *why* it ended the way it did," she said, and it was she who looked at Kiril.

He took her hand. They walked up the steps together and left Brenner standing in the cellar.

25

"What do you think?" Albert pushed his chair back.
"Nothing wrong with the fit of the clothes," Erich
observed.

"Gunther?"

"They look like what they're supposed to be—brothers."
He chuckled. "Zind, this time around, instead of Andreyev.
What happened to your white hair?" he asked Brenner.

"Brown rinse. I'm told dark hair will be less noticeable."

"They'll be on the lookout for his white hair," Kiril
explained. "Besides, you and Erich both have brown hair."

"Good thinking, Kiril," Albert said. "Stand alongside
each other for a moment, will you?" He scrutinized the
four of them: Erich and Gunther were a little shorter and
stockier, and their hair was finer.

"No problem with the hair, if that's what you're thinking.
We'll be wearing these, remember?" Erich clapped a steel
helmet on his head. "We switch helmets for caps just
before they leave the flatbed."

Erika Holzer

"What about a helmet for Mrs. Brenner?" Kiril asked.

"Only ironworkers and riveters get to wear helmets," Gunther said with mock pride. "Don't worry, the cap Erich gave her will conceal her hair. See what I mean?"

They turned to look at Adrienne, standing in the parlor doorway.

Gunther smiled at her reassuringly and said, "Good," in English. His voice lacked conviction.

Albert and Erich looked at each other.

There was an awkward silence.

Erich broke it. "Otto's close enough to her size, all right. No problem with the hair, either," he added lamely. Her thick auburn hair was almost hidden under a cloth cap.

"Do you have any elastic?" Kiril asked, trying unsuccessfully not to smile.

"A roll of tape for bandages. Will that do?" Albert said, trying and succeeding.

"Sure."

"What's wrong?" Adrienne asked tensely.

"Nothing we can't fix." Kiril took the tape Albert handed him and led her back to the parlor. "Be grateful you're not a sturdy, robust specimen like so many of our Russian women," he said, smiling openly.

She flushed and closed the parlor doors, then took off her shirt. She hesitated. "The bra, too?"

"You're supposed to be a man. The straps would be a dead giveaway."

She took it off.

"This is going to feel uncomfortable, but I want it as tight as possible."

"Just so long as I can breathe," she said lightly. *But I can't. Not with your hands on me.*

"Too tight?"

"No." She concentrated on the elastic he was winding around her breasts, feeling the heat of his hands.

He finished, but his hands stayed on the tape. When he took them away, she thought they were shaking.

There was a light tapping on the door. "Otto just pulled up with the flatbed," someone said.

"Be right out." He handed her the shirt. "When they do a body search, they'll move their hands up and down and all along your sides," he said, all business. "They'll feel the elastic but nothing much underneath it, so don't worry. And try not to tense." She finished buttoning the shirt. "Much better. Since they might ask you about the bandage, you should add the words 'Unfall' and 'Verletzung' to your German vocabulary."

"Meaning?"

"Accident. Wound. If they think you've been injured, they might not explore that area with their usual thoroughness."

"Unfall," she said uneasily as he opened the door.

The man waiting outside extended his hand in greeting. "We meet again," said Otto Dorf.

"We're in your debt," Kiril told him.

"I'm here to repay one."

Albert started to check his watch, then remembering that he'd given it to Kiril, glanced at the kitchen clock. "Plenty of time yet," he said. "Let's go over the work routine one last time. Erich?"

"The cables we installed yesterday aren't up to a full supporting load, and won't be until the new struts go into place. Once they're in, remember to tighten the cables. That will bring the bridge into perfect stress. If you run into problems, Albert will guide you."

"What's he saying?" Adrienne asked Brenner. "Some last minute instructions?"

"He's telling us about struts."

"Struts?"

"The steel webbing along both sides of a bridge that brace everything. You've seen a thousand struts, for Christ's sake."

"What *about* them?"

"Must you know even the details that don't concern you?"

"It's not knowing any details that terrifies me."

"Let me interpret," Kiril offered. "You've seen drawings of how and where the bridge was damaged. Ironworkers have to replace those charred struts with new ones, but they can't remove the old struts until after they've put up cables for temporary support. The cables went up yesterday. Today, your husband and I will help put in the new struts. Erich is saying they have to be in solidly before we remove the cables."

"At what point does the riveting begin?" Brenner asked.

"That's the next step," Erich said. "The riveter's job is to attach the struts to the main stringer and—"

"Stringers are those long steel spans, one on each side of a bridge," Kiril explained. "They start low, gradually sweep up to a peak, then dip again to a low point at the middle of the bridge. That's where most of the construction is being done—on the right-hand side, near the middle."

"So close to the border," she whispered.

"And closely guarded. The flatbed will be parked much farther back, unfortunately."

"—and if the riveters get through before quitting time, which I doubt," Erich was saying, "you simply remove the cables."

"Tell me, again, what the riveters will expect us to do." Brenner sounded nervous.

"You'll light a fire inside the pen and lay the rivets on top of the charcoal, that's step number one. Step number two is to toss them, one at a time, to the riveters, like we showed you," Erich went on. "Try not to drop one on your toe because you're not wearing the proper shoes. The damn thing would burn right through."

"That hot?" Brenner said uneasily.

"That hot."

"And try not to hit the riveter," Gunther joked. "He'd be sure to take offense."

"What exactly will *I* have to do?" Adrienne asked Kiril.

"A cleanup man does not do much of anything," Albert said in heavily accented English, surprising them.

"I should have known you'd speak my language," Adrienne said, smiling.

"Not good," he said, returning the smile. "Where is the spare ignition key?" he asked, switching back to German. Kiril held it up. "Your passes to the bridge site. Frau Brenner . . ." Albert handed her a card in Otto's name, then gave Kiril and Brenner the cards for his brothers. "Take good care of these. I'll be wanting them back once you're on the site."

"*We'll* be wanting them, you mean," Gunther laughed.

"Where's the petrol tank on the flatbed?" Albert asked Kiril abruptly.

"On the left rear side of the cab," Kiril shot back. "It will be uncovered. I'll be able to reach it by crawling onto the steel coupler that connects the cab of the truck with the flatbed part."

"Good."

339

"I'm still not clear on how I get from the workers' hut to the coupler when I'm ready to pour the petrol."

"You'll see. Where will the flatbed be parked?" he asked Brenner.

"On the bridge site, right behind the pen where we heat the rivets."

"Right. Don't forget about those two guards posted at the middle of the bridge. *That's* the weak link."

"They never used to post guards there until that center barrier was knocked out of commission. The thing operated by remote control," Erich remarked.

"Well, they're there now. Once you're out on that coupler ready to pour the petrol, Kiril, you'll be right in their line of vision. Don't try to crawl out there until the shift changes. What time does it change?"

"Five o'clock sharp," Brenner said.

"We'll wait," Kiril promised.

Albert led the way out. "Take a good, long look at the flatbed," he cautioned Kiril and the Brenners at the foot of the steps. "You won't get another chance at the site. I'll be keeping you too busy."

They looked. The truck parked in front of the house was roughly twenty feet from its cab to the tail of its flatbed. Perched on the forward end of that flat, open platform was the workers' hut—a three-sided structure with a roof, about five feet wide all around. A steel coupler, several feet long and a foot-and-a-half wide, connected the flatbed platform with the cab of the truck.

While Otto and Gunther helped the Brenners onto the platform, Kiril jumped up, hurried inside the workers' hut, and took a close look at its back wall. Along its entire length ran a wooden bench with some tools underneath. Some work clothes hung from a couple of hooks.

Otto came up behind him, pushed some of the clothes aside, and showed him an opening in one corner. It was just large enough for a man to crawl through. Admiringly, Kiril touched the wood of the false back wall.

"It's a cramped little closet, but wide enough for three people to stand shoulder to shoulder," Otto observed. "Everything you'll need is stashed back there—the can of petrol, a piece of hose and a funnel, a flashlight and a hammer—"

"And one of the revolvers?" Kiril interrupted.

"It's back there, just in case."

"We drilled a couple of air holes, just in case you wanted to breathe," Gunther said, trying to lighten the moment.

Otto showed Kiril the way to the coupler outside: low down on the actual rear wall of the hut, a square-shaped piece of wood had been cut out and nailed in again, like a plug. "Just use the hammer to remove the nails," he said. "You can barely see the cut from the outside, by the way."

After Kiril stood up, Brenner knelt to examine the hole and the space behind it. "I wish we could stay back *here* all morning instead of playing ironworkers," he said regretfully.

"I wish you could, too," Gunther said, "but it's too tight a fit and there isn't much air. You'd probably collapse after a few hours. Besides, they're sure to spray tear gas back here, since the flatbed's going on the site."

They all turned at the sound of footsteps. Albert and Erich were making their way across the long platform toward them.

"Anything wrong?" Gunther called out.

"We just wanted to wish you luck. And goodby."
Albert was looking at Kiril.

They shook hands all around.

"Good luck in all things," Albert said in careful English to Adrienne, warmth in his handshake and his smile.

She held onto his hand for a moment. "I'll see you again some day. I won't forget." He was about to jump down from the platform when she stopped him. "Why?" she asked him. "Why are you doing this?" She looked around at the others. "All of you?"

Albert shrugged. "It is not so different from what Kiril did for us. It is simple . . ." He looked to Kiril for help, speaking in German.

"A simple act of humanity," Kiril translated.

As simple as that, she thought.

And couldn't stop thinking about it, as she followed Kurt through the opening, into the narrow concealed space. She stood between Kurt on her left, Kiril on her right. The space went suddenly dark; someone had draped clothing back over the opening. She tensed at the roar of the motor as the truck moved forward. She heard the angry, unexpected splatter of raindrops on wood over her head. And she heard the question coming back, like an old refrain: I'm not my brother's keeper—I've never believed in that wretched slogan. Why do I take things *personally?*

I know the answer, she thought. It's simple, after all, though far from self-evident. A simple act of humanity. Brotherhood. Not— She closed her eyes. Not brothers. Not blood or race or genes or government edicts trying to force an issue that can't be forced. It's happened without force so many times, she thought. History was filled with stories. Workers who threw down their tools to join the resistance or go on suicide missions. Farmers who defied storm troopers in France and Belgium and Holland—and died for it. Families who hid Jews in their homes and paid the price of becoming fugitives themselves. Men who faced firing squads rather than betray other men. But it isn't just wartime heroics. What about the person who hears a stranger's cry for help and plunges into a river, or, unarmed, tries to disarm some mugger, or, with his CB radio tuned to the emergency channel, dashes off to help someone on the highway? People at their best, she thought, at their most human—even if, much of the time, their best seems buried and needs to be triggered by some crisis. My own response isn't limited to wartime or near-drownings or even concentration camp victims. It's spurred by a lot of different things and . . . and by the same thing, she realized. Different forms of the same issue. Someone suffering through no fault of his own, someone wronged. Injustice in the subways or in some bureaucrat's office or in the halls of a courtroom. Injustice in the form of barbed wire and a concrete wall. The act of caring about it, she thought, that act comes from something universal. A bond. She thought of a timeworn slogan . . . and reversed it. Man's humanity to man.

The heavy rain stopped abruptly, as if someone had turned off a faucet. The truck's motor died. She heard retreating footsteps . . . Otto and Gunther leaving the hut to help with the loading. She heard a series of metallic sounds . . . steel beams being rolled around on pipes, hitting the deck of the flatbed with a startling clatter . . . chains scraping, being wrapped around the beams to hold them in place. She heard the motor again, then Otto's voice, competing with it. They were through loading, apparently; they were leaving the yard.

It seemed a long time before she heard Otto's voice

343

again. She didn't have to strain to hear it, even though it was in a whisper; the motor had died. We're here, she thought.

They came out in reverse order—Kiril, Adrienne, Brenner—and spotted Erich cutting across steel struts with the agility of a squirrel.

Kiril took two cigarette lighters out of his pocket and bent down to shove them behind the false wall. As he started to get up, he heard Erich's voice: "Put this on." He was handed a helmet. "Careful when you climb over this stuff," Erich cautioned all of them. "The edges are sharp and the steel isn't chained down too well." Kiril translated for Adrienne and reached for her hand.

"Let Dr. Brenner guide her across. We need your help for something," Erich told him. "Go off to the left and start mingling with the crew," he told Brenner. "We go right, Kiril. Let's pray Albert can keep the guard distracted until we're ready."

From the sideview mirror in the cab of the flatbed, Albert watched the Brenners head for the workcrew and Kiril, Otto and his brothers head for the back of the panel truck.

Bruno had just come out of the guard-duty shack. Albert pressed the horn and tossed him a friendly salute. "We're an even dozen again today," he called out cheerfully. "Four riveters—no carpenters, this time—two ironworkers, three cleanup men—lots of debris, today—two flagmen, and one tired sonofabitch of a foreman."

Bruno chuckled as Albert slid over. "Always wanted to get the feel of a flatbed under my hands," he said, taking the wheel.

Albert raised his arms in the air and said with a half-grin, "Not going to make me line up with the others?"

"Have I made you do it yet?" Bruno said gruffly as his hands did a quick, thorough search of Albert's body. "You being such a wiseguy, I ought to, but I'm in too good a mood today." He said it as if he had a secret he was eager to have pulled out of him.

"Yeah?" Albert glanced casually out the window. The little runt of a guard who counted noses was looking impatient, waiting for the last of the workcrew to line up. Albert glanced in his sideview mirror. The last of the crew was Kiril. He was just closing the back of the panel truck—closing Erich, Gunther and Otto inside. "Why are you in a good mood?" he asked Bruno.

"I did something last week for somebody big, that's why, and now he—" He broke off, as if deciding he'd better keep his mouth shut. "I had something good happen to me last night, is all."

"In that case, how about doing something good for *me* right now?"

"Like what?"

Albert looked pointedly out the window. "That spray-gun fanatic is on his way over here. Every time he lets loose in the back of my panel truck, the men complain about the smell. Can't say I blame them. That crap gets all over the equipment, the tools, the work clothes—"

Bruno shrugged. "It's routine."

"Not today, it isn't. We're using the flatbed. The panel truck's not going anywhere near the goddamn bridge. Let him spray up my flatbed, if he has to. Hey, Bruno, you got the authority to stop him, don't you? Or maybe I'm wrong about that," he said nonchalantly.

"I damn well got the authority," Bruno said hotly.

Albert looked down at his hands, amazed to see how steady they were. "Thanks, pal. Tell him to go easy with the tear gas. Tell him to stick to the undersides and avoid the steel, okay? And have him stay the hell away from the hut. I got tools back there I'll be using right away."

"Anything else, Boss?" Bruno said as he got out.

"Hell, you're the boss," Albert laughed. "There is one thing more, though. Better have him make sure everybody's cleared away from the back of the hut before he starts. I had a few men ride back there with the steel on the way over."

"I *thought* I saw workmen coming out of there before."

"Just proves how alert you are." And how it always pays to cover yourself, he thought.

"Be right back," Bruno said, looking pleased.

A stubby little guard stood in front of the crew, shifting one foot back and forth and sniffing the air like a bull getting ready to charge. He was counting blank faces and peering at passes held in the air. "Eleven," he called out shrilly to Bruno. "Twelve, counting the foreman," he amended, eyeing the flatbed.

"Yeah, yeah," Bruno yelled back, and kept going.

Albert was torn. He couldn't decide whether to concentrate on the frisks just getting under way or on the imminent explosion between Bruno and Spray Gun. He compromised. Number three and four in the crew lineup were Kiril and Dr. Brenner. He watched while the little runt did a painstaking body search of the "Zind brothers." Not a hitch. Then his eyes and ears sought out the explosion. But the guards were too far away. Their confrontation was all emphatic gestures and raised voices. The two of them started walking his way. The flatbed, he wondered, or the panel truck? He stuck a cigarette in his mouth, struck a light—and smelled an acrid smell. Christ! He'd lit the filter end. He flipped it out the window, ready to hop out of the truck and make one last stand—

"—just following orders," the guard with the spray gun was saying sullenly.

Officiousness had triumphed over literalness. Albert let out a long breath as Spray Gun headed for the back of the flatbed. His eyes returned to the crew. Mrs. Brenner was at the end of the line.

The guard got to her.

His hands slid rapidly at both sides of her body, then paused at her rib cage. Her eyes had been averted; now she looked at him.

"Was ist dir denn passiert? Bist du von dienem Fahrrad gefallen?" he chuckled.

The match Albert had just struck for a fresh cigarette burned his fingers. He shook it out, straining to hear.

"Ein Unfall . . . meine Verletzung," she mumbled, half-closing her eyes as if she were in pain.

"Ja, ja, du hast eine Verletzung. Alt oder neu?"

Albert's hand automatically moved to the door of the truck. The guard's hands had started to explore the elastic that bound Adrienne's breasts.

She opened her eyes and winced hard.

"Neu," the guard said. "Tut es weh?"

She hesitated. "Ja, ja."

"Also ich passe auf," he said, and continued his exploration. He would go more lightly now, Albert thought, watching as the guard finished with the rib cage and moved onto the head, patting all around the top of Mrs. Brenner's cloth cap. He turned, finally, and gave a signal to another guard—Spray Gun.

Albert exhaled slowly. Spray Gun's other duty was to

347

walk the crew to the site. He watched as the signal was given to move forward, watched Mrs. Brenner drift into the middle of the group. Her head was slightly bent and her feet farther apart than usual, with her hip movement squared off—a creditable job, he thought admiringly, of transforming her graceful stride into an awkward masculine gait.

And if any of the workers noticed that the man bringing up the rear seemed different in appearance from the one who'd driven them out in the panel truck, they said nothing. The difference was not so apparent that they could be held accountable for failing to notice it. Not being held accountable and not getting involved, Albert thought, was all they cared about.

Bruno got back in the flatbed. "That bastard gave me an argument!" He turned the key in the ignition. The engine sputtered briefly and died. As he gave it some gas, his glance automatically went to the gas gauge. "What, again?" he said incredulously.

"Relax, pal. The gauge must be broken. You don't think I'd forget to fill *this* baby, do you? Did it myself right before we left the yard."

"Maybe the gauge sprang a leak somewhere."

"You're just full of optimism this morning, aren't you? The last thing I need is a goddamn leak."

The engine caught and the truck moved forward.

"Well, how do you like the feel of a flatbed under your hands?"

Bruno grinned. "I like it fine. They use some powerful engine to pull these heavy loads, don't they?"

It was easy after that to keep things amiable, to launch into a discussion about trucks and truck driving, and from there to pleasure driving and how a real man ought to be driving something more powerful than those anemic-looking pieces of tin that passed for automobiles around here, and if *that* wasn't bad enough, having to wait a goddamn eternity before you got yours—

And then they were on the cobblestone square and Bruno was asking. "Where do you want it?"

"Same place you parked the panel truck yesterday— right behind the rivet pen."

Bruno advanced on it, barely kissing the back of the pen with the nose of the truck. He switched off the engine and pocketed the ignition key.

"Beautiful," Albert sighed.

"You really are a wiseguy," Bruno said.

26

Albert took a moment to look around and check everything. Kiril and Dr. Brenner were working in the rivet pen. The heat in there was stifling, Albert knew—charcoal fire and hot metal, sun and hot pavement. The two men were awkward with the rivets, but so far no one had noticed and the work was going well. He glanced at the middle of the bridge; Spray Gun and Bruno were at their posts there. Bruno was surveying everything and looking bored.

Satisfied, Albert turned back to explain something to one of the riveters. It took him several minutes to notice that Bruno was no longer at his post; he had sauntered over to the pen. Albert cut off his explanation in mid-sentence and hurried across the bridge.

"—after we get off work," Bruno was saying as he got there. "You two sure look as if you could use it. Like I said, the beer is on me."

Albert tensed. Of all days for Bruno to be feeling generous!

"Thanks, but we can't." Kiril's head stayed bent over the fire, waiting for a rivet to get hot. Brenner was resting for a moment, kneeling beside a pile of unheated rivets.

"Why can't you?" Bruno pressed.

"Quitting time is half-past five. You're through at five, aren't you?"

"How'd you know that?"

Albert's eyes shot to Kiril's face. "It's not my first day on the job," Kiril drawled. "Who do you think helped string all those cables?"

Albert took the cue quickly. "And a good job, too. Did you take a hard look at them?" he asked Bruno.

Bruno scrutinized the cables like an expert on an inspection tour. "Looks good, all right." His eyes moved to some new steel struts that were propped against the undamaged left-hand side of the bridge. "Pretty soon there won't be a trace of the damage left. I was on duty when it happened, you know," he said expansively. "Some swine of a Russian officer thought he could get past *me*. He was a spy as well as a traitor—I helped prove it." His voice warmed to his subject. "He died right over there," he said, swinging around to the railing on his left, "but he didn't die right away. I watched him crawl through his own blood . . ."

Bruno went on talking as a red-hot rivet slipped out of Kiril's tongs.

Albert had seen it coming; he grabbed the tongs just as Brenner snatched his hands out of the way, but he was too late. The rivet hit the floor of the bridge and rolled.

Bruno turned around.

Brenner whipped off his goggles and sprang to his feet, clutching his right hand; he had scraped it against the pile of unheated rivets and drawn blood. In his face was blind rage at Kiril, ready to erupt into words.

In German—please let the words be in German, Albert prayed.

Brenner seemed to become aware that Bruno was watching; he turned away and snarled, "Blöter hund!"

Bruno's stare became open-mouthed.

And Albert realized that the tongs was still in *his* hand— realized how the scene must look to Bruno. His mind raced over possible courses of action; the best one, he decided, was to get Brenner out of there. He watched Brenner pull out a handkerchief and waited while he bound the wound. Then he picked up Brenner's goggles, held out one hand for his helmet, and snapped, "I'll take your place here. You work on cleanup for the rest of the day. And be careful with that precious hand of yours. No more accidents, do you hear?"

Brenner crossed hurriedly to the other side of the bridge.

"You stand for *that*?" Bruno said. "The Boss drops a rivet, and one of his crew calls him a stupid dog?"

Albert made himself shrug. "Just a flash of temper. Or nerves. These things happen when they're new on the job." A split second later, he thought of a more obvious explanation—and a safer one. Why hadn't he just said that the worker with the explosive temper was his own brother, Gunther Zind?

Bruno, thumbs hooked into his belt, looked across at Brenner. Albert followed his glance and saw the confident bearing, the distinguished profile. "An aristocrat, that one," Bruno jeered. "An ironworker who dares to raise his voice to the Boss. And for someone who ain't a leftie, he sure did a helluva job on that injured hand of his. Maybe the sonofabitch is a doctor as well as an ironworker," he said acidly.

The heat from the fire seemed to leap into Albert's face. He forced a weary sigh. "It's that goddamn labor pool arrangement they put me through each morning. Most of the men I pull are either incompetent fools or prima donnas like that guy."

He waited until he had elicited a reluctant expression of sympathy from Bruno before putting on Brenner's goggles and helmet. As he joined Kiril over the charcoal fire, he felt Bruno's glance on him.

Bruno wandered back to his post at the middle of the bridge.

Yes, he thought, you could feel sorry for a man like Zind who had a job to do and was saddled with idiots or with big-shot types, like millstones around your neck. But a man who was in charge—who was the *Boss* and didn't act like it—that was something else. He himself was a man who knew how to give orders, when he had to, and how to obey them. A man should respect and obey his superiors without question—he had always believed that. And a man in charge should punish disobedience. He thought of the ironworker-aristocrat. He thought of the foreman. He simply had no category for men who did not live by his own code. How often had *he* been commended by his superiors for his efficiency? He avoided thinking of the one blot on his record—the recent border incident. After all, he had made up for that, hadn't he? He comforted himself by concentrating on the impressive little bundle in his pocket; Colonel Von Eyssen, his powerful protector, had been generous with him the night before. And here he had offered to spend some of his good fortune on a prima donna aristocrat!

It hardly seemed to him that any time had passed when another accident occurred—some damn-fool workman had let the fire in the pen get out of control. How the hell had that happened? He watched while work on the bridge halted and the fire was put out. What would Mr. Foreman do now? he wondered. How would he deal with the guilty man? He saw Zind put a whistle to his lips. Quitting time? He checked his watch. It was only 2:30.

Zind strode toward him, his expression dour. "To hell with their breakneck schedule," he muttered. "I need carpenters again to repair this mess. Time enough tomorrow, with a fresh crew. Maybe tomorrow, my biggest problem will be the heat or the puddles these goddamn downpours leave behind. Clear everything off the roadbed!" he shouted to the cleanup men. "Move the rest of those struts over to the side! Call the flagmen up from the riverbank! Hurry it up, will you? Do you want to walk back, the whole damn lot of you? The rest of you men, hop on the truck!"

"I'll move them along," Bruno volunteered, feeling sorry in spite of himself. Some people just didn't know how to handle authority.

He began to hustle the men onto the platform of the flatbed. Some of them went inside the workers' hut. He started to gesture for the last man to jump up. Then he got a better idea.

Zind was standing right there. "What's *this* one's problem?" he asked.

"The aristocrat?" Bruno sneered. "The way I figure it, an aristocrat's got no business riding in the back like some peasant. I say he rides up front with us. What do *you* say?"

355

"The others won't like it."

"An aristocrat don't care what peasants think of him, *do* you?" he needled, enjoying the expression on the worker's face. "Let's get started," he said, chuckling, and led the way to the cab of the truck. "Get in the middle, Mr. Aristocrat," he ordered, and still chuckling, slid behind the wheel.

He turned the key in the ignition. Nothing. He checked the petrol gauge. Empty.

Before he could react, he heard Zind cursing the truck, the bridge, the weather, the bad luck that had made him foreman of such a luckless job. "I don't believe this day!" Zind howled, hopping out of the cab. "If I didn't know better, I'd think it was Friday the thirteenth!"

"It's Friday the fourth," Bruno retorted, "and don't say I didn't warn you."

He watched Zind walk around to the driver's side, uncap the cover of the petrol tank, and stick a wire inside. He pulled it out and, cursing again, tossed the cap aside. "Bone dry!" he said, holding up the wire.

"What'd I tell you?"

Then Zind dropped out of sight, apparently to peer under the truck. "You were right," he called out, "the damn thing must have been leaking ever since I left the yard!" He stood up. "You were right," he repeated, looking sheepish.

Bruno could afford to be generous in the face of such an admission. He said nothing. But he felt smug. He slipped the ignition key into his pocket and got out. The iron-worker followed him.

"*Everybody* out—get out of the damn truck!" Zind shouted. "Today we *walk* back!" The minute the crew began to leave the platform, he grabbed the ironworker

356

roughly by the arm and shoved him forward. "Check the work bench, you. Make sure no one's left anything behind."

But Bruno wasn't finished with his little joke. "You giving a menial job like that to Mr. Aristocrat, here? We can't let him get away with that, can we?" He slapped a comradely arm around the man's shoulders and started walking him off the bridge.

Kiril was crouched in one corner of the hut, not quite hidden behind a pile of clothing. "Where's my brother?" he whispered when Albert entered.

"We've got trouble. Get behind that wall. Mrs. Brenner okay?"

Kiril nodded.

"Hurry." Albert pretended to examine some clothes while holding them up like a curtain.

Kiril disappeared into the opening.

Albert draped a pair of trousers over it. "Dr. Brenner is being watched," he whispered. "I'll find another way to get him out. There's nothing you can do, understand? Wait for the shift to change at five o'clock. Pour the petrol. Then get the hell out of here."

He left the truck, looking casual, walking fast and wishing the others didn't have such a headstart. Wondering whether he could get to the panel truck before Otto and his brothers slipped out and started mingling with the crew. *He had to stop one of them.*

He got as far as the shack with the sign that said, NO CIVILIANS BEYOND THIS POINT—and saw that he was a few minutes too late. Otto, Erich and Gunther had slipped in among the others, not noticing that Brenner was among them, too. Could one of them be smuggled back into the truck before the count?

He peered through a window of the guard shack. Bruno was inside, but the damage, he thought, was done. The little runt of a guard was dancing around, yelling for the men to line up next to the panel truck. His face impassive, Albert leaned casually against the shack. And braced himself.

The nose count began. "Twelve?" the guard said, looking as if someone had just announced that two plus two equaled five. He counted again. "Twelve—not counting your foreman. How can there be *twelve* of you?"

No one answered him.

He counted a third time. "Twelve!" he shouted. "I demand an explanation!"

No one moved. No man looked at his neighbor.

The guard spotted Albert leaning against the shack. "You! How do you explain this?"

Albert shrugged. "I can't," he said, walking over to the crew.

The guard pulled out his revolver and fired three times in the air. Bruno came running out of the shack. "There was eleven of them this morning. I called out eleven, remember? Now I get twelve!"

Albert took advantage of the moment to slip Otto and his brothers their bridge passes.

"You're crazy," Bruno muttered. But he counted for himself. When he got to Brenner, he paused before going on to the end of the line. "Twelve," he confirmed. His eyes returned to Brenner, to the bandaged right hand. "I'll be back in a minute," he told the guard. "Don't anybody move," he warned over his shoulder. He hurried into the shack.

Von Eyssen was halfway out the door when the buzzer rang on his desk. He frowned with annoyance and went back for it, hoping whatever it was wouldn't make him late for his appointment with a major general who didn't like to be kept waiting.

"It's that border guard from the Potsdam checkpoint calling," his secretary apologized. "He insists on speaking with you."

"Put him through." The major general would have to wait.

"I've got him!" The voice was triumphant. "Colonel, I've got the Russian spy—the one we were talking about last night!"

"Doctor Andreyev? Are you *sure?*"

"It's him, all right! I just checked out the latest bulletin— two doctors, right? And the one with the dark hair is Andreyev? He fits the description all the way."

"Did you find that cigarette lighter I told you about?"

"I haven't searched him yet."

"What about the American couple?"

"He's alone."

"Have the Russians been informed?"

"They have, by now. I just called the guardhouse to confirm my suspicions, and they said they'd be sending a man across the square right away."

Too bad. "All right, quiet. Let me think." What would Colonel Andreyev do when they contacted him? Make haste for Glienicker Bridge. He was probably only minutes away, somewhere in Potsdam. If Andreyev got there first and got his slimy hands on that lighter, he might destroy it—along with his brother, probably. Then it would *still* be his word against mine, he reasoned.

"You want me to search him before the Russians take him, Colonel?"

"Take him where?"

"Their own guardhouse on the square. When I called, they told me—"

"Search him, God damn it! You *must* get that lighter. Get it and keep it for me. Do you understand?"

"Yes, sir!"

Silence. The bastard was waiting for a compliment! Why the hell did he have to call in the first place and put me in the position of—

"How soon will you get here, Colonel?"

"How soon?" Von Eyssen stared off into space, wondering how he dared risk going anywhere near Glienicker after what had happened a few weeks ago. If there were trouble again and he were in the *vicinity* of that border area, he would get more than severe criticism this time—much more. But a major general was waiting to hear about the circumstances surrounding Ernst's death. If I could get my hands on that lighter first, he thought, I wouldn't have to walk into his office with empty assertions. I'd have proof that Ernst was innocent, that the intelligence leak had nothing to do with me. I'd have witnesses to show that the brother of Colonel Aleksei Andreyev was caught trying to escape with the incriminating lighter in his pocket . . .

"You still there, Colonel?"

"Yes. Quiet." There wouldn't be any trouble at the border; the fugitive was already apprehended, wasn't he? Whatever sweet revenge Andreyev had in mind for his traitor-brother would be a private affair—Andreyev's own interests demanded that. A family is a real liability in our business, he thought. Andreyev did me a favor getting rid of Ernst. "Search Dr. Andreyev," he said aloud. "Then stay with him until I get there."

* * *

Brenner still stood where Bruno had ordered him to wait. He concentrated on keeping calm. But when he saw the guard emerge from the shack, he started.

"Come with me," Bruno ordered. "Dismiss the others," he told the nose-counting guard.

"This man has no bridge pass," the guard said ominously.

"I'm aware of that," Bruno snapped. He gripped Brenner's arm.

Is it just the pass business, Brenner wondered, or does he suspect the truth? Stay calm, at least until you know . . . He moved obediently toward the guard shack. *This* one has the smell of a man who likes to spread money around, he thought hopefully, remembering the beer-buying offer on the bridge.

Bruno took a chair and offered him one. He took his time lighting a cigarette. And offered him one. Then some matches.

Brenner reached for the matchbook with a steady hand.

"What, no light of your own? I heard a rumor you had a cigarette lighter on you. Mind if I check?"

"Suit yourself," he answered in German. Calmly.

Bruno's hands were swift but thorough. They found nothing. He cursed and went through it again, with the same result.

Brenner started to light his cigarette.

"Had a trying morning . . . Dr. Andreyev? Going to waste my time denying who you are?" he sneered.

This time Brenner's hand shook. He stared at the guard, and realized the man was confused by the dark hair. He felt an insane desire to laugh in the damn fool's face. But he wasn't about to. He had just had a very sane idea. His instinct for survival hadn't deserted him, after all.

The phone rang. Bruno answered, listening for a moment, hung up. "Your brother is on his way."

"Here?"

"Close enough. They'll be taking you to the bridge any time, now."

Aleksei has some kind of a personal stake in all this. He probably regrets losing you even more than he does me. "What time is it?" Brenner said tensely.

"See for yourself."

The hands of the wall clock were locked together at 3:15. Less than two hours before the guard still at the middle of the bridge changed shifts. *As far as the Soviet authorities are concerned, you're a Russian citizen, now. That makes you a fugitive . . . a lawbreaker . . . a lawbreaker . . . a lawbreaker . . .* Two hours. Plenty of time yet. Time for one last trade.

They heard a jeep pull up outside.

"How shall I introduce you?" Bruno quipped. "Mr. Aristocrat? Mr. Ironworker? Dr. Kiril Andreyev?"

"Suit yourself," Brenner said with matching sarcasm.

Some guards in Russian uniforms came rushing through the door.

Brenner went up to the one who was obviously in charge. "Has my brother arrived yet?" he said in German, glancing at Bruno as if he were speaking in German rather than Russian in deference to him.

The Russian officer replied in German. "He's on his way."

The young West German policeman stood like a statue outside his gray sentrybox. Unable to stand the suspense any longer, he walked warily toward the middle of the bridge, one hand touching the rifle slung over his shoulder.

He stopped just short of a small yellow rectangle. DEUTSCHE DEMOKRATISCHE REPUBLIK, POTSDAM.

A lone East German guard who was marching back and forth on the other side of the sign, also carrying a rifle, glared at him. He looked both nervous and resolute at the same time, the policeman thought, as he walked to one side of the bridge and peered across the river. He resisted the impulse to use his binoculars—too conspicuous. All he saw were concrete slabs posted like disciplined guards along the shoreline, and a barbed-wire fence where the river widened. But no activity of any kind, none that he could see, anyway.

He retraced his steps and started to enter his sentrybox. He hesitated in front of another sign—five-inch-high letters, spelling out a message in four languages: YOU ARE LEAVING THE AMERICAN SECTOR. He shrugged and walked across the way to a wooden shack. He went in.

"Any idea what's going on?" asked a fellow policeman who was sitting behind a desk. He looked apprehensive.

"I couldn't see much. Just a lot of equipment lying around the roadbed. The construction crew left early today."

"I guess we were imagining things."

"We didn't imagine those gunshots, did we? Three of them," the young policeman said tensely.

"That was over ten minutes ago."

"They got only *one* guard posted, which is unusual— and he looks nervous as hell. I wonder what about?"

"The gunshots, probably, same as us."

"Something is in the air, I tell you—I can *feel* it out there. I think we should contact *Die Mauer*."

"Maybe you're right."

"What the hell, if I turn out to be wrong, they'll have sent someone over for nothing, that's all."

"Quit worrying. They get a lot of bum tips. They make the rounds and go with the percentages."

"You been here a long time," the young policeman said. "Anybody ever make it across this bridge?"

"One guy, only he don't count. That American U-2 pilot who got shot down over Russia, remember? They exchanged him for some KGB colonel right in the middle of Glienicker Bridge."

"Anybody trying to escape ever make it?"

"Nope."

"Anybody get . . . killed?"

"Yeah. The last one wasn't even running. He was already here, poor bastard."

"What do you mean?"

"I was thinking of that tourist from Hamburg who strayed too close to the center of the bridge last year. I heard shots and saw him spin off his feet and fall backward, like he'd taken a spill on roller skates."

"I read about that," the young policeman said grimly. "What's *Die Mauer's* telephone number?"

"Right over there. Downtown Berlin. Ever take a look through that magazine?"

"Once. Once was enough." He shivered. "You could be wrong, you know," he said as he dialed the number.

"About what?"

"About nobody making it across."

"I didn't say they couldn't. I said it's never been done."

"There's always a first time," the young policeman said. But skepticism crept into his voice, along with hope.

27

Kiril heard her take a deep breath and then let the air out slowly. "How are you doing?" he whispered.

"There's barely enough air for breathing, and all I can think of is how desperately I want a cigarette."

"I know what you mean. Legs getting tired?"

"Terribly. I think they'll hold up."

"Lean against me instead of the wall when you want to shift position. It will relieve some of the pressure."

"Kiril?"

He closed his eyes.

"Why don't you answer?"

"I want to hear you say it again."

". . . Kiril."

"What?"

"There's something I want you to know. In case anything else goes wrong. I came to East Berlin because—"

"Don't explain. I knew from the beginning you weren't

some apolitical wife along for the sightseeing. You're a journalist. You write medical articles.''

"The article I wanted to do wasn't really medical. It was more like an exposé . . . complete with photographs. I'll write that article, and I'll use the photographs your brother Aleksei dropped in my lap—if we ever get out of here.''

"How can you— What happened to those photographs?''

"I used to complain about my thick head of hair,'' she said lightly. "It finally came in handy.''

"You hid them under your cap?''

"They're still there.''

"You *never* should have taken the risk.''

"The photographer took the same kind of risk. Kiril, they're photographs of your friend, Brodsky. On this bridge.'' She touched his arm.

"I'd like to see them,'' he said. "Wait, I'll get the flashlight.'' He slid down gingerly, felt around on the floor, and touched a substitute for the light.

She had her cap off and was exploring a tangled mass of hair. "Ready,'' she whispered.

He flicked a cigarette lighter. His or Stepan's? He couldn't tell.

He looked at the photographs, one by one.

I will never leave for America unless I first find a way for you to follow. You said that once, Stepan. You found a way, didn't you? Did you arrange your own death to help me? You steal a limousine and smash into a bridge. And here I am, repairing what you smashed for me. Helping to erase every physical trace of your last violent encounter with life on this wretched, wonderful place. This bittersweet bridge. Your end, and my beginning. This photograph, where your hand hangs over the edge of the bridge—you

tried to destroy the lighter . . . your final, protective act.
Thank you, my friend, my fellow exile. My brother.

The flame went out.

Adrienne took the lighter from him. Her finger followed the outline of outstretched wings. "What do the wings stand for?"

"Somewhere in his travels, my friend Stepan managed to pick up a pair of American lighters. He had the emblems put on himself. The black wings are your American eagle's. It was our symbol of hope—that, and a toast we used to make. I've read your Declaration of Independence. Many times." He sounded wistful. "Is it still the freest place on earth, the United States of America?"

She shifted her body, leaning against his, as if she needed a contact more personal than words. "Whatever else it is . . . or isn't," she answered finally, "it's still the freest place on earth." Then she said, "I was wondering about Kurt," and he heard reluctance in her voice as she went on. "Maybe he was caught. What else could those shots have meant?"

"Trouble of some kind," he answered. "Not necessarily that kind of trouble."

"If they caught him—" She hesitated.

He finished her thought. "He might tell them where we are? I don't think so."

"He tried, once, to turn you in."

"He didn't know we were brothers." The lighter flashed for a moment. "Another hour to go." He was uneasy.

"I'd feel safer if we had gas in the tank."

He sighed. "So would I. I don't think we should wait. I'll need room. Slide down and move as far to the right as you can. As soon as I've pried off the nails, grab the wood as it comes loose and pull it out of my way."

"No—don't," she said. "There's at least one guard out there, patrolling the middle of the bridge. He's bound to see you."

"Maybe not. It depends on where he's standing and what direction he's looking in."

"What if the other guard comes back—if he hasn't already?"

"What if those three shots are bringing half a dozen guards out here? What if they've sent someone for petrol so they can move the truck away?"

"What if Kurt betrayed us? We have no choice, do we?" She slid down and moved to the right.

"I won't try to crash through—not with a guard right in front of us," he reassured her. He found the flashlight, then the hammer. "I just want to be ready by five o'clock. I want petrol in the tank. Are you willing to chance it?"

"Let me have the flashlight first."

When he gave it to her, she turned it on. Her mouth found his.

"Now let me have the gun."

Von Eyssen paced back and forth in the Soviet guard-house, seemingly oblivious of the Russian guards who sat sipping coffee and looked alternately amused and disdainful. Abruptly he brought his fist down on the table, startling the guards and rattling their cups. "I do *not* understand," he said. "*Why* would you give the cigarette lighter with the film to Dr. Brenner?"

"I told you—for safekeeping." Brenner could feel the effort behind his pose of nonchalance. He took a long drag on his cigarette. "His escape plan involved less risk than mine. Why is that so difficult to understand?"

"What risk? What plan? How is it you managed to slip

in among these construction workers but *he* did not? Where is his wife?''

Brenner shrugged.

"How did you get here?"

"I can answer that, Colonel," Bruno volunteered. "The foreman's got no control over the makeup of his crew so he don't know from one day to the next who he'll be pulling from the labor pool. Dr. Andreyev must have bribed his way into the pool, rode over in the panel truck with the crew, and kept out of sight, somehow, when the count was going on—I don't take the count," he added quickly. "He must've had in mind to jump over the side of the bridge when my back was turned. That what you had in mind?" he asked Brenner.

Brenner smiled enigmatically. The fingers of his freshly bandaged hand toyed with one of the two megáphones he'd discovered in a corner of the room. He was aching to know what time it was.

"Was that your plan—to swim for the other side?" Von Eyssen said slowly. "You should have tried it. You might have died quickly—from a bullet as you dove for the water. Or you might have caught a piece of barbed wire in your gut and died from loss of blood. Or one of the dogs on a patrol boat—" He stopped himself. "Where is Dr. Brenner?" he demanded.

"I'll tell you in the presence of my brother Aleksei—*if* he agrees to let me go."

"Now, why would I do that?" said a voice from the doorway. It was Aleksei, patting a bulge under his jacket and smiling, positively radiating good cheer.

"You'd do it to get your hands on Dr. Brenner," Brenner said, wishing he felt as confident as he sounded.

"Brenner has the cigarette lighter with the film," Von Eyssen volunteered eagerly.

"Ah yes, that intelligence leak you're so concerned about. *My* major concern is sitting right on that chair." Aleksei took out his pipe and began filling it. "Good to see you again, Kiril." He went on conversationally, but the words were unintelligible to Brenner; they were in Russian. His mind went blank. He heard a sound at the door.

Rogov came lumbering in. His military cap had been changed for a headdress of bandages—for which, Brenner realized, he would be blaming Kiril.

Luka, his eyes gleaming, started toward Brenner—and stopped when Aleksei spoke softly to him in Russian.

Brenner stood up. "Let's stop playing games," he said in German, looking pointedly from Aleksei to Von Eyssen and back again. "I knew you had a personal stake in this Brenner affair. I knew he was important to you. I never realized just *how* important until Colonel Von Eyssen took me into his confidence. Isn't that so, Colonel? Without Brenner, you can't hope to salvage your career. Without *me,* you won't find Brenner. It's as simple as that. He's almost out of your reach, Aleksei. Let me go, now, and you still have time to get him back—Brenner *and* his wife."

"A world-famous surgeon in exchange for a glorified mechanic?" Aleksei said, lapsing back into German. "By some people's standards, that's an excellent trade, eh, Colonel? There's only one problem." His eyes bored into Brenner's. "You're lying, Kiril. Either you don't know where Brenner is, or you're ready to give me false information." He lit his pipe calmly. "I can't believe that after your noble sacrifice in Zurich, you'd do a complete turnabout and sell him out."

Brenner wished he hadn't made a show of standing up. He felt a sudden, urgent need for support—a chair to sit on, a wall to lean against. "I . . . don't believe in sacrifice," he said slowly. "My—our country is a sewer of sacrifice. I came back because I thought I had a better than even chance of diverting your plane to the West." He shrugged. "I came close to succeeding. I ran into bad luck, that's all. Now, it's . . . Kolya's turn for a run of bad luck. I've paid my dues. I have much more to lose than he does if I don't strike a bargain with you. What are a few years in Moscow to a world-famous surgeon, compared to a firing squad for a glorified mechanic?" He relaxed a little; the Colonel looked convinced.

"Tell me where he is. *Then* I'll let you go," Aleksei offered.

"Now, who's lying?" Brenner scoffed.

"How do you propose we go about this swap?" Aleksei snapped. "Do you really expect me to release you and hope that somehow you'll send me word from across the border? How will you do it—by carrier pigeon?"

"I have it all worked out. Let me show you." Brenner picked up a megaphone. "Let's go outside," he said.

He waited until they had followed him out—Aleksei, Luka, Von Eyssen, and Bruno—and then began to explain. As he talked, they all looked out over the cobblestone square toward the starting point of the bridge, roughly a hundred feet away.

"—and I'll stop walking just short of the dividing line in the middle of the bridge. That's when I'll reveal their hiding place. With this." He held up the megaphone.

"What kind of fool do you take me for? You'd be a few

steps away from safety." Aleksei scanned the bridge area. "I'll let you go halfway"—he pointed—"directly opposite the flatbed truck that's parked behind that wooden pen. Do you see it over there, on the right side of the bridge?"

"I see it." Brenner had difficulty keeping his face impassive.

"That's where you'll stop until I can prove that your information is accurate. *Then* I'll let you go the rest of the way."

"In that case, I don't go alone, and I don't go unarmed." Brenner suddenly recalled a startling scene by the roadside when he and Kiril had taken over the limousine. "Your . . . trained bear goes with me," he said. "I see that he has a gun to replace the one I took away from him. That goes, too."

Two small, red blotches began to spread over Aleksei's milk-white complexion, as if a drop of food coloring had been added to each cheek. "I won't do it!" he cried.

I was right, Brenner thought; Rogov *is* my insurance. He'll never give an order to fire if Rogov is with me on the bridge. "So you won't do it, Colonel?" he said. "Why not, if you don't intend to have me shot in the back?"

"I won't expose Luka to any unnecessary danger."

"What danger? After I've told you what you want to know, you'll give me a signal. I'll start walking the rest of the way. As soon as I get to the middle of the bridge, I'll send Rogov back to you." Brenner turned to Von Eyssen. "I want that East German guard out there to start walking this way—now."

"He's due to change shifts soon, anyway," Bruno sniffed.

Von Eyssen cleared his throat; he was staring at the peculiar look in Aleksei's eyes.

"What's the time?" Brenner said nervously.

Bruno checked his watch. "4:50. How come you're always asking the time?"

"Because my brother Aleksei has ten minutes left." Ten minutes before the shift changes and Kiril pours the gas, he thought. "After that," Brenner said out loud, "it will be too late. Well, Brother?"

"You leave me no choice."

"You agree to everything?"

"You leave me no choice!"

"What a revealing last-minute show of affection. How you must hate to lose me," Brenner said with a vicious smile.

Von Eyssen wasn't smiling. "Listen, Colonel," he said uneasily, "we can't afford another border incident—especially not here. Neither of us can afford it. If anyone were to get hurt . . ."

"Including my buddy in the middle of the bridge," Bruno chimed in. "You know what happened the *last* time some Russians tried to cross over."

"That's true," Brenner said slowly. "I read that an East German guard was killed." He turned to Von Eyssen. "You'd want to protect your man, just as my brother wants to protect his, wouldn't you? I think your guard should stay where he is—right in the line of fire. Just make sure he knows not to use his rifle. I don't want him pointing it at me, understand? Go get that other megaphone."

Von Eyssen snapped at Bruno. "Do as he says!"

"And now your gun, Rogov."

"Give him your gun, Luka." Aleksei's voice was flat. There was unquestioning obedience, and devotion, in the look Luka gave his Colonel. He allowed Brenner to take first his gun, and then his arm. He didn't resist when he was given a slight push forward.

Brenner kept Luka in front of him and slightly to one side as he moved across the square toward the bridge. With his left hand, he kept a firm grip on the megaphone. His bandaged right hand pressed a gun into Luka's back. His own back felt vulnerable . . . exposed to unseen machine guns. Yet he felt inexplicably calm, completely in control, except for one thing. He couldn't seem to get a firm grip on his mind—he couldn't control its direction. It kept retreating to the past, throwing off images of whimpering children crossing this same bridge. In the opposite direction. In the eerie light from makeshift lanterns . . .

They had reached the starting point of the bridge. Brenner felt water seeping into his shoes and realized he'd stepped in a puddle. His foot slid, but he caught his balance, using the megaphone as a brace between his body and some steel struts propped against the left side of the bridge. Ahead and to his right, the rivet pen loomed, and behind it, the flatbed truck.

*Think of this as an ordinary suspension bridge under repair. Steel struts. Lumber and rivets. The paraphernalia that construction crews are always leaving behind after a day's work. If you must think, think of that instead of . . . a man's photograph in an envelope . . . a newspaper headline—*LATEST COLD WAR CASUALTY—*and a name: Stepan Brodsky. Ukrainian . . . Stepan Brodsky, lawbreaker. Don't think! Walk. Keep walking straight ahead. Keep walking toward West Berlin. Why are you stopping?*

Because I'm here, he realized. Because I'm standing opposite the truck. Because it's time.

He turned around to face the way he'd come, forcing

Luka to turn with him. He raised the megaphone. He lowered it again. His mind leapfrogged to the present, to Adrienne. Nothing would happen to her, he reasoned. The moment he was out of their clutches, they would have to let her go. As for the man in the truck with her, there was nothing he could do . . .

For a moment he permitted himself to know that the man in the truck had risked his life to come back for him, and was his brother.

I have no choice! He put the megaphone to his lips.

Aleksei was ready. He raised the megaphone Bruno had brought him.

"I think I should leave," Von Eyssen said cautiously. "I think you have no intention of keeping your word so—"

"I think you will stay." Aleksei checked to make sure Bruno's eyes were fixed on the bridge, then pressed the muzzle of his revolver against Von Eyssen's side. "I need you," he told Von Eyssen softly. "I need you to give the order, because I cannot give it myself. I cannot. You understand that, don't you?" He sounded like a reasonable man raising a reasonable question, but the gun was shaking in his hand.

Von Eyssen looked into his eyes, numbed by what he saw there.

They heard Brenner's voice, carrying back clearly to the square. "Tell your guard to stop pointing his rifle at me!"

"The guard's name—quickly," Von Eyssen asked Bruno. "Reiss."

Von Eyssen seized Aleksei's megaphone. "Listen to me, Reiss! This is Colonel Von Eyssen speaking! I want you to walk over to that wooden pen and stand in front of it! You are *not* to point your rifle at the two men standing to the left of the truck!''

Aleksei grabbed the megaphone back. "Your move, Little Brother!''

The voice shouted back—in English. "Dr. and Mrs. Brenner are in the back of the truck! The truck can't move! The gas tank is empty!''

"You bastard!''

The cry—also in English and clearly a woman's—came from the back of the flatbed truck.

Comprehension flared in Aleksei's eyes, then excitement. "Dr. and Mrs. Brenner!'' he shouted in English. "Stay where you are until someone comes for you! I repeat—*stay where you are* and you will *not* get hurt!'' He raised the megaphone higher and switched to German. "Reiss! There are people in the truck but no petrol! Guard that truck but *do not fire on the people!*'' He turned the megaphone to his right and shouted in Russian. "You men in the watchtowers! When the order is given by Colonel Von Eyssen, do *not* aim at the truck—avoid hitting it at all costs! Aim your weapons at the tall man on the right and *shoot to kill!*'' He aimed the megaphone at Brenner as if it were the telescopic sight of a rifle. *"Did you hear me, Little Brother?''*

Brenner heard, but could not understand. He assumed the words were the signal that he could start walking again—his part of the bargain was fulfilled and he was free to go. He turned again toward West Berlin, walking cautiously, forcing Luka in front of him, his gun against Luka's back.

Luka also had heard. He understood the words, but not how the machine gun bullets could hit his Enemy without hitting *him.*

In the truck, Kiril understood everything. "Don't move, don't cry out, no matter what happens," he told Adrienne. He crawled through the opening, dropped to the ground, and climbed into the cab.

The guard Reiss saw an unarmed man getting behind the wheel of a truck with no petrol. He hesitated, remembering his orders not to fire on anyone in the truck.

He saw two other men, one of them armed, slowly advancing. He forgot about the order not to point the rifle at the two men. He pointed at them.

As soon as he saw it, Aleksei shoved his megaphone at Von Eyssen's face. "Give the order to fire, Colonel."

"Give it yourself, damn you! You have the authority. There are as many Russians as there are Germans in those watchtowers!"

"I'll kill you if you make me do it. *Give that order.*"

Von Eyssen seized the megaphone and pointed it to the right—at the machine gun emplacements in the watchtowers. "Feuern!"

This time Brenner understood. But he had no time to translate his understanding into action.

Long, hot streaks of red and orange and yellow tore across the cobblestone square and across the bridge—and keeping obediently to the right-hand side, connected with the objects of their fiery mission. The earsplitting clatter of the guns blotted out two other sounds: Aleksei screamed Luka's name. Brenner screamed as he fell, bleeding, to the pavement.

He gasped into the megaphone, lying useless, near his lips. "No . . . don't. I'm not . . ."

"Feuern aufhoeren!"

It was the last thing Brenner heard. The last thing he saw, as he struggled to raise his head, was the burst of a flashbulb on the West Berlin side of the bridge. The last thing he felt, as his cap slipped off and his head fell back again into a puddle, was the cooling touch of water on his face.

Flashbulbs burst in quick succession—triggered by the sight and sound of the flatbed as it roared to life, ramming the wooden pen. The pen collapsed under the impact like a house of cards, and the guard crouched in front of it barely had time to leap aside with the debris that scattered in every direction.

In the confusion of wailing sirens and shouted orders, two men raced for the bridge. Aleksei got there first. He bent over Luka's body, moaning. Von Eyssen nudged Brenner's head with the toe of his boot—and saw dark stains seeping into a puddle, leaving behind them patches of white hair.

"We've killed the wrong man," he groaned. "We've killed your famous American surgeon! Look at the hair!"

"Don't *say* that! Kiril's hair was white, too—it was part of his disguise!" Aleksei dropped to his knees, oblivious of the muddy water seeping into his pants. He seized the head with both hands and pulled it up to stare into lifeless eyes. His fingers touched a small lump on the scalp. He screamed.

On the West Berlin side of the bridge, three men raced for the flatbed truck. The young policeman got there first and yanked the man out from behind the wheel. The other policeman helped the woman out of the opening in the rear of the hut. A photographer from *Die Mauer* helped them half drag, half carry their burdens toward the safety of the guard-duty shack. Once inside, the two policemen looked at each other self-consciously, waiting to discover which agency to alert. The United States Mission, they concluded. The man had just mumbled something in English.

"Free." Tears spilled down Kiril's face. Then, "Kolya is dead."

"Kurt . . ." Adrienne said, mingling her tears with his for the man she had loved long before she had learned to despise him.

After a while, she was able to look at Kiril. Then they were crying and laughing and clinging to each other. When she thought she had breath enough to speak, she spoke the words against his chest, but they came out a whisper: "Welcome home."

EPILOGUE

The cover story was by-lined: Adrienne Brenner. The magazine's cover looked like a horizontal split-screen image in a movie: the photograph on top was of Stepan Brodsky, the one on the bottom of Dr. Kurt Brenner. Across the middle ran a headline—FREEDOM BRIDGE: A CONTRADICTION AND ITS CONSEQUENCES.